ACCLAIM FOR JAYNE ANN KRENTZ'S SPLENDID *NEW YORK TIMES* BESTSELLERS

EYE OF THE BEHOLDER

"The prolific Krentz...once again demonstrates her knack for page-turning plots that masterfully inveigle and misdirect readers up to a surprising denouement."

—*Publishers Weekly*

"In the eye of the romance reader, Jayne Ann Krentz remains one of the great authors of the decade....This wonderful writer always provides an entertaining story. Readers will relish the exciting story line. The lead protagonists are a warm, intrepid duo."

—barnesandnoble.com

"Krentz weaves her magic in this exciting and passionate tale. She leads us into a maze of puzzles and adventures which we don't want to end. Read, absorb, and enjoy."

—*Rendezvous*

"[A] fun-filled and sensational tale by the incomparable Jayne Ann Krentz. Ms. Krentz is batting a thousand."

—*Romantic Times*

FLASH

"Once again, Jayne Ann Krentz brings wit and intelligence to her distinctive, sure-fire recipe for contemporary romantic suspense....As always, Krentz pairs two equally strong people, endowing them with just enough quirks to make them real, and provides plenty of plot twists to keep her story humming. *Flash* is romantic suspense of the highest order."

—amazon.com

"*Flash* glitters and glows with all of Jayne Ann Krentz's patented humor and spice. Chalk up another winner for this perennial favorite."

—*Romantic Times*

"[A] dazzling tale....With superb style and skill, Krentz creates a series of false trails that cloak the identity of the threat...until the final, dramatic unveiling. This new element of suspense, plus Krentz's trademark family squabbles and strong characters, will thrill her fans."

—*Booklist*

"*Flash* has everything a reader could want—mystery, romance, humor, murder, and blackmail....The final pages bring a surprising twist."

—*The Southern Pines Pilot* (NC)

SHARP EDGES

"A fast-paced mystery."

—*Chicago Tribune*

"Entertaining....The dialogue cuts through with...sarcasm and snappy double entendres."

—*People*

"A fast-paced, sexy, romantic mystery...with dangerous and passionate results."

—*Library Journal*

"A little mystery, a little romance, a lot of fun."

—*Minneapolis Star Tribune*

"[A] brisk tale....A risky time is had by all. And a good time is had by the reader."

—Associated Press

Books by Jayne Ann Krentz

The Golden Chance
Silver Linings
Sweet Fortune
Perfect Partners
Family Man
Wildest Hearts
Hidden Talents
Grand Passion
Trust Me
Absolutely, Positively
Deep Waters
Sharp Edges
Flash
Eye of the Beholder

By Jayne Ann Krentz writing as Jayne Castle

Amaryllis
Zinnia
Orchid

Published by POCKET BOOKS

JAYNE ANN KRENTZ

EYE OF THE BEHOLDER

POCKET BOOKS
New York London Toronto Sydney Singapore

This book is a work of fiction. Names, characters, places and incidents are products of the author's imagination or are used fictitiously. Any resemblance to actual events or locales or persons, living or dead, is entirely coincidental.

 POCKET BOOKS, a division of Simon & Schuster Inc.
1230 Avenue of the Americas, New York, NY 10020

ISBN: 1-4391-5453-8
ISBN-13: 978-1-4391-5453-3

First Pocket Books paperback printing December 1999

10   9   8   7   6   5   4   3   2   1

POCKET and colophon are registered trademarks of Simon & Schuster Inc.

Cover illustration by Tom Hallman
Cover lettering by Jim Lebbad

Book design by Irva Mandelbaum

Printed in the U.S.A.

QB/✶

This one is for Alberta Castle,
the best mother in the world.
And she just happens to be my mother.
Thanks for everything, Mom!

PROLOGUE

Avalon, Ariziona
Twelve years earlier. . .

He swept into the house out of the hot desert night, an avenging warlock from the dark canyons carrying thunder and lighting in his fists.

Alexa froze at the top of the stairs when she heard his voice in the hall. Her sudden stillness was instinctive, the immediate, elemental reaction of any creature to the presence of a potential predator.

"I don't know whether it was you or Guthrie who killed my father, Kenyon," he said. "Hell, for all I know, the two of you planned it together."

The night was warm, but Alexa shivered in the shadows above the hall. John Laird Trask was young, somewhere in his early twenties, but the taut control he exerted over his icy rage would have done credit to a man twice his age.

"You listen to me, son, and you listen good." Lloyd Kenyon spoke with a calm authority that reverberated with an underlying sympathy. "No one murdered your father. Once you've had a chance to cool down and think about it, you'll accept the facts. It was a tragic accident."

"Bullshit. Dad was a good driver, and he knew that road. He didn't go off Avalon Point by accident. One of you forced him over the edge."

Alexa felt suddenly lightheaded. A strange, unfamiliar panic left her fighting for breath. *Trask was threatening Lloyd.* He was not only a much younger man, he was even bigger than Lloyd, who still had plenty of bulk and muscle left over from the days when he had run construction crews.

Her anxiety for Lloyd's safety took her by surprise. Until tonight she would have sworn that she had no strong personal attachment to him. She and her mother had moved in with him eighteen months ago following her parents' divorce. She had been careful to keep a cool distance between herself and this very large, unexciting, rock-steady businessman Vivien had married; careful to make sure Lloyd understood that he could never take the place of the charismatic hero who had been her real father.

It had been a year since Crawford Chambers had been killed by a sniper's bullet. He had been halfway around the world at the time, photographing the latest in the long list of small, brutal civil wars that had made him a legend in journalism circles.

Crawford had been everything that Lloyd was not, a rakish, dashing, larger-than-life figure who lived life on the edge.

Her father would have been able to deal with Trask, Alexa thought. But staid, steady, unflappable Lloyd probably didn't stand a chance.

Trask's accusations were nothing but crazy talk, she told herself. Lloyd would never harm anyone.

She had to get to the phone.

The nearest instrument was at the foot of the stairs. With an enormous effort of will, she fought through the temporary paralysis. She went silently, cautiously, down the steps.

"It was raining that night." Lloyd's voice was calm, infused with reason. "This is what we call our monsoon season. Downpours are common. That stretch of the road is treacherous. Everyone around here knows that. I've always said that portion of Cliff Drive should be closed during a storm."

"The rain had passed by the time Dad got into the car," Trask said. "I checked with the cops."

"The roads were still wet. Even the best driver can make a mistake."

"This was no mistake," Trask said. "I know all about the partnership between the three of you. And I know about the offer from that hotel chain. Dad was murdered because someone wanted him out of the way."

Alexa realized he believed every word he said. She knew that he was wrong, at least about Lloyd. But Trask was clearly convinced that his father had been murdered.

She sensed her mother's presence on the steps behind her. She glanced over her shoulder. Vivien's fine-boned, ascetic face was taut with anxiety as she listened to the two men quarrel.

"You.think I was involved in some kind of bizarre conspiracy to kill your father?" Lloyd's voice rose in disbelief. "That's outrageous."

"I looked through some of Dad's papers this afternoon. I heard about the quarrel at the country club the night he died. It didn't take me long to put it all together."

"Business partners sometimes disagree. It's a fact of life, son."

"That argument was more than a disagreement. I talked to the bartender at the club. He said the three of you nearly came to blows."

"Guthrie gets a little hotheaded when he drinks," Lloyd admitted. "But I restrained him. There was no physical stuff."

"Maybe not then. But you and Guthrie knew that Dad would never agree to sell the Avalon Mansion property to that chain. So one of you found a way to get rid of him."

"Damn it, I've had enough." Lloyd's voice hardened. "I'm trying to be patient. I know you've had a hellish few days, and I know you've got a lot of responsibility to shoulder. But you're going too far here."

"Believe me, Kenyon, I haven't even started."

"You're going to have to get your priorities straight, Trask. You've got your brother to think about. He's only seventeen, and you're all the family that boy has left in the world."

"Thanks to you or Guthrie."

"That's a damn lie. When you come to your senses and calm down, you'll see that. Meanwhile, you'd better start thinking about the future. You've got your work cut out."

"Don't talk to me about my *work*, you son-of-a-bitch."

"Someone better talk to you about it. You're going to have to get through the fallout from your father's bankruptcy and take care of your brother at the same time. That's a man-sized job. You need to get focused and stay that way. You can't afford to waste your energy chasing a wild conspiracy fantasy."

"I don't need you to tell me what I have to do, Kenyon. I'll take care of Nathan, and I'll take care of myself. But one day I'll find out what really happened at Avalon Point the night Dad died."

Alexa reached the bottom of the stairs. Neither man noticed her. They were intent only on each other. Lloyd had his back to her as he confronted Trask.

This was the first time she had seen John Laird Trask in person. She knew from what Lloyd had said that his family came from Seattle. It had been Harry Trask's plan to restore the old Avalon Mansion and turn it into a destination resort. The project had brought him to Arizona on a frequent and regular basis during the past year. His two sons had remained in Seattle.

Alexa paid little attention to Lloyd's business affairs even though he managed the inheritance she had received from her grandmother. As a result, she knew almost nothing about Harry Trask and even less about his sons.

But after tonight she knew that she would never forget John Laird Trask.

From where she stood she could see him looming in the hall, taking up far too much space. The warm glow of the overhead fixture did nothing to soften the sinister angles of his face and jaw. She could feel the energy waves of his fury.

She was only a step away from the phone now. She took a deep breath, stretched out her hand, and picked up the receiver.

"If you don't go away right now, Mr. Trask, I'm

going to call the police," she said with a fierceness that startled her as much as it did everyone else.

Both men swung around to stare at her, but it was Trask's relentless green-gold gaze that riveted her. For an instant she could not move. Her hand clenched around the phone.

"It's all right, Alexa." Lloyd's face gentled as he looked at her standing there with the phone clutched in her hand. "Everything is under control. Trask is leaving now. Isn't that right, Trask?"

Trask continued to watch Alexa for another second or two, as if assessing both her and her threat. Abruptly he turned away, dismissing her with a cold disdain that sent another chill through her.

"Yeah, I'm going now, Kenyon," he said. "But one day I'll come back for the truth. And when I do, someone will pay. Count on it."

Without another word, he walked out into the night.

A startling silence gripped the entire house for a few endless seconds.

Then Lloyd exhaled deeply and quietly closed the front door. He turned to give Alexa a reassuring smile.

"Don't worry, he didn't mean any of that nonsense."

She thought about the pitiless determination she had seen in Trask's eyes. "Yes, he did."

Outside a pickup truck engine roared to life.

Vivien came slowly down the stairs. "He sounded very serious, Lloyd. Do you think he might come back to cause trouble?"

"Nah. That was the pain of a young man who has just lost his father talking." Lloyd put his arm around his wife. He looked at Alexa with perceptive eyes. "You know what he's going through, don't you, honey?"

The phone buzzed. Alexa realized that she still held the receiver in a death grip. Slowly she replaced it. "Yes," she said. "I guess I know how he feels."

"He was just lashing out at the nearest target and I was it." Lloyd shook his head. "Trask has got some tough times ahead of him. His father was a great one for dreaming up projects, but he wasn't much good at the bottom line. He left his finances in a shambles. And then there's young Nathan to worry about."

"Do you think that Trask will be able to handle things?" Vivien asked uneasily. "He's only twenty-three years old."

"He'll be okay." Lloyd raised his bushy gray brows. "But I'll contact the lawyer who's handling Harry's estate in the morning and see what I can do about arranging some financial assistance."

Alexa hugged herself and listened to the pickup roar off into the night. "Trask won't take your money, Lloyd."

"After he calms down and realizes what he's up against, he'll see that it's the only reasonable thing to do," Lloyd said.

"No." Alexa thought about the savage determination that had blazed in Trask's eyes. "He won't accept any help from you or anyone else."

"Thank heavens he's gone," Vivien whispered. "I don't mind telling you that he scared me."

"Once young Trask is back in Seattle he'll settle down and get on with his life," Lloyd said.

Alexa stared at him. In the short time she had known him, she had learned that he was usually quite accurate when it came to judging people. She was amazed by his failure to comprehend the obvious.

"You're wrong," she said. "He's gone for now. But he'll come back someday."

1

Seattle, Washington
The present . . .

"Damn it, this isn't about opening another hotel, JL, it's about your obsession with revenge." Nathan planted his hands on the polished glass surface of the desk and scowled at Trask through the lenses of his gold-rimmed glasses. "This is about what happened to Dad all those years ago. Admit it."

"For the last time, I'm going to Avalon on company business." Trask leaned back in the gray leather chair and steepled his fingers. "I thought I'd made that clear."

Only Nathan still called him by the initials, JL. To the rest of the company and the world he was simply Trask, president and CEO of Avalon Resorts, Inc. It had been that way for five years, ever since he had left his position with Carrington-Towne Hotels to go out on his own.

"I don't like it." Nathan shoved himself away from the desk and thrust his hands into the pockets of his trousers. He stalked to the window and stared moodily out at the soft rain that drizzled over Seattle. "You've been obsessed with that property down in Arizona ever since you managed to buy it from Carrington-Towne two years ago."

"I'm focused on it, not obsessed with it. There's a difference."

"There sure as hell is, and take it from me, your attitude toward this project definitely comes under the heading of obsession. There was no good reason for us to acquire the old Avalon Mansion in the first place."

"Yes, there was," Trask said. "It was a steal."

Nathan snorted. "Only because it's been a financial disaster for every hotel and resort development company that has ever tried to do anything with it. Dad wasn't the only one who went broke trying to make it work. Even Carrington-Towne decided it wasn't worth the cost of gutting the old mansion and turning it into a hotel."

"It won't be a disaster for us," Trask said with absolute certainty. He was not the dreamer Harry had been, but he knew that he was very good at the hotel business. "Dad always said that Avalon would eventually become the next Sedona. He was right. He was twelve years ahead of his time, but he was right."

Nathan raised his eyes to the ceiling, apparently seeking patience from on high. "I'm not arguing the point. And I'm not saying that the new resort won't fly. Unlike Dad, you can make it work."

"Damn right, I can make it work." Trask felt no particular obligation to be modest about what was a simple, incontrovertible fact. "I may not be the creative type, but I know a good fantasy when I see one. And that's what we're in the business of selling. Fantasy."

Avalon, Arizona, with its surreal landscape of sculpted red rocks, mysterious sandstone canyons, and shatteringly spectacular sunsets, had caught the attention of artists, writers, retirees, and the New Age crowd several years ago.

A handful of small inns and bed-and-breakfasts as well as a trendy metaphysical retreat called the Dimensions Institute had operated successfully for several years in Avalon. The new Avalon Resort & Spa, however, would be the first large, world-class hotel designed to attract the increasing number of tourists who had begun to discover the region.

"Avalon is going to be very hot in the next few years." Trask watched the cold rain come down outside the window and thought of the heat of that Arizona night twelve years ago. "We'll be there to ride the wave."

"I'm not doubting your instincts for this kind of thing." Nathan glanced uneasily at him. "It's just that I have a feeling this property is different from the others for you. The closer we get to the opening, the weirder you get."

"There's nothing weird about my going down for the official opening of the resort. I go to every opening."

"Sure, but you don't make plans to hang around for a month or two afterward."

"You know that I've been thinking that it might be a good idea for me to spend more time in the field." Trask smiled. "What's the point of having an office and an owner's suite at each of the properties if I don't use them once in a while?"

Nathan swung around abruptly, intelligent eyes

narrowed behind the lenses of his glasses. "Let me handle the opening down in Avalon, JL."

Trask tapped his fingers together very gently as he considered the best way to deal with his brother.

Nathan had graduated from the University of Washington with a degree in architecture. He was the creative powerhouse responsible for the unique design concepts of each Avalon Resort.

Their mother, who had died shortly after Nathan was born, had bequeathed not only her artistic flair but also her light brown hair and warm hazel eyes to her youngest son.

Women considered Nathan good-looking. He had never lacked for dates. But he had been politely oblivious to every woman who had come along until he had fallen like the proverbial ton of bricks for Sarah Howe. The two had been married within four months of meeting each other. Trask had had his reservations, the chief one being that he considered Nathan too young to marry.

But, then, what did he know about marriage? His own had been a carefully considered decision made with the same attention to detail he applied to all his business affairs. It had proved to be a spectacular failure.

Nathan and Sarah, however, seemed blissfully happy. Any day now they would become parents.

Parents. It struck Trask as very strange to think of his little brother becoming a father.

From out of nowhere, he had a sudden, searing memory of standing with Nathan at Harry's funeral. That was when it had hit him for the first time that Nathan was now his responsibility. It would be his job to make sure that his younger brother had a roof over his head, went to college, and got started in life.

Trask knew he would never forget the raw fear that had descended on him at that moment. He had just come from the lawyer's office, where it had been explained to him that Harry had died on the brink of bankruptcy. Every major possession left, including the house in Seattle, was in jeopardy.

With an effort of will, Trask blanked the screen inside his head. He wondered if he should be worried about the fact that the old images were coming back with increasing frequency.

He had thought that the disturbing mental snapshots had all faded to distant memories. They had not troubled him much in recent years, perhaps because he had been consumed with one major crisis after another. Back at the beginning there had been the basic problem of keeping Nathan and himself afloat financially. Simultaneously he'd had to deal with his brother's grief, as well as his own mixed bag of anger and guilt.

When the dust had settled after the bankruptcy, he had focused on his long-term goal, the creation of Avalon Resorts, Inc. He'd continued to work construction for a couple of years, the kind of hard, heavy jobs that had financed his and later Nathan's education. And then he'd gone to work for Carrington-Towne. His success with the dynamic hotel conglomerate had helped him launch Avalon Resorts, Inc.

The business had been a godsend in ways other than financial. It had provided an outlet for the restless energy that burned within him. It had forced the shards of memories to the distant corners of his mind.

But now the unpleasant pictures were becoming sharper and more vivid again. All of them had one thing in common. They were connected to his father's death.

He didn't need a shrink to tell him that it was the plan to return to Avalon that was causing the images and the guilt that went with them to flash across the screen in his mind.

Nathan stared glumly out the window. "I don't like this, JL. I wish you weren't going down there. I've got a bad feeling about it."

"You know Glenda wants me there. She says she's pulled in a lot of media because of the hotel's art collection, and she wants to take advantage of it."

"I know." Nathan massaged the back of his neck. "We'll get a tremendous amount of press out of that collection."

"You'd better be right. When I think of what we paid that consultant . . ."

Nathan smiled wryly. "Edward Vale was worth every penny. He's one of the best corporate art consultants in the country. He's got contacts throughout the art world, and that's what it takes to pull together a great corporate art collection. Contacts."

"All I care about is that the company gets its money's worth."

"Does it ever worry you that you might be a little too focused on the bottom line, JL?"

Trask contemplated that briefly. "No."

"We're talking about art here. There are reasons

other than the bottom line for putting together a great collection."

"Not for a corporation."

"What about the prestige factor?" Nathan swept out a hand as he warmed to his topic. "What about good corporate citizenship? Responsibility to the community?"

Trask grunted.

"What about the knowledge that Avalon Resorts, Inc., will be doing its share to make a fine collection of art and antiques available for viewing by thousands of people who might not otherwise have the opportunity? What about the duty to preserve and protect some of the most interesting objets d'art of the early twentieth century for generations to come?"

"We operate hotels. Bookings are the bottom line."

Nathan gave him an exasperated look. "I'm not worried about the collection, I'm worried about your fixation with the new resort. I want you to swear to me on a stack of Avalon Resorts quarterly reports that you're not going back for revenge."

"I'm going back to open the hotel that Dad dreamed of creating in Avalon," Trask said softly.

He did not tell Nathan about the private investigator he had hired six months ago. He knew the information would only fuel his brother's concern.

He was not going back for revenge, Trask thought. He was going back to get the truth.

After he had the answers to his questions there would be plenty of time to think about revenge.

2

Avalon, Arizona
The present . . .

Alexa Chambers walked slowly around the slender bronze satyr set in the green marble and wood base. She paused to trail a palm across the muscular hindquarters of the half-man, half-goat figure. Her gaze fell on the satyr's lovingly detailed genitalia.

She grimaced and looked up quickly. She could have sworn the satyr gave her a lewd wink.

Something was wrong with the bronze. She recognized the craftsmanship all too well.

Anger hummed in her, but she forced herself to remain calm and professional. There was too much riding on this project. She could not screw up now.

"It's one of the best fakes I've ever seen, Edward," she said evenly, "but it's definitely a fake. This is not an Icarus Ives piece."

"A fake?" Edward Vale's chin dropped visibly. "Are you mad? I paid Paxton Forsyth a fortune for *Dancing Satyr.*"

"It was Avalon Resorts' money, not your own. Call Forsyth, tell him you've had *Dancing Satyr* independently appraised, and you want to return it."

Edward briefly closed his eyes. A shudder went through his elegant frame. "You know I can't do that. It would be as good as telling Forsyth that he had been fooled himself. Or, worse, that he'd deliberately misrepresented the piece. Either way, if word got out that I'd questioned his opinion, he'd be furious. He'd never deal with me again."

Alexa met Edward's eyes over the top of the satyr's horned head. "Want me to talk to him for you?"

"No, no, for God's sake don't even think about it." Edward flapped his professionally manicured hands wildly. "If you call Forsyth to tell him you think *Dancing Satyr* is a, uh, reproduction—"

"Not a reproduction, Edward. A fake. A forgery. A fraud."

"We don't know that." He eyed the figure. "It could be an honest copy, some artist's homage to Icarus Ives created years ago that accidentally got passed off as the real thing."

"If you believe that, I've got a genuine Avalon energy vortex tuning fork that I can sell you."

Edward groaned. "We both know that you can't call Paxton Forsyth. If you do he'll suspect that you're my Deco authority on this project. I would be ruined."

Alexa propped one shoulder against the plaster replica of a Roman column that stood behind her. She folded her arms.

"Ruined?"

"Let's be honest here, Alexa. Neither of us can afford to take any risks at this delicate stage. From all accounts Trask has got a thing about getting his money's worth. He approved me as art consultant on this project on the basis of my reputation. If he gets word that you're working with me, he might very well explode."

"How bloody inconvenient."

Edward bounced a little on the toes of his beige oxfords. He fixed her with a grim look. "More to the point, he'll probably fire me and we'll both be out our commissions."

Alexa pursed her lips. "I guess that is the bottom line, isn't it?"

"It certainly is. And Trask is said to be very big on bottom lines." Edward gave her a pleading look. "I don't suppose there's any chance that you're wrong about *Dancing Satyr?*"

Alexa gave a ladylike snort. "Take a good look at the thing."

"I did take a good look at it when I bought it from Forsyth. I didn't see a damn thing wrong with it." Edward glared at the bronze. "It's a magnificent satyr. A perfect example of the French influence on American sculpture during the Deco period."

"That's the whole point," Alexa said softly. "It's a little too good."

Edward blinked and then scowled. "I beg your pardon?"

She waved a disgusted hand at the bronze. "Look at the finesse of the zigzag design worked into the hair. And the sense of balance in the Egyptian-style pose of the arms. The energy in the arrangement of the feet or hooves or whatever it is satyrs have. What about the, shall we say, earthy expression on the features?"

"A sense of sophisticated sensuality is a classic element of the Art Deco style," Edward reminded her quickly.

"Deco sensuality is icy and dark. This is too warm and lively. Besides, Ives's work is more heavy-handed than this." Alexa paused, searching for the right words. "It's colder."

"Are you sure?" Edward studied the figure.

"I'm sure." There was no point in being self-deprecating about it. When it came to this kind of thing, she was almost never wrong. Edward knew that better than most.

"The provenance is impeccable." Edward sounded as though he was trying to convince himself rather than her. "After all, the piece came from the Paxton Forsyth Gallery. He's been dealing to the most important collectors for over thirty years. His reputation is—"

"I know," Alexa interrupted. "His reputation is everything that mine is not."

Edward drew himself up, an impressive sight in his off-white linen jacket and matching, pleated trousers. Alexa allowed herself a tiny spark of pure envy. Edward was one of those rare individuals whose innate sense of style allowed him to actually wear summer-weight linen suits without looking like an unmade bed.

"Not to put too fine a point on it," he said, "yes. Your reputation is downright shaky, and we both know it. Damn it, Alexa, there are times when we in the trade have to consider the pragmatic angle."

"Pragmatic?"

"You know what I'm trying to say here. Trask is a corporate collector. We both know that guys like him buy art to get publicity and to impress their fellow corporate honchos. It's an image thing."

"I can just see Trask out on the golf course with his corporate buddies," Alexa mused. " 'My hotel's art collection is bigger than your hotel's art collection.' "

Edward's mouth twisted. "Crude but accurate. Corporate art collections are trophies for CEOs, just like new, young wives. The point is, Trask will never question a work purchased through the Paxton Forsyth Gallery and neither will anyone else."

"Because the Forsyth reputation is unassailable."

"Exactly. No offense, but the truth is Trask would have every reason to discount your professional opinion." He swept out a hand to indicate Alexa's cluttered stock room. "I mean, just look at what you're doing for a living these days. The word *tacky* comes to mind."

Alexa refused to acknowledge the hit. She did not even wince. But then, she reflected, she'd had a lot of practice keeping her expression cool and unfazed whenever the subject of her past arose.

It had been a little more than a year since the art forgery scandal that had crushed her budding career as an expert in early-twentieth-century art and antiques. In the blink of an eye, she had lost her most important asset in the world of art, her reputation as an honest dealer.

Following the humiliating debacle at the once-prestigious McClelland Gallery in Scottsdale, she had returned to Avalon to lick her wounds and plot her comeback. Step One of her big plan was to go to ground while the worst of the gossip dissipated.

Her small business, Elegant Relic, was only a

stopgap measure designed to occupy her time and energy while she schemed to make her triumphant return to the art world.

The shop specialized in inexpensive replicas of ancient, medieval, and gothic relics. She did a lively trade with the New Age and metaphysical types, as well as people who were fascinated by the symbolism and pageantry of the past.

She could not complain, she thought. She had even learned to take some satisfaction in the success of Elegant Relic. As Lloyd had promised, she had learned a lot about running her own business in the process. She had certainly come a long way since the disaster at McClelland.

Like the replicas she sold, she was very good at presenting a false facade to the world. She could fake a cool nonchalance about her former career. But deep inside, the hunger to reestablish herself smoldered.

Edward Vale and the Avalon Resort & Spa collection of Art Deco was her ticket back to the world she loved. She must not blow this golden opportunity.

"What do you want me to say, Edward? You paid for my opinion on *Dancing Satyr*, and I gave it to you. You know I'm right."

Edward pushed back the edges of his off-white jacket and planted his hands on his hips. He glared at the bronze statue. "Damn, damn, damn."

"You should have had me examine the piece before you bought it."

"I told you, there was another bidder. I had to make a decision on the spot." Edward groaned. "Who'd have thought that Forsyth would make a mistake like this?"

Alexa said nothing. The professional opinions of dealers of Forsyth's stature were almost never questioned.

"Damn, damn, damn," Edward said again.

Alexa eyed him. "What are you going to do about *Dancing Satyr?*"

"I don't know." Edward slanted her a sly, speculative glance. "I've got to think about it."

A tingle of alarm zinged through Alexa. "What's to think about? It's a fake."

"According to you," he murmured.

Panic replaced alarm. "Edward, you know I'm never wrong about this kind of thing."

His gaze slid away from hers. "No one is right one hundred percent of the time. If push comes to shove, it's Forsyth's opinion against yours. As the corporate art consultant for Avalon Resorts, Inc., I have every right to go with Forsyth's verdict. In fact, I've got a clear responsibility to credit his professional expertise."

Alexa straightened abruptly away from the Roman column. "Don't tell me you're planning to add this piece to the hotel's collection."

"Why not?" Edward's artificially tanned jaw set in mutinous lines. "It's been certified by no less than Paxton Forsyth himself."

"Damn it, Edward, you can't put *Dancing Satyr* into the Avalon Resort collection."

"Give me one good reason why it shouldn't be added."

She took a step toward him. "I've given you the best possible reason. It's not an Icarus Ives. It's a fake."

"So you say."

"Yes, so I say."

She was stunned to realize that she was on the verge of losing her temper. This was crazy. She had to watch her step or risk destroying everything she hoped to gain with this venture.

Edward had every right to take Forsyth's opinion over hers, she told herself. As he had just pointed out, most people would say that he had a duty to take the reputable gallery's opinion over hers.

This was business, she reminded herself. Her future was at stake. She must stay calm. The last thing she wanted to do was jeopardize her new working relationship with Edward Vale.

They had known each other since her days with the McClelland Gallery. When she'd learned that he had landed the plum assignment to select the Art Deco pieces that would be installed in the new Avalon Resort, she had approached him with her offer to consult anonymously.

Edward had leaped at the opportunity to take advantage of her expertise. He knew better than anyone else just how good she was at her work. On top of that, he had reason to be grateful to her. She had saved him from becoming one of McClelland's victims. He owed her, and he knew it.

They had struck a bargain. She had been his secret consultant on the Avalon Resorts project. She had done all the work, but Edward would take all the credit, at least initially.

If things went well and the reviews were favorable, he would leak the fact that she had assisted him on the project. The reviewers and others who considered themselves experts on the Art Deco style would not be able to retract their authoritative opinions without making themselves look like fools.

Alexa's vision of her potentially rosy future shimmered before her. With luck the reviews, articles, and feature stories in the major journals and publications that served the art world would bring in other consulting opportunities. Private collectors would seek her out. Museum curators and gallery owners would begin to call on her again.

It would take time, but she was determined to shed the taint of fraud that had tarnished her career.

Everything depended on this project, she thought. The glittering reception the hotel management planned to celebrate the opening of the new resort would attract a host of VIPs. There would be influential people not only from the tourism industry, but also from a variety of Southwest and West Coast museums and galleries.

Edward had told her that a reporter for *Twentieth-Century Artifact* was scheduled to attend the reception. The journal was considered a bible to everyone involved in the business of buying and selling the art and antiques of the twentieth century. It was *TCA's* "Insider's Notes" column that had done the most damage to her reputation following the McClelland fiasco.

No, she definitely could not afford to annoy Edward Vale.

On the other hand, she could not abide the thought of *Dancing Satyr* in the Avalon Resort collection. She had invested too much time, energy, and sheer passion on that collection. It was perfect, and it was *hers*.

"I understand your position." She gave him her

best shot at a placating smile. "But you've said yourself there will be a lot of experts at the hotel when it's opened. Why take a chance that one of them will recognize *Dancing Satyr* as a fake?"

Edward shook his head. "Highly unlikely that will happen. It's good enough to fool me and Paxton Forsyth. What are the odds that there will be someone in the crowd who's got your instincts? I've never met *anyone* else who's got your feel."

She had nothing left to lose. It was time to grovel. "Please, Edward. I'm throwing myself on your mercy. Leave it out of the collection as a favor to me."

He looked pained. "This is business. I spent a good-sized chunk of my total budget on *Dancing Satyr*. Trask may not know art, but he does know money. Sooner or later someone will take a look at the invoices. What the hell am I supposed to say? 'Sorry, Mr. Trask, I dropped a bundle of your money on a fake statue and had to throw it away'?"

"We've got time." Alexa tried for a cross between coaxing and persuasive. "It's not as though Trask will personally inspect the invoices. This is a corporate project. Heck, he'll probably never even see the bill. It will be handled by the company accountants, and it will take months to go through the process."

Edward hesitated. "I don't know, Alexa. From what I've been told, Trask keeps an eye on every aspect of his business."

She cast about in desperation. "Look, I'll make a deal with you. Promise me you'll leave *Dancing Satyr* out of the collection until after the opening night reception."

"Alexa—"

"Let the art critics and the gallery crowd see the good stuff that night. Give the media a chance to write the reviews. Wait until *TCA* tells the world that Avalon Resorts, Inc., houses a museum-caliber display of Art Deco. Then you can slip this stupid statue back into the collection if you really think it's genuine."

Edward bounced on his toes again while he considered her offer. Alexa waited, intensely aware of the swift beat of her own pulse.

"I'll think about it," Edward said finally.

Alexa breathed deeply and allowed herself to relax slightly.

"Thanks." She smiled. "You'll be doing yourself a favor by leaving this piece out. Like I said, why take the risk that someone else might recognize that it's a fake?"

"You're the only one who seems to think it's not a genuine Ives." He shot the cuff of his pale linen jacket and recoiled in apparent shock when he saw the face of his black and silver watch. "Look, I've got to run. There are a million things that have to be done to prepare for the reception."

"I understand."

"Give me a hand with this, will you?" Edward stooped to grasp the hindquarters of *Dancing Satyr*.

"Sure." Alexa took hold of the figure's head. "Sheesh. Not exactly a lightweight piece, is it?"

"No." Edward backed cautiously through the cluttered stockroom toward the rear door. "By the way, the Clarice Cliff teapots arrived from Harbin's this morning. They'll be gorgeous in that display case in the east wing."

"Yes, I know. I chose them, remember? It took me months to hunt down a good representative selection. Then I had to pry them out of the collectors 'hands."

"Bribe them, you mean."

"The good stuff rarely comes cheap." Lugging her half of the bronze, she followed him through the maze of artistically broken columns, scrolled pedestals, and winged lions that littered the back room of Elegant Relic. "Edward, about *Dancing Satyr* . . ."

"Get the door, will you?"

"Right."

She lowered her end of the figure to the floor and hurried around Edward to open the rear door. She peered out into the alley that served the boutiques and galleries in Avalon Plaza. It was too early in the day for any of the other establishments to be open, but she nevertheless took pains to be certain that there was no one around.

It would not do for anyone to notice her and Edward carrying a large Art Deco–style statue out of Elegant Relic.

She and Edward had not concealed the fact that they were acquainted with each other, but they had kept absolutely mum about the extent of their past and present association.

"All clear."

She went back to help Edward hoist the statue.

Together they carted it out to the unmarked white van that stood in the alley. Edward set his end down and slid open the vehicle's side door.

"Ready?" he asked.

"Ready."

They maneuvered it into the van. Edward quickly slammed the door closed.

Alexa dusted off her hands. "Edward?"

"Yes?" He dug out his keys and started toward the front of the van.

"There's just one more thing," she said very firmly.

He glanced warily back over his shoulder. "What's that?"

"I haven't received my invitation to the hotel opening yet. It should have come by now."

"Yes, I suppose it should have arrived," he said vaguely.

"I'd use the one that got sent to my mother and Lloyd since they're both in Maui for a month. But it very clearly states that it's for Mr. and Mrs. Kenyon."

"I'll look into it," Edward said much too glibly.

"You promised, Edward." It was time to get tough. Edward was very good at weaseling if he was given half a chance. "It was part of our arrangement, remember?"

He sighed. "I know, I know. But it's risky. What if Trask recognizes you and somehow puts you together with the McClelland forgery affair?"

"I told you, Trask has only seen me once, and that was only for a few minutes twelve years ago. I was a scrawny teenager at the time, and he had other things on his mind. He wouldn't remember me even if he did happen to see me at the reception. And there is no way he could tie me to the McClelland affair unless someone told him about it."

"I don't know." Edward looked dubious. "I hear he's a take-no-prisoners kind of guy if he thinks he's been crossed."

"No one's crossed him. He's getting what he's paid for."

"Yes, of course," Edward said quickly. "But you know that perception is everything in our business. If he even suspects that he's been had, we're doomed."

"Even if, by some hellacious bit of luck, Trask does see me at the reception and even if he does happen to recognize me and if he can associate me with the McClelland scandal, which is highly unlikely since he's not into art, he'd *still* have no way of knowing that I was the expert who selected the art in his new hotel."

"Well . . ."

"I haven't said a word about working for you on this project, and I know you've kept quiet about it. Who's going to tell Trask?"

"I suppose that's true."

Sensing weakness, Alexa pounced. "Look, I give you my word I'll wear black and stay out of sight behind the potted palms. There will be a huge crowd at the hotel on the night of the reception. Trask will never even know I'm there."

Edward studied her with an unusually thoughtful glint in his light gray eyes. "Are you sure you want to attend?"

"Are you kidding?" She stared at him, outraged. "I've put several quarts of my life's blood into assembling the Avalon Resort collection. Of course I want to be at the reception. I told you at the start that it was important to me."

"I thought maybe you might have changed your mind," Edward mumbled.

"What on earth made you think I'd do that?"

Edward twitched his discretely padded shoulders. He was clearly uncomfortable. "During the past few days it has come to my attention that not everyone here in Avalon is thrilled to have Trask back in town, even for a short time."

"So?"

Edward gave her a straight look as he opened the driver's door. "So, according to the talk I heard, one of the people who apparently would rather not have Trask here is your stepfather."

"Lloyd is not my stepfather," she said automatically. "He's the man my mother married after my parents were divorced. There's a difference, at least as far as I'm concerned. And what do you know about Trask and Lloyd, anyway?"

"As little as possible, I assure you." Edward shot her a meaningful look as he got behind the wheel. "You know my motto. Never get too curious about the client. That way lies madness."

"Edward, who told you about Lloyd and Trask?"

He inclined his head significantly at two of the other doors in the alleyway. "I overheard Joanna Bell and that fellow who owns the bookstore, Dylan Fenn, talking about it. I got the impression there was some bad blood between Trask and a couple of folks who had once been in a partnership with his father. True?"

Alexa glanced at the doors in question. One was the rear entrance of Joanna's Crystal Rainbow, a popular gallery that featured stone and crystal jewelry.

Alexa had met Joanna shortly after Elegant Relic

had opened. They were not close friends, but they had gotten to know each other as business neighbors. Joanna was the half-sister of the charismatic Webster Bell, owner and resident guru of the trendy metaphysical retreat called the Dimensions Institute.

The second door was the rear exit of Spheres, a metaphysically oriented bookshop owned and operated by Dylan Fenn.

Alexa turned back to Edward. "Whatever gossip you heard is more than a decade out of date. Forget it."

"Happy to oblige." Edward turned the key in the van's ignition. "As I said, my policy is not to get curious about the client."

"Edward, about my reception invitation . . ."

"All right, all right." He gave her a smile that showed off his nicely capped teeth. "If you're sure you really want to go to the ball, Cinderella, I'll arrange it. Just remember to stay out of sight while you're there. I have it on good authority that, whatever else he may be, Trask is no prince."

"I'm not looking for a prince. All I want is to get back my career."

Understanding softened Edward's expression. "I know, Alexa. Hang in there. If anyone can make it happen, you can."

She stood watching as Edward drove slowly out of the alley. After a while she turned and went back into the crowded stock room.

She wondered why she had not told Edward that *Dancing Satyr* was not just a very skillful forgery. It was a McClelland piece.

Mac was back in business.

3

She saw the Jeep first. A layer of desert grit dulled the dark green paint, evidence of a long drive. The vehicle was parked on the side of the road above Avalon Point. The sight of it brought her to a halt on the path.

It was not unusual to see a tourist stopped here at the Point. The sun was about to set, and the view of the stark, red rock landscape with its towers and canyons was magnificent at this time of day.

Alexa glanced around, searching for the Jeep's driver.

It took her a moment to find him. He stood deep in the long shadow cast by a stone outcropping.

The first thing that struck her was that he was on the wrong side of the waist-high metal rail that had been erected a few years ago to protect sightseers. Alarm shot through her. He was much too close to the edge of the Point.

He seemed oblivious to the vibrant beauty of the spectacular terrain set afire by the dying light. As Alexa watched, he gazed broodingly down into the brush-choked canyon. There was a dark intensity about him, as though he were engaged in reading omens and portents.

Sometimes an overly ambitious amateur photographer took one too many risks in an attempt to get the perfect sunset shot.

"Excuse me," she said loudly. "That guard rail is there for a good reason. It's dangerous to stand on the wrong side."

The man in the shadows turned unhurriedly to look at her.

Her first thought was that he could have stepped straight out of a Tamara de Lempicka painting.

The artist who had become known as the quintessential Art Deco portraitist would have loved him, Alexa thought. De Lempicka had excelled at creating a dark, sinister, edgy energy around her subjects. She had been able to endow them with a highly charged sensuality and an icy, enigmatic aura.

But in this man's case, she thought, de Lempicka would not have had to invent the ominous illusion. The painter's only task would have been to capture the unsettling reality of it.

The jolt of recognition hit Alexa with such force she froze in mid-step.

Trask.

Twelve years older, harder, more dangerous, but unmistakably Trask. He looked even bigger than he had the last time. Lean and broad-shouldered, he still took up a lot of space. It was a wonder light did not bend to get around him.

He contemplated her for a moment.

"Thanks for the warning," he said.

He made no move to get back behind the guard rail. It figured, she thought. This man was accustomed to standing on the edge of cliffs. She could tell that just by looking at him.

She realized she was holding her breath, waiting for him to recognize her. But he gave no indication that he remembered her from that long-ago scene in Lloyd's hall. She told herself she should be enormously relieved.

She released the breath she had been holding.

A gust of wind broke the peculiar little trance that had gripped her. She managed to keep her polite-to-the-tourist smile firmly fixed in place.

"You really should move back to the right side of that railing." She was horrified by the slightly breathless quality she heard in her own words. *Get a grip, Alexa.* "Didn't you see the sign?"

"Yeah, I saw it."

His voice was low and resonant. The voice of a man who did not have to speak loudly in order to get the attention of others. The voice of a man who was accustomed to giving orders and having them obeyed.

She had pushed her luck far enough. Time to take her leave before he recalled her face. No sense taking chances. She searched for a suitable exit line.

"Are you lost? Can I give you directions?" she asked.

He looked amused. "I know where I am."

"Well, in that case," she said briskly, "I'll be on my way. It's getting late."

He watched the breeze tangle her hair. "Can I give you a lift?"

"What? *No.*" Startled, she took a hasty step back, although he had made no move toward her. "I mean, thanks, but I live near here. I use this path for exercise." Lord, now she was babbling.

His brows rose. "It's all right. I'm not a serial killer."

She kept smiling. "Yeah, sure, that's what they all say."

"I take it you're the type who doesn't take lifts from strangers?"

"No intelligent person accepts rides from strangers in this day and age."

"Maybe I'd better introduce myself. My name is Trask. My company owns the new resort here in Avalon."

Stay cool, Alexa. "Nice to meet you, Mr. Trask."

"Just Trask."

"Yes, well, best of luck with the new resort." She retreated another step. "Everyone in town is very excited about it."

"Is that so?"

"Yes, it is."

"I'm glad to hear that."

She did not trust the cool amusement she saw in his eyes. She dropped her own polite smile.

"Welcome to Avalon, Trask."

She turned quickly and walked swiftly away from him.

"Better hurry," he said much too softly behind her. "I hear that night falls fast in the desert. It'll be dark soon."

She resisted the sudden urge to break into a run. With grim determination she kept moving, listening intently for the sound of the Jeep's engine.

She finally heard it come to life with a low, throaty growl. She did not look back, but neither did she take a deep breath until the sound receded into the distance.

Then and only then, did she allow herself to quicken her step.

Adrenaline rushed through her, creating a tingling in her hands and feet. She was both hot and cold. It was the sort of feeling one got after having had a very close call.

The other shoe had finally dropped. Trask was back in Avalon.

4

An hour later, dressed in a black satin robe splashed with an intricate, flowing Deco design worked in gold, Alexa stretched out on one of her most prized possessions, a chaise longue. The wrought iron piece was a sleek, 1920s-era creation, cushioned in black leather and ornamented with legs and arms in the shape of palm trees.

The chaise longue had been a gift from her former employer, the person she had once considered her closest friend and mentor but who had ultimately betrayed her.

Alexa's jaw tightened as she reached for the phone. Thoughts of McClelland had hung heavy on her mind all day, thanks to Edward. She pictured *Dancing Satyr* again as she picked up the phone. She had not been wrong. It was definitely one of Mac's pieces.

How like McClelland to send a piece into the Paxton Forsyth Gallery, the very bastion of the twentieth-century arts and antiques establishment. It had been a test, no doubt. Mac had wanted to see if the bronze could get past Forsyth himself. Which, of course, it had.

"Hello?" Vivien Kenyon's warm voice came clearly over the line.

"It's me, Mom." Alexa took a sip of the wine.

"Alexa, dear. Is anything wrong?"

"No, of course not. Everything is fine here." Alexa settled deeper into the chaise. "I just called to see how things were going there."

"Maui is great, as always." There was a smile in Vivien's voice. "Lloyd is out on the golf course as we speak. He'll be back soon. You're sure everything is okay back there? I wasn't expecting you to call."

Alexa took a sip of sauvignon blanc and contemplated the Cubist-inspired geometric pattern of her black, brown, and yellow rug.

"I met the owner of the new Avalon Resort & Spa today," she said.

There was a short, brittle pause on the other end of the line. "You met young Trask?"

"I wouldn't call him young. Not anymore. Maybe never."

"It's all relative, isn't it? But, yes, I suppose he would be twelve years older now, wouldn't he? That would make him, what? Thirty-four?"

"Thirty-five."

"Did he remember you?"

"No, thank goodness. And it was a very casual sort of meeting. I didn't even give him my name."

"I see." Vivien sighed. "Well, it's not as though we didn't know that he was coming back to Avalon for the opening of the resort."

"When are you going to admit that you scheduled your vacation so that you and Lloyd wouldn't be here while Trask was in town?"

Vivien hesitated. "I suppose it was rather obvious, wasn't it?"

"Uh-huh."

"Lloyd refuses to be concerned, but I felt that, at best, it would be awkward for both of them to come face-to-face at the reception."

"Ever the diplomat, hmm?"

"Ever the coward." Vivien chuckled. "Besides, Lloyd and I were long overdue for this vacation."

"You just got back from a cruise."

Vivien let that pass. "I'm sure that Trask has made his peace with his father's death."

Alexa thought about Trask standing on the wrong side of the guard rail, gazing down into the canyon below Avalon Point. "What makes you so certain of that?"

"Well, it's obvious, isn't it? He's been a wealthy, successful man for several years. He's got resources. If he'd intended to rake up the past, he would have done so long ago."

"Maybe."

"He didn't even bother to visit Avalon during the construction of the resort," Vivien reminded her. "He let his staff handle everything."

Alexa sipped wine. "True."

"I'm sure he's only there now to handle the formalities associated with the opening of the hotel. He won't stay more than a few days, at most."

"Probably not." There was a beat of silence. "Mom?"

"Yes?"

"About what happened twelve years ago?"

"What about it?"

"What if Trask hasn't made peace with the past? What if he's back in town to cause trouble?"

"I really don't think he would have waited this long to come back if he'd had revenge on his mind." Vivien's own anxious uncertainty was painfully clear beneath the surface of her assured words.

"I was too young to pay attention to the details of the events," Alexa said slowly. "But I do remember that Lloyd was involved in a partnership with Harry Trask and another man."

"Dean Guthrie."

"Right. Guthrie. That's the name. He's still around, isn't he?"

"Yes, of course. I never did care for the man. He drinks too much and he's got a violent temper. I forget how many wives he's had. Three, at least. He divorced the last one a few months ago. Someone said she's a jewelry designer. Lives out in Shadow Canyon, I believe."

"Looking back on it, Mom, do you think there's any chance that Trask was right about his father's death not being an accident?"

"My God, Alexa, you can't possibly believe that Lloyd would—"

"No, of course not," Alexa said hastily. "Never in a million years. But what about Guthrie? You just said he drinks too much and he has a temper. Do you think he might have had something to do with Harry Trask's death?"

"I talked to Lloyd about it at the time," Vivien said quietly. "He has always been convinced that, even though Guthrie has a temper, he's not a killer."

"Lloyd was always pretty good at figuring out what made people tick," Alexa admitted.

"You should know," Vivien said gently.

Alexa recalled how patient and understanding Lloyd had been with her during those tumultuous years after she and Vivien had moved into his home.

She had fiercely resisted the notion of anyone trying to take her father's place. Lloyd had never tried to do that. She still remembered the conversation she had overheard between her mother and Lloyd shortly after they had married. Vivien had been worried about Alexa's failure to accept her new husband.

Lloyd had been as steady and calm about Alexa's icy attitude toward him as he was about everything else. "That girl doesn't need another father in her life," he'd said. "She needs a man who can show her that not all men are like her father."

Somehow in his own quiet, solid, dependable way, he had become very important to her over the years. It was Lloyd who had taught her how to drive, helped her select a college, instructed her in the fundamentals of running her own business.

Patient, solid, dependable Lloyd. She was surprised by the hot rush of protective loyalty she felt toward him.

"When it comes to judging people, Lloyd's track record isn't perfect," Alexa said.

"What do you mean?"

"Don't you remember? Twelve years ago he said that Trask would not come back."

"I remember." Vivien paused. "I also recall that you said Trask would return some day."

"I was right."

5

Trask stroked the stylized wings of one of the two massive marble condors that guarded the lobby staircase.

"It looks like something that fell off the top of the Chrysler Building," he said.

A pained expression appeared in Edward Vale's eyes. It vanished as quickly as it had come, replaced by the serene arrogance of authority.

"It's considered an excellent example of the Aztec and Mayan influence on the Deco sculptural style."

"How much did I pay for them?"

Edward was unable to conceal another wince. "I'd have to check the paperwork, but I believe we purchased the pair of condors for something in the neighborhood of twenty thousand."

It was Trask's turn to wince. "That's a hell of a neighborhood. Twenty grand? For two marble birds?"

"We were fortunate to get them," Edward assured him. "They were previously in the hands of a private collector. If it hadn't been for my, uh, contact in the Deco market, I wouldn't have even been aware that they were for sale."

"Guess I should be grateful that your contact found a couple of condors instead of a pair of pink flamingos."

Edward cleared his throat. "The sculptures make a brilliant frame for this truly outstanding staircase."

Trask took a step back and studied the unabashedly exotic lines of the cascading staircase. It was the focal point of the ornate lobby, the sort of staircase that women clad in satin evening gowns descended with languid grace in old Cary Grant films.

Trask reminded himself that he knew a good fantasy when he saw one.

"You're right, Vale. The birds suit the staircase."

Edward relaxed slightly. "I'm glad you're pleased."

Trask turned slowly on his heel, surveying the rest of the lobby. From the elaborate wrought iron and etched glass fixtures that produced a sultry ambient light to the richly lacquered end tables and the low, sweeping curves of the chairs, it was a complete universe. The lobby reeked of a dark, smoldering sexuality and between-the-wars decadence. The entire effect was anchored by the antiques and objets d'art that were strategically showcased throughout the hotel.

He knew that when guests stepped through the front doors they would walk into another time and place, a world in which sophisticated romance and dangerous intrigues seemed possible.

He had bought and paid for a fantasy, and that was exactly what had been delivered.

"You did a good job, Vale. Looks like I got my money's worth."

"Thank you." Edward glowed with relief. "May I say that you've created a very unique vision here at the Avalon Resort & Spa. I'm sure your guests will be enthralled."

"Has all of the art arrived on site?"

"Yes." Edward cleared his throat. "With the exception of one bronze that will be installed at the end of the hallway in the west wing this afternoon."

"Fine. Then we're set."

"Yes, indeed." Edward smiled broadly. "I can assure you that, so far as the art collection is concerned, everything will be in place for the reception."

"Good. My PR people are counting on the art and antiques to pull in the media."

"I understand. I'm sure it will have the desired effect."

"It damned well better have the right effect," Trask said. "I paid enough for it."

The sound of footsteps on tile caught his attention. He glanced over his shoulder and saw Pete Santana striding swiftly toward him.

Pete had worked for Avalon Resorts, Inc., for four years. He was an outgoing, high-energy type with a keen eye for the subtle details that made the difference between four stars and five in the travel guides.

"Sorry to interrupt." Pete came to a halt. He acknowledged Edward with a quick nod and then looked at Trask. "I've got a meeting with the head of security in a few minutes. We're going to go over some parking and crowd-handling issues for the night of the reception. Thought I'd better check to see if you wanted to join us."

Trask shook his head. "No, thanks. You're in charge of running this hotel, Pete. I told you, I'm only here to help draw the press and the VIPs. After that, I'm strictly on vacation."

"Right." Pete hid his obvious skepticism behind a professional smile. "Well, I'd better get to the meeting. Let me know if there's anything you need, sir."

"I'm not one of the guests, Pete. I can take care of myself."

"Right," Pete said again. He looked even more doubtful.

"Oh, yeah, one more thing," Pete added. "About those two particular RSVPs you wanted Glenda to follow up."

Trask stilled. "What about them?"

"I checked with her a few minutes ago. She told me that Guthrie never bothered to respond so she called his office and was told that he definitely will not attend the reception."

Interesting, Trask thought. The hunt had barely begun, but the quarry was already running for cover.

"What about Kenyon?" he asked. Out of the corner of his eye he saw Vale stiffen. You knew you were in a small town when even your overpriced art consultant had heard the local gossip.

"Glenda mentioned that she had received written regrets from Mr. and Mrs. Kenyon," Pete said. "Seems they're in Hawaii for the month."

Santana looked as wary as Vale, Trask thought. Apparently everyone had leaped to the conclusion that he was back in Avalon to do more than just open a resort. Fine by him. When you wanted something at the bottom of the pot to float to the surface, you got out a spoon and started stirring.

"All right, Pete. Thanks for the update."

"Sure. Like I said, let me know if there's anything else." Pete glanced at Edward. "By the way, Glenda got your last-minute addition to the guest list, Mr. Vale. She sent out an invitation to Alexa Chambers."

"Thank you," Edward said in a strangled voice.

"No problem." Pete smiled. "It's standard Avalon Resorts procedure to allow all major subcontractors and suppliers on a project to invite a few guests to the opening night reception."

"Very kind." Edward dug out a pristine white handkerchief and blotted his forehead. "A bit warm in here, isn't it? Perhaps the air conditioning needs adjustment."

Trask watched with interest as Edward wiped away perspiration. Outside, the late spring sun had driven the temperature into the mid eighties, but here inside the lobby the atmosphere was cool and comfortable.

"I'll have someone check the equipment," Trask said softly.

"Yes, well, just a suggestion." Edward smiled weakly. "If you'll excuse me, I'll go see about that bronze."

He swung around and fled toward the massive etched glass doors at the front of the lobby.

Trask waited until he had disappeared. Then he

walked past the very expensive condors and went up the staircase to the second floor.

At the top of the stairs he turned and went down the carpeted hall to the owner's suite at the far end of the west wing.

He opened the door and entered a room that exuded raffish elegance, a place designed for midnight seductions and the hatching of dark plots.

Subdued, milky light from the frosted glass wall sconces gleamed on the abstract design of the red and gold screen. The vermilion and yellow tapestries that covered the furnishings added a rich, decadent touch. According to Nathan, the sofa and armchairs were replicas of designs featured in something called the 1925 Paris Exposition. When Trask had asked what that was, Nathan had groaned. Trask had been left with the impression that the event had been a defining moment in Deco style.

He went to the black lacquered cabinet and switched on a lamp that looked like a hood ornament from a 1927 Packard. He opened the cabinet doors to reveal the state-of-the-art business work station inside. Picking up the phone, he punched in a downstairs extension.

Glenda Blaine, his unnervingly efficient head of public relations, answered on the first ring.

"Blaine here," she said with the brusque precision of a military officer reporting in from the front.

Glenda had worked for him since the inception of Avalon Resorts, Inc., but he still found himself tempted to salute every time he spoke with her.

"I understand we sent out an invitation to someone named Alexa Chambers."

"Yes, sir. It was a last-minute request. I handled it myself."

Trask leaned back against the edge of the desk and studied the graceful, marble-topped console in front of him. "I believe that her name was submitted by the art consultant."

"That's right."

"Do we have any record of what Alexa Chambers did on the project?"

"Let me check."

Trask listened to the faint rustle of papers on the other end of the line. An image of Glenda's terrifyingly efficient desktop floated through his mind.

She came back a few seconds later.

"Here's the list, but there are no details concerning her connection to the resort project. All I have is an address for her here in Avalon."

"See if you can pin down her connection to the project. Find out if she was a supplier or a sub, will you?"

"Certainly, sir."

"And, Glenda?"

"Yes?"

"Be discreet will you?"

"I'm in PR, sir." There was no hint of amusement in her words, only firm, professional assurance. "I am nothing if not discreet."

"Sorry. It's just that I'd rather Vale didn't find out that I'm questioning any of the names on his list."

"I understand. He might take offense. Artistic types can be temperamental."

"Yeah, just like us business types."

Glenda paused for a beat or two. Trask wondered if she was rerunning the conversation through her neatly organized brain to see if she was supposed to laugh. She evidently concluded that a polite chuckle was unnecessary because when she resumed speaking her inflection did not alter.

"Ms. Chambers may not have had anything at all to do directly with the project," she warned. "You know how the architect and design people are. They often use their invitation privileges for clients, friends, and relatives. Opening night receptions provide an opportunity to show off their work."

"I'm aware of that. Get back to me when you find out which category Ms. Chambers falls into."

"Yes, sir."

Trask slowly put down the phone. He straightened away from the desk and walked across the thick carpet to the French doors.

He twisted the ornate brass knob and stepped out onto the balcony. A warm breeze, as light as a woman's silk scarf and infused with the clean scent of the desert, drifted over him.

He wondered if Harry would have been pleased with the way the resort had turned out. He knew that he would get some answers here in Avalon but that would not be one of them.

Nathan had come up with the design based on Harry's original concept. The resort had been constructed on the bones of the old Avalon Mansion, which had been built in the 1930s by a retired mobster who had moved to Arizona after Prohibition was repealed.

Nathan claimed the end result was a cross between Frank Lloyd Wright and the Spanish Colonial style. In Trask's opinion it was a Hollywood fantasy straight out of a thirties film.

Fine by him. He knew the power of a good fantasy.

Down below, the hotel's fancifully sculpted outdoor pool sparkled in the afternoon sun. Beyond lay the verdant green fairway of the Red Canyon Country Club's twelfth hole. The frivolous luxuries of civilization were framed by the bleak, timeless elegance of the desert's towering sandstone spires and rust-colored ramparts.

After a lifetime spent in the cool, cloudy realm of the Pacific Northwest, the starkly surreal cliffs and canyons of Avalon should have felt alien to him, Trask thought. He had been completely unprepared for the impact the place had had on him when he arrived three days ago. He still could not understand why, at thirty-five, he suddenly found himself drawn to this science fiction landscape.

He had not taken any pleasure in the scenery twelve years ago. On that occasion he had spent forty-eight hellish hours arranging his father's funeral, sweating the future, and dealing with the guilt that had gnawed at his insides. The only emotions he had felt toward Avalon then had been rage.

But this time it all seemed different somehow. It had started feeling that way the day he got into town—the day he met the woman with the crystal-gazing eyes at Avalon Point.

Her image flickered through his mind again. He remembered the way her sleek, dark hair had curved just beneath her high cheekbones, saw again the distinctive line of her nose and the deep, steady watchfulness in her blue-green eyes.

When she had walked away from him, there had been an unconscious sensuality in her stride that had made him think of full moons and scented, sultry bedrooms.

She had not been wearing one of the turquoise and silver bracelets that half the town sported. As far as he could figure out, the lack of one indicated that she was not affiliated with the Dimensions Institute crowd.

Then he thought about the fact that there had been another item of jewelry missing from her hand. A wedding ring.

The disturbing sense of awareness that had whispered through him that afternoon at the Point returned.

The skinny teenager with the big, anxious eyes had grown up. She'd been scared to death of him that night twelve years ago, but she'd hung on to the phone and ordered him out of Kenyon's house with a gutsy determination that he had never forgotten.

Thanks to the private investigator he had hired a few months ago, he now had a name to go with the face.

Alexa Chambers.

What the hell was she doing trying to sneak into his reception?

6

"I think that does it for Avalon Plaza's segment of the Gallery Walk." Alexa put down her pen and picked up her tea. "Anything else?"

"I don't think so." Foster Radstone's distinctive Dimensions bracelet, a unique, intricate design rendered in turquoise and silver, glinted when he reached for his own tea. "I don't see any major conflicts. Things won't really get into high gear at the Institute until after eight on Saturday night. Plenty of time for stragglers to drive out there to hear Webster speak and to see the fireworks."

"Is parking going to be a problem at the Institute?" Seated on the other side of the small Café Solstice table, Alexa closed the binder that contained her copies of the Avalon Spring Festival committee notes. "The officials are all saying that there will be more people in town for festival weekend this year than ever before."

Foster was unfazed. "We'll manage. Plenty of room outside the gates for the overflow."

The green awning that overhung the café's outdoor terrace reflected the warmth of the sun. It was
getting late in the day. The lunch crowd had thinned
out. It had been replaced by Avalon Plaza shoppers
seeking a reviving cup of one of the many tea
blends that were specially concocted by Stewart
Lutton, the owner of Café Solstice.

Alexa searched for an excuse to return to Elegant
Relic. She did not relish the frequent meetings with
Foster that had been required by her duties on the
festival committee. She had not been keen on vol-
unteering for the job in the first place, but her mother and Lloyd had talked her into it.

*"A good way to expand your circle of friends," Vivien
had said.*

*"Great for making business contacts," Lloyd had
added.*

Alexa knew full well that what they'd both
meant was that she might meet someone of the male
persuasion and get herself a real, live date.

Instead, she had wound up spending far too
much time with Foster Radstone, the financial guru
of the Dimensions Institute.

Who could have foreseen that she would be forced
to meet regularly with the only man in Avalon whom
she actually had dated since her return?

This experience would teach her to volunteer, she
thought grimly.

Business concluded, Foster lounged back in the
spindly little metal chair and propped one ankle on
the opposite knee. He showed no signs of preparing
to rush off to meet one-on-one with the other committee members who were scattered around town.

Instead he looked ready to spend the rest of the afternoon under Café Solstice's awning.

"Everything all set for the psychic fair?" Alexa asked, more for something to say than because she was genuinely interested.

The fair, with its colorful collection of self-proclaimed psychics, crystal analyzers, aura readers, channelers, and mediums, was a popular part of the festival. Every year it drew thousands to the grounds of the Dimensions Institute, which provided space for the event.

"We'll have twice as many booths this year as last," Foster said with complacent satisfaction. "Webster is pleased."

Alexa did not doubt that. As far as the Institute was concerned, anyone who attended the fair was a potential customer for one or more of its seminars. For all its metaphysical pretensions, Dimensions was, at its core, a business. The Institute had been Avalon's largest employer for years. When the new resort opened, Dimensions would take second place.

"Next year the committee had better think about using shuttle buses to handle some of the traffic between downtown and the Institute," Alexa said. ‹

Foster gave her an approving smile. "You're absolutely right. Next year's committee will have to consider the idea."

Alexa knew that she was supposed to feel warmed by Foster's approving smile. But for some reason it made her want to grind her teeth.

"Well, here's to the end of committee meetings," she said, raising her cup in a mock toast. "I, for one, can't wait for this year's festival to conclude."

"I know it's been a lot of hard work, but I think it

was just what you needed, Alexa. It was good for you to get involved."

As usual, Foster's well-meant comments ruffled her feathers. She could not get past the sensation that she was being patronized.

She reminded herself that it was only natural that Webster Bell's acknowledged right-hand man came across as a self-confident fount of insight. What else could one expect from the number two man at a metaphysical retreat?

In all fairness, Foster was the living embodiment of the sensitive, New Age male. He was also well educated. On their first date he had skillfully inserted into the conversation the fact that he held two academic degrees, one in philosophy and one in business.

She refused to be impressed. Deep down inside she knew that she was just as smart as he was. Okay, maybe she was not as *enlightened*, but she was definitely just as smart.

On their second date she had asked him why, with his academic leanings, he had gone into the assistant guru business. After they had gotten past her insensitive and unenlightened terminology, he had launched into a two-hour lecture on the importance of the search for spiritual meaning in the modern world.

"Ultimately, I will be able to do more good working with the Dimensions Institute than I will ever be able to do in the academic or business world," he'd concluded earnestly.

Alexa had felt extremely shallow and unenlightened for about a day after that conversation. But she had gotten over it.

In addition to all his other sterling qualities, Foster was good-looking. Maybe a little too good-looking, Alexa thought. Then again, she was probably just being picky.

She had seen photos of Foster in the Institute's brochures and, from time to time, in the *Avalon Herald*. The camera loved him. The pictures emphasized the burnished quality of his golden brown hair and the heroic line of his jaw. In person, however, his greatest feature was the overwhelmingly direct, I-am-deeply-interested-in-you expression in his amber eyes.

Foster's seminars were almost as popular as those of Webster Bell himself, especially among the female students.

No one had been more surprised than Alexa when he had asked her to go to dinner with him shortly after she had dropped out of one of the Institute's popular meditation seminars. But she had sensed from the start that a relationship with Foster would end the way all of her relationships ended: with a whimper, not a bang. She had been right.

"Have you given any more thought to signing up for another seminar?" Foster asked.

"No."

"I really think you would benefit from one of our intensive classes, Alexa."

"I know you mean well, but I've been very busy lately. Besides, that metaphysical stuff just isn't for me."

"It's for everyone." He gave her a smile of gentle encouragement. "You didn't give the program much of a chance, admit it."

"All right, so I quit after three weeks."

"It takes longer than that to begin to obtain the full effects, especially for someone like you."

"Someone like me?"

"I watched you while you were with us at the Institute. You have a long way to go, Alexa. You need to learn how to let yourself feel, how to live in the here-and-now, how to be free."

"Thanks, but I'm doing okay."

"But you could be doing better than okay. That's my whole point." Foster leaned forward. "You have the power within to set yourself free. Why not use it?"

"Because I'm one of those poor, unlucky stiffs who work for a living." Alexa glanced at her watch. "Speaking of which, I'd better get back to the shop. Kerry will wonder what happened to me."

"All I ask is that you think about signing up for another guided meditation seminar. You need to open yourself up to the flow of positive energy. You're missing so much in life because you've allowed the negative forces to enter your consciousness."

A large, dark shape blotted out the light. Awareness tingled through Alexa. She did not have to look up to know who stood there.

"Am I interrupting anything?" Trask asked.

"Speaking of negative forces," Alexa murmured.

"What was that?" He gave her a look of polite inquiry. "I didn't quite catch it."

She looked up with a deliberately vague smile. "Have we met? Oh, yes, now I remember. Avalon Point. You're involved with the new resort or something like that."

Amusement flickered in his green eyes. He gave

her a small salute with the cup of coffee he held in one hand. "I can see I'm going to have to work on making a stronger first impression."

Alexa flushed. Fortunately, there was no need to come up with a brilliant rejoinder. Foster was on his feet, hand extended.

"Foster Radstone. I'm with the Dimensions Institute. I don't believe I've had the pleasure."

"Trask. Like the lady said, I'm with Avalon Resorts."

Foster chuckled. "You mean you *are* Avalon Resorts. Welcome to Avalon, Trask. I take it you and Alexa know each other?"

"We've met," Trask said.

Alexa tensed. The enigmatic expression in his eyes was worrisome. Did he recognize her or not? The suspense was maddening.

She decided to take the initiative.

"I was in a hurry to get home that day," she said casually. "I don't believe I gave you my name."

"No, you didn't. You were distracted."

She frowned. "Distracted?"

"You didn't like the fact that I was on the wrong side of the guard rail, remember? Tell me, do you patrol that stretch of the road on a regular basis looking for tourists who don't follow the rules?"

Out of the corner of her eye she saw Foster's startled stare. She set her jaw and refused to blush again.

"I'm Alexa Chambers," she said very firmly.

Trask inclined his head. "Nice to meet you, Ms. Chambers. Again."

There was no flash of recognition in his expression, merely a cool, enigmatic amusement.

She reminded herself to breathe. It was okay. Nothing to worry about. He had not yet made any connection between herself and Lloyd. He had been in town for several days now, and the Chambers name still meant nothing to him. She could relax.

"Do you always follow the rules yourself, Ms. Chambers?" he asked.

She certainly had until recently, she reflected. It occurred to her that before she had concocted the scheme to revive her dead-on-arrival career, she'd never had any real incentive to break rules. Contrary to her former therapist's opinion, it wasn't fear that had kept her from taking risks, she thought. It was the fact that, until now, there had been nothing she had wanted badly enough to warrant a walk on the wild side.

"Unlike some people, I assume rules exist for a purpose," she said.

"Sure. To be broken."

"Fortunately not everyone holds the same opinion," Alexa said through her teeth. "Like it or not, rules are the glue that holds a civilization together."

"I'm not in favor of breaking all the rules," Trask said. "Just the ones that get in my way."

She gave him a steely smile. "Tell me, do you find that there are a lot of rules that get in your way, Trask?"

He shrugged. "I admit that, on the highway of life, I tend to ignore the occasional guard rail warning sign."

Foster glanced from Alexa to Trask and back again. He looked politely baffled. "Guess I'm missing the joke here. What's this about guard rails and signs?"

"Ms. Chambers happened to notice my Jeep at Avalon Point the day I arrived," Trask said. "She saw me standing on the wrong side of the guard rail. Made her nervous."

"I see."

"Then I offered to give her a ride home." Trask watched Alexa's face. "But she said that she didn't think it was safe to accept lifts from strangers."

Foster smiled expansively. "I think I get the picture. Obviously a little misunderstanding. So you stopped at the Point to admire the scenery? It's pretty incredible, isn't it?"

"I wasn't admiring the scenery," Trask said.

Alexa raised her brows. "I imagine our landscape must come as something of a shock after Seattle."

"It's different."

Foster changed the subject with a diplomatic aplomb that Alexa could only admire.

"Congratulations on the new hotel," he said. "It's going to be a major asset to Avalon."

Trask nodded. "Thanks. We're pleased with it."

"You certainly chose the ideal time to open," Foster enthused. "The Spring Festival is the big event of the year. The town will be filled with visitors."

"I think it will be a good launch," Trask said. "The hotel officially opens to guests two days after the reception. We're booked solid, not only for the festival, but for the next several months."

Foster nodded. "I'm not surprised. Avalon is becoming a major destination point in the Southwest. The positive energy of the vortices in this region make this a very special place."

"Generally speaking, I'm not into metaphysics."

Trask glanced at Alexa. "But I do believe in the old saying that what goes around, comes around."

"Interestingly enough," Foster said, slipping into his pedantic mode, "that adage is based on ancient karmic doctrine which holds that all actions have consequences, not only in the material world but in the personal and metaphysical realms as well."

Trask did not take his gaze off Alexa. "Translated, that probably means that no good deed goes unpunished."

"I'll keep that in mind the next time I see you standing on the wrong side of the guard rail," Alexa said. "How long do you plan to be in town, Trask?"

"As long as it takes."

Alexa could have sworn that she felt a chill wind blow across the café terrace. But the scalloped edge of the green awning did not so much as flutter.

He was playing games, she thought. Why? Were the rumors right after all? Had he returned to Avalon on a mission of vengeance?

Trask sampled his coffee. The hard line of his mouth curved in rueful dismay. "The quest goes on."

Alexa tensed. "What quest?"

"I've been looking for a decent cup of coffee ever since I arrived in town. So far no luck."

Foster laughed. "I've heard that people from Seattle have an obsession with coffee."

Alexa raised her brows. "If you want coffee, Trask, you came to the wrong place. Café Solstice is known for its tea. The owner blends it himself."

"Looks like I've got a problem," Trask said.

"Could be." Alexa had had enough. She scooped up the festival binder and rose to her feet. "You just said you don't put much stock in metaphysics, Trask, but maybe the fact that both our scenery and our tea leaves you cold is a sign that you won't be staying too long in Avalon."

"Depends."

"On what?" she snapped.

"On whether I find something else besides the scenery and the tea here. Something that won't leave me cold."

7

The Guardian drank the last of the herbal tea and watched the rays of the setting sun paint the canyons and spires of Avalon in shades of rust and blood.

Night descended. After a while, the outlines of reality shifted, altered, and took on new dimensions.

Here in this realm of enhanced consciousness the power and direction of the energy vortices were clear and easy to analyze if one was gifted, as the Guardian was, with the ability to see the deeper truths.

The vortices were in flux, as expected. Trask's arrival, after all, had been anticipated for months. The harmonic balance of powers in the region had shifted violently. The negative energy fields were surging to the surface.

It was a dangerous state of affairs, this imbalance in the vortices. But the Guardian reveled in it, drew power from it.

The Guardian went deeper into the trance, found

the place where the most volatile energy pulsed and seethed.

After a while, when the time was right, the Guardian surrendered to the swirling forces with a shuddering cry of raw, sexual release that reverberated endlessly against the cavern walls.

The climax was a real mind-blower. But then, it had been twelve years since the last really good one.

8

She kept her promise to Edward. She wore black to the opening night gala at the resort, and as soon as she was inside the lobby, she made every effort to fade into the woodwork.

Alexa drifted, ghostlike, along the fringes of the crowd and listened to the scraps of conversation around her. She was careful to keep a watchful eye on Trask, making certain that they were separated by a sea of people or a jungle of potted palms.

There were several familiar faces in the throng. She exchanged nods with some friends of Vivien's and Lloyd's and smiled at a couple of Elegant Relic customers. Although all the local VIPs were present, including the mayor and her husband, many of those in attendance were from out of town. In addition to the architect, design, and construction teams that had worked on the resort project, there were representatives of various sectors of the tour industry.

Travel writers from the Tucson and Phoenix papers were among the invitees, and the reporter from *Twentieth-Century Artifact* had arrived.

The sheer numbers present made it easy to remain unobtrusive. Alexa told herself that all she had to worry about was staying out of Trask's path.

It was not difficult to know where he was in the room at any given moment. Some sixth sense warned her whenever the natural ebb and flow of the crowd brought him too close.

The odds of accidentally stumbling into him were minimal, she thought. Even if she had been trying to get close, she would have had to work at it. As the host for the occasion, he was constantly surrounded.

A tall, statuesque, middle-aged woman wearing a pair of red-framed reading glasses and a no-nonsense haircut hovered constantly at Trask's elbow. Alexa concluded that she was Glenda Blaine, the Avalon Resorts, Inc., PR person Edward had mentioned.

Center of attention though he was, Trask was not the only major attraction in the room tonight. Many of those who could not get close to him formed a tight cluster around the charismatic figure of Webster Bell, the head of the Dimensions Institute.

Alexa halted near a pillar and watched Bell for a moment. She had spoken with him on occasion when he had visited his half-sister, Joanna, at her shop in Avalon Plaza. He had always been gallant and charming.

Webster would have been hard to miss in any gathering. He had what, in the theatrical world, was called *presence*. Tall and dynamic, he was endowed with a rugged, handsomely weathered face that would have done credit to one of the legendary gunslingers of old Arizona.

Bell was somewhere in his early sixties. He wore his silver hair in a ponytail secured with a black thong. His rakish black shirt and black trousers were set off with a wide silver and turquoise-studded belt. There was another loop of turquoise and silver around his throat. It matched the bracelet that circled his wrist.

Many in the crowd wore similar bracelets. They were fashionable among the locals and sold well to souvenir-seeking visitors. Alexa thought about the one that Foster had given her. It was an expensive version, made with real silver and quality turquoise, unlike the cheap imitations the tourists bought in large quantities. Presently, it was sitting in the bottom drawer of her jewelry case.

"There you are, Alexa." Edward, resplendent in an all-white tux, materialized at her elbow. "Personally, I can't usually abide the guru type, but I have to admit that Bell seems decent enough. He certainly cuts an impressive figure."

Alexa grinned. "I suspect there's a bit of the showman inside every successful guru."

"True." Edward popped a canapé into his mouth and munched. "I'm a little surprised to see that he was invited to Trask's opening."

"Professional courtesy," Alexa said. "When you stop and think about it, he and Trask are both in the hotel business."

"You have a point. From what I hear, the Dimensions Institute gets almost as many paying guests each year as a major resort."

"Bell and Trask have something else in common," Alexa said. "They're both catering to the high end of the market. Being trendy has its price. It costs as much to stay at Dimensions for a week as it does to stay at an Avalon Resort."

"Given the choice, I'll take a week at an Avalon resort over two weeks at Dimensions, any day." Edward shuddered. "At least at an Avalon hotel the client isn't forced to eat tofu and meditate with crystals."

"There is that." Alexa turned around to face him. "Level with me, Edward. What is the art crowd saying about my collection tonight?"

"They're going wild over it." Edward chuckled. "You should hear the reporter from *TCA*. He's raving about the depth and scope of the collection. No one knows it yet, but you, my dear, are a brilliant success. In the meantime, I, of course, am accepting all the credit."

An exuberant anticipation bubbled up inside Alexa. "I can live with that for now."

"I'm going to take a little group through the east wing to look at the Deskey textiles and the Steuben glass." Edward cocked a brow. "Want to trail along behind us and listen in?"

"No, thanks. I think I'll take my own private tour."

"Just be sure you stay out of Trask's path."

"Don't worry," Alexa said. "He's too busy with his guests to notice me tonight."

"You're probably right. Still, we wouldn't want to take any chances."

"Don't worry, I have it on good authority that I'm the risk-averse type."

"Who told you that?"

"My therapist."

Edward gave her an amused, skeptical look. "If

you're so risk-averse, why are you here tonight?"

She tightened her hand around the strap of her small evening bag. "Because tonight is very, very important to me."

Edward gave her a knowing look. "Some risks are worth taking, aren't they?"

"Yes."

"Don't worry, Alexa. It's all going to work out. You'll see. In a few months, you'll be back in business."

"For myself, this time," she vowed. "If there's one thing I've learned since McClelland left me to the wolves, it's that I much prefer to be my own boss."

"I can't blame you for leaping to that conclusion." He started to saunter off.

"Edward?"

He stopped and looked back. "Hmm?"

She smiled. "Regardless of what happens to my career, I want to thank you for everything you've done."

"My pleasure. Besides, we both know I owed you." He raised his well-manicured hand in a small, negligent wave. "Well, I must be off. My tour group awaits."

When he disappeared into the crowd, she turned and made her way in the opposite direction.

She slipped into the west wing and wandered slowly along the carpeted hall, pausing occasionally to savor some of the 1920s-era paintings she had chosen for this corridor. They were all Southwestern landscapes.

Deco art, she reflected, had been particularly suited to the dramatic play of light and shadow in

the desert. The Santa Fe and Taos region had lured
the most famous names such as Hartley, Dasburg,
and Georgia O'Keeffe. But Avalon had attracted the
attention of some very special artists, too.

At the end of the hall, she turned a corner and
went up a flight of stairs. On the second floor she
was relieved to find herself alone. The entire hotel
with the exception of the spa was open tonight, but
none of the other guests had migrated this far. She
could take her time enjoying her own handiwork.

She moved slowly along the west wing hall. Her
high heels sank deeply into the thick carpet. The
sounds of music and laughter down below seemed
to come from a great distance.

She was bending over a cabinet filled with a representative sampling of Modernist ceramics when
she caught the unmistakable gleam of a bronze horn.
The light from the 1920s-style wrought iron and
etched glass sconces was subdued, but she could
have sworn that a lecherous eye winked at her.

She straightened abruptly and stared, outraged,
at the familiar bronze peeking out of the small reading alcove at the far end of the hall.

"Edward Vale, you son-of-a-bitch," she breathed.
"I take back everything I just said about being grateful. How could you do this to me, you little twerp?"

She hiked her long, narrow black skirt up above
her knees and rushed the entire remaining length of
the west wing.

She came to a halt in the alcove and glared at
Dancing Satyr.

"I'll strangle him," she told the beast. "I swear, I
will."

She glanced around and saw what looked like

the door of a closet or utility room. Perfect. She could hide the fake Icarus Ives sculpture inside until the reception ended.

Flinging her tiny black handbag onto the nearest chair, she seized the tail end of the figure with both hands and started to drag it across the carpet.

Despite her best efforts, the bronze shifted only a scant few inches in the direction of the closet.

She had forgotten how heavy it was. She could only be grateful that Edward had not had it bolted to the floor for security purposes as he had done with most of the other freestanding pieces.

She tightened her grip on the Satyr's tail and leaned into her task. There were some side benefits to working in the art and antiques field. One of them was that one developed muscles when one spent one's days handling hefty pieces of early-twentieth-century furniture.

She had not gone soft during the past year at Elegant Relic, she discovered. Evidently unpacking and arranging countless stone gargoyles and a few life-sized suits of sixteenth-century armor kept one fit, too.

She managed to get *Dancing Satyr* as far as the closet door before an all-too-familiar voice sent a chill up her spine.

"I'm not real fond of it, either," Trask said. "But I apparently paid more for it than I did for my Jeep, so I'm afraid I can't let you just cart it off, Ms. Chambers."

Alexa saw the vision of her reconstructed future flash before her eyes.

"Oh, damn." Very slowly she released her grip on *Dancing Satyr*.

She straightened and turned around to face Trask.

He stood on the thick carpet that had swallowed the sound of his approaching footsteps. He looked very large and very solid in the expensively cut tuxedo. The muted glow of the hall lamps gleamed on his dark hair and glinted on the icy shards at his temples. There was no expression at all in his eyes.

She sighed. "Nice party."

He glanced meaningfully at the statue. "I'm surprised to hear you say that. I assumed that since you're up here rearranging the furniture, you must be bored."

She followed his gaze to *Dancing Satyr*. "It's a long story."

"Why don't you give me the short version?"

Damned if she would allow him to intimidate her, she thought. "I wasn't trying to steal it, you know."

"Could have fooled me."

"I only wanted to get it out of sight before anyone sees it." She waved a hand at the closet door. "I was going to stash it in there until later."

He gave that a moment of what appeared to be thoughtful consideration.

"Why?" he asked eventually.

She hesitated. This was the tricky part, but the entire project had been a calculated risk from the start. Now she had no option but to fight for her future.

"There's been a mistake. *Dancing Satyr* should never have been installed. It's not a genuine Icarus Ives piece."

"Are you telling me that I paid big bucks for a fake statue?"

"It's just a little mix-up," she said smoothly.

"I don't like mix-ups that cost me money."

"I'm sure everything will be straightened out very quickly after the reception. But in the meantime, I don't want it in my, uh, I mean, in the *hotel's* collection. At least not tonight when there are so many people from the art world here."

"*You* don't want it in the collection?" Trask eyed her with grave interest. "Why do you care what the art crowd thinks about *my* collection, Ms. Chambers?"

"Because I assembled it." The fat was in the fire. There was no point playing any more games. "I was Edward Vale's special Deco consultant on the project. I did not approve *Dancing Satyr*. Obviously there was a failure of communication somewhere along the line."

"The same sort of communication failure that took place at the McClelland Gallery two years ago?"

Alexa was stunned into silence. Her mouth opened but nothing emerged. This was worse than she had imagined. He knew about the McClelland scandal.

He pinned her with cold eyes. "Well, Ms. Chambers? Do I have to wonder about the authenticity of any of the other items in my very expensive new collection of Art Deco?"

Fury flared, white-hot and intense. "Gee, I don't know, Trask. Maybe you do. Just like I have to wonder whether or not you're here in Avalon to open a resort or because you intend to take your revenge against Lloyd Kenyon."

His brows rose. "So you do remember me. I couldn't be sure the other day when we met at the Point. You played it pretty cool."

"So did you."

"Guess we're both cool. Let's return to the subject of your reputation, which is not so cool. I understand that it was shredded two years ago when you were involved in that art forgery scam in Scottsdale."

She held his gaze. "I had nothing to do with the McClelland forgeries. As a matter of fact, I was the one who blew the whistle."

"Got any proof?"

"Probably not the sort you'd accept. There was no criminal investigation because none of McClelland's clients wanted to press charges."

"Convenient."

"It's a common enough reaction in the art world."

He gave her an expression of polite disbelief. "What the hell kind of client would sit still for being conned?"

"The kind who values his or her own reputation," she said.

"Meaning?"

"Look, the situation is not unlike what happens when a big business discovers that one of its employees has embezzled money from client accounts or that a hacker has gotten past its computer security. The corporation generally wants to keep things quiet because it fears the publicity of an arrest and trial. Clients and customers would question its ability to provide privacy and security."

Trask's eyes narrowed. "I'm aware of how things work in the business world."

"They aren't that much different in the art world. McClelland sold almost exclusively to high-priced art consultants and acknowledged experts who bought art and antiques for their own exclusive clientele."

"I think I'm getting the picture," Trask said. "No so-called expert likes to admit that he or she was fooled by a series of good forgeries."

"Exactly. Bad for business. After the McClelland incident everyone involved had a vested interest in keeping as quiet as possible. Reputations and careers were at stake. McClelland, of course, counted on that attitude. There was no investigation, no trial, and no arrest. Just lots of rumors and innuendos."

"Rumors and innuendos, I'm told, in which your name figured prominently."

She folded her arms beneath her breasts and angled her chin. "Actually, my name got savaged by a particularly nasty bit of insider gossip in a very influential trade magazine called *Twentieth-Century Artifact*. The idiot reporter who wrote the piece did so without having all the facts. He managed to imply that I was actively involved in selling the forgeries at McClelland."

"What happened to the forger?"

"McClelland?" Alexa glanced morosely at *Dancing Satyr*. "Disappeared and left me holding the bag."

Trask said nothing for a while, but the calculating look in his eyes told Alexa that he was processing the information she had given him.

He stirred eventually, sliding one palm along the polished veneer of a lacquered cabinet in an absent caress. "Can any part of your story be verified?"

It took every ounce of willpower she possessed to produce a careless shrug. "It's possible that one or two of McClelland's clients, those who are grateful to me for saving them from buying a lot of very expensive, very fake early-twentieth-century art and antiques, might be willing to talk off the record."

"Only one or two?"

"Only one or two listened when I warned them not to trust McClelland. Edward Vale was among that rather select group. That's why he—"

The Valkyrie-like figure of Glenda Blaine bustled up out of the stairwell before Alexa could finish.

"There you are, sir." Glenda hurried toward him down the hall. "I've been looking everywhere for you. One of the Phoenix TV stations sent out a camera crew. I've scheduled an interview with you standing in front of those big marble birds at the foot of the lobby staircase in five minutes."

Trask did not take his eyes off Alexa. "I'm a little busy at the moment, Glenda."

"Sir, I worked very hard to pull in this interview for you." Glenda gave him a reproachful glare. "You told me you wanted all the media coverage you could get."

Trask's jaw tightened. "I'll be down in a moment."

"I need you to be there *now*, sir."

To Alexa's astonishment, Trask inclined his head in an acquiescent gesture.

"All right, Glenda. I'll come down."

Apparently satisfied, Glenda swung around and strode off toward the stairs.

Trask looked at Alexa. "You and I aren't finished. When this reception is over, I'll take you home. I want to talk to you."

Without waiting for her to acknowledge the order, Trask turned and walked toward the stairs.

Alexa waited until she was alone before she responded.

"I don't think so," she whispered into the hushed silence of the empty hall. "I may have taken a few risks lately, but I haven't lost my mind. I'm not about to start accepting rides from strange men."

She whirled around, seized *Dancing Satyr* in a fierce grip, hauled it into the closet, and slammed the door.

9

Alexa was in bed but still wide awake when she heard the heavy growl of an engine in the drive. Outside the window, the twin beams of a pair of headlights sliced through the night. A moment later the vehicle came to a halt. The engine was switched off.

She had known all along that he would follow her home.

She tossed aside the covers, stood, and reached for the black and gold satin robe. A dark sense of inevitability settled on her as she thrust her feet into a pair of fluffy gold mules.

She crossed the room to another one of her handful of treasured Deco-style pieces, a glorious green-glass-and-lacquered-wood dressing table. Designed in 1927 in the sophisticated tradition of Paul Frankl, it was a blatantly sensual thing with its sleek curves and gleaming surfaces. In Alexa's mind it transformed her bedroom into a fantasy version of a boudoir.

She switched on a lamp and almost turned if off

again when she saw her reflection in the oval mirror.

She had scrubbed her face before retiring. Without even a vestige of liner to brighten them, her eyes appeared to be sunk deep in shadows. Her hair was wildly tangled from a lot of tossing and turning on the pillow. Tension had tightened her features.

All in all, not a pretty sight, she decided. On the other hand, there was no point trying to impress Trask. It wasn't as if he was here to seduce her.

She scowled at the mirror. Where had the word *seduce* come from? It had certainly never been a heavily used term in her personal vocabulary.

An ill omen if ever there was one.

Three demanding knocks rang out.

It was like a scene out of a bad fairy tale, Alexa thought. Trask had followed her home from the ball but, as Edward had warned, he was no prince.

On the other hand, she wasn't exactly Cinderella.

Uneasily aware of her pulse, which was beating much too quickly, she left the bedroom and went down the short hall into the darkened living room.

Another brusque knock echoed. She ignored it long enough to turn on a 1920s-style glass-and-chrome lamp. Then she went to the door and peered cautiously through the peephole.

Trask stood on the front step. He had obviously driven here with the windows down. His dark hair was roughened from the night breeze. He had discarded the jacket of his black tux. The ends of his bow tie trailed loosely down the front of his crisply pleated white shirt.

He had removed his cufflinks and rolled up his sleeves. Alexa could see the strongly detailed contours of muscle and sinew beneath his skin.

Somewhere along the line this man had done something else in his life besides sit behind an executive's desk.

He looked as if he were about to pick up a rapier and do battle with an opponent over a point of honor.

Lucky for him he had not come here to seduce her, Alexa thought. No telling what might have happened.

She took a deep breath. *Think: wild woman.* She flung open the door.

"It's late," she announced.

"I know." He contemplated her with an unreadable expression. "The party's over. Offer me a drink."

The flames of reckless abandon shriveled a bit when it occurred to Alexa that the harsh glare of the porch light was probably not doing much for the shadows beneath her eyes.

Not that she cared.

She stepped back into the subtly lit living room.

And immediately realized her mistake.

Trask glided over the threshold before she could think of a way to regain the territory she had just yielded.

"About that drink," he said.

"You just came from a party."

"That was business. I never drink when I'm working." He glanced around at the interior of her snug little house, openly curious. "Looks a little like one of the suites in my hotel. You're really into this Deco stuff, aren't you?"

"I told you, it's my specialty."

He looked at her. "If you won't offer me a drink,

the least you can do under the circumstances is make me a cup of coffee."

She turned and walked into the kitchen. "I'll fix you a cup of tea."

"I'll settle for that." He followed her as far as the doorway and watched as she filled the kettle. "No one around here seems to know how to make good coffee anyway."

"There's a simple solution to that problem."

"I know. I'm going to call my office in Seattle and have someone ship down an emergency supply of coffee via overnight express carrier."

"I had in mind an even easier solution," she said sweetly. "You could just go back to Seattle."

"I will." He propped one shoulder against the door frame and folded his arms. "Eventually."

She set the kettle on the burner. "Why did you come here tonight, Trask?"

"I told you I wanted to talk to you."

"I don't think we have anything left to talk about."

"You're wrong."

She gave him a wary glance. Then she opened the cupboard and took down a teapot decorated with a bright, geometric, Deco design and two matching mugs.

She decided to ask the question that had been worrying her most since she had left the hotel.

"Did you confront Edward Vale about my role in putting together your new collection?"

"You know damn well I didn't," Trask said.

Her hand stilled on the jar of loose green tea. "Why not?"

His mouth crooked humorlessly. "Because I find

myself in the same position as those McClelland clients you told me about. The ones who got defrauded and did not want to admit it publicly."

"I see." She met his eyes. "It would be embarrassing for you and your company if anyone were to question the authenticity of the resort's new collection, wouldn't it?"

"Very."

She spooned the tea into the pot. "Want my advice?"

"Why not? You're the only expert I can consult, given the situation."

She thought about that. "You are in an awkward position, aren't you? My recommendation is that you continue to keep quiet about your suspicions until the reviews appear. After the so-called experts have declared your collection brilliant and dazzling in print, you'll be home free."

"Yeah?" He did not bother to conceal his skepticism. "How do you figure that?"

"Don't worry, the critics aren't likely to change their minds after they've committed their opinions of the collection to print."

"In other words, they don't want to look like fools, either."

"You got it."

"What about you?"

She smiled slowly. "With any luck, once those reviews hit, especially the one in *Twentieth-Century Artifact*, I'll be home free, too."

"Bottom line is that you want me to keep my mouth shut."

"Just for a few weeks. A couple of months at the outside." She was taking yet another risk, she thought. This was not the kind of man who could be threatened or intimidated. He had to be convinced. Mentally she marshaled her arguments.

"Deal," he said.

She nearly dropped one of the mugs. "Do you always make decisions that quickly?"

A laconic gleam lit his eyes. "I made this particular decision before I left you in that second-floor hallway tonight, Alexa."

A sharp frisson of unease went through her. "Why?"

"Because you're right. I don't have much choice. I've also got other issues that will require my full attention here in Avalon for the next few weeks. Whether or not I've been defrauded with a lot of phony Deco art and antiques is not the most important item on my agenda."

"I was afraid of that." The piercing whistle of the tea kettle made her jump. She turned quickly and seized the kettle. "So the rumors are right. You have come back with some off-the-wall notion of revenge."

"I'm here to get some answers."

"It's been twelve years, Trask. How can you possibly find any after all this time?"

"For the past six months I've had a private investigator looking into the backgrounds of the two men who were my father's partners at the time of his death."

"Lloyd and that other man, Dean Guthrie."

He nodded. "I've got information on Kenyon's and Guthrie's financial and personal situations twelve years ago that I did not have access to at the time."

"And just what do you plan to do with that information?"

"Use it to stir the pot until something boils over."

"You sound like Machiavelli." She finished pouring the hot water and set the kettle down with more force than she had intended. "Listen, Trask, I don't know what information you *think* you've got about the past, but I want you to leave Lloyd alone, do you hear me? I know him as well as I knew my own father. Better in some ways, truth be told. He would never have been part of any conspiracy to murder anyone."

"If that's true, you've got nothing to worry about, do you?"

"Is that a threat?"

"No. It's a statement of fact."

"Damn it, if you think I'll stand by while you dig up the past in order to hurt innocent people . . ."

"I'm not after innocent people." His voice hardened appreciably. "I want the truth, and I intend to get it."

She searched his face, shocked in spite of herself by the relentless determination she saw in him. "You really do believe that someone murdered your father, don't you?"

"Yes."

"But what possible motive could there have been?"

"A business deal gone sour."

"A lot of business deals go bad because the partners have a falling out. People don't murder other people because of that."

"You're wrong," he said. "Sometimes they do."

"Not Lloyd Kenyon." She was startled by her

own fierce certainty. "He's a gentle, good-hearted man. He's not a killer."

"I don't know yet if Kenyon was involved. Even if he wasn't, that still leaves another possibility."

"Dean Guthrie."

Trask watched her closely. "Do you know him?"

"No," she admitted. "My mother told me that Lloyd hasn't done any business with him since that deal with your father."

"According to my investigator, she's right. Kenyon and Guthrie went their separate ways after that partnership was blown apart. Maybe whatever happened the night my father went off Avalon Point made it impossible for either man to trust each other again."

"Great." She threw her hands into the air. "Now you're weaving conspiracy theories. You're obsessed with this plot you've invented, aren't you?"

"So my brother tells me." He glanced at the pot. "Is that tea ready?"

She was so focused on trying to figure out how to handle an obsessed conspiracy theorist that for a second or two, she could not figure out what he was talking about. Then she turned her head to stare blankly at the teapot.

"Yes." She seized the handle. "Yes, it is."

She poured the tea, not because she wanted to be a good hostess but because she needed a moment to collect her thoughts into some logical sequence.

She met Trask's eyes when she handed him one of the cups. "Tell me the truth. Have you got any hard evidence against Lloyd or Guthrie?"

His fingers brushed hers as he took the cup from

her hand. She could have sworn she saw sparks, the kind that crackled when she walked across a rug and touched something metallic.

"Not yet," he said.

She allowed herself to relax slightly. "Other than this thing you have about the past, you seem to be an intelligent man."

His brows rose. "Gee, do you really think so or are you just saying that?"

She pressed on grimly. "If nothing else, you've got your business reputation to consider. I assume it's important to you."

"I think that goes without saying. Why?"

"You won't do anything stupid until you've got your facts straight, will you?"

"Stupid?"

"Something really dumb." She paused deliberately. "You know, the kind of thing that might make you and, therefore, Avalon Resorts, Inc., look bad."

"I didn't build Avalon Resorts by doing stupid stuff."

"Good." Picking up her own cup, she stepped around him and led the way back out into the living room. "I'll cling to that straw, if you don't mind."

"You don't look like the clinging type, but suit yourself." He followed her and watched her curl up on the chaise longue. "It won't make any difference one way or the other."

She studied him over the rim of her cup, wishing she could read his mind. "You'll probably say that I don't have any right to ask this, but I want you to promise me something."

He looked cautiously intrigued. "What's that?"

"I want your word of honor that you will talk to

me about any so-called evidence you turn up here in Avalon before you leap to any conclusions concerning Lloyd Kenyon's role in your father's death."

He pondered that for a while. "Why not?"

Too easy, she thought. She had a feeling he had spotted some loopholes that she had not noticed. She'd better tighten the net. "Or before you make any similar leaps concerning Mr. Guthrie."

"What the hell do you care about Guthrie?"

"Very little. I don't even know the man. But since he and Lloyd were once partners, I don't want you putting two and two together and coming up with five."

Trask grunted but said nothing.

"In other words," she continued very deliberately, "I want you to run any and all your evidence by me before you conclude that the two of them formed a conspiracy to get rid of Harry Trask."

"Alexa—"

"Hear me out." The unfamiliar adrenaline of recklessness surged through her again. "You don't know it yet, but when those art critics write their reviews you're going to find out that I have made Avalon Resorts, Inc., the owner of one of the most distinguished corporate collections of art and antiques in the Art Deco style outside of New York."

He was silent for a couple of heartbeats. Then he gave her a quizzical look. "So?"

"So you owe me."

Mocking disbelief flashed in his expression. "I beg your pardon?"

"I worked for a fraction of the consulting fee I should have charged you through Edward Vale.

The least you can do to make up for taking advantage of me is give me your word."

"What the hell are you talking about?" Genuine outrage replaced the cold amusement in his eyes. "I didn't take advantage of you."

"Yes, you did. You just weren't aware of it at the time. I'm willing to overlook that in exchange for your promise not to move against Lloyd or Guthrie until you've talked to me about any facts you uncover."

He fell silent again. For a long time. Longer than she could hold her breath, she discovered.

"All right," Trask said after an eternity. "I promise."

He finished his tea and put down the cup. Then he got up and walked out the front door without once looking back.

Yes, indeed, Alexa thought as she listened to the sound of the Jeep's engine recede into the night. Lucky for Trask he hadn't come here bent on seduction.

No telling what might have happened, her being such a wild woman and all.

A few minutes later, when she went to put the empty cups into the sink, she discovered that her hands were still trembling slightly.

The thing about taking risks, she decided, was that it was hard on the nerves.

She was as aware of the attraction between them as he was. He had seen it in her fortune-telling eyes. He wondered what would have happened if he'd kissed her.

Dumb question. Trask tightened his hand on the

wheel and watched the narrow strip of pavement unwind in front of the Jeep. He should not even think about getting involved with Alexa Chambers.

She was Lloyd Kenyon's stepdaughter. And if that wasn't messy enough, she was a scandal-tainted art expert who, at the very least, associated with a known forger by the name of McClelland. She might well have made Avalon Resorts, Inc., the proud owner of the largest collection of fraudulent early-twentieth-century art and antiques on the West Coast. Hell, maybe the whole damn country.

When the reviews and articles appeared in the trade journals he could wake up one morning to find himself a laughingstock among corporate art collectors throughout the nation. The headline in the business sections of every major newspaper in the country etched itself in invisible letters on the windshield in front of his eyes.

AVALON RESORTS CEO VICTIM OF ART SCAM

No question about it. An affair with Alexa Chambers would seriously complicate an already labyrinthine situation.

He tried to analyze her motives.

Maybe she thought she could influence the direction of his investigation into Harry's death.

Maybe she figured that sleeping with him would be an effective way to deflect his attention from her stepfather.

Damn. He was still half erect.

Maybe she was right.

10

Alexa parked the Camry in the section of the Avalon Plaza parking lot reserved for shopkeepers and their employees, got out, and checked her watch.

There was time to pick up some tea and a muffin from Café Solstice before she opened Elegant Relic.

She slung the strap of the large black leather satchel that doubled as both purse and briefcase over her shoulder and started toward the café.

Avalon Plaza was a trendy architect's version of an eighteenth-century Spanish Colonial village. Vine-draped trellises shaded the terra cotta walks. Red tile roofs gleamed in the morning sun. Artistically worked wrought iron benches surrounded a sparkling yellow, blue, and white tiled fountain.

The shops in the Plaza catered to tourists and locals who were into the metaphysical aspects of the Avalon area. It wasn't where she had envisioned Elegant Relic when she first came up with the notion for the shop, but there had not been a lot of choice in the matter.

After making the decision to return to Avalon to lie low for a while following the debacle at McClelland, she had faced the problem of finding a suitable retail location. Business rental space had been at a premium in town due to the increased number of people moving into the vicinity and the surge in tourism.

Lloyd had put out some feelers for her. Luckily one of his business contacts had passed along a rumor that Avalon Plaza was looking for a new tenant.

Although not New Age or metaphysical in focus, Elegant Relic, with its gargoyles, medieval map reproductions, and imitations of ancient Egyptian jewelry, had settled in well with its neighbors.

After all, it was only for a year or two, she reminded herself, as she did every morning when she arrived at the Plaza.

"Peace and serenity, Alexa."

Alexa glanced at the arched stucco doorway of Spheres Books and saw Dylan Fenn, the proprietor. He was a striking contrast to the faux-Spanish Colonial architecture of his shop. Unless, of course, short, razor-cut, platinum-tinted hair, a single gold earring, and a taste for 1960s tie-dye and platform sandals had been a fashion statement in the eighteenth-century Southwest.

She guessed Dylan to be somewhere in his forties, although it was hard to be certain. There was a curiously androgynous air about his pale, slender frame. If he had a love life of any kind, straight or gay, she had never seen any indication of it.

She reminded herself that she was hardly in a position to question the excitement quotient of other people's sex lives. It had been so long since she'd had one herself, that she'd almost forgotten what a sex life felt like.

She halted on the sidewalk and smiled. "Good morning to you, too."

Unlike half the town and all of her fellow shop-keepers, she had not picked up the habit of using the Dimensions Institute greeting, "peace and serenity."

"What do you think of the display?" Dylan's turquoise and silver Dimensions bracelet gleamed in the sun as he swept out a hand to indicate the array of books on the other side of the shop window. "Is it a grabber?"

Alexa studied the window arrangement. It consisted of several dozen copies of *Living the Dimensions Way: Building a Life Based on the Principles of Peace and Serenity*. The books were artistically stacked in circles and pyramids.

A huge picture of Webster Bell in his signature black, silver, and turquoise dominated the display. The sign beneath the photo read, *Meet the Author.*

"Looks good," Alexa said. "I'm sure you'll have a line of people around the block for Bell's auto-graphing this time, just like you did when his last book came out."

"I hope so. This new book is a follow-on to last year's title. It goes deeper into the metaphysical concepts relating to the Dimensions diet and exer-cise programs."

"You've read it already?"

"Sure." Dylan's sky-blue eyes shone with pride. "Webster always makes certain that I get an advance copy from the publisher."

"How long have you been selling his books?"

Dylan's thin shoulders lifted in a small shrug. "Ever since he started writing them. The first one came out about four years after he opened the Institute. Let me see, that would be—"

"Seven years ago, to be exact," said a familiar voice. "Webster owes you a great deal, Dylan. I have a hunch you've sold more of his books than all of the shops in Tucson and Phoenix combined."

Dylan grinned. "Peace and serenity, Joanna."

Alexa turned to see Joanna Bell walking briskly toward them along the terra cotta sidewalk. She had a plastic container of Café Solstice tea in one hand. Stewart had created a special blend just for her. He called it Joanna's Rainbow.

Joanna was a few years younger than her half-brother, which put her somewhere in her mid-fifties, Alexa guessed. She was a striking woman with dark eyes and patrician features.

She wore her discreetly tinted hair in a sophisticated knot at the nape of her neck. Like Webster, she favored turquoise and silver jewelry. In addition to her Dimensions bracelet, she wore several silver and stone-studded bangles, a modern interpretation of a traditional squash blossom necklace, and enough rings to blind a deer on the highway at night.

"Hello, Joanna," Alexa said.

Joanna smiled at her, but there was an oddly tense, searching expression in her eyes. "Didn't I see you at the Avalon Resort reception last night? Thought I caught a glimpse of you in the crowd, but I lost you again."

"I just dropped in for a few minutes."

"Did you get a look at some of the art and antiques? Edward Vale did a magnificent job. I'm not a great fan of the Deco style, but I have to admit that it's perfectly suited to the Avalon Resort."

Alexa hid her surprise with some effort. She told herself that it was a good sign that the other woman had noticed the hotel's collection. But it nonetheless struck her as strange. Until today the only art Joanna had ever shown any interest in was the craft of jewelry design.

Alexa studiously avoided the subject of her former career with anyone at Avalon Plaza. It was all part of the grand plan to keep a low profile until she made her comeback.

She was wondering how to change the topic before it strayed into dangerous territory when Dylan took the problem out of her hands.

"Were you okay with everything last night, Joanna?" he asked gently.

Alexa glanced at him, startled by the unmistakable note of concern in his voice.

"Yes, of course, Dylan." Joanna gave him a wan smile. "Thank you for asking. I'm fine. It's been a long time, after all."

Alexa suddenly felt very awkward. She glanced from one to the other, sensing undercurrents.

"You two will have to excuse me," Joanna said quickly. "I've got a shop to open. Things are getting busy around here. The tourists are really starting to pour into town for the festival."

"See you later." Dylan watched her walk away toward the door of Crystal Rainbow.

"Am I missing something here?" Alexa asked. "Or is it any of my business?"

"What?" Dylan blinked a couple of times and then shook his head. "Sorry. I just figured you knew."

"Knew what?"

"Joanna was engaged to Harry Trask, the guy who tried to turn the old Avalon Mansion into a resort twelve years ago. When he died in a car crash, she was pretty shaken up for a while. Had a bout with depression. I was a little worried about her last night. Didn't know if seeing Harry's son again after all this time would bring back some unhappy memories."

At four o'clock that afternoon, Alexa found herself alone in Elegant Relic. Through the front window, she watched a truck bearing the logo *Avalon Herald* pause in front of the vending machine outside her shop. A young man hopped out of the back and filled the box with several copies of the town's only daily newspaper.

She grabbed some change from her satchel and raced outside. She plunked the money into the slot and seized a copy of the *Herald.*

Back inside Elegant Relic, she opened the paper on the counter beside the cash register and scanned the front-page article on the Avalon Resort & Spa reception.

The *Herald* was a typical small-town paper. Cheerful and folksy in tone, it tended toward stories on local tourism, Avalon High School football games, and the annual Spring Festival. She told herself it did not matter whether or not the paper had said anything about her art collection at the new resort. She was pretty sure the *Herald* did not even have an art critic on the staff.

She reminded herself that it was entirely possible that whoever had covered the reception for the newspaper had not even noticed her spectacular collection.

She read through the entire article before she finally found a single sentence near the end.

... Several influential members of the Tucson and Phoenix art world turned out to view the hotel's collection of art and antiques from the early twentieth century.

"That's it?" Outrage poured through her. "That's all you turkeys can say about one of the finest collections of Deco in the country?"

A figure loomed in the open doorway of the shop. "Is this a private conversation or can anyone join in?"

She looked up at the sound of Trask's voice. Dressed in a work shirt and a pair of jeans, he looked as if he had just walked in off a construction site.

She blurted out the first words that came into her head. "What are you doing here?"

"I came to see you." He walked into the shop and halted in front of the display of stone gargoyles. He picked up one of the smaller figures, a fist-sized, goggle-eyed little monster with elfin ears and a pair of leathery-looking wings. "So this is what you do when you're not acting as a secret art consultant for Edward Vale."

"I don't have much choice." Alexa straightened and slowly refolded the newspaper. "Secret art consulting jobs are hard to come by."

He walked through a maze of faux Greek urns

and came to a halt in front of the Egyptian-style chair that Alexa had privately dubbed Cleopatra's throne.

"Not exactly museum-quality art and antiques," Trask said.

"No, they're not." She heard a crackling sound and looked down to see that she had crumpled the newspaper in her hand. "I don't pretend that they are. Everything in this shop is clearly labeled as a replica."

"Clearly labeled," he repeated. "Unlike the proprietor."

"What's that supposed to mean?"

"Nothing sinister. I just can't quite figure you out, that's all. Will you have dinner with me tonight?"

She stared at him, dimly aware that her mouth was hanging open. She got it closed with a monumental effort of will. "You think you can figure me out over dinner?"

He smiled slightly. "I've got a feeling that it will take a little longer than that. But I can at least get started on the problem. We'll go to the country club, if that's all right with you."

"I'm not a member of the club."

"I am. The hotel has a corporate membership and guest privileges."

"Oh."

He watched her very steadily. "Is that a yes or a no?"

"I'm thinking about it."

"I was under the impression that you wanted to keep tabs on my every move while I'm here in Avalon."

"You mean you're going to take me out to dinner and tell me all the details of your paranoid conspiracy theories?"

"Depends on how good a listener you are."

Alexa took a deep breath. "Well, okay. I guess."

"I like enthusiasm in a woman." He inclined his head with mocking grace. "I'll pick you up at seven-thirty."

He turned on his heel and walked toward the door.

"Hold it." She met his eyes across the top of the King Tut mask. "Mind if I ask why?"

"I told you that I came back to Avalon to make some waves. I can't think of a better way to start than to have the country club crowd see me having dinner with Lloyd Kenyon's stepdaughter."

She froze. "You intend to use *me* to stir up trouble?"

His mouth curved in a small, grim smile. "In exchange, you'll be in an ideal position to know exactly what trouble I manage to stir up."

"What makes you think that taking me out to dinner at the country club will give you the kind of results you want?"

His eyes glinted with amusement. "Avalon may have become trendy in the past few years, but at its heart it's still a very small town. That means it runs on gossip, rumors, and speculation."

She watched him uneasily. "How will stirring up a lot of wild speculation help your so-called investigation?"

"I'm here to find some answers. It's been my experience that there's nothing like a lot of rumors and gossip flying around to make people talk."

"That's what you want?" She stared at him. "To make people gossip about the past?"

"Gotta start somewhere."

"I keep telling you, there is nothing sinister to uncover."

"In which case, you'll get a free dinner out of the deal."

Trask went out the door.

Through the front window, Alexa watched him walk back down the terra cotta path toward the parking lot.

Unsettling though it was to know that he had invited her out to dinner solely to roil the seas of old gossip, there was an even more unpleasant possibility.

Maybe Trask had invited her out to dinner in order to pump her for information on Lloyd. What better way to dig up inside data about one of his father's ex-partners than by dating said ex-partner's stepdaughter?

Any way you looked at it, dinner with Trask was a dangerous proposition.

It occurred to her that his scheme was potentially a double-edged sword. There was, after all, nothing to stop her from using the dinner invitation to do a bit of pumping herself. The more she knew about Trask and his plans for vengeance, the better positioned she would be to protect Lloyd.

Her stomach suddenly felt disconcertingly weightless. She wondered if her former therapist, Dr. Ormiston, would approve of her new, high-risk lifestyle.

11

The trip across the candlelit restaurant proved to be the longest trek Alexa had made since the day she walked out of the McClelland Gallery for the last time. The sudden hush that had fallen when Trask had escorted her through the doors of the Red Canyon Country Club soon gave way to a buzz of conversation that was just a bit too loud to be natural.

She glanced at Trask as the waiter pulled out her chair. The cool amusement in his eyes told her that, unlike her, he had been fully prepared for the reaction to their presence in the club.

This new, reckless approach to life might be all very well, she thought, but it was possible that she was playing out of her league. She probably stood a better chance of having an out-of-body experience during a Dimensions Institute seminar than she did of tricking Trask into spilling his dark secrets.

"Don't let it get to you," Trask said as he opened the tasseled menu. "It's why we're here, remember?"

She leaned forward slightly and lowered her voice. "You knew it would be like this, didn't you?"

He looked up. "Do you want to go somewhere else?"

It was a direct challenge, one she could not ignore. She straightened her shoulders and picked up the menu as though it were a gauntlet.

"No, of course not," she said, trying to focus on the appetizers. "It would only make things worse if we got up and left now."

"You're right," he said. "Trust me, the best way to handle this kind of scene is to ignore it."

"I know." She thought about the grim days after the McClelland affair, when she had been the subject of every speculative tongue in the Southwest art world. "I have, as the saying goes, been here and done this before. I had rather hoped not to repeat the experience, however."

He smiled faintly. "If it's any consolation, most of the people who recognized us when we walked in a few minutes ago are probably genuinely concerned about you."

"Me?"

His eyes did not leave her face. "I'm sure they're all wondering if I'm dating you because I've got some diabolical scheme to use you against Kenyon."

She held his gaze. "Do you?"

His smile took on a thin, lethal edge. "What do you think?"

Folks who courted risks were supposed to be cool types, she reminded herself. "Let's just say I'm reserving judgment."

"Hard to go wrong that way."

"You sound as if you don't approve of that approach."

"I was thinking that our relationship would function as a partnership," he said with a considering expression. "I was hoping for a measure of trust between us."

"Trust?" She gave him amused disdain. "Don't talk to me about trust. You don't trust me any farther than you can throw me. You're still waiting for the reviews of your new art collection to hit before you decide whether or not I've defrauded you, remember?"

There was a beat of silence.

"You've made your point," Trask said finally.

"Good." It was a small victory, but, she discovered, a heady one. It emboldened her. "By the way, you may be wrong."

One dark brow climbed. "About what?"

"About the possibility that everyone here tonight is concerned with your intentions toward me. I suspect that quite a few people may be wondering if I'm with you because I've got a deep, dark scheme of my own."

His eyes gleamed. "Did you agree to go out with me in order to seduce me into agreeing to abandon my plans?"

She felt herself turn very warm and was suddenly grateful for the low light level in the restaurant. "What do you think?"

"I think it might be interesting from my point of view, but not particularly effective from yours."

She closed the menu with a smart snap. "Okay, we'll take it as a given that I can't talk any sense into you. I can promise you that I'm not going to give

you any inside information that concerns Lloyd
Kenyon, either. Guess we're even, hmm?"

"Sort of limits the scope of the conversation,
doesn't it?"

"Yes, it does." She gave him another cool smile.
"So what are we going to talk about?"

"Us?"

The suggestion caught her completely off guard.
"Us?"

"Why not?"

"Uh . . ."

"We'll stick to strictly neutral territory."

"Well . . ."

The return of the waiter rescued her from having
to come up with something more intelligent.
Unfortunately, the reprieve did not last long. When
they were alone again, Trask looked at her.

"Let's get the basics out of the way," he said. "I'm
not married and neither are you."

She stared at him. "How do you know that I'm
not married?"

He flicked a glance at her left hand. "My first clue
is that you don't wear a wedding ring. Just to be on
the safe side, I asked around."

"You asked around? About *me?*"

"Don't worry, I was discreet. Now, moving right
along—"

"Stop right there." She eyed him narrowly.
"What do you mean, you were discreet?"

"Don't go getting paranoid. It was just a simple
precaution."

"A precaution?"

He watched her very steadily. "I don't date married women."

"I see." She wanted to accuse him of something, but she was not sure what. She could hardly fault him for his policy.

"Are you going to tell me that you didn't know whether or not I was married when you accepted my invitation?" he asked.

She hesitated and then shrugged lightly. "I'm aware that you're divorced."

"Who was your source?" he asked very casually.

"Edward Vale mentioned it in passing."

Trask nodded. "Fair enough. As I said, moving right along, care to tell me why?"

"Why what?"

"Why you're still single?"

She summoned up a breezy little smile. "It's a matter of opinion. My therapist, Dr. Ormiston, whom I saw for two whole months, told me that I'm not very good at commitments. She said that I'm overly cautious and risk-averse, especially where men are concerned."

"Risk-averse?"

"Uh-huh. Means I'm afraid to allow myself to be vulnerable. A result of having had an unreliable father."

"Ah." Trask nodded wisely. "Risk-averse. Got it. What did you say when she came up with her diagnosis?"

"I told her that I just hadn't met the right man yet."

"I see." He eyed her with a considering gaze. "Which opinion is the correct one? Yours or Dr. Ormiston's?"

"Danged if I know." Alexa decided it was time to turn the tables. "Why did your wife leave you?"

"Let me see." He looked briefly thoughtful. "As I recall, she said that I was obsessed with building an empire, that I didn't understand her needs, and that I failed to share my deepest feelings."

Alexa cleared her throat. "But other than that it seemed like a pretty good marriage?"

"Yeah. But I didn't have much to compare it with."

"Was any of it true? The empire building and the failure to communicate, etc., etc.?"

"Probably. But personally, I think the real reason she walked out was that she never really forgave me for insisting on a prenuptial contract."

Alexa slowly lowered the chunk of bread she had been about to put into her mouth. "I see."

"She left me for a software zillionnaire from Seattle who retired at forty and bought a house in the South of France. She said that he might be a nerd, but he was more of a romantic than I would ever be."

"Meaning he didn't insist on a prenuptial contract?"

"That seemed to be the bottom line as far as I could tell."

Alexa hesitated. "Why did you insist on one?"

"I'm a businessman. I believe in contracts, not fairy tales."

"Funny you should say that."

"Yeah?" He looked intrigued. "Why?"

"I never discussed it with Dr. Ormiston, but I think one of my problems with men revolves around the same issue."

"A prenup contract?"

"Yes. I received a rather hefty inheritance from

my grandmother on my father's side. It came to me after Dad was killed. Mom turned it over to Lloyd to manage." She paused. "Lloyd is very good at managing money."

"So I hear," Trask said softly.

"Early on he convinced me that no matter whom I married I'd better make certain that I had a prenuptial agreement. I agreed with him. But wouldn't you know it? Every time I bring up the subject with a date, the relationship always seems to cool off in a hurry."

"Hell of a coincidence," Trask said.

"Struck me that way, too."

"How come you never explained the facts of life to that therapist who told you that you just couldn't commit?"

"Like your ex-wife's zillionaire, Dr. Ormiston was, at heart, a romantic. I didn't think she'd understand about prenups."

Trask grinned slowly. "Well, I'll be damned. Looks like you and I have something in common, after all. We're both afraid of being married for our money."

The sort of silence that could be termed pregnant descended. Alexa felt the immediate onset of panic. Mercifully the waiter chose that moment to show up with the cilantro-and-lime-laced avocado salads.

When he disappeared again, she fumbled to change the conversation.

"I think that's enough on the topic of marriage," she said in a voice that sounded too brittle, even to her own ears. "Let's find something more interesting to talk about."

Trask picked up his fork. "Such as?"

She thought quickly and leaped at the first obvious notion that sprang to mind. "Careers. That should be safe enough. You know a lot about mine. Tell me about yours. Obviously you followed in your father's footsteps."

Without any warning, the incipient warmth vanished from Trask's eyes. His expression became shuttered and withdrawn.

"I'm very different from my father," he said. "He was a dreamer."

She realized she had wandered into treacherous territory. The smart thing to do was to retreat to safer ground. But the newly discovered, decidedly more daring element of her nature lured her forward.

"What kind of dreams did he have?" she asked gently.

"It's a long list. I guess you could start with his dream of playing pro baseball. That bombed, I gather, shortly after I was born." Trask forked up a bite of avocado. "Not that the failure of that particular fantasy stopped him from trying to turn me into a major league pitcher."

"What happened?"

"I played ball all the way through high school to please him, but when I got into college I drew the line. My excuse was that between work and studies, I didn't have time for it. Truth was, I just wasn't interested in living his dream. We had our first big battle over my decision to pursue a business career."

"Why business?"

He shrugged. "I wanted something I could control."

"What were some of your father's other dreams?"

"He tried to make his fortune in real estate. When that failed, he ran for the state legislature. Lost in a landslide. He hatched a scheme to operate a private ferry service on Lake Washington. He went bankrupt before the first boat got launched. He came up with a plan to market hot air balloon rides . . ."

"I think I get the picture. How did your mother cope with all this?"

He hesitated. "It wasn't easy on her. But she endured. She died right after my brother Nathan was born."

"I'm sorry."

"I have a hunch that if she'd lived, there would have been a divorce. I don't have a lot of memories of her, but the ones I do have mostly involve listening to her plead with my father to be sensible. After she was gone, I guess I tried to take over that job."

Alexa nodded. "Hard for a kid to parent a parent. All of the responsibility and worry but none of the power of an adult."

His mouth twisted wryly. "I can tell you've been in therapy."

"No wonder you pursued a career that allows you plenty of personal autonomy."

"What can I say? I'm a control freak."

"What about your brother?"

Trask's expression lightened into something that resembled an almost paternal pride. "Nathan and I are a team. He's the creative one. Hell of an architect. He was the lead on all three Avalon hotels, including the one here in town."

"If he's the creative one, what part do you play?"

"I look after the bottom line. No creative talent necessary, but lots of control."

"Why do you say you're not a creative thinker?" She tilted her head slightly to the side to study him. "Avalon Resorts has a reputation for crafting fantasy vacation worlds."

"My brother comes up with the big concepts. All I do is figure out which ones will work financially."

She propped her chin on the heel of her hand. "I think that's very definitely a creative talent."

"I don't see it that way." He shrugged. "But I do know that I never make the mistake my father always made."

She watched him. "What mistake was that?"

"I know a great fantasy when I see one, but I never allow myself to get caught up in it."

Alexa thought about that from her new risk-taking perspective. "What good is a fantasy if you don't get into it?" Belatedly old habits kicked in. "At least for a while."

12

Trask was aware of a deep reluctance to end the evening. He tried to think of a way to make it last a little longer as he escorted Alexa out of the restaurant.

The warm, velvety darkness of the desert night settled over them.

He wondered what Alexa was thinking. Covertly he studied her as they walked between the rows of cars in the club's dimly lit parking lot.

The handkerchief points of her weightless little blue-green silk dress floated around the elegant curves of her calves. He had been studying the garment all evening, wondering if it was really a slip or a sexy nightgown in disguise. It had tiny little straps and it was cut so that it skimmed over her high, apple-shaped breasts and elegant thighs.

It was exactly the sort of dress a woman could wear to descend the staircase in his new hotel.

The high heels of her strappy sandals clicked on the parking lot pavement. The sleek, sophisticated curve of her bobbed hair swung forward, just past the high arch of her cheekbones, partially veiling her face.

She appeared to be lost in deep, mysterious female thoughts. He wanted to haul her back out of that dark pool and get her to focus on him again as she had during dinner. But he had no inkling of how to go about it.

He wondered if she considered the evening a total waste because he hadn't confided any of the substantive details of his plans.

Alexa halted without any warning. Her eyes widened. "Trask, your Jeep."

The shock in her voice got his full attention. He looked at the Jeep, which was parked between a BMW and a mammoth SUV. There was something wrong with the way the light hit the front windshield. Then he saw the web of glittering glass shards.

"My insurance company is not going to be thrilled."

"Trask." Alexa's voice was infused with shocked urgency. "Behind you."

He heard the soft thud of heavy-soled boots on the pavement and turned quickly.

They exploded out of the dark void between parked cars: two men dressed in denim shirts, jeans, and ski masks. One of them carried a length of metal. The tire iron that had been used on the Jeep's windshield, Trask thought.

He had only a fleeting second to contemplate the incongruity of ski masks in the desert before they closed in.

"Get out of here, Alexa. Run, damn it."

He saw her mouth open on a scream that was

probably meant to summon help. The man in the red ski mask seized her from behind, threw an arm around her throat, and hauled her back against his chest.

The second man, the one in a blue mask, came straight at Trask, tire iron raised.

"You're lucky," Blue Mask snarled. "Tonight all you get is a warning and a little something to think about."

He swung the metal rod in an arc intended to connect with Trask's ribs.

There was something to be said for having worked heavy construction to pay his way through college and to support Nathan for a few years, Trask decided. Life occasionally got rough on job sites. He had broken up more than one fight in the past, had more than one enraged combatant turn on him in frustration.

He leaped back. Heard the whoosh of air as the tire iron skimmed past, inches from his rib cage.

"Listen up," Blue Mask said, dancing closer. "You're not wanted here in Avalon. Understand?"

"Who sent you to tell me that?" Trask moved back into the narrow space between the Jeep and the BMW. "Guthrie?"

"All you need to know is that you're supposed to go back to Seattle." Blue Mask advanced, coming forward between the two vehicles.

He raised the tire iron again and brought it down in a savage motion.

Trask was already moving. He vaulted up onto the hood of the Jeep. There was another rush of air as the tire iron whizzed past his thigh.

He heard the crack of metal on metal, knew that the tire iron had collided with the Jeep's fender. Irresistible force meeting immovable object.

Blue Mask grunted in pain and staggered under the jolt. Trask launched himself from the hood of the Jeep before the thug could recover.

He dropped straight down on Blue Mask. The weight of his body carried them both to the pavement. Blue Mask, however, was on the bottom. He took the brunt of the impact.

It probably did not help that his head struck the Jeep's fender a glancing blow on the way down, Trask thought.

Blue Mask lay stunned and unmoving. Trask grabbed the tire iron.

"Sig?" Red Mask sounded alarmed. "Sig, what the fuck is going on? Finish it, man, or I'm gonna get outta here. The bitch is too much trouble."

Trask got to his feet and moved out of the dark place between the Jeep and the BMW.

"Your friend decided to take a little nap." Trask did not look at Alexa's face. He walked straight toward Red Mask, the tire iron dangling loosely from his hand. "Let the lady go."

"Sig?" Red Mask tightened his arm around Alexa's throat. "Sig? Where are you? We gotta get outta here."

"Let her go," Trask repeated softly.

"Get away from me." Red Mask sounded truly freaked now. "Stay back, you hear me? Or I'll hurt her. I swear, I will."

Trask stopped. He kept his voice low and calm. "Let her go and get out of here while you still can. I hear some people coming out of the restaurant. They'll see what's happening."

"We were just supposed to give you the warning, man." Red Mask's voice rose on a shrill whine. "That's all."

"Tell Guthrie to deliver his own warning next time."

Car lights flashed on at the far end of the parking lot. Red Mask's head whipped around to stare in that direction.

Trask saw Alexa's knee come up. She brought the high heel of her sandal back smartly against Red Mask's shin.

Red Mask screamed with rage and lurched to the side. He fetched up hard against the grille of the car parked directly behind him. He still had his arm around Alexa's throat. She fell back heavily. Her weight destroyed what was left of Red Mask's balance.

Trask dropped the tire iron and leaped across the small distance that separated him from the struggling pair.

Red Mask had had enough. He shoved Alexa into Trask's path and tore off down the aisle of parked cars. The second man, the one called Sig, had managed to drag himself to his feet. He chased after Red Mask, albeit unsteadily.

Trask caught Alexa close. "You okay?"

"Yes." She sounded breathless and scared but still in command of herself. "What about you?"

Trask listened to the echo of two vehicle doors slamming shut. Headlights flashed. He glimpsed a battered pickup as it roared out of a parking space and careened toward the exit.

He thought about how Red Mask had put his filthy arm around Alexa's throat.

"Me?" he said. "I'm swell. No more than semi-hysterical."

She uttered something that sounded like a cross between a mad laugh and a sob and huddled against him. "Oh, my God, Trask. Oh, my God. That man with the tire iron . . ."

"It's all right." He stroked her back with an awkward motion and tried to think of something reassuring to say. "It was me they were after. You were in the wrong place at the wrong time."

"If that's supposed to make me feel better, you're on the wrong track."

A heavy white Lincoln pulled out of a space at the end of the aisle and drifted swiftly toward them. It came to a halt when it was directly opposite. The driver's window slid down.

Trask looked at the bulky, florid-faced man behind the wheel. The yellow light from the parking lot lamps gleamed on his balding skull and gave his features an unhealthy sheen.

"Hello, Guthrie," Trask said softly. He felt Alexa freeze against his side. "Your two goons went thataway. You know, if you paid more than minimum wage, you'd probably be able to hire better talent."

"I don't know what the fuck you're talking about, Trask." Guthrie's hoarse, rasping voice was slurred with alcohol. "I didn't see anything."

"I've heard that too much booze affects the eyesight."

Fury flashed in Guthrie's face. "I know you've come back here to make trouble, you SOB. But you

damn well better not mess with me. You unner-
stand? Nobody messes with Dean Guthrie."

"He's drunk," Alexa whispered. "Let's get out of
here."

Trask ignored her. "There's something you need
to understand, Guthrie. This is between you and
me. You made a mistake tonight. You involved Ms.
Chambers. That's against the rules."

"I don't give a fucking damn about your threats,
Trask." Guthrie's voice rose. "Got that? Not a fucking damn. Come near me again and I'll go to the
cops."

Trask realized that Guthrie had raised his voice
because they had drawn a small audience. Two
middle-aged couples had emerged from the restaurant and now stood watching the scene with
shocked expressions. The gossip about the confrontation in the Red Canyon Country Club parking
lot would be all over town in the morning.

"I think we'd better have this conversation some
other time," Trask said.

"Bullshit. We'll have it now. You still think I had
something to do with your father's death, don't
you, you crazy bastard?"

Trask watched him. "Did you?"

"Goddamnit, you're as stubborn as he was."
Guthrie's face worked. "I knew you'd come back. I
knew it that night you charged into my house. My
wife said you were just letting off steam, but I knew
better."

"You were right," Trask said.

"That's enough, please." Alexa's voice sharpened. "There's no point talking to him."

Guthrie peered at Alexa and then his big head

swiveled back toward Trask. "So what's the master plan, here, Mr. Fucking Hot Shot CEO?"

"Alexa's right. You're drunk." Trask took her arm. "Get out of here, Guthrie."

"Think you can get your revenge on Kenyon by fucking his stepdaughter? Is that it?"

Rage exploded in Trask's veins. He released Alexa and started toward the Lincoln. "I said, that's enough."

"Trask, no." Alexa snatched at his sleeve.

He ignored her.

Guthrie's eyes glinted with malice as Trask neared the car. "Maybe you're gonna try to get your hands on her money, huh? That would sure piss off Kenyon."

Trask did not respond. He was only a yard away from the Lincoln.

"Who the hell do you think you are, you son-of-a-bitch?" Guthrie's voice rose. "Leave me alone. I'll have you arrested if you so much as come near me."

He gunned the Lincoln. It shot forward, tires screaming, just as Trask started to reach for the door handle.

The two middle-aged couples stood statue still. They stared, bemused, at Trask and Alexa.

Trask watched the Lincoln disappear into the night. Then he turned to look at Alexa. She was watching him with huge eyes. He groaned.

"I realize that I didn't make a good impression twelve years ago. And this scene probably didn't do much to improve my image as a fun date. But I wouldn't want you to get the idea that every time I go out I end up in a brawl."

She blinked a couple of times. Then her mouth

curved in a shaky smile. "I'll try to keep an open mind."

Trask glowered at Calvin Strood, Avalon's chief of police, across the expanse of Strood's dented metal desk. "I told Alexa that this would be a waste of time."

Alexa, seated next to him, frowned in disapproval. "Don't be ridiculous. We had to report what happened in the parking lot."

Strood's rawhide and leather features grimaced in a pained expression. He had made it clear that he was not happy about being pulled away from the late-night television news to come down to Avalon's small police station to take the statements. Trask was pretty sure that the only reason he hadn't let one of his officers handle the complaint was because the complainant had recently become the town's biggest employer.

"We'll keep an eye out for those two who mugged you," Strood said patiently. "But my guess is they're already long gone to Phoenix or Tucson. Even if they're still in town it'll be hard to pick 'em out in the crowd. Avalon is filled with visitors this week. Festival time, you know."

"Talk to Guthrie," Trask said evenly.

Strood's brows rose. "You sure that's what you want me to do? According to what I hear, you and Guthrie were seen engaged in an argument. I believe the exact phrase was, in a *heated argument*. No one saw the two men you claim tried to mug you."

"Talk to Guthrie," Trask repeated. "Ask him about the two thugs."

"Okay, okay." Strood sighed heavily. "But I'm not going to promise anything. You got no names, no descriptions, and no license plate. Hell, neither of you is even hurt and nothing got stolen. All you've got is some wild theory that Guthrie sent two men to rough you up."

Alexa sat forward tensely. "Are you implying that we made up the whole thing?"

Strood shook his head. "No, Ms. Chambers. I'm just saying that I haven't got a lot to work with here. I'll do what I can."

Translated, that meant nothing, Trask thought.

13

The heels of Alexa's sandals tinged on the mosaic tiles. She came to a halt just inside the vast, unabashedly ornate spa and allowed the sultry atmosphere to envelop her.

The warmth felt good. The adrenaline had evaporated from her system, but it had left an unpleasant, shivery chill in its wake.

"This is incredible," she said.

Water the color of liquid aquamarines lapped at the edges of the room's three freeform pools. In addition to the soaking areas there were two fountains. Neither was operating at the moment. Tiled and gilded pillars rose gracefully into the shadows of the high ceiling. Ranks of webbed loungers and draped massage tents were flanked by an array of palms and ferns.

An eerie silence hung over the steamy chamber. She and Trask had the place to themselves. The hotel was not scheduled to open until tomorrow. Only a skeleton staff was on duty tonight.

"Edward told me the architect had done a magnificent job in here, but I had no idea it had turned out like this." Lord, she was babbling. Another aftereffect of the night's violence, no doubt.

"The spa wasn't open to the public last night." Trask closed the heavy opaque glass doors behind him. "The PR people were afraid someone might drink too much champagne and fall into one of the pools."

He opened a side door and stepped into a small room. Alexa caught a glimpse of glowing dials on a control panel. Trask contemplated the switches for a moment and then flipped two of them.

A melodic, burbling sound made Alexa turn back to the two fountains. Water spouted from each and cascaded into the low blue-green bases.

She smiled faintly. "It looks like a fantasy version of an ancient Roman spa."

"Fantasy is what an Avalon hotel is all about." Trask watched her from the shadows. "Feel free to look around, but you'd better take off your shoes first. This floor is designed for bare feet and rubber soles."

"All right."

She could feel his brooding gaze on her as she stepped out of her high heels. Neither of them had said much since they had returned from the interview with Chief Strood. Trask had used one of the resort's cars to drive to the station.

After they had talked to Strood, Trask had brought her back here to the resort instead of taking her straight home. She had made no protest. The truth was she was not particularly eager to be alone just yet, she thought.

The tiles were warm beneath her stocking-clad

feet. She went to the edge of the largest of the three soaking pools and looked down.

Trask had not turned on all of the lights, only those beneath the surface of the water in the three pools. The submerged glow, made blue and hazy from the steam, enhanced the otherwordly atmosphere.

Trask took off his own shoes. Barefoot, he walked slowly toward her across the mosaic floor.

An atavistic thrill went through her at his approach. Another symptom of adrenaline withdrawal? she wondered. Instinctively she moved out of his path. He paused, watching her.

She went to stand at the edge of one of the tiered fountains. After a few seconds, he changed course to follow, halting less than a yard away from her. She stared at the bubbling water and tried to think of some clever, offhand remark. It wasn't easy. The unfamiliar energy of naked physical attraction was suddenly swirling up through the mists.

The genie was out of the bottle.

"There is nothing so seductive as water in the desert," she said softly.

"You're wrong. There are more seductive things."

She glanced quickly over her shoulder. It was a mistake. The expression in his eyes sent a wave of heat through her. Alarmed, she sought to regain control of herself and the situation.

She opted for the direct approach.

"Why did you bring me here?" she asked.

"Two reasons. I wanted to apologize again for what happened to you in the parking lot. It was my fault. I should never have—"

"Forget it." She cut him off with an impatient wave of her hand. "It wasn't your fault. You can't take responsibility for everything, Trask."

His eyes narrowed, but he did not respond to that. "The second reason I brought you back here was that I wanted to tell you that what Guthrie said was a lie. I don't have any plans to use you against Lloyd Kenyon."

"Because you don't think you can?" She turned completely around to face him. "Or because you draw the line at that kind of thing?"

"What do you think?"

She hesitated. "As I said earlier, I'm reserving judgment about you, just as you are about me. But I will tell you one thing, Trask. If you do have plans to use me against Lloyd, you can forget them. You'll be wasting your time."

He eyed her thoughtfully. "This relationship is not exactly getting off to a great start, is it?"

"This relationship," she said deliberately, "is business, not personal. You've agreed to share your conspiracy theories with me before you take any action, and I'm going to hold you to that bargain."

"You're sure this is the way you want it?"

"I'm sure." She studied the tiles at the bottom of the fountain pool. "Guthrie threatened you tonight. It's obvious that your presence here in town has scared him badly."

"I told you that I came here to stir up trouble."

"Congratulations. You've obviously succeeded." She glanced at him. "You could have been seriously injured tonight."

He smiled slightly, but his eyes were cool and unreadable. "Does that worry you?"

"Yes." she said.

He took another step toward her, closing the small distance between them. "Why?"

His question unnerved her. It also made her angry. "I'd like you to stay in one piece long enough to read the reviews of your hotel's new art collection. I've got something to prove, and I can't do it if you get clobbered by Dean Guthrie's hired thugs."

"Nice to know you care." His smile was cold. "But you don't have to worry. I can handle Guthrie."

She wrapped her arms around herself. "I'll admit you handled the situation tonight."

"I had help. That was a neat trick with the heel of your shoe, by the way."

"Lloyd taught me that before I went off to college."

"I see."

Another of the unpleasant, involuntary shivers went through Alexa. "Guthrie's dangerous, Trask."

"Guthrie's temper and his drinking problem are two of the reasons why he's at the top of my list of suspects."

"What are your other reasons?"

Trask was quiet for a moment. She sensed that he was debating how much information to give her. For a while she thought he would simply brush her off. Then to her surprise, he started to talk.

"According to the information my investigator turned up, Guthrie was in major financial hot water twelve years ago. He was severely overextended. Facing bankruptcy. Something had to give."

Alexa considered that and then shook her head. "Guthrie's a developer. According to Lloyd, developers always seem to be overextended and teetering on the edge of bankruptcy. It's a way of life for most of them."

"As far as I'm concerned, Guthrie's financial situation at the time of Dad's death gives him a motive," Trask said evenly.

"A dubious one, if you ask me. What information have you got on Lloyd that makes him number two on your list of so-called suspects?"

"Kenyon also had invested money in several projects."

She shot him an exasperated glare. "Lloyd's a real estate investor. Arranging finance money for other people's projects is what he does. He's good at it. I told you, he manages the inheritance I got from my grandmother. My portfolio has increased in value every year, even during the last economic downturn."

"I never said Kenyon was bad at what he did." Trask's jaw tightened. "Just the opposite. Twelve years ago he concluded that Dad's dreams of turning the old Avalon Mansion into a world-class resort was never going to work. He wanted to get his clients' money out of the project. Dad threatened to make that difficult."

"Lloyd has dealt with developers and complex financial situations for years. He knows how to handle people and money. I can guarantee you that he doesn't resort to murder whenever someone makes life difficult for him."

Trask said nothing for a moment. He contemplated the water spilling down the sides of the fountain.

"They were both right, you know," he said eventually.

Alexa frowned. "What do you mean?"

"Kenyon and Guthrie were both right to pull the plug on Dad's Avalon Mansion project. They would have lost a lot of money if it hadn't been halted."

Alexa heard the underlying frustration and something else, something that might have been pain, in his voice. She did not know what to say.

"I see," she managed.

Trask put a bare foot on the low rim of the fountain. He leaned forward, braced one forearm on his knee, and looked down into the foaming water.

"I told you, my father was a dreamer," he said.

"Yes."

"He was a man of vision, but he was not very good when it came to the bottom line. The Avalon Mansion project was a disaster waiting to happen. It was undercapitalized and poorly managed from the start. But Dad wouldn't listen to—"

He broke off abruptly. The fingers of his left hand flexed once.

Comprehension crashed through Alexa. "Your father would not listen to you? Is that what you were about to say?"

"He was obsessed with the Avalon project. He had a vision of what it could be." Trask's mouth was a grim line. "When Dad was riding the wings of a fantasy, he couldn't see the reality of a stone wall looming in front of him."

Alexa drew a deep breath. "You tried to tell him, didn't you?"

"I argued with him until I was hoarse. He said I was only twenty-three. What the hell did I know?"

"But you knew, didn't you?"

Trask turned his head slowly. His eyes were pitiless. "It was the worst of all our head-on clashes. Much worse than the one we had when I told him I didn't want to play college ball, let alone try for the pros. Worse than the battle we fought when he used the money my mother had left for Nathan's college education to finance his doomed private ferry scheme."

Alexa realized that the chilling blame in Trask's gaze was not directed at the memory of his father. It was aimed at himself.

"I used up all of my logic and reason that night, and then I lost my temper," Trask continued softly. "I told him that he was going to bankrupt us again. I pleaded with him to ditch the Avalon project. I told him to think about Nathan's future. Dad was furious. He said I had no vision. He slammed down the phone and so did I."

"That night?" A terrible sympathy flashed through Alexa. "You quarreled *that night*, didn't you? The night your father was killed in the accident."

Trask's eyes were hooded now. She knew that he had said far more than he had intended.

"Three hours after I put down the phone I got the call from the Avalon cops telling me my father had driven his car off Avalon Point."

"Oh, Trask." Not knowing what else to do, she reached out to touch his shoulder. "No wonder you've been obsessed with finding answers. Deep down you're afraid that you might have been the one who was responsible for your father's death, aren't you?"

His eyes gleamed with sudden fury. "What the hell are you talking about? I told you, Dad was murdered, and I'm going to prove it."

"You're afraid that what really happened after that last quarrel was that he got into his car and drove off without being in full control of himself. You think you were a contributing factor in his death, don't you?"

"That is pure, undiluted bullshit."

"Yes, it is," Alexa said. "But deep down inside, you're worried that it's the truth. You've come back to Avalon because you have to know if you've been right to blame yourself all these years for what happened that night."

He said nothing.

Alexa gripped his shoulder. "Listen to me, you were not responsible for your father's death. But that does not automatically imply that someone else is."

"I'm going to find out what happened that night," he said very steadily.

"Trask, listen to me. I know what it's like to get that kind of call in the middle of the night. I know what it's like not to have had a chance to say goodbye."

"Alexa—"

She tightened her hand. "I know how it feels to wonder if, just maybe, I'd been prettier or more clever, or, better yet, if I'd been a son, if maybe my father would have spent more time at home. Maybe he wouldn't have gotten bored and traveled halfway around the world to risk his neck taking pictures of other people's wars. Maybe he wouldn't have gotten himself shot by some anonymous sniper who probably never even knew his name—"

She broke off abruptly, shocked by the rush of

words. She had never said those things aloud, not even to Dr. Ormiston.

Trask watched her with an unblinking gaze. "I'm sorry."

Alexa fought a short, ferocious battle to pull herself together.

"Sometimes there are no answers," she said.

"Sometimes there are answers. I'm going to get them."

"I never thought I'd say this," she whispered. "But I wish you luck. I think you're going to need it."

On impulse she stood on tiptoe and brushed her mouth lightly across his. He did not respond.

She took her hand off his shoulder and turned away toward the exit.

"Alexa."

She paused and looked back. "What is it?"

"I don't want or need your sympathy. Do you understand?"

She could feel the tension in him, a live wire dancing with dangerous electricity. "Got it. No sympathy."

"And the next time you kiss me, by God, make sure it's for real. I don't need little butterfly pecks to make me feel better. I'm not some kid with a skinned knee."

She braced herself. "What do you need, Trask?"

Without warning, he took two steps toward her and pulled her into his arms. "This is what I need."

His mouth came down on hers, fierce, hot, demanding. The kiss exploded through her senses, pulling her deep into the vortex of sensation that had opened at her feet.

She discovered in a sudden rush of heat and lightning that she did not want to give him another little butterfly caress. She did not want to brush her mouth across his in a misguided attempt to communicate her understanding of what he had gone through all those years ago.

She wanted to crush herself against him so that she could feel the kiss all the way to her bones.

She wrapped her arms around his neck and sank deeper into the whirlpool of sensual energy.

14

Her response swept away everything else that should have mattered to him tonight, everything that should have commanded his full attention at that moment. Everything that he had been thinking just a few seconds earlier.

It was not that he forgot about Guthrie and Kenyon or what had happened twelve years ago. It was just that, right now, while he was holding Alexa in his arms, those things could be put aside for a while.

The past could wait until tomorrow.

He tightened his hold on Alexa. She was soft and vibrant. Her scent captivated him on an elemental level. He'd known women who smelled good, but none of them had smelled *this* good.

The contours of her body were exquisitely satisfying. They seemed to fit him perfectly. It was as though she had been made just for him. When she sighed and opened her mouth he wanted to go out and conquer a large chunk of the civilized world and maybe finish exploring the Amazon.

But first he wanted to make love to her. He had to make love to her. And he had to do it now, tonight.

He eased her closer. Her thigh brushed against the inside of the leg he had braced on the fountain rim.

There is nothing so seductive as water in the desert.

Without breaking the kiss, he closed his hands around Alexa's waist, scooped her up, and stepped into the low fountain pool with her in his arms. The soft, warm rain cascaded over them.

Alexa gasped and pulled back a little, but her hands still clung firmly around his shoulders. She stared at him through the gentle mist. Her eyes gleamed with astonished wonder as the water plastered her hair to her elegantly shaped head.

He could not tell her that he was even more amazed than she was by his exuberant passion. For some reason it felt perfectly natural to make love to this woman in a fountain tonight.

"*Trask.*" She caught his face between her palms, closed her eyes, and nibbled hungrily along the line of his jaw until her teeth closed around his earlobe.

He slid his hands down the length of her body, savoring the feel of her. The water had turned the tissue-thin dress into a second skin. He was aware of every inch of her through the wet fabric. When he curved his fingers around her breasts he discovered that her nipples were tight and full beneath a near-transparent bra.

The vapors that filled the spa chamber created a dream world, a place where reality could be checked at the door. For the first time in his life, he

did the unthinkable. He knowingly allowed himself
to enter the fantasy.

He could always step back out of it when this
was finished, he thought. He could deal with the
facts. He always understood the bottom line in any
given situation. But just for tonight he would revel
in the fantasy. He needed it.

Just for tonight.

Alexa made no protest when he eased the zipper
of her dress down to the small of her back. He
peeled the wet silk away from her body and let it
sink into the churning pool. Then he unfastened her
bra. It, too, fell into the water and floated away.

He shuddered when he felt her hands on his bare
chest. He realized with a shock of excitement that
she had unbuttoned his shirt.

"You feel so good," she whispered against his
shoulder.

He heard the unveiled appreciation in her voice.
The knowledge that she wanted him was the ulti-
mate aphrodisiac.

As if he needed any other drug tonight.

He went down on one knee, hooked his thumbs
in the waistband of her pantyhose, and stripped
them down to her ankles.

Slowly he drew his palms upward from ankle to
thigh. He urged her legs apart and slid his finger
into her. She gave a choked moan and clutched at
his shoulders to steady herself. He felt her nails sink
into his skin.

He wrapped his hands around her buttocks and
found her clitoris with his tongue. The taste of her
was utterly unique in all the universe. It made him
ravenous, insatiable.

She trembled violently.

He could feel himself, hard and full, inside his trousers.

He rose in the sparkling water until he was once more standing in front of her. He looked into her eyes and saw the sultry yearning there.

He reached down and unbuckled his belt.

It took him only a moment to get out of his trousers and retrieve the foil packet from his wallet.

When he lifted Alexa high into his arms and carried her to the nearest lounger, she whispered his name. He considered it a near-miracle that he did not climax then and there.

He put her down on the cushions and lowered himself on top of her. She folded one leg around his thigh. He discovered that she was damp and slick all over.

And hot. So very, very hot.

With a groan, he thrust deep into her snug body. She lifted herself, straining against him. He found the swollen nub between her legs again, this time with his thumb.

The waters of the spa bubbled, lapped, and surged around them.

He sank deeper into Alexa.

She cried out, shivered, and climaxed beneath him. He tried to hold himself back long enough to savor her response, but the delicious demands of her body proved irresistible.

Somewhere in the shimmering void a bell rang, warning him about the risk of getting caught up in the fantasy.

He ignored it. He would worry later about climbing back out of the illusion.

*   *   *

Alexa sat up on the edge of the lounger and pulled the oversized bath sheet more closely around her breasts. She glanced around surreptitiously, part of her still half-convinced that she might have hallucinated the entire experience. But the steamy atmosphere, the frothy fountains, and the gleaming tiles were definitely real.

This wasn't her. It couldn't be her. She didn't do things like this.

Wild woman had struck, big time. But now the real Alexa had to deal with the aftermath.

She watched Trask walk back toward her through the mist. He wore a toweling robe that he had found in one of the changing rooms. He carried a second robe in his hand.

She studied the veiled expression in his eyes as he drew closer. Had he planned to seduce her tonight? Or had he been as caught up in the heat of the moment as herself? Was he already regretting the interlude? Or did he think he could control her with passion?

Dr. Ormiston, if you could only see me now. Risk city.

Trask halted near the fountain to scoop up their sodden clothing and her small evening bag. Then he walked over to the lounger and handed her the extra robe.

"You can wear this home," he said.

She got to her feet, still clutching the bath sheet around herself with one hand. She took the robe from him.

"Okay." She wondered why she suddenly felt uncomfortably warm. To her chagrin, she realized that she was blushing.

This was ridiculous. She had to pull herself together or she would collapse from humiliation.

She gave him what she hoped was a bright, sophisticated sort of smile. *Be cool, Alexa. Risk-takers are nothing if not really, really cool.*

"It's going to be a little awkward explaining to your staff why we're not wearing the clothes we had on earlier, isn't it?" she said.

"No big deal. We'll say we took an unanticipated swim in one of the spa pools. Don't worry, a good hotel staff knows better than to ask questions." His mouth curved at one corner. "Especially of the boss."

"That won't stop people from speculating about us. As you have so frequently pointed out, this is a small town."

"If it will make you feel more comfortable, I'll take you out the back way."

She pursed her lips while she considered that. Then she shook her head. "That might make things even worse."

"You're really sweating this out, aren't you?"

"It just occurred to me that the repercussions could be a bit awkward, that's all." The bath sheet slipped precariously as she fumbled to hold it in place while she put on the robe. "For both of us."

"I'm not going to worry about it," he said. "Are you?"

"Heavens no." Sheesh. Her voice was much too high. She fought to bring it down to a more normal level as she struggled with the robe. "What's to worry about? We're consenting adults. I mean, it's not as if this sort of thing is any big deal these days."

Damn. She'd missed the sleeve. It flapped use-

lessly. She readjusted her grip on the bath sheet and
tried again.

"Here. Let me help you." Trask took the robe
from her and held it ready.

Alexa turned her back to him and froze, both
hands clutching the bath sheet to her breasts.

"You're going to have to let go of that bath sheet
if you want to put on the robe," he said.

"I know that."

She took a deep breath, closed her eyes, released
her death grip on the bath sheet, and plunged both
arms into the sleeves of the robe.

To her everlasting relief, she made it on the first
attempt. She seized the dangling ends of the sash
and tied them swiftly.

Be cool, wild woman. You can do this.

She opened her eyes and saw that Trask was
watching her with grave amusement.

"I may be able to find a comb for your hair," he
said.

Her hair. She raised a hand to the damp tangle.
She could feel bits and pieces sticking out at crazy
angles.

"I've got one in my purse." She yanked the bag
from his hand, jerked it open, and snatched out the
comb. She tried to drag it through her snarled hair.
"Ouch."

Trask studied the results. "Want me to do that?"

"No, no, I'm fine. Thank you." She gave up the
attempt to put her hair into some semblance of
order and glanced at her watch instead. It appeared
to have survived the soaking in the fountain. "It's
getting late. I have a busy day tomorrow."

"Yeah. Me, too."

The odd edge in his voice brought her head up sharply. His gaze, dark and brooding, trapped hers.

"Trask, I—" She broke off, floundering.

"Wondering if you've just made a serious mistake?" he asked much too evenly.

Anger shot through her, mercifully vaporizing some of the awkwardness and the uncertainty.

"I thought maybe you were asking yourself the same question," she said.

"I'll guess we'll both have to wait and find out, won't we?"

Alexa came awake so suddenly and with such a surge of adrenaline that for an instant she was certain there was an intruder in her bedroom.

Panic froze her. She lay motionless, listening with preternatural intensity for the slightest scrape of a foot or the sound of an indrawn breath. *Pretend you're still asleep.*

The phone rang again.

A shudder of relief went through her. Not an intruder, after all.

"Okay, I can deal with this."

She glanced at the glowing numbers on the clock as she reached for the bedside phone. Two-fifteen in the morning. No one called with glad tidings at this hour.

She thought of Vivien and Lloyd in Maui. If something had happened to one or both of them . . .

Obscene phone calls also came in the middle of the night, she thought, trying for a note of optimism. At that moment there was nothing she wanted to hear more than a heavy breather on the other end of the line. Anything would be better than bad news from Maui.

She tightened her grip on the phone, raised it to her ear. "Hello?"

"Trask has aroused the vortices of dark energy. Stay away from him."

The voice was low and muffled, as though the caller was holding a wad of fabric over the mouthpiece.

"Who is this?" Alexa sat up against the pillows. "If this is some kind of weird joke, I can tell you right now, it's not appreciated."

"The vortices will not grow calm again until he is gone. There is great danger."

"Who are you?" She listened closely, straining to detect a familiar note in the oddly flat voice. She thought she heard a car's engine start up. Other voices in the background. Laughter. Teenagers?

"You have been warned. Stay away from Trask or you will be caught up in the dark storm."

"Listen, you little creep, there are laws against—"

There was a click. The line went dead.

Alexa slowly replaced the receiver. She switched on the light and sat up on the edge of the bed.

Opening the drawer of the bedside table, she pulled out the phone book. She flipped swiftly through the pages of helpful information on voice messaging services, long distance calling instructions, area codes, and time zones.

She found the instructions she wanted and followed directions for returning the last call.

The phone rang on the other end. She waited

tensely for someone to respond. She had read somewhere that most victims of obscene phone calls
knew the caller.

On the other hand, threats about dark vortices
didn't sound exactly obscene.

"*Yeah?*"

The voice was young. The accent was pure
teenager.

"Who is this?" Alexa asked.

"*Duh. Me Tarzan. You Jane?*"

Muffled giggles sounded. A car's engine revved.
Another voice spoke in the background.
"*Damnit, you kids stop fooling around with that phone
or, so help me, I'll have the phone company take it out.*"

A seriously annoyed adult, Alexa realized.

"*If you're callin' someone to come down and buy
booze for you, you can forget it.*"

There was more teenage laughter.

"*Let me have that phone.*" A new voice came on the
line, gruff and aggressive. "*Who the hell is this?*"

"I'm sorry to disturb you," Alexa said in her
plummiest antique gallery tones. "Someone called
me from this number a moment ago and hung up. I
was trying to find out who it was."

"*Probably one of the punks hangin' around out front
here.*" The irritation leaked out of the voice. "*There
was a dance after the game tonight. Some of the kids are
still out cruising. You know how it is. They all oughta be
home in bed, but parents these days just don't seem to
care where their kids are.*"

"Excuse me, out in front of where?"

"*You got the pay phone outside Avalon Quick Stop.
I'm the night manager.*"

"I see. Thanks for explaining things. You know how it is with that kind of call."

"*Sure.*" The manager was not unsympathetic. "*But I wouldn't worry too much about this one. I know most of these kids. If you get any more calls, let me know. I'll put a stop to 'em.*"

"Thank you."

Alexa hung up the phone. She turned out the light and slipped back under the covers.

She did not sleep for a long time. Instead she stared up at the ceiling and thought about the voice of the person who had called earlier.

It had not sounded like a youthful voice. Furthermore, it was highly unlikely that any kid who was into cruising and hanging out with his friends at the Avalon Quick Stop would have any interest in Trask, dark vortices, or what, for a teenager, was truly ancient history.

She was all too well aware that sex with Trask had its risks. She certainly did not need a late-night phone call to warn her.

15

"How did the reception go?" Nathan asked. "I tried to get hold of you yesterday to get a firsthand report, but you weren't answering your phone."

"I got your messages. Everything went off on schedule." Phone in hand, Trask walked to the French doors. "You know Glenda. She never leaves anything to chance."

"Right. So, out of curiosity, what did you think of the art collection?"

"Interesting." Trask opened the doors and stepped out onto the balcony. "At least there aren't any pink flamingoes out on the front lawn."

The late morning sun was high overhead. The sculpted buttes and towering rock spires were silhouetted against an impossibly blue sky.

"You'll like Deco well enough when the publicity hits." Nathan paused. "Still planning to stay down there in Arizona for a while?"

Trask looked down at the sparkling pool. Memories of last night drifted through his mind. "Yeah."

Nathan groaned. "I don't suppose it would do me any good to try to talk you into coming back to the home office?"

"No. But that reminds me, I do need something from your end."

"What?"

"Coffee. Ask Bernie to ship down a couple of pounds of my usual. Tell him to overnight it."

Nathan grunted. "What, exactly, are you doing down there, JL?"

"You really want to know what I'm doing on my spring vacation? Well, let's see. Last night I went out on a date."

There was a stunned pause on the other end of the line. "You did *what?*"

"You don't have to make it sound as if I've taken up bungee jumping or sword swallowing."

"You haven't been out on a real date in months." Nathan was clearly intrigued. "What's going on? Who is she?"

"Her name is Alexa Chambers. She owns a shop here in town. Sells those tacky museum replicas. You know, gargoyles and statues of winged lions and suits of armor."

"Didn't know you were in the market for that kind of thing."

"A man never knows when he might need a full suit of armor."

Nathan laughed. He sounded vastly relieved. "How'd you meet this Alexa?"

"She showed up at the reception."

"Well, all I can say is, I'd rather worry about you remembering to practice safe sex than wonder if you're still obsessing on the past."

Trask said nothing.

There was a beat of silence.

"Damn." All of the brotherly amusement evaporated from Nathan's voice. He sounded grimly resigned. "I knew it was too good to be true. What's the connection between Alexa Chambers and your obsession?"

"Alexa is Lloyd Kenyon's stepdaughter."

"Shit."

"Thanks for your good wishes, little brother." Trask turned away from the stark landscape and walked back into the cool suite. "I'm going to hang up now. I've got an appointment in five minutes."

"Wait," Nathan said swiftly. "Listen to me, JL, I don't know what you're up to, but I don't like the sound of this Alexa at all."

"Your opinion is duly noted."

"Any way you look at it, dating Kenyon's stepdaughter is a really bad idea. People are going to wonder if you've got ulterior motives. Damn it, *I'm* going to wonder . . ."

A knock sounded. Trask glanced at the door. "I've got to go."

"Don't hang up on me, JL. I've got to talk some sense into you. You're the CEO of Avalon Resorts, Inc. The company doesn't need this kind of trouble—"

Trask gently hit the disconnect button on the phone. He set the instrument on the desk and crossed the room to open the door.

Joanna Bell stood in the hall. There was a fine trembling around her mouth when she smiled. "Hello, Trask."

He moved aside. "Come on in, Joanna."

*   *   *

"I just dropped in to say good-bye." Edward Vale stood in the opening of the back door of Elegant Relic. He was his usual dapper self in a beige linen sport coat, pale cream shirt, and matching trousers. "I'm on my way back to Phoenix."

Alexa eyed him grimly. "You've got a heck of a nerve showing up on my doorstep after pulling that stunt with *Dancing Satyr*."

He winced. "I know, I know. I hoped that if I gave you a day to cool off you'd be a little more open-minded—"

"Open-minded? About a fake in my beautiful collection?"

"I had to make an executive decision."

"You sneaked that statue into the west wing hoping I wouldn't notice it, didn't you?"

"Try to understand. I simply could not pretend it didn't exist. Trask demanded to see every item listed in the catalog of the collection."

There's was no point beating up on Edward, Alexa thought. For better or worse, the damage had been done. And she *had* managed to hide the statue before any of the art crowd had seen it. Her future was still reasonably secure. She could afford to let bygones be bygones.

"Forget it." She gave him a wry smile. "Other than *Dancing Satyr*, things went well. Thanks, Edward. I know you took a chance on me, and I appreciate it."

"Think nothing of it." Edward turned a delicate shade of pink. "I am enormously grateful to you. This was an important client, and I wanted to be sure Avalon Resorts got the best. I knew I could depend on your eye. Besides, I owed you for saving me from getting scammed by McClelland."

"We're even now."

"If everything goes well with the reviews, I'll call you again," Edward promised. "I've got other clients, corporate and private, who want to add to their early-twentieth-century collections."

"You know where to find me."

On impulse, Alexa stepped forward and gave him a quick hug. When she moved back she was surprised to see the concern in his eyes.

"Alexa, my dear, I hesitate to say this, but given our long-standing professional association and what I feel has become an ever-deepening friendship—"

"Just say it, Edward."

"Very well, I'll come straight out with it. I heard that you were seen at the country club last night."

"So?"

Edward cleared his throat. "According to the rumor, you were with Trask."

"You know, Edward, for a man who swears he does not want to know too much about a client, you always seem to be first with the latest gossip."

"Actually, I believe I was at the end of a rather long line of people who got this bit of information. To be blunt, the rumors are all over town."

"Everyone is talking about the fact that I had dinner with Trask? Must be a slow news day here in Avalon."

"Not just dinner," Edward said very deliberately. "The word is that there was some sort of unpleasant scene in the parking lot afterward. And then you went back to the hotel with Trask and left dressed only in a spa robe."

Alexa drew herself up and looked down her nose. "A couple of muggers accosted us and smashed the windows of Trask's Jeep. And then Guthrie appeared. Some unpleasantries were exchanged. As for the bath robe, we took a late-night swim. That's all there is to your rumors."

"Damn." Edward grimaced. "I knew I shouldn't have started this conversation. It's really none of my business."

"No, it's not."

"Still, you are a friend and I am indebted to you." Edward hesitated. "I don't suppose it would do me any good to warn you to keep a safe distance from this particular client?"

Alexa remembered her late-night caller. "Safe?"

"I must be honest, my dear. You're a charming, interesting, attractive woman."

"Why, Edward, you'll make my head spin."

"It's the truth. If I were so inclined in that direction, I'd have asked you out myself long ago."

Alexa grinned. "But you're not so inclined, and Roger would be insanely jealous."

"Yes." Edward braced himself. "Back to my point. I've heard enough of the local gossip to know that any personal interest Trask shows in you must be viewed as highly suspect."

Wild woman surged to the fore without warning. "Oh, yeah? How about any personal interest I show in him?"

Edward looked deeply distressed. "I beg your pardon?"

"You're afraid Trask may be trying to use me. But has it occurred to you and everyone else that I might have my own sneaky reasons for dating him?"

Edward blinked a couple of times, assimilating that concept. "No. To be frank, it hadn't occurred to me."

"Look, I appreciate your concern. But I lost my girlish naiveté and innocent trust in my fellow human beings in the McClelland affair."

Edward grimaced. "Well, yes, I suppose you did."

"I'm well aware that Trask may have asked me out for reasons other than my charm, wit, and personality."

Edward looked mortified. "I never meant to imply that you lack wit and charm. Or personality, either, for that matter."

"Gee, thanks, Ed."

"I'm not handling this well, am I?"

"It's okay." She tried for a reassuring smile. "I know what I'm doing." *I think.* Mentally she crossed her fingers behind her back.

"Yes, of course." Edward made himself very busy adjusting the sleeves of his linen jacket. "Well, then, I'd best be off. I told Roger I'd meet him in Scottsdale in time for dinner."

"Good-bye, Edward." Alexa went to stand in the doorway. "Give my best to Roger. And, again, thanks for everything. Except *Dancing Satyr*, of course."

"Think nothing of it, my dear." Edward climbed into the white van. "I've always said, you're the best in the business when it comes to the early twentieth century. One of these days everyone else will know it, too."

He raised his neatly manicured hand in farewell and put the van in gear.

"I don't know quite how to say this." Joanna put her coffee cup down on the room service cart and got to her feet. She walked to the French doors and looked out at the sun-drenched view. "You certainly have every right to tell me to mind my own business."

Trask leaned back against the desk. "This is about last night, isn't it?"

She bowed her head. "Yes. I heard you took Alexa Chambers to the club. I also heard that there was a scene between you and Guthrie in the parking lot afterward."

"I don't know why the *Avalon Herald* even bothers to put out a daily edition of the paper. News travels so fast around this town that it seems pointless to take the time to put it in print."

Joanna looked at him with agonized eyes. "I'm sorry, Trask, but I must ask if the rumors are true."

"Which ones?"

"Are you here in Avalon to . . . to open up the old wounds of the past?"

"Does that possibility worry you?"

"Yes."

"Why?"

"Because even though I know that you won't find any answers to your questions, I'm afraid that you'll stir up a lot of unpleasantness, not only for yourself but for some other, innocent people."

"Which innocent people?"

Joanna clasped her hands very tightly together. "Alexa Chambers, for one."

The swiftness of her response disturbed him. He shoved the flicker of guilt aside. "What makes you so sure I won't find any answers to my questions?"

"There aren't any to find. At least, not the kind I think you want. Please listen to me, Trask. I was devastated by what happened twelve years ago. I loved your father."

"I know."

"But the crash was a terrible accident. A tragedy, not an act of violence. I've made my peace with the past. I assumed that you and your brother had done the same."

"What, exactly, are you worried about?"

"I don't know." Joanna's mouth trembled. "But I'm afraid that there will be more incidents like the one between you and Guthrie last night. Someone might get hurt."

"I can handle Dean Guthrie."

"Can you? His drinking is worse now than it was twelve years ago. So is his temper. I know because I'm a close friend of his last ex-wife, Liz. Why do you think she divorced him? And what about Lloyd Kenyon? What do you think will happen when he finds out that you're dating Alexa?"

Trask shrugged. "Damned if I know."

"Don't give me that." Desperation flared in her eyes. "You know as well as I do that when Kenyon hears about this, he'll assume that you're somehow trying to use her. He'll be furious."

"Alexa is an adult, and she's aware of the facts. She knows what happened twelve years ago. She can make her own decisions."

Joanna met his eyes very steadily. "She may have her own reasons for seeing you. She may believe she can manipulate you. Have you considered that?"

"It's a risk I'm willing to take."

"Why? What do you hope to accomplish?"

"I just want some answers. Is that so hard to understand? I want to know what happened twelve years ago."

"I've lived in this town for nearly fourteen years. I know everyone who knew your father, and I am telling you that there is no great conspiracy for you to uncover. Go back to Seattle and leave us in peace."

"I'm sorry, Joanna. I can't do that. Not yet."

The line of people who showed up to purchase a copy of *Living the Dimensions Way* and have it personally autographed by Webster Bell stretched past the front door of Alexa's shop. It did not begin to shorten until the very end of the scheduled signing.

A handful of Webster's fans wandered into Elegant Relic to browse, but sales were not brisk. They had come to the Plaza to buy books, not suits of armor and Egyptian tomb jewelry. Between them, Alexa and her assistant, Kerry, sold only a set of gargoyle bookends and a Crusader's shield.

Shortly before the end of Webster's appearance at Spheres, Alexa decided business was not going to pick up any time soon. She left Kerry in charge of Elegant Relic and went to fetch two iced green teas from Café Solstice.

Dylan Fenn stuck his head out of the doorway of Spheres and crooked a finger at her as she went past. His angelic platinum hair shone in the sun. He looked very pleased with himself.

"You're in luck, Alexa. Webster is still here and I've got some copies of *Living the Dimensions Way* left."

"That's not fair, Dylan. When was the last time I coerced you into buying a gargoyle?"

"Let me see." He pretended to ponder the matter for a brief moment. "Last December twenty-ninth, I think it was, when you realized that you were going to get stuck with all those little gargoyles dressed in Santa Claus outfits."

"Okay, okay, I'll buy a book. But I've got to tell you, living the Dimensions Way is not really my thing."

"So you keep telling me, but I'm not giving up. One of these days the positive energy vortices will start to exert their influence. You can't resist them forever. This is Avalon, after all."

"Meaning I'm doomed to think positive?"

Dylan grinned. "Something like that."

There was a blaze of silver and turquoise as Webster appeared in the doorway behind Dylan. He gave Alexa his charismatic smile. His eyes, brimming with a patented expression of insight and understanding, were the color of ancient amber.

"Don't push her." Webster clamped a fatherly hand around Dylan's shoulder. "Those who are destined to find their way to Dimensions must do so in their own time. How are you, Alexa?"

"Fine." She felt herself turn red. "Of course I'd love an autographed copy of your book, Webster."

He chuckled. The sound was almost musical,

dark and rich. "Please, don't feel you have to buy one just because you know the author."

"No, no, I want one. Really, I do."

Dylan stood aside. "Come on in. I'll get a copy for you. Webster can sign it."

"Great." Alexa tried to infuse some genuine enthusiasm into her voice. She smiled brightly at Webster. "It looked like you had a great crowd."

"It was a gratifying turnout, thanks to Dylan."

"All I do is sell the books." Dylan picked up a copy of *Living the Dimensions Way* from the small stack of books that was left from the signing. "You're the one who brings in the crowds, Webster."

"This one does seem to be doing quite well." Webster glanced at the cover of his book. "Let's hope it changes a few lives."

Changes a few lives? Compared to that goal, her own career aspirations seemed downright mundane, Alexa thought.

Webster opened the book and removed an expensively worked silver and turquoise pen from his pocket. He scrawled a short message and his name across the inside page.

"There you go." He handed the book to Alexa.

"Thank you." She would put the book on the shelf in her living room, she decided. No one would ever have to know that she was one of probably no more than three people in Avalon who hadn't actually read a Webster Bell book all the way through.

A couple walked through the door. The woman asked Dylan for a guide to the metaphysical "hot spots" in the surrounding desert. Dylan drew her

and her friend to a shelf of books at the far end of
the room.

Alexa found herself alone with Webster. She
thought about edging back out the door but paused
when it occurred to her that she had not yet paid for
Living the Dimensions Way.

"I hope you find my book useful," Webster said
very quietly. "The Dimensions Way is the way of
peace and serenity. Most of us lead lives that are
filled with too much stress. The key to fulfilling our
true potential is to resist the negative forces that sur-
round us."

Something in his voice made her look at him
more closely. The intensity with which he was
watching her made her uneasy.

"Right," she said. "Peace and serenity."

"Alexa, I hesitate to make a personal comment."
Webster glanced at the far end of the store, where
Dylan was still occupied with his customers. Then
he lowered his voice slightly. "After all, we aren't
close. But I know that you and Joanna are friends.
May I be blunt?"

"Uh—"

"I sense a severe disturbance in your personal
aura."

"Dang. Funny you should mention that. I've
been worried about my aura lately."

He smiled ruefully. "I know that to those who
have not yet found their own touchstones of power,
people like me can be a source of amusement."

She was instantly embarrassed. "I'm sorry. I
never meant to imply that you were funny. I
mean—"

"It's all right." He gave her a self-deprecating grin. "I don't mind. What the heck, if the bottom ever falls out of the metaphysical business, I can always get a job as a stand-up comedian."

Alexa relaxed slightly. "Sorry. I get a little nervous around gurus."

Webster's smile faded. He gave her a troubled look. "I don't consider myself a guru, you know. I'm only trying to help others find some of the inner peace that I, myself, have found here in the red rock country around Avalon."

"Sure," she said quickly.

"But that's not what I wanted to talk about. I heard about what happened last night at the Red Canyon Country Club."

"I'm beginning to think that there's not a single person left in town who doesn't know that I went out to dinner with Trask."

"Please believe me when I say that I am speaking up only because I am genuinely concerned. Joanna tells me that Vivien and Lloyd Kenyon are out of town. They may not have told you that there's a history between Trask and Lloyd."

Alexa angled her chin. "I'm well aware of what happened twelve years ago. I don't want to discuss it."

Webster made a face. "I guess that puts me in I my place."

"I'm sorry. I don't wish to be rude, but I really don't think that there's anything to be gained by rehashing old gossip."

"I could not agree with you more, Alexa. Gossip is, generally speaking, an extremely negative force.

What worries me is that Trask may have returned to Avalon to reopen the past. It's possible he believes that he can use you to accomplish his ends."

"I appreciate your concern," Alexa said stiffly.

"But it's none of my business, right?" Webster gave her an oblique smile. "All right, I'll shut up about it. But please allow me to pass along an ancient bit of metaphysical wisdom."

"What's that?"

Webster leaned in very close and lowered his voice. "Watch your ass around Trask."

He straightened quickly. Ignoring Alexa's widened eyes, he raised a hand in casual farewell to Dylan. Then, with a wink, he walked out the door.

Alexa managed to get her mouth closed. She waited until Dylan's customers had left before she carried her copy of *Living the Dimensions Way* to the counter.

"Don't tell me, let me guess." Dylan gave her a meaningful look as he took the book from her hand. "Webster gave out a little fatherly advice?"

"How did you know?"

"Get real." He punched in the numbers on the cash register. "Everyone knows about you and Trask at the country club last night. And about the fight between Guthrie and Trask later."

"There was no fight. Trask chased off a couple of would-be muggers and had a few words with Guthrie. That was all there was to it." She wondered how many more times she would have to tell the story.

"Whatever you say." Dylan gave her an assessing glance. "For what it's worth, my advice would be to steer clear of Trask."

"I seem to be getting that advice a lot today." Alexa hesitated. "Dylan, were you living here in Avalon twelve years ago?"

"Sure was." Dylan slipped the book into a paper sack. "I ran the bookshop up at the Institute in those days."

"No kidding? You worked for Webster Bell?"

"What's so strange about that? Until the resort opened, Dimensions was always the largest employer in Avalon." Dylan set the sack aside and folded his elbows on the counter. "It was Webster who encouraged me to open Spheres a few years ago. He urged me to stretch and grow both personally and professionally. I'll always be grateful to him."

"He seems nice enough, and I'm fond of Joanna, but I've got to admit that I've been put off by the guru thing. Career-wise it's a little too close to televangelism and carnival huckstering for my taste."

Dylan smiled. "There's always been a lot of the phony stuff going around because there's money involved in metaphysics. But with Bell it's the real thing. People respond to him. You saw some of the folks who came to buy his book today. He can touch them. He makes a difference in their lives."

"Joanna tells me that the retreat here in Avalon has been so successful, Webster's going to open another one near Santa Fe."

"It's true." Dylan contemplated the shady scene out in front of his shop. "The man's got a mission. Since his wife died twenty years ago he's focused all of his attention on his message."

"He never remarried?"

"No."

"Joanna's not married, either," Alexa said. "Doesn't that strike you as a little weird?"

"I don't think there's room in Webster's life for a wife," Dylan said. "And as for Joanna, she hasn't shown any interest in marriage since Harry Trask died."

"She and Webster seem to have a very close relationship."

Dylan nodded. "The only time I've ever heard them argue was when Joanna told Webster that she was going to marry Harry Trask."

Alexa looked at him, surprised. "Webster was against the marriage?"

"From day one."

"Any idea why?"

Dylan shrugged. "Joanna never said much, but it was obvious that Webster wanted to protect her. He was probably afraid that Harry Trask was after her money."

"From what I hear," said a familiar dour voice, "Webster had good reason to be concerned. Folks who knew him say that Harry Trask had a reputation for dreaming up big, expensive ideas that never quite worked out."

Alexa turned and saw Stewart Lutton standing in the doorway. She smiled.

Stewart did not return the smile. She did not take it personally. Stewart never smiled. It wouldn't have suited his intense image. Alexa had occasionally been tempted to ask him where and when he had acquired the tattoos that decorated his arms and shoulders, but she'd never quite worked up the guts to inquire.

Stewart's personal artwork was on display most

of the time because he wore the same style of clothing virtually every day of the year. Rain or shine, hot days or cool ones, he could be counted on to show up at Café Solstice in a tank top with a motorcycle emblazoned on the front, and pair of cargo shorts and sandals. He kept his long, graying hair out of his eyes with a length of fabric wrapped around his forehead to form a headband.

The only bright spot in Stewart's attire was the Dimensions bracelet on his left wrist. No one at Avalon Plaza knew much about Stewart, but everyone acknowledged that when it came to blending and brewing teas, he was a true artist.

"I was on my way down to Café Solstice when Dylan, here, dragged me into his shop and made me buy a book," Alexa said.

"Hey, don't blame me." Dylan gave her a beatific smile. "Must have been the power of the energy vortices under my shop."

"Yeah, right." Alexa turned back to Stewart. "So you think Webster had a reason to worry about Joanna losing her inheritance?"

"Everyone around here pretty much agrees that Harry Trask would have squandered it." Stewart's eyes narrowed. "That would have been wrong."

Alexa thought about it. "Joanna's an intelligent woman. She probably could have handled her own money."

Stewart's expression darkened. "Even if that was true, the money would have been lost to Dimensions."

Alexa stared at him as the facts clicked into place. "Are you saying that Joanna invested in Dimensions?"

"Didn't you know that?" Dylan glanced at her in surprise. "Who do you think provided the seed money to get the retreat and the seminar building off the ground? No bank would touch Webster at the time."

Stewart looked at Alexa. "And who do you think is helping him finance the new retreat in Santa Fe?"

"Joanna?"

Stewart nodded. "She's always been there to help finance Bell's work. Without her, his message would never have reached beyond a handful of people."

Dylan shrugged. "She's not the only investor involved, of course, but she's a major one. Back at the beginning, her money was particularly crucial. And it's vital again now because of the Santa Fe project."

"I see," Alexa said.

Dylan looked down at his hands for a moment. When he looked up there was concern in his light blue eyes. "I know this is none of my business, but about your dinner with Trask last night . . ."

"You're right, Dylan," she said gently. "It's none of your business."

His pale skin flushed a dull red. "Sorry."

Now she'd embarrassed him. She smiled to erase the sting. "I know you mean well. But don't worry about me, Dylan. I can take care of myself."

"Sure." Dylan gave her a rueful grin. "Didn't mean to play big brother. It's just that, well, this business of Trask coming back to Avalon doesn't feel right somehow."

"What do you mean?"

"He means," Stewart said in ominous tones, "that it feels like there's going to be trouble. Stay away from Trask or you might get caught up in whatever bad energy is going down here in Avalon."

Alexa stared at him. "You're serious, aren't you?"

"Stewart's always serious, you know that." Dylan said dryly. "And he has strong feelings about Dimensions, don't you, Stewart?"

A fervent gleam appeared in Stewart's eyes. "Dimensions changed my life."

"Right." Dylan made a face as he turned back to Alexa. "But enough of the melodrama. Let's get to the important stuff."

"Which would be?" Alexa asked politely.

He rolled his eyes. "Don't act dense. It doesn't suit you. Obviously what everyone in town really wants to know is whether or not the rumors are true."

Alexa vowed to stand her ground as long as possible. "What rumors?"

He grinned. "Did you and Trask really engage in a wild orgy in the spa at the new Avalon resort last night?"

"Beats me," Alexa murmured. "It's been so long since my last orgy that I've forgotten what one looks like."

At five o'clock that afternoon a large, dark shadow fell across the model of Stonehenge displayed in Alexa's front window. She paused in the act of turning over the *closed* sign and looked out at the trellised sidewalk.

Trask stood there. In spite of all her best intentions she felt butterflies flutter in the pit of her stomach. He watched as she finished flipping the sign.

Then he walked through the open door into the shop.

"Can I assume that you spent your day the same way I did?" he asked without preamble.

"That depends." Alexa put the sales counter between them. For some obscure reason the bulwark gave her confidence. "How did you spend yours?"

"Getting warned off."

"What a coincidence. That's exactly how I spent mine."

He nodded. "For the record, how many people took the trouble to tell you that they'd heard about the brawl in the parking lot and the orgy in the spa and that it might not be a good idea for you to date me?"

She leaned on the counter, held up one hand, and began to tick off her fingers. "Let me see, if you count the obscene phone call that I got last night . . ."

His brows climbed. "You got a call?"

"Some jerk stopped at one of the local convenience stores long enough to call me up and tell me that the dark vortices have been aroused."

"Aroused, huh?"

She beetled her brows at him. "Don't start. As I was saying, if you count the phone call, I guess the number of warnings I got would hover somewhere in the range of half a dozen."

He wandered over to a large tapestry that featured a unicorn and a lady dressed in medieval garb. "How do you generally respond to that kind of thing?"

"Getting warned off?" She sighed. "I realize

everyone means well. But on the whole, I would have to say it annoys me."

"Yeah. Me, too. The implication seems to be that one of us is a slave to passion and the other is a manipulative seducer who will not scruple to use sex to achieve his or her ends."

She cleared her throat. "Have you detected a consensus concerning which one of us is the slave to passion and which one is the unscrupulous seducer?"

"The betting at the moment is that you're passion's slave. I've got the other role."

"Darn. I was afraid of that. It's not fair."

He continued to contemplate the tapestry. "You don't care for the slave-to-passion part?"

"Strikes me as an insult to my intelligence."

"There is that." He turned away from the maiden and the unicorn scene to meet her eyes. "So, you want to go out to dinner again tonight and discuss the subject of who gets to play which role?"

She drummed her fingers on the counter. "Might be better if we stuck to discussing our business arrangement."

"Is that how you see our relationship?" He gave her an inquisitive look. "As a business arrangement?"

Think: wild woman. "That's what it is, isn't it?"

He was silent for a couple of counts.

"I guess, when you get right down to it," he said, "that pretty much describes it."

She was in control, she told herself. No problem. Obviously, the more risks you took, the better you got at it. She straightened briskly away from the counter.

"Dinner sounds fine. My place. I'd like some privacy, and I don't think we'll get it at any restaurant in town."

He gave her a knowing look. "Also, you want to be on your own turf this time, right?"

"Yes." She gave him a bright smile that she hoped made it clear that she really was in control. "I want to be on my own turf this time."

16

The soaring stone palisades that dominated the Avalon landscape glowed a brilliant orange-red in the fires of the dying sun. Trask walked to the edge of the patio, braced one foot on the low rock wall, and watched the night descend.

He could not see Avalon Point from where he stood, but he knew that it was close. The natural rise of the land in front of Alexa's patio hid Cliff Drive from view, but he could hear the occasional sound of a car engine in the distance.

The screen door slid open behind him. Alexa's sandals scraped lightly on the paving stones.

"Dinner will be ready in a few minutes." She handed him a beer. "Hope you like Southwest fusion cuisine."

He caught the faint tang of freshly cut lime when he took the bottle from her. "Is that anything like Pacific Rim fusion cuisine?"

"I wouldn't be surprised. Except we probably use more tortillas and chilies." She looked out over the red canyons. "You want to tell me who gave you your warnings today?"

He took a swallow of the cold beer and considered for a moment. "One of them came from Joanna Bell."

"No kidding?" She looked briefly startled. "I got one from her brother."

That gave him pause. He turned his head to look at her. "You got a warning from Webster Bell, himself?"

"Uh-huh." Alexa made a face. "Of course, I also got one from Edward Vale and Dylan Fenn, who owns the bookshop at Avalon Plaza, and another from the guy who runs the café there, Stewart Lutton."

"What did they all tell you?"

"It pretty much came down to the same thing. Everyone thought it would be a really swell idea if I stayed clear of you."

He studied the Mexican label on the beer bottle. "Joanna didn't like the concept of me dating you, either. But she went a little farther with her warning."

"How much farther?"

"She told me that I should not stir up the past."

"Well, well, well." Alexa took a sip of the wine that she had poured for herself. "Did she give you a specific reason?"

"She implied that innocent people might get hurt."

Alexa groaned. "I suppose her warning made you all the more certain that there are great mysteries and dire conspiracies to be uncovered in Avalon, just as you suspected."

"If what happened twelve years ago was just an accident," he said softly, "why the hell would my asking questions hurt anyone or even make someone nervous?"

Alexa met his eyes. "Did it occur to you that Joanna was afraid that you might be the one who would be hurt? Everyone says she loved your father. Perhaps she's just trying to protect you."

"From what? Finding out that Dad was responsible for his own business problems? That he was so caught up in his private fantasy that he lost his perspective? That he would have dragged Guthrie and Kenyon into a financial quagmire if he wasn't forced to sell out?" Trask tightened his grip on the beer bottle. "I already know all that."

Alexa gazed pensively out at the desert. "Yes, I guess you do."

Silence fell. Darkness settled around them. Trask saw lights come on in some of the windows of the neighboring homes scattered lightly across the landscape. Alexa made no move to go back indoors to check on her dinner preparations. He sensed the tension in her.

He realized he was waiting, but he was not sure why. "Am I missing something here?"

She looked down at her wine. "I hesitate to mention this because I don't want to add any more fuel to your theories."

"They're already stoked."

"I found out today that Webster Bell may have been seriously opposed to the idea of Joanna marrying your father."

Trask swung around so sharply that Alexa gave a small, startled squeak and stepped back.

He searched her face. In the deepening shadows it was impossible to read her eyes. "Are you certain of that?"

"No," she said quickly. "It was just gossip. I got it from Dylan Fenn and Stewart Lutton, the two shop owners I mentioned earlier."

"Did they say why Bell didn't want Joanna to marry Dad?"

Alexa hesitated. "Apparently Webster was afraid that your father would have siphoned off a substantial portion of Joanna's inheritance in order to build his new resort."

His jaw tightened. "I can't blame Bell for worrying about that possibility. In Dad's defense, all I can say is that he wouldn't have seen it as using Joanna's money. He would have called it an investment."

"Yes, well, I guess Webster considered your father a financial risk."

Trask swallowed more beer. "He was right."

There was another short silence from Alexa.

"I got one other bit of old gossip out of my pals today," she said eventually.

"You're a regular gold mine of information this evening, aren't you?"

"I'm rationalizing it by telling myself that it's in my own best interests to help you get your questions answered as quickly as possible."

"Meaning that the sooner I'm satisfied about what happened here twelve years ago, the sooner I'll be gone?"

She looked at him, but there were too many shadows on the patio now for him to read her expression.

"The other tidbit I picked up," she said very steadily, "is that, although Webster Bell may have opposed the marriage because he wanted to protect Joanna, there is another possibility."

"I'm listening."

Alexa took an audible breath and released it slowly. "Bell apparently needed Joanna's money to help finance the expansion of his retreat. Joanna was one of his cornerstones, financially speaking."

Trask was surprised at the jolt her words gave him. Damn. How could he have overlooked such an obvious possibility as Webster Bell?

He let the implications sink in for a long moment. They were not very palatable. Surely he hadn't been looking in the wrong direction all these years. But then, that was the problem with an obsession. It tended to blind you to other possibilities.

He searched swiftly for more angles.

"What's your strategy here, Alexa? Are you trying to point me toward Bell in the hopes that I'll forget about Guthrie and Kenyon?"

"I knew I shouldn't have said anything." She turned her back on him and started toward the kitchen. "Have you always been this suspicious, Trask? Or is it a bad habit you've developed?"

"I was born this way."

"I see. Well, that's as good an argument for genetic engineering as I've heard to date."

Alexa was right about the food, Trask thought. Southwestern fusion cuisine looked a lot like Pacific Rim fusion cuisine with the addition of tortillas and chilies. He could get used to it.

They ate out on the patio. Moonlight poured

down, mingling with the flickering lights of the candles on the table. The sky was a dark, cobalt blue bowl studded with diamonds. The air was a warm caress.

Hard to imagine a more romantic setting, Trask thought. Too bad he'd screwed up earlier. Conversation had not been going well since he'd practically accused Alexa of trying to deflect his investigation.

He wondered if Alexa planned to kick him out the door immediately after dinner, or if she would offer him tea first.

He also wondered how she would react if he kissed her again. He was not particularly optimistic. Although she had not specifically brought up the subject of their encounter in the spa, he was getting the strong impression that she considered last night's lovemaking a serious mistake.

The screen door opened again. Alexa walked out of the kitchen with a pot in her hand.

Hope soared. It looked like he was going to get tea at least.

She sat down and poured the brew into two cups. "What will you do now that you've stirred your cauldron?"

"Sit back and let things boil for a while."

Her head came up swiftly. "Are you going to just ignore the information I gave you about Bell?"

"No. I'll call Okuda in the morning—"

"Okuda?"

"Phil Okuda is the investigator I hired to do the initial background work on this thing. I'll tell him to check out the situation at the Institute twelve years ago. But my money's on Guthrie at the moment."

She raised her brows in disbelief as she took her seat. "Just because of that little incident in the parking lot last night?"

"*Little incident?*"

"Granted, Guthrie went a bit over the top with the two goons. But you've got to admit, he's got a right to be annoyed. How would you feel if someone started digging around in your past, trying to find evidence that you'd committed murder?"

"He's rattled. I have a hunch that if I apply a little more pressure, he'll crumble."

"I don't think you're approaching this situation the right way."

"So now you're an expert?"

"I've lived in this town longer than you have. I understand how—"

A distant, muffled *whoomp* interrupted her.

They both turned to look out across the desert toward Cliff Drive.

A cold foreboding swept through Trask. He shoved his chair back. "That came from the road. Sounded like a car. I'll go take a look."

"I'll come with you."

He got to the edge of the patio before he saw the glow of orange flames in the distance. "Better call 911 first. And bring a flashlight, if you've got one handy."

He vaulted the low rock wall and headed toward the fire.

She followed hard on his heels a moment later. He realized she had grabbed her cell phone.

"No, I don't know exactly what the problem is," she said urgently into the phone. "But there are flames. A car, I think."

Trask turned and stretched out his hand. Alexa slapped a flashlight into it. He switched it on and aimed it at the ground to light their path.

The red glow in the distance burned brighter now.

"My God," Alexa whispered. "That's the Point."

Trask reached the embankment above Cliff Drive and dropped to the pavement. Alexa clattered down behind him. A small shower of pebbles and loose sand cascaded onto the road.

Somewhere in the distance a siren began to wail.

They crossed the road and started toward Avalon Point. Flames flared from the rocks below.

"Stay back." Trask went through the gaping hole in the shattered guard rail. "There could be an explosion."

"Trask, come back. It's too late. There's nothing you can do."

He stood at the edge of the Point and looked down into the mouth of hell. She was right.

A disorienting sensation swept over him.

For an instant past and present fused in a nightmarish glare.

This was how his father had died. This was *where* his father had died.

But it was not his father's car that lay on the rocks below Avalon Point tonight. The roaring flames provided more than enough light for Trask to see the remains of a familiar white Lincoln.

Dean Guthrie.

17

Alexa was staring at the ceiling of her bedroom when the phone rang hours later. She reached for the receiver, hoping that Trask would be on the other end.

"Hello?"

"The dark vortices are in flux. The energy storm grows more powerful and more dangerous with each passing moment. Death and destruction have come to Avalon. Seek cover while you still can."

"Screw you." Alexa slammed down the phone.

She went back to contemplating the shadows above the bed. She knew she would not sleep tonight. Every time she closed her eyes she saw the fire and the white Lincoln.

The night was warm but she shivered beneath the covers.

The nightmare came an hour before dawn. Searing flames and twisted metal were prominently featured.

The truly horrifying part was the vision of

Guthrie staring calmly at him through the blackening glass of the driver's window.

Trask awoke, cold and clammy. For a moment he could not remember where he was. He could not even recall the year.

Then he realized that the phone beside the bed was ringing. He reached for it, profoundly grateful to whoever had interrupted the dream.

The image of Guthrie's face was a figment of his imagination, he told himself. The fire had been too intense to make out anything or anyone inside the burning vehicle.

Later, when the medics had removed the body, he and Alexa had mercifully been occupied giving their statements to Chief Strood.

"This is Trask."

"I called to see if you were getting any sleep," Alexa said.

The dream fragments disintegrated at the sound of her voice. "Not much." He shoved aside the covers and swung his legs over the edge of the bed. "What about you?"

"My semi-obscene caller struck again."

"Bastard." Trask was quiet for a moment. "What did he say?"

"Something about an energy storm and dark vortices in flux." She paused. "Death and destruction were mentioned. I got the impression he knew about what happened at the Point tonight."

"By this time, half the town probably knows about Guthrie's crash."

"I imagine so." She paused. "One of the medics told me Guthrie probably died instantly. At the very least, he would have been unconscious when the fire broke out."

It was, Trask reflected, the same rough comfort the authorities had offered him after Harry's crash at Avalon Point. Something in Alexa's voice told him that a long time ago someone had given her similar assurances about her own father's death.

He listened to the silence on the line. They both knew the truth, he thought. No one could be certain how long either of the victims had lived after disaster struck. No one knew how much awareness the men had had of their terrifying last moments.

But Trask also knew that, for the sake of those who were left behind, it was important to preserve the fiction that neither had suffered for long.

"I'm sure the medic was right," Alexa said. "The impact must have killed Guthrie instantly."

"Yeah."

Silence hummed again on the line.

Trask looked at the faint glow in the sky. "Maybe you should stay home from work today. Get some rest."

"I've got a shop to run. Besides, I think it would be better if I kept myself busy."

"Sure." He understood all too well that work was a useful narcotic for dulling unpleasant memories. He'd used it to take the edge off a lot of things, including a failing marriage.

She hesitated. "What are you going to do today?"

"Me? I'll be busy, too. Didn't I tell you? I've got another hot date with Chief Strood."

"You're going to talk to him again? Why? We told him everything that we saw last night."

"Seems he wants to revisit the subject of my little parking lot altercation with Guthrie."

"Oh, *no*. Surely he doesn't think that you—?"

The alarmed concern in her voice warmed him for some obscure reason.

"Strood just wants to clear up a few questions," he said. "Can't blame him. He's got a job to do."

"Do you think he might try to involve you in this in some way? Why? Strood wasn't even the chief of police here in Avalon twelve years ago. He didn't take the job until after Wilcox died. That was only about five years back."

"Strood has heard the rumors, same as everyone else in town."

"I can call Lloyd's lawyer if you think you should have one."

"Don't worry, Avalon Resorts, Inc., has a herd of lawyers on retainer." Trask smiled slightly. "If I need one, I know where to get one."

"There is absolutely no way anyone can connect you with Guthrie's accident. Remind Strood that you were with me when it happened."

"Yeah." Trask smiled to himself. "I'll do that."

The cloud of morbid curiosity was thick in Café Solstice. Every eye in the place shifted toward Alexa when she walked through the door shortly before ten.

She came to a halt and gazed around at the ring of familiar faces. "I take it everyone has already heard the news?"

Murmurs of assent went through the small crowd of shopkeepers huddled over their tea and muffins.

Dylan, propped against a counter, looked at Alexa with a troubled expression. "Is it true that you and Trask were first on the scene?"

Alexa shuddered. "Yes. It was awful."

Joanna gazed down into her tea. "Poor Guthrie."

Brad Vasquez, the owner of the Out Of Body Experience travel agency, shook his head. "The courts should have yanked Guthrie's license years ago. Everyone knew he had a serious drinking problem."

"He nearly sideswiped me once on that sharp curve on Bandit Road," Stewart said as he poured boiling water into a pot. "A couple inches closer and he would've hit me. I called him up later and told him that he could have gotten both of us killed."

Alexa went to the counter to collect her tea. "What did he say?"

Stewart shrugged. "He got mad. Yelled and screamed a lot. Claimed he'd been in complete control."

"I wonder how his ex-wife is taking the news," Brad mused.

Stewart looked up. "Which one? There were at least three at last count."

Joanna raised her bowed hed. Her face was tight and bleak. "Liz is having a tough time. I talked to her this morning. She and Dean were still seeing each other, you know, even though the divorce was final a few months ago."

Brad raised his brows. "Guthrie was sleeping with his ex-wife?"

Joanna's mouth tightened primly. "They had a relationship, yes."

Alexa glanced at her. "How do you know that?"

"Liz is a good friend of mine," Joanna said quietly. "I've carried her jewelry designs in Crystal Rainbow for years. She's active out at the Institute. We've served on several committees together."

Dylan screwed his features into a quizzical expression. "Why'd she marry a mean drunk like Guthrie?"

"The usual reason." Joanna returned her attention to her tea. "She thought that she could change him."

"Yeah, I've heard that one before," someone muttered.

Stewart's gaze was somber. "When you stop and think about it, you gotta admit, there's something really weird about Guthrie's death. I mean, what are the odds?"

A short, charged silence fell on the small group. Alexa noticed that no one met her eyes.

"Odds about what, Stewart?" she asked quietly.

Dylan stirred against the counter. His gaze flickered to Stewart and the others. Then he looked at Alexa. "He means the odds that Guthrie would die now. Like Brad says, he drove drunk for years. By rights he should have run himself off that cliff a long time ago."

Alexa watched him very steadily. "What are you saying, Dylan?"

It was Joanna who answered the question.

"He's saying what everyone else who knew Guthrie in the old days is saying this morning. It's a very strange coincidence that Guthrie died only a few days after Trask returned to Avalon."

"And even weirder that he was killed at the same place where Harry Trask died," Dylan whispered.

Alexa's temper flared without warning. "If you're implying that Trask had anything to do with Guthrie's accident, you can forget it. Trask was with me when Guthrie drove off Avalon Point. There is no way he could have been involved."

"Take it easy, Alexa," Stewart said. "No one is saying that Trask killed Dean Guthrie."

"Hell, no," Brad said quickly. "No one's claiming that Guthrie's death wasn't an accident. It's just, well, strange, that's all. The timing, I mean."

"And the place where it happened," Stewart added softly. "Avalon Point. The very same place Harry Trask—"

"Don't say it," Alexa warned.

Stewart raised one big tattooed shoulder in a massive shrug, but he did not finish the sentence.

Dylan's gaze slid away from Alexa's. "According to the theory of Dimensions, there are no coincidences in the universe."

Alexa realized her hand was trembling from the effort it took to control her fury. Very deliberately she set her cup down before it slipped from her grasp. She looked at each member of the small group in turn.

"Contrary to popular opinion," she said, "Trask had no reason to want Dean Guthrie dead. I don't think it's any secret that he has some questions about what happened to his father twelve years ago, but he won't make any moves until he has answers."

"Maybe it was the pressure," Brad mused. "Maybe it pushed Guthrie over the edge in more ways than one."

"What pressure?" Alexa snapped.

"The pressure Guthrie must have felt." Brad gave her an apologetic look. "The way I heard it, Trask's return to Avalon had really agitated him. There was that scene in the country club parking lot the other night . . ."

"It was Guthrie who threatened Trask, not vice versa," Alexa said tightly. "Furthermore—"

Joanna gave a short, muffled cry. Her plastic cup fell to the floor. Hot tea splashed across Alexa's sandal-shod feet. She stepped back hastily.

"I was so afraid something like this would happen," Joanna whispered in a choked voice.

Her low, anguished words riveted everyone's attention. Alexa turned toward her and saw that tears glistened in her dark eyes. Instinctively she took a step forward and put out a hand.

"Joanna?"

"I'm sorry." Joanna evaded Alexa's outstretched hand. "It's late. I've got to open my shop." She seized a tissue from her purse, buried her face in it, and rushed out the door.

Alexa felt the eyes of everyone in the shop turn to her.

"Joanna's right," she said. "It's getting late."

She did not look back as she walked out the door.

Joanna looked up from a tray of colored crystals when Alexa walked into Crystal Rainbow a few minutes later.

"That was very embarrassing," Joanna said quietly. "I don't know what came over me. I didn't mean to make a scene. Did the tea burn your foot?"

"No. I'm fine, Joanna."

"I upset you." Joanna blinked rapidly. "I've been

very tense lately. Stress, you know. My doctors gave me some pills. I should probably take another one."

"I've been a little tense myself." Alexa walked past an array of sparkling, glittering stone and crystal jewelry. "Will you tell me what that was all about, Joanna? I think I've got a right to know."

"Yes. Yes, you do." Joanna closed her eyes and massaged her temples. When she looked at Alexa again, it was clear she had herself back under control. "But I really don't know what to tell you, Alexa."

"What do you think happened to Harry Trask twelve years ago?"

Joanna picked up one of the crystals, an amber-hued stone. Her fingers tightened around it as if it were a talisman.

"It was an accident, just as the police said," she whispered. "We'd had one of our summer monsoons. A lot of rain had fallen. The roads were wet and slippery. Harry lost control of his car and went off the Point. But I always knew that his son did not believe that explanation."

"But you believed it?"

"Yes, of course I did." Joanna gripped the amber-colored crystal so fiercely that her fingers whitened at the knuckles. "When young Trask left and did not return to Avalon, I assumed that he'd come to terms with Harry's death, too. Then Avalon Resorts announced that the company was planning to build a new hotel here. I knew then that Trask was finally coming back."

"Now he's here."

"Yes." Joanna opened her hand and stared at the amber stone. "He's here. And someone else is dead."

"Are you afraid that Trask is somehow responsible?" Alexa took a step closer. "Listen to me, Joanna, I swear that Trask was with me all evening. We were together when we heard the crash."

Joanna stared at the amber crystal. "I believe you."

"Then why are you so frightened?"

"Only a fool would deny that there are things in this world, especially here around Avalon, that we do not fully comprehend."

Alexa gazed at her, appalled. "Are you telling me that you actually believe that some mysterious negative force has been awakened by Trask's return? That some dark energy vortex is responsible for Guthrie's death?"

"There's no reason to look for supernatural causes. Human beings generate more than enough negative energy all on their own to account for most of the problems in the world."

"On that, we agree," Alexa said firmly. "From what I've seen and heard of Dean Guthrie, he was his own worst enemy."

"You're right," Joanna whispered. "Everyone knows that."

Alexa took another step, reached out, and put her hand on Joanna's arm. "Talk to me. Tell me why you're so scared. What do you think Trask might uncover here in Avalon?"

"*I don't know.*" The skin of Joanna's finely molded face drew very tight. "That's the problem. Don't you understand? I don't *know* what Trask will find out if he continues to dig up the past. Opening old graves is always a dangerous business."

Old graves.

It was a good thing she did not believe in negative auras and bad vibrations, Alexa thought. Joanna's anxiety and barely controlled fear lapped at her in dark waves.

"Joanna—"

"You want to know why I'm scared? I'll tell you why." Joanna hurled the amber crystal onto the counter. "Twelve years ago the man I loved was killed in a terrible accident. His son vowed revenge. Now that same son is here in town, and one of the men he threatened all those years ago is dead. No, I don't think it's a coincidence."

"Are you telling me that you think Trask murdered Guthrie?"

"No."

"Then what are you saying, Joanna?"

"I'm saying that I think Trask should go away before someone else dies."

A tiny, trembling movement caught Alexa's eye. She glanced down. Joanna's hands were shaking so violently that her turquoise and silver Dimensions bracelet was dancing on her wrist.

"I need my pills," Joanna said.

The day did not improve markedly as time passed. Trask did not call, but a reporter from the *Avalon Herald* did.

"Rich Rudd, Ms. Chambers. Just following up on what I got from the cops. Guthrie was one of the movers and shakers here in Avalon for a long time, you know."

"Yes, I know."

"I understand that you and JL Trask, the president and CEO of Avalon Resorts, were first on the scene?"

"That's right. We were just finishing dinner when we heard the crash."

"Dinner?"

Alexa drummed her fingers on the counter. "We had dinner together."

"I don't recall a restaurant near Avalon Point . . ."

In for a penny, in for a pound, Alexa thought. "JL Trask was a guest in my home last night, which happens to be close to Avalon Point."

"A guest." The sound of rapid-fire typing on a computer keyboard echoed down the line. "Have you and Mr. Trask been acquainted long?"

"That question doesn't sound relevant, Mr. Rudd," Alexa said coolly. "Unless you're also doing the Society column for tomorrow's edition?"

"Trask and Avalon Resorts are big news here in town. There's been some talk about an old feud."

"Really?" Alexa infused as much innocence as she could into her tone.

"A feud that involved Dean Guthrie and Lloyd Kenyon."

"Fascinating," Alexa said, deliberately vague.

A large object obscured the light in the doorway of the shop. Alexa looked around and saw Trask. She clutched the phone in her left hand, stabbed a finger at it, and mouthed the word *reporter*.

Irritation narrowed his gaze. He walked toward her.

"Guthrie was said to be visibly upset by Trask's presence here in Avalon," Rich Rudd said on the other end of the line. "Would you care to comment?"

"No."

Trask crossed to the counter and took the phone from Alexa's fingers. "Rudd?" he asked softly.

She nodded.

"I've been ducking his calls all day." He spoke into the phone. "This is Trask."

Alexa heard a buzzing sound. She realized it was Rich Rudd firing questions. There was a short pause while Trask listened.

"It's personal, Rudd. Sorry, that's the only question I'm going to answer today."

He replaced the receiver very gently.

Alexa eyed him. "What was the question?"

"He asked me if our relationship was business or personal."

"Oh." Alexa could not think of anything else to say on that topic.

"How was your day?" Trask asked.

"Lousy. Joanna Bell and some of the other shopkeepers here in the Plaza seem to think that dangerous metaphysical forces have been unleashed in the vicinity of Avalon. On top of that, I only sold two winged lions and a reproduction of a medieval map that showed the edge of the world. How about you?"

"The good news is that I'm not officially a suspect in Guthrie's death. The bad news is that there are some seriously disappointed people in town."

Alexa was incensed. "There was never any question of you being a suspect."

"That appears to be a matter of opinion in some quarters. Chief Strood, however, is currently treating Guthrie's death as an alcohol-related accident. I got the impression that he is no more eager for it to turn into a murder investigation than I am."

"Of course it was a drunk driving accident." Alexa frowned. "What did you mean about the seriously disappointed people?"

"Let's just say that the story of Dean Guthrie's death would be a lot more exciting to some folks around here if there was a way to tie it to me and to those threats I made twelve years ago."

"Fat chance." Alexa gave a ladylike snort of disgust. At least she hoped it was ladylike. "There is no way anyone can do that. It was just a horrible coincidence."

Trask looked thoughtful. "I'm not so sure about that."

Alexa went cold. "Don't do that."

"What?"

She waved a hand. "Don't start talking about negative vortices and a lack of coincidences in the universe. I can't take any more metaphysics today."

"My theories don't have anything to do with metaphysics. But I have to admit that I'm not a big believer in coincidences."

"Damn. I was afraid of this." Alexa grabbed her satchel from the small closet beneath the cash register and slung it over her shoulder. She fished her keys out of her pocket. "It's closing time. Let's go." She started toward the door.

"Where are we going?"

"Someplace where we can have a little privacy."

Trask followed her toward the door. "Why?"

She paused to flip over the sign that hung in the window. "We need to talk."

18

Trask lowered himself onto one of the rocks that rimmed the natural, spring-fed pool. The damp walls of the canyon cave loomed around him. Through the opening he could see the hot afternoon sunlight, but here inside the cavern, the hidden desert oasis was cool and serene, a shady retreat from the strong, bright sun and the stark landscape. *There is nothing so seductive as water in the desert.*

An inexplicable restlessness shivered through his senses. He suppressed it with an act of will and forced himself to examine the stone cave that shielded the crystal-clear water.

This place was beautiful, fascinating, mysterious. Wet.

He realized that he felt like an intruder here.

"It's called Harmony Spring," Alexa said as she dropped down onto a stone on the opposite side of the rocky pool. "It's supposed to be one of the hot spots in the area. The energy vortex here is feminine, by the way."

Trask grunted. "Didn't know vortices came in different genders."

"Just ask any of the locals. Energy vortices are either positive or negative, and they're either male or female."

"Uh-huh. Come here often?"

"Sometimes." She tossed a tiny pebble into the spring. Water rippled gently. "When I need to think. I spent a lot of time here after Mom and I first moved to Avalon."

"Yeah?" He tried to feel amused. "I didn't think you were into that metaphysical stuff."

"I'm not." She tucked one leg under herself. "But I must admit that I always feel calmer and more peaceful when I leave this place. Stronger, somehow."

Trask had a sudden memory of how she had looked when she had faced him twelve years ago, phone clutched in her hand. He recalled the big, haunted eyes filled with gutsy determination and courage. Those qualities were still there, he thought. They were a part of her.

She looked at him across the deep pool. "What did you mean earlier when you said that Guthrie's death could be connected to you and to what happened twelve years ago?"

He contemplated the depths of the spring. "At the risk of confirming your belief that I'm slipping ever deeper into my conspiracy theories, I've got to tell you that I don't buy Guthrie's death as an accident."

She stiffened and then dropped her forehead down onto her upraised knee. "I've already had this conversation with Joanna. Are you seriously going to tell me that you believe some malevolent force has been unleashed here in Avalon?"

"Is that what Joanna said?"

"Not exactly." Alexa raised her head. "But I got the feeling that she views you as the eye of the storm. She thinks that if you just go away, things will return to normal."

"Depends on your definition of normal, I guess." He shifted position slightly, trying to shake off the disturbing sensation that had settled between his shoulders. "Look, you're the one who insisted that I confide everything in you before I acted. You want to hear my new theory or not?"

"It's not like I have a lot of choice here. Give it to me in easy sentences."

"I don't have a lot to go on at the moment—"

"You can say that again."

"Just a hunch."

She wrinkled her nose. "Just a hunch, huh?"

"The kind of hunch I get when I'm in danger of getting screwed in a business negotiation," he said deliberately. "The kind I got just before I found out my wife was going to run off with another man."

She raised a brow. "The kind that brought you charging into Lloyd's house that night twelve years ago?"

He met her eyes. "Yeah. That kind of hunch."

She sighed. "Okay, tell me how Guthrie's death could possibly be connected to your father's death?"

She sounded much too reasonable now. Probably trying to humor him, Trask thought.

"I'm not sure yet," he admitted.

"Why now? If someone wanted Guthrie dead, why wait until you returned to Avalon?"

He shrugged. "The obvious reason that springs to mind is so that if anyone got suspicious the finger of blame would point my way."

"You're saying that someone tried to set you up?"

The doubt in her voice bothered him. He realized that it was very important that she be convinced of his new theory. Somewhere along the line she had become both partner and ally in this thing.

"Think about it. Folks around here have known for several months that I'd be coming back to Avalon to officially open the resort," he said. "If someone wanted to get rid of Guthrie, it would have paid to wait until I was in the vicinity."

Her brows came together in a grim, skeptical line. "It's awfully far-fetched."

"I know there are a lot of questions to be answered. All I'm saying is that I think there may be a connection."

"Such as?"

"All along I've had a feeling that my father's death was related to his business dealings. If I'm right, then it stands to reason that Guthrie's death might also be linked to his financial affairs."

She gave him an incredulous look. "*Twelve-year-old* financial affairs? You're seriously suggesting that someone waited all this time to kill him because of a business deal that went bad more than a decade ago?"

"No, of course not. I'm talking about his current financial situation."

"What are you saying?" She spread her hands. "That it may have been a crime of opportunity? That someone just happened to want to get rid of Guthrie and decided to do it while you were in town?"

"That pretty much sums up my current working hypothesis, yeah. You've got to admit that if I hadn't had a solid alibi last night, I'd have made a handy distraction for the cops in case they started asking questions."

"Only if the investigation didn't conclude that Guthrie's death was the result of his own drunk driving."

"No killer, no matter how careful, can be absolutely certain that some evidence won't survive," he said evenly. "Makes sense to have a fallback plan if you can. I was handy. Why not use me?"

"Let's try for some logic here, Trask. If someone planned to murder Guthrie and pin the crime on you, he would have made certain that you *didn't* have an alibi for last night."

He met her eyes. "Maybe he figured that the fact that I was with you, assuming that he knew where I was, wouldn't be viewed in court as a really strong alibi."

"What's that supposed to mean?" Alexa scowled. "That he thinks I'm such a slave-to-passion that I'd lie under oath for you?"

He did not want to test that particular theory, he thought glumly. "There's another possibility."

"What?"

"A jury could probably be convinced that I used you to give myself an alibi. You've seen enough films to know that there are ways of tampering with cars to make them unsafe. The killer doesn't have to be anywhere near the scene of the crime."

"But even if someone did mess with his car, what are the odds that it would have gone off the road right at Avalon Point?"

"Not that bad, when you think about it. If Guthrie got drunk, got into a car that had been sabotaged, and took Cliff Drive home, Avalon Point is as likely a place as any to go over the edge. It's the sharpest, steepest curve on that stretch of road."

Alexa pounced. "Exactly. And Guthrie *had* been drinking. He wasn't in any condition to give that curve his full attention. There's no need to construct a conspiracy theory to explain his death."

Trask said nothing.

Alexa made a face. "Okay, I can't talk you out of it. So, who do you think killed Guthrie?"

"Very likely the same person who had a reason for wanting my father dead twelve years ago. Webster Bell."

She stared at him, open-mouthed. *"What?"*

"You heard me."

"This is madness." She closed her eyes. "The only upside is that you seem to have dropped Lloyd from your list of suspects."

"I'll admit that the likelihood of Kenyon being involved is fading rapidly."

She opened her eyes and glared at him. "That's some comfort, I suppose. Trask, you can't go jumping to wild conclusions. This is Webster Bell you're talking about."

"I know you think I'm going off the deep end here, but if I'm right, I may not have much choice."

"What do you mean?"

"It's possible that whoever killed Guthrie may come after me eventually."

She stared at him. "Why?"

"Because by returning to Avalon after all these years I've confirmed what has to be his deepest fear."

Realization dawned in her eyes. "That you won't ever stop asking questions about the past?"

"Yeah."

"Oh, my God," she whispered. "What are you going to do?"

"What I started out to do. Find the evidence I need to prove that someone killed Dad."

"How?"

"By finding out who killed Guthrie."

He was not making a great impression. Alexa had looked both resigned and wary on the drive back into town. He was pretty sure that she was toying with the possibility that he was a full-fledged wacko.

He was almost positive that she would not jump into bed with him again until she had decided just how far gone he was.

On the other hand, he thought as he walked into the lobby, she had agreed to have dinner with him tomorrow night. He allowed himself to entertain a cautious note of optimism.

"Good afternoon, sir." Eric Emerson, busy with some colorful walking maps at the concierge desk, gave him a professional smile. "An overnight courier left a package for you while you were out."

The coffee had finally arrived. Trask's mood escalated another notch. "About time."

"I'll get it for you."

Eric rose and disappeared into a small office. Trask glanced toward the front desk while he waited. A small crowd milled about in the lobby. There was an air of expectation. The first of the resort's paying guests had arrived.

A sense of satisfaction hit him when he saw the expressions on the faces of those who were surveying the glowing glass bricks, lacquered wood, and scrolled steel of the lobby desk. He'd been in the business long enough to know when the fantasy was working.

Eric reappeared bearing a carefully wrapped and taped package.

Trask inhaled deeply as he took the sealed box from Eric. He caught the faint aroma of rich, dark-roasted coffee.

"I think I'm going to survive after all, Eric."

Eric grinned. "I'm delighted to hear that, sir, given the fact that you pay my salary. I assume those are whole beans?"

"Naturally."

"There's a coffeemaker in your suite, but you'll need a grinder for the beans." He reached for the phone. "I'll have the kitchen send one up."

"Thanks. I always say, a good hotel concierge should be able to read minds." He inclined his head toward the group at the reception desk. "Looks like our guests are starting to arrive."

"You're looking at the first trickle. According to Mr. Santana, we'll be one-third full tonight. Sold out by the weekend. Scheduling the opening to coincide with the Spring Festival was a great idea, even if things will be a bit hectic."

"Nothing like opening with a bang. Hotels are like restaurants. They're either hot right from the start or they're doomed."

Eric chuckled. "Judging by the bookings, we're definitely going to be hot. Must have tapped into some of the positive energy vortices in the ground around here when they dug the hotel's foundation."

"Yeah, right," Trask muttered. "Positive energy vortices. I wonder if they were masculine or feminine."

Eric shrugged. "According to the people up at the Institute, it doesn't matter. Both kinds are equally strong. The important thing is that they're positive, not negative."

Aware that he was rapidly getting out of his metaphysical depth, Trask nodded and headed toward the staircase.

On the second floor he went down the west wing corridor to his suite. Cradling the fragrant package in one hand, he paused to dig out his card key.

A glint of bronze caught his eye. He glanced into the alcove and saw *Dancing Satyr.* He could have sworn that the damn statue winked at him.

He remembered how he had caught Alexa trying to stuff the figure into a closet on the night of the reception. He smiled to himself.

"I may keep you even if you do turn out to be a fake," he said aloud.

He slid the card key through the lock and pushed open the door. The suite was cool and dark. Sort of like Harmony Spring cave, he thought as he put the coffee down on the counter. But at least here he didn't experience that weird sense of being an intruder in a mysterious world.

The housekeeping team had closed the drapes and turned on the air conditioner when they cleaned. He paused at the thermostat and switched it back to the off position. Then he opened the French doors onto the balcony. He much preferred the fresh air of the desert, even when it was on the hot side.

He slid aside the screen that concealed the desk with its array of high-tech business accoutrements.

For a moment he studied the miniature office, trying to decide what was wrong.

Housekeeping had strict instructions not to straighten any papers or personal items that a guest had left on a desk. That policy went double in the owner's suite.

He was almost certain that he had left the notepad on top of the morning edition of the *Avalon Herald*. The pad was sitting beside the phone now.

The entire housekeeping staff was new. It was possible someone had forgotten the instructions regarding desks.

He opened the first drawer, picked up the small stack of papers inside, and thumbed through them quickly. There was nothing of critical importance in the pile of notes he had made. Most concerned minor management details he intended to discuss with Nathan and Pete Santana. One or two related to public relations matters he wanted to hand off to Glenda Blaine.

The important file, the one compiled by Phil Okuda, was safely locked in the suite's wall safe.

The only interesting thing about the small stack in his hand was that it seemed to be out of order. He was willing to bet that someone had rifled through it.

A curious or poorly trained employee *might* have flipped through the papers out of curiosity. That kind of thing was not supposed to happen in an Avalon Resort hotel, but occasionally the wrong person got hired.

It was also possible that someone had searched his room while he and Alexa were at Harmony Spring. Given the general chaos that attended any hotel opening, it would have been possible for someone to slip through security.

"You're getting nervous, aren't you, you son-of-a-bitch? That's good. That's very, very good. Nervous people make mistakes."

19

The Guardian downed the last swallow of the herbal tea and watched the sun set outside the cave. The light was slowly, inevitably consumed by the dark. The symbolism appealed.

Consciousness expanded in the absence of light. Awareness deepened. Perception strengthened.

The Guardian studied the ebb and flow of the shifting vortices. The negative energy was running high now. Dangerous stuff if one were not careful. *But what a rush.*

It had been twelve years since that intoxicating power had been tapped; twelve years since the last time it had been necessary to kill in the line of duty. The surge of personal energy was unbelievable.

It was amazing how much easier it had been this time. How much more satisfying.

Looking back, the Guardian understood that it was not a lack of necessity that had kept the defender of the Institute from killing for the past twelve years. It had been fear. A simple, paralyzing fear of getting caught.

But now it was clear that would never happen.

Last night's triumphant success was a sign. The great work must go forward. It all had to be done quickly while the dark energy storm pulsed so strongly below the surface of Avalon.

The Guardian was ready. The last of the old anxiety and the terrible fear that had been so overwhelming twelve years ago had died along with Guthrie. Power had taken the place of those incapacitating emotions.

This time the sexual release was shattering in its intensity.

20

Alexa hunched over the phone. "I know we've never met, Mrs. Guthrie, but I'm a friend of Joanna Bell's."

"She's mentioned you." Liz Guthrie sounded impatient and distracted on the other end of the line. "But I really don't have time to talk right now. This is my meditation hour. My Dimensions guide says I must develop more self-discipline. I'm trying to meditate every day at the same time."

"I understand. I just want to ask you a few questions."

"Questions about what?"

"This is a little awkward, but I wanted to ask you about your ex-husband."

"Dean?" Liz's voice sharpened in alarm. "He's dead. Why do you want to ask me about him?"

"I'm very sorry about your loss . . ."

"We were divorced," Liz said stiffly.

"Yes, I know." Now what? Alexa wondered. She could hardly say, *I've heard that you and Dean were still sleeping together, and I was wondering if he ever mentioned what happened to Harry Trask twelve years ago, and by the way did he indicate he might have any current enemies other than JL Trask?* There were limits to her powers of subtlety.

"I'd rather not talk about Dean," Liz said. "My guide says that I focus too much on the negative forces around me. Dean was a negative force."

"The thing is, I was one of the first people at the scene of his accident."

"I see." Surprisingly, Liz's voice softened slightly. "It must have been very traumatic for you."

"Yes, but that's not what I wanted to discuss."

"I suggest you get counseling. Dimensions has an excellent staff. I'm sure someone there could assist you. They've done wonders for me."

"Thank you. But what I wanted to ask was whether or not Dean ever mentioned any personal concerns he might have had."

There was a distinct pause on the other end of the line. "Concerns about what?"

"It really would be easier if we talked in person."

"I don't think I can manage—"

"Please, I just want to ask you some questions. It's very important to me." Alexa thought swiftly. "I believe that it would help me, uh, realign my inner peace and serenity. There are some unresolved issues, you see. Because of the trauma of the accident and all."

Liz hesitated. "All right. I suppose it can't do any real harm. Be here at ten. I'll be busy with my personal guide until then. Oh, here he is now. I've got to go."

"Thank you, I'll see you at ten."

Alexa hung up with a sense of relief. Then she quickly punched in the number of her part-time assistant.

"Kerry, can you open the shop for me today? Something has come up. I'm going to be a little late getting to work."

No matter what the hour of the day, Shadow Canyon was cloaked in perpetual twilight. It was a popular tourist destination in the summer when its year-round creek and canopy of green offered respite from the heat. There were several large swimming holes in Shadow Creek that were much prized by the locals as well as outsiders.

The flora and fauna of the canyon's higher elevation provided a striking contrast to the desert a short distance down the road. The cool, dark caverns and crevasses that had been etched into its rock walls drew hikers and bird-watchers.

But even at the height of summer, when the sun beat down relentlessly on the town of Avalon, Alexa was not a great fan of Shadow Canyon. The cool shade it offered could not overcome the mild sense of claustrophobia that she always felt here.

She brought the Camry to a halt and studied Liz Guthrie's home through the windshield. It was an expensive-looking, stylish affair with a lot of glass walls and a wide, encircling deck. There was no sign of a light in the windows. Granted, it was nearly ten o'clock in the morning, but given the general gloom of the canyon, it was a little surprising, she thought.

Maybe people who lived in a world of eternal twilight learned to adapt.

She opened the car door, got out, and eyed the thick stand of trees. There was something vaguely menacing about the way they loomed over the house.

She hurried toward the front steps.

The decision to talk to Dean Guthrie's last ex-wife was the result of an impulse. It had struck when she first awakened that morning.

Trask was convinced that money lay at the heart of the conspiracy theory he had woven. But she was not so certain. The late-night phone calls had a very personal feel.

She had tried to argue herself out of the notion of talking to Liz Guthrie, but the more she thought about it, the more important it seemed.

Liz was the one person who appeared to have had a close relationship of any kind with Guthrie.

Chances were Guthrie had not been the confiding type, but if he had talked to someone, that someone might have been the woman he had slept with during the past few months.

The rustling sighs of the branches overhead sounded unwholesome. There was a hungry, yearning quality to the soft whispers. An unpleasant tingling sensation brushed across the nape of Alexa's neck.

No one came to answer the door.

She exhaled slowly, aware of a curious sense of relief. She had not been all that enthusiastic about talking to Liz Guthrie anyway.

She turned away from the door, intending to walk back down the steps to her car. But something made her glance to the side of the house. The door of the garage was closed. Liz's car might or might not be inside.

It would be simple enough to check.

And just what the heck was she going to do if the car was parked inside the garage? she wondered. The woman had a right not to answer her door.

Nevertheless, she had driven several miles out of her way to talk to Liz. She had been invited, more or less. There was no harm in ascertaining whether or not her reluctant hostess was home.

She went swiftly down the steps and around the corner of the house. There was a single, grimy window on the side of the garage wall.

She peered. through the darkened glass. There was no car inside.

Maybe Liz had changed her mind.

But she had been home little more than an hour ago and had planned to meditate with her personal guide until ten, Alexa reminded herself.

She turned to retrace her steps and paused when she noticed that the blind in the kitchen window was raised. A deep, intuitive disquiet swept through her.

She walked hesitantly up the rear steps of the deck and glanced into the kitchen. She was not spying, she told herself. It was a casual glance.

Who was she kidding? She might as well admit that she was getting nervous. Something felt wrong.

An empty cereal bowl and a mug sat on the tiled counter near the sink. *And what can we deduce from that, Ms. Sleuth? That Liz was definitely home this morning? We already know that much.*

She walked around the side of the house. The drapes were pulled across a wide bank of windows. The living room, no doubt. She walked farther along the deck and turned a corner.

Ahead of her a small sun room projected out from the wall of the house. It was windowed on two sides and the ceiling. A sliding glass door formed the third wall.

The slider was open two or three inches. The edge of a long, cream-colored curtain fluttered in the breeze.

Alexa walked along the deck to the glass door.

"Is anyone home?" she called through the crack. "Liz? It's Alexa Chambers. If you're in there, I'd really like to talk to you."

There was no response.

The wind sighed eerily in the thick branches behind her. Shadow Canyon was really getting to her today.

"Mrs. Guthrie? It's important."

She gave up trying to shake off the sense of impending disaster. Opening the slider, she grasped a handful of curtain and lifted it out of the way.

She found herself staring into a small, minimally furnished room done in neutral shades. There were no chairs, only a single pale pillow placed in the center of the milk-colored carpet. There was also a bookcase and a low, wooden table. A large chunk of rose-pink crystal sat in the center of the table.

A pair of shoji screens paneled with squares of a white, translucent fabric sealed the glass chamber from the rest of the house. The screens were closed, blocking the view of the room or hall beyond the chamber.

Liz Guthrie's meditation room.

Alexa knew that the Dimensions seminar program emphasized the necessity of creating a personal, private space in which to meditate. In terms of priorities, it was right up there with keeping one's personal meditation journal up to date. In the course of her short affiliation with the Institute, she had failed in both endeavors. Privately, she put the blame on the boredom that had overcome her every time she tried to get into meditation mode.

She glanced at the low bookcase and was not surprised to see that the shelves were crammed with a variety of Dimensions Institute publications, including Liz's copy of *Living the Dimensions Way*.

A familiar volume sheathed in a turquoise and white dust jacket lay open on top of the bookcase. A Dimensions personal journal.

Alexa thought about the one she had been given when she took the Beginning Guided Meditation Seminar. She had dutifully written in it for three whole days before concluding that her progress in the Dimensions Way was not only going to be quite brief, it would also be extremely dull.

She hesitated. She had no right to enter the house. But the feeling of wrongness was getting stronger by the minute.

"Liz?"

She drew a breath and stepped into the meditation retreat.

A sudden shifting of the light on the other side of the closed shoji screens made her flinch. Her pulse, already trotting along at a brisk clip, broke into a wild gallop. She stared at the white panels.

"Liz, it's me, Alexa Chambers." Her voice sounded unnaturally loud and a little too thin and high to her own ears.

A dark figure loomed on the other side of the semitransparent panels. The head was too round.

There were no arms or legs, just a long, shadowy form. It moved slowly toward her.

A scream surged up out of nowhere. Alexa fought it with every ounce of willpower she possessed.

The figure came closer to the screen.

Common sense finally returned. Alexa realized that what she was looking at was a person dressed in a hooded robe. Liz Guthrie must have been in the shower.

"I'm so sorry, I hope I didn't scare you, Liz." Lord, now she sounded much too bright and cheery. "I know I had no right to intrude like this, but when you didn't answer the door I was afraid something might have happened."

There was no verbal response from the person on the other side of the screen. But a shadowy arm rose. Alexa could see quite clearly the outline of the long-bladed knife in the hand.

A knife.

She was finally ready to believe in malevolent vortices and dark forces. She could literally feel them emanating toward her from the figure on the other side of the screen.

Probably not Liz Guthrie.

Whirling, she leaped back through the open glass door.

The car. She had to get to it.

No, not the car. That was exactly what the guy with the knife would expect her to do. The Camry was parked at the front of the house. She was all the way around at the back.

The intruder could easily beat her to the car by running through the house and out the front door.

Her only hope was to lose herself in the heavy stand of trees or in one of the little caves that dotted the walls of Shadow Canyon.

She felt her heavy satchel start to slide off her shoulder as she dashed across the deck. She was about to let it go so that she could run unencumbered. Then she recalled the cell phone inside. She tightened her grip on the strap, jumped off the low deck, and flung herself into the trees.

Branches and scrubby underbrush closed around her before she had taken a dozen strides. She glanced back over her shoulder. She could no longer see the entire deck, but she heard footsteps pound on the wooden planks.

The intruder was pursuing her.

She glimpsed the edge of a flapping black robe. Dead leaves and needles crackled and snapped.

It was a scene out of a nightmare, the awful kind in which one was pursued by a faceless menace.

Alexa plunged deeper into the woods, afraid that she might be running for her life.

21

The ground sloped upward rapidly. Her sandals slipped and skidded on dead pine needles. She put out a hand and managed to catch hold of a trailing branch; used it to haul herself forward.

Branches slapped her in the face as she plowed through the maze of trees. Her breathing was already labored. How long could she run flat out?

Even though it was unlikely her pursuer could see her any better than she could see him, she knew she gave away her position with every move she made.

She could hear him, too. He was not pounding through the woods the way she was. He was taking his time, pausing to listen for the sounds she made, closing in on her.

She could not go on like this. She had to go to ground long enough to call 911 on the cell phone. If she could get to one of the caverns that studded the area, she might be able to conceal herself inside.

The hulking trees stepped up the side of the ancient canyon. The incline sharpened still more.

The first rocky opening loomed without warning, a pitch-black lair that could have concealed anything from a rattler to a family of coyotes.

Not that she was fussy at the moment, Alexa thought. Still, instinct sent her racing past the opening. It was too obvious.

She glanced back over her shoulder. She thought she caught another glimpse of the black robe. It vanished almost instantly behind a veil of fir boughs.

The climb grew steeper and more treacherous. Small pebbles shifted beneath the soles of her sandals. The remains of an old rock fall littered her path. She worked her way around the largest of the tumbled boulders. The larger stones offered some cover.

She paused once to listen. Over the groans and sighs of the trees she heard the steady, oncoming footfalls. The hooded figure was not hurrying, but he was still in relentless pursuit. It was as if he was confident that he would overtake her when she eventually tired.

He was probably right.

She hitched the satchel higher on her shoulder and reached out to grab hold of an outcropping of rough stone. More loose rock fragments slithered beneath her feet. She realized that if she was not very careful she would start a small landslide that would carry her down with it.

A landslide. She looked around. There was evidence of several of them in the vicinity.

She searched the mounded boulders and chunks of stone for another dark opening. She passed up three before she noticed one that was partially blocked by a heap of tumbled rock debris.

It looked impossibly far away. She thought about the knife and renewed strength flowed from somewhere. She managed to climb to the dark entrance. Praying that she would not come face-to-face with some creature who might take offense at the intrusion, she worked her way over the barrier of loosened stones.

Nothing hissed, rattled, or roared out of the inky darkness.

She crouched behind the bulwark of stones and rocks and let the satchel slide off her shoulder. She dared not look out over the rocky barricade for fear her pursuer would spot her. In hindsight, her orange and yellow striped blouse had probably not been a wise fashion choice this morning, she thought. It was as bright as a beacon. All too easy to see.

She sank deeper into the darkness and strained to listen for sounds of her pursuer.

Pebbles rattled down below. He was still in pursuit.

She gripped the largest of the rocks that half-closed the opening of the crevasse and shoved with all of her might.

For a terrifying instant, nothing happened.

And then, with a grinding, grating rumble, the mount of rock debris in front of the small cave began to shift.

Slowly, but with gathering energy and noise, the small avalanche of loose stones picked up momentum. Alexa pushed several more chunks of jagged rock over the edge of the opening.

"Nooo . . ."

The cry was high and shrill. A scream of fright

and rage. Alexa could not tell if it was male or female.

There was no way to hear footsteps above the sound of falling stones, but she sensed that the other was frantically scurrying to get clear of the shower of rock.

The noise of the cascading debris seemed to go on forever.

A rush of triumph brought a strange euphoria.

"Don't mess with the wild woman," she whispered as she pushed a few more pounds of rubble down the slope.

She huddled in the shadows of the crevasse and listened until an unnatural silence fell. The brief thrill of victory dissipated as quickly as it had come. An annoying series of shivers took its place.

For the first time she became aware of the dark, close confines of her hiding place. Claustrophobia squeezed through her. She fought it with deep breathing. The Dimensions Institute training had been good for something after all, she thought.

After a while, when she heard nothing moving on the path beneath the cave, she opened her purse and took out the cell phone.

Punching out the emergency number was not easy. The stupid little instrument would not hold still in the palm of her shaking hand.

22

"Why in hell didn't you tell me what you were going to do?" Trask paced back and forth across Alexa's living room. It took everything he had to hold back the storm of unfamiliar emotion that threatened to swamp his control. "Of all the damn fool stunts. Do you have any idea what could have happened?"

"You don't need to spell it out for me." Alexa sat on the edge of the sleek chaise longue, huddled over a mug of hot tea. "I was there, remember?"

The first thing she had done after walking through the front door was take a long shower. Trask had seethed quietly while she bathed and changed into a pair of jeans and a white cotton shirt.

After an eternity she had emerged from the bedroom. Her damp hair was combed straight back from her forehead and anchored behind her ears with a faux tortoiseshell headband. The strict line emphasized the shadows in her eyes and the tautness around her mouth.

He had wanted to take her into his arms and

crush her close just to reassure himself that she was safe. Unsure of how such a gesture would be received, he had opted to chew her out instead. Every successful CEO lived by some very simple rules. One of them was, when in doubt, start yelling.

He paused in front of the window. "You should have called me before you went off on your own."

"Please stop shouting at me. It was bad enough that Strood and his officer thought I was hallucinating."

"They didn't think you were seeing things." Trask glanced over his shoulder. She gave him an ironic look. He forced himself to unclench his jaw. "Not exactly. They just thought you might have been a little shaken up because of Guthrie's accident and overreacted to a shadow."

"Bull. They think I'm flaky."

He decided not to argue the point further. She was right. Strood and Officer Clarke had been polite and professional, but the bottom line was that they had discovered no evidence to support her tale of being pursued up the side of Shadow Canyon by a knife-wielding figure in a hooded robe.

The only indications that anything out of the ordinary had occurred that morning were the dirt stains on Alexa's linen trousers and her scraped knees and torn nails.

No one doubted that she had made a mad dash through some underbrush, Trask reflected. It was the reason for her wild run that was in question, at least so far as Strood was concerned. The menacing shadow behind a shoji screen had not stood up well to investigation.

The officer who had responded to Alexa's frantic 911 call had found no sign of an intruder inside Liz Guthrie's home. According to the official report, there had been no evidence of forced entry or foul play. Nothing of value appeared to be missing from the house. An expensive audio system sat untouched in the living room.

After Alexa had given her statement, the chief had taken Trask quietly aside.

"She may be having some problems because of Guthrie's accident," Strood had said, not unkindly. "That kind of thing can shake someone up. Cause bad dreams and so on."

Trask had decided not to mention his own nightmare following Guthrie's accident. "She's not the type to invent bizarre stories out of thin air. Something scared her."

Strood's heavy features softened. "Look, I've been in this business a long time. I can tell you from experience that people react to a severe shock in unpredictable ways."

"I know that."

"Take her home. Make sure she gets some rest. If things get worse, you might want to advise her to get some counseling."

Trask shoved the memories of the less than satisfying interview with Strood aside. The chief was right. There was no evidence of a crime.

He rubbed the back of his neck, trying to unknot muscles that had been rigid since he had gotten Alexa's phone call two hours earlier. "Why in hell did you go out to Shadow Canyon?"

"I told you, I wanted to talk to Liz Guthrie in person."

"What did you expect to learn from her? She's not involved in any of this."

Alexa hesitated. "From all accounts, she and Dean were still lovers."

That news made him go very still. He swung around to face her. "Are you sure?"

"That's the rumor." Alexa gripped the mug tightly in both hands. "I thought she might be able to give me some indication of Guthrie's state of mind the night of the accident."

"Strood says there's every indication that Guthrie's state of mind was seriously stoned, as usual. You heard him. He's not pursuing any other line of inquiry because there's absolutely no reason to believe that the crash was anything other than an accident."

"But we are pursuing another line of inquiry," Alexa said deliberately. "Aren't we?"

The prospect of being hoist on his own petard was not pleasant. "Let's get something clear here. I'm the one pursuing it. Not you."

"We're supposed to be partners in this thing, Trask."

"I said I'd keep you informed. That is not the same thing as being a team."

"I'm involved in this just as much as you are, and I've got just as much right to pursue a line of inquiry as you do. If you don't want to work as partners, fine. I'll go my way and you can go yours."

"The hell you will." He started toward her with no clear objective in mind other than to make her see reason. He stopped halfway across the room as the full impact of what she had just said finally hit him. "Damn. Are you telling me that you think there's something to my conspiracy theory after all?"

She watched him with intense, shadowed eyes. "I did not invent that intruder in Liz Guthrie's house. I did not imagine being chased up a mountainside by some thug with a big knife. It's possible that what happened to me this morning had nothing whatsoever to do with your conspiracy theory. Maybe I interrupted a burglary in progress."

He did not move. "Possible."

"But like you said, coincidences in a situation such as this are a little hard to swallow. Liz Guthrie was home earlier this morning. I told you, I talked to her on the phone. She agreed to see me. I was supposed to wait for an hour because she wanted to do her meditation exercises first. She said her—" Alexa broke off.

Trask lowered himself into a chair. He did not take his eyes off her face. "What is it?"

"In all the excitement I almost forgot. Liz told me that she was going to meditate with her Dimensions guide this morning. When we spoke on the phone she said he had just arrived."

"He?"

"I think ... No, wait." Alexa tapped one finger on the side of the mug. "She didn't specify. She just said that her guide was there."

"Okay, so he or she could have left with Liz before you got there."

"But, why?"

"A million reasons, just like Strood said."

Alexa wrinkled her nose. "You're starting to sound a little too reasonable. This is not the Trask I know and—" She stopped very quickly and smiled coolly. "The Trask I know and whom I consider a world-class conspiracy theorist."

Trask studied the flags of pink in her cheeks. He wondered why she was so embarrassed about having almost said, "the Trask I know and love." It would have passed easily enough as a flippant, off-the-cuff crack. No one would have taken her seriously, least of all him.

"I'm trying to be reasonable," he said, "because I'm not so sure it's a good idea for both of us to go off the deep end. At least, not simultaneously."

"You're probably right. Obviously this conspiracy thinking stuff is contagious." Alexa took another sip of tea. "I'd sure like to know where Liz went and how long she intends to stay gone."

Trask settled deeper into his chair and eyed the toes of his shoes. "Assuming she stays gone, we can probably get the answers to those questions."

"Think so?"

"I told you, I've had a private investigator on this project for months. Finding people is bread-and-butter work for him. I'll give Phil a call this afternoon and add Liz Guthrie to his to-do list."

"Could be a little embarrassing, not to say expensive for you, if it turns out she just went to the library or the grocery store."

"Embarrassing, yes. Financially speaking, it'll only be a drop in the bucket compared to what I've already spent on this thing."

"I see."

Absently he contemplated the set of orangy-green plastic bookends that framed a set of volumes on a nearby shelf. The sweeping, molded curves told him he was looking at more Deco. He remembered Edward Vale telling him that old Bakelite plastic was very collectible.

"Something wrong?" Alexa prompted.

"Maybe." He looked away from the bookends. "There's one other angle we should probably consider."

"What's that?"

"Someone tried to terrorize you today. Could have been an angry burglar. Could have been person or persons unknown. Hell, it could have been Liz Guthrie herself, dressed in a robe."

Alexa frowned. "That's a weird thought."

"But there is one other remote possibility. And I stress remote."

"Which is?"

Trask paused. "There could be a link between those late night phone calls you've been receiving and the creep who chased you today."

She stared at him. "Why would someone go to all the effort to scare me?"

"I don't know. But it occurs to me that whoever he is, he might not like the idea of the two of us forming a . . ." He groped for another word; could not find it. "A partnership."

She watched him with brooding eyes. "This is getting murkier by the minute."

"Better get used to it. We conspiracy theory buffs thrive on murk."

23

Trask was out on the balcony of his suite when he heard the fax machine hum to life again shortly before five that afternoon. This time he did not rush back through the open French doors to check out the data that was being sent to him.

He'd had enough of hovering over the fax as if it were some pagan oracle that could give him answers to his questions. He'd spent most of the day standing in front of the machine's receiving tray, snatching up each new page as it appeared. When he hadn't been obsessed with the fax, he'd been on the phone.

He had a mountain of information on the investments of Guthrie Enterprises, past and present, piled high on his desk. Thus far, however, none of it looked useful.

Unless, of course, you wanted to prove that there was no conspiracy.

He lounged in his chair, heels propped on the railing, and gazed out at the rust-colored monoliths.

After a while he opened the door in his mind

and looked at the ghost in the closet. He had known all along that his belief that his father had been murdered might be a fantasy, a dark vision he had conjured so that he would not have to think too much about that last phone call between the two of them.

He had avoided looking into the closet during the past twelve years. Now he forced himself to examine the specter of his own guilt. If he was wrong, he would have to expose it to the light of day and deal with it.

But he could not do that until he knew for certain whether or not the ghost was real.

He closed the door again and switched his thoughts back to Alexa. He recalled her torn clothes and scraped hands. His insides went cold all over again. He remembered the shadows he had seen in her eyes. Someone had scared the hell out of her this morning.

Regardless of the outcome of his own quest, he would not leave Avalon until he found out who was terrorizing Alexa.

It occurred to him that he was in no rush to leave Avalon at all. Leaving town meant leaving Alexa. The thought of doing that filled him with a disturbing sense of incompleteness.

Whatever existed between himself and Alexa needed to be finished before he could return to Seattle.

Behind him the fax sang its siren song to itself and then fell silent. He waited a while longer. Eventually he took his feet down off the railing, stood, and went through the French doors.

He crossed the room to the desk and picked up

the pages that were stacked neatly in the tray. More financial data.

He poured himself another cup of coffee. Then he took the pages out onto the balcony, sat down, and put his feet back up on the railing. Methodically he began to read the information Phil Okuda had transmitted: More info on the status of Dean Guthrie's recent financial affairs and the projects he had been involved with at the time of his death.

A single word leaped out from the second paragraph of the first page.

Trask took his feet off the railing.

"Guthrie, you son-of-a-bitch. I knew there had to be a connection."

He reached for the phone.

Alexa eyed the stack of plastic containers in Trask's hands and tried not to salivate.

"I thought when you said you'd bring dinner you meant pizza." She opened the door wider. "This looks like room service with all the stops pulled out."

"I own a hotel, remember?" Trask carried the fragrant packages toward the kitchen. "My new chef is trying to impress me."

She watched him set the containers out on the counter. "Well, I don't know about you, but I am definitely impressed."

It was the food she was drooling over, she thought, not Trask.

He turned around, a bottle of dark red zinfandel in one hand, a corkscrew in the other. She looked into his gleaming eyes and knew that she was lying to herself. It was definitely Trask that was making her drool.

Dressed in a khaki shirt and a pair of black chinos, he looked far more appetizing than any of the gourmet delicacies he had brought with him. The kitchen was charged with the sexual energy that emanated from him.

Unfortunately, he had made it clear on the phone that he wanted to talk about his conspiracy theories tonight, not their relationship.

It was probably better that way. Certainly much less hazardous to her emotional health. Besides, she was hardly in a position to complain. After all, she was the one who had backed away from a sexual liaison after that one night of sizzle and burn in the spa.

"I've got news that should interest both of us," Trask said.

"That's nice." She moved closer to the counter and started to pry the lids off the plastic containers. "Are there any hors d'oeuvres?"

"The little package on the right."

"Got it." She peeled the lid off the small plastic container and helped herself to a salsa-laced canapé. She plucked out another. "Want one?"

"Sure." He did not stop work on the cork.

She realized that he was waiting for her to put the canapé into his mouth. She hesitated and then, feeling very daring, leaned across the counter and popped the tidbit between his teeth. She snatched her fingers back immediately.

"Relax," he said around the canapé. "I usually don't bite the hand that feeds me."

"An excellent policy." She watched him pour two

glasses of the ruby-colored zin. "Let's hear your big news."

"I found a link." Cold satisfaction made his eyes very green. He handed her one of the wine glasses. "It came through the fax this afternoon just after five o'clock."

"What sort of link?"

"A connection between Dad's death and Guthrie's so-called accident."

She paused with the glass halfway to her mouth. Slowly she set it back down on the counter. "You're talking about your conspiracy theory?"

"I like to think of it as *our* conspiracy theory now."

She studied him warily. "You're serious, aren't you?"

He touched his glass to hers and then raised it to his mouth. "I have never been more serious in my life."

"I'm listening."

"In a word, *Dimensions*."

She blinked. Whatever she had been expecting, that wasn't it. "What about Dimensions? You're not suggesting some kind of metaphysical aspect to this thing, are you?"

He pondered that. "Maybe."

"Come on, Trask."

"This afternoon I found out that, at the time of his death, Guthrie was heavily invested in several construction projects."

"So?"

"According to my information, he wanted to pull out of one of the deals because he had to raise cash in order to get into a hot mall project outside of Phoenix."

"Wait a second, are you saying that someone may have murdered Dean Guthrie because he was threatening to yank his investment funds in a development?"

"I think it's a real possibility."

"That sounds like a replay of your theory about your father's death."

"I know. That's exactly what it is."

She shook her head. "It doesn't make any sense."

"Go with me on this, Alexa. Twelve years ago Guthrie was in a financial bind. He had to raise cash quickly to meet his investment commitments. My father was standing in his way."

"I've heard this part of your theory before. What does it have to do with the present scenario?"

"Guess which investment commitment Guthrie met twelve years ago with the money he pulled from Dad's project."

"I don't have a clue."

Trask savored a long, slow swallow of wine. "Guthrie had committed himself to a line of credit for the Dimensions Institute."

She stilled. "You're moving too fast for me. Slow down and tell me exactly where you think you're going with this."

"There are still some crucial pieces of the puzzle missing, but here's what I've got so far." Trask leaned back against the counter. "Twelve years ago Guthrie had to choose between two investments, Dad's resort project and the Dimensions Institute. He chose the Dimensions project, but Dad threatened to tie up both him and his money in court for months."

"You think someone killed your father to free up Guthrie's money so that he could sink it into Dimensions?"

"Yeah. I can't prove murder yet, but I can sure as hell prove that Dimensions is where Guthrie's money went after my father was killed. There's a nice, neat paper trail."

"Okay, go on. But remember to keep it slow and easy."

Trask took another swallow of wine and set the glass down. He met Alexa's eyes. "I think history has just repeated itself. Only this time it was Guthrie at the wheel."

"What do you mean?"

"I just told you Guthrie was in another cash bind just before his death."

"You said he was trying to get out of his commitments to one construction project in order to free up cash for another."

"You get one guess to name the project he wanted to pull out of."

"How in the world would I know—" She broke off as her intuition took over. "Oh, my God. You said the link was Dimensions. Are you talking about the new Dimensions Santa Fe project?"

"Welcome to Business 101. You may go to the head of the class."

"Do you realize what you're saying?" She struggled to absorb the implications. "If you follow this to the logical conclusion, it means that someone may have murdered both your father and Guthrie for the same reason. Dimensions."

"Right." Trask picked up his glass and studied the blood-red zin. "Twice during the past twelve years crucial investment cash intended for a Dimensions Institute project was jeopardized. I think that on each occasion someone stepped in to get rid of the investor who was standing in the way."

Alexa suddenly recalled the conversation she'd had with Dylan Fenn and Stewart Lutton in Spheres. An image of Joanna's tense, anxious face loomed in her mind. Her mouth went dry.

"You do realize what this means, don't you?" Trask said with icy anticipation.

"Yes." She rested her elbows on the counter and let the conclusions sink in. "As far as you're concerned, it's more evidence against your newest suspect."

"Webster Bell. Everything fits."

Two hours later Trask settled into the patio lounger and contemplated the star-studded sky. He could get accustomed to this, he decided. It was strange that, after living in the Northwest all of his life, he should find himself so content here in Avalon. There was something deeply satisfying about watching a full moon rise over the desert.

He hoped a coyote would howl at some point. It would add just the right touch. Plus, it would make a pleasant change from listening to Alexa. She had not stopped talking since they had sat down to eat.

"We've got to move slowly on this, Trask. We've got to be very sure. You can't just accuse Webster Bell, of all people, of murder. The man is a guru to thousands. People look up to him."

He decided that he'd had enough of Alexa's litany of caveats, warnings, and arguments. He was starting to lose patience. He wanted to make some solid plans, but he was having a hard time getting past her demands for caution. It was a wonder she hadn't made herself hoarse.

She pushed aside her unfinished flan and sat forward.

"Listen to me," she said very earnestly. "You're a businessman. You know as well as I do that we've got to stick to the facts, and we don't have very many of those yet."

"The Dimensions Institute is at the bottom of this, I can feel it. It's the single common denominator. Everything comes back to it." He was getting bored listening to himself repeat his own counterarguments. "And Webster Bell is the Dimensions Institute."

"I'm not denying that everything we've got so far points to a connection. All I'm saying is that we've got to get some hard evidence before you go riding off on your big horse to challenge Webster Bell to a gunfight out in front of the saloon at high noon."

He was briefly amused. "I'm from Seattle. We don't do gunfights at high noon. We prefer a more subtle approach."

"Oh, yeah? What's subtle to you?"

Trask shrugged. "There are a variety of alternatives. A man can accidentally fall off a ferry in the middle of Puget Sound and disappear into water so cold and deep that the body might never be found. Or he can go for a hike in the Cascades and never return. Then there's the ever-popular skiing accident or boating disaster . . ."

She stared at him with mounting horror. "My God, you're serious. Trask, you can't possibly mean that you would . . . would . . ."

"Relax. I'm not interested in getting myself sent to prison on a murder charge. I've got other plans for the rest of my life."

"I'm very glad to hear that." She flopped back in her chair. Her eyes were still wary. "You've got a business to run."

"Among other things." For the first time since Jennifer had left him for her software zillionaire, it occurred to him that maybe he did want to do something else with his life besides add a few more fantasy resorts to the Avalon chain. Like what? he wondered.

Alexa scowled ferociously across the patio table. "Trask?"

Like make love to Alexa, he decided. That would be as good as any other way of filling up the empty places in his life.

"Trask? Did you hear me?"

"Sorry. My mind wandered. What did you say?"

"I said, what about using your private investigator to get the information you need?"

"I called Okuda this afternoon. Told him to start digging around in Bell's background. I also asked him to find out what happens to Guthrie's estate now that he's dead."

Alexa raised her brows. "I hadn't thought about that. He had no family as far as anyone knows. I wonder who takes control of his finances?"

"That's the big question at the moment. "

"There's another looming issue."

He cocked a brow. "Liz Guthrie?"

Alexa tilted her head. "Still no word on her whereabouts?"

"No. Phil says it'll take him at least twenty-four hours to locate her, maybe a little longer if she's trying to stay hidden."

"She still isn't answering her phone, so I think we can assume she didn't just go out to the store."

"Yeah, I think that's a reasonable assumption." Trask watched the moon rise above a rocky spire.

"I wonder where Liz fits into this thing," Alexa said after a while.

"I don't know yet. But there is one indisputable fact. She has ties to the Dimensions Institute."

"So she takes some guided meditation seminars." Alexa lifted one shoulder. "Big deal. Half of Avalon has been involved in a Dimensions class at one time or another. I took a course at the Institute myself, after I moved back here."

That startled him. "You did?"

She gave him a fleeting grin. "Mom and Lloyd thought that it would be a good way for me to meet people. They're worried because I don't have much of a social life."

"Guess they'll be surprised when they get home and find out that you're involved in a flaming affair."

Alexa's eyes widened and then instantly narrowed. "I am not involved in an affair, flaming or otherwise. I think that what we had could more properly be classified as a one-night stand."

So much for his own lousy ability to tap into the positive energy vortices around here. He wondered if it would help to take one of the Dimensions Institute classes.

"I suppose it depends on your definition of a one-night stand," he said carefully.

"It happened once. That makes it a one-night stand."

"All right, you've made your point." He hesitated. "So, did you?"

"Did I what?"

"Meet people and develop a social life when you took the class at the Institute?"

Her face was serenely unreadable in the shadows. "I met some people."

He thought about the day he had found her having tea at Café Solstice with Foster Radstone. "Yeah, I guess you did. What happened between you and Radstone, anyway?"

She blinked and then frowned in what appeared to be genuine bafflement. "How did you know that Foster and I dated for a while?"

"The guy was leaning in a little too close." How did you explain that kind of thing to a woman? It was something another man would have understood intuitively. "You know, like he thought he had a right or something."

"Hmm." She did not look pleased. "Well, whatever we had, it didn't last long. I met him when I took a class he taught at the Institute. When I dropped out, he called me up for a date. We saw each other a few times, but that was the end of it."

"Another example of your, uh, inability to commit?"

"Not exactly." Alexa flashed him an unexpected grin. "Foster's idea of scintillating dinner conversation was to explain to me how I could benefit from classes at the Institute."

"Why did you drop out of the one you did take?"

She rested her chin on the heel of her hand and regarded him with an enigmatic expression. "It wasn't my kind of thing. Besides, I was too busy with another, much more interesting project that was chewing up all of my free time."

"What project was that?"

"Selecting early-twentieth-century art and antiques for your resort."

"Yeah?"

"Trust me, it was a full-time job. And I already had a full-time job running Elegant Relic. The combination did not leave me much time for meditation seminars or dates."

He nodded. "So, in a way, you could say that I was the reason you haven't had much of a social life for the past year."

"Yes, you could say that. Now, if we might return to the subject at hand?"

"Sure. Why not?"

"What do we do now? Sit back and wait until we get more data from your investigator?"

"No."

"No?" Curiosity flickered in her intelligent eyes. "Just what do you think you can do that a professional investigator can't?"

"I'm not sure yet. I'm still thinking about it."

"I was afraid of that."

"I've got a couple of ideas." He met her eyes across the table. "But the first priority is to make sure you're safe."

She stared at him. "I beg your pardon?"

"If I'm right about Bell being behind this, he wants

you out of the picture, but he probably doesn't want to take the risk of doing something too drastic."

"I don't know about that. What happened this morning at Liz's house seemed pretty drastic."

"I think the son-of-a-bitch may have sent someone to frighten you."

"Why do you say that?"

Trask hesitated. She'd been through enough today. He did not want to add to her anxiety level. On the other hand, she was as involved in this as himself. She needed to look at the whole picture. He decided to lay it on the table.

"Bell's not stupid. Killing you is not only unnecessary, it would be an extremely risky move. Two violent deaths in one week in a town the size of Avalon would probably make even Chief Strood start asking questions."

She gave him a knowing look. "Especially after you leaned on him a little?"

"I'd have done some leaning, all right." He helped himself to one of the leftover chocolate mints. He munched without tasting anything. It would probably make Alexa nervous if she knew that he would do more than lean on Strood if anything happened to her. He would tear Avalon apart.

"If your reasoning is right," Alexa said, "then we can conclude that the last thing whoever is behind this wants is a serious criminal investigation. That means I'm probably safe."

"I'm not making any assumptions."

"What do you mean?"

"Even though Bell probably doesn't want to do

anything more than scare you into staying out of the picture, I think we should take precautions."

"Trask, try to bear in mind that we don't know that Webster Bell is behind any of this."

"That's beside the point. We're discussing precautions, remember?"

She sighed. "Okay, okay. What precautions do you suggest?"

He thought about it. "As far as the days go, a few prudent steps should be sufficient."

"What steps?"

"We'll make sure you're not alone or isolated for any extended period of time, the way you were yesterday. He's not likely to try anything chancy in broad daylight if there are witnesses."

Alexa considered that. "A comforting thought, I suppose. But, for the record, I think you're overlooking a really large issue here."

"Which is?"

"If you're right about any of this, *you're* the one who's in danger, not me."

His spirits lifted. "Worried about me?"

"Well, yes, now that you mention it, I am."

"Thanks. I'm touched. Now then, as far as the nights go—"

She gave him a sharp look. "What about the nights?"

"There are a couple of ways we could go about this." He kept his voice calm and deliberate. He wanted to make himself sound rational, logical, and reasonable. He did not want her thinking that he'd gone over the edge with his paranoia. "You could stay with me at the hotel."

"Move into your hotel?" She stared at him. "Are you crazy?"

"Alexa, be reasonable. Avalon Resorts provides round-the-clock security for all guests. It's discreet but professional. You won't even be aware of it."

"Forget it." Her chair scraped as she shoved herself back from the table. "I have absolutely no intention of moving into the Avalon Resort & Spa. I want to stay right here in my own home, thank you very much."

"All right, plan B is to send a member of the Avalon security staff over here in the evenings to keep an eye on things."

"Now you're talking about providing me with a bodyguard." She folded her arms beneath her breasts. Her shoulders made a stiff, angular line. "I don't like the sound of that either."

"There is a third alternative," he said as casually as possible.

She gave him a suspicious look. "If you're about to suggest that I leave town for a while, you can save your breath. I've got a business to run. Besides, I'm not about to walk away from this thing."

"I know you won't leave town. I'm not even sure that would be a good idea." He made himself sound patient. "What I was about to suggest is that I stay here at night with you."

She said nothing, just looked at him as if he had suddenly begun to speak in an incomprehensible foreign language.

"I would, of course, sleep on the couch," he added politely.

"The couch?"

"I realize that your neighbors won't understand the situation. Conclusions might be drawn."

"The neighbors? I don't give a damn about the neighbors. Everyone in town has already concluded that we're involved in a torrid affair." Her jaw tensed. "Even though it was only a one-night stand."

He looked at her. "I don't know how it was for you, but for me it was definitely a very *torrid* one-night stand."

She gaped, clearly bereft of words.

"Alexa, be reasonable. Given the Dimensions connection and the fact that Guthrie may have been killed because of it, we have to take your experience today very seriously. If I'm not with you at night, I'm going to lie awake sweating."

"Why?"

"I won't be able to sleep because I'll be worrying about your safety."

"Oh."

"I need my rest."

"Uh-huh."

"It's settled, then," he said. "I'll spend the night here. On the couch."

"That won't be very convenient for you, will it? All your things are back at the hotel."

He thought of the small, plastic Avalon Resorts amenities kit he'd stashed in the Jeep's glove compartment before coming here tonight. It included a razor and a condom. Who said he couldn't think positive?

"I'll get by," he said.

24

The ringing of the phone brought Alexa out of the first decent night's sleep she'd had in days. She came awake thinking that her alarm had gone off early.

The phone rang again, shrill and menacing. She glanced at the window and realized it was still dark outside. The numbers on the clock glowed green in the shadows. Two-fifteen A.M.

"Oh, damn."

She sat up in bed and stared at the phone as if it were a cobra.

A shifting of the shadows in the doorway broke the spell. Trask. She was suddenly very glad that she had allowed him to sleep on her couch. The sight of him reassured her in ways she did not want to examine too closely.

He had taken the time to put on his chinos, but he had not yet zipped them. She glimpsed a wedge of white.

Another ring sounded. *Pull yourself together, Alexa. And for heaven's sake stop staring at the man's briefs.*

"Answer it." Trask came toward her through the shadows. Moonlight glinted on the fierce planes of his face. "Make sure he knows you're not alone."

She reached out and picked up the phone.

"Who is this?" she demanded.

"Think he'll still want to go to bed with you after he finds out about the McClelland Gallery forgeries?"

Alexa froze. "What do you know about McClelland?"

"Enough." The voice was muffled and distorted again. *"This will be your last warning. Stay away from Trask or he will be told everything."*

"He's right here. Why don't you tell him everything right now and save yourself the time and—"

Alexa broke off, wincing when the caller slammed the receiver down in her ear.

"Let me have that." Trask took the phone from her hand and quickly punched in the code to activate last call return.

Alexa held the sheet to her throat and waited tensely. Eventually someone picked up the phone on the other end.

"I know this is a pay phone," Trask said roughly. "Did you see whoever it was who just used it?" There was a pause. "Kids? Are you sure there aren't any adults around? Did anyone just drive off?"

Alexa listened as he went through the same litany of questions she had asked the night she had tried to trace the call. She was not surprised when he got nowhere. Eventually he hung up the phone and turned to look at her.

"Another all-night convenience store," he said. "No one saw whoever used the pay phone last."

"Why am I not surprised?" Alexa muttered.

"Who would notice anyone using a pay phone at a convenience store unless he tied up the line for a long time?"

"What did he say this time?"

"The caller? He was a little more direct and to the point than usual." She tightened her grip on the sheet. "He didn't mention dark vortices and approaching storms. He tried blackmail instead."

"The McClelland scandal?"

"Uh-huh." She watched him out of the corner of her eye.

"Interesting that Bell knows about that." Trask sounded thoughtful.

"As I keep reminding you, we don't know for sure that Webster Bell is the one making those calls. Besides, everyone in Avalon recognizes him on sight. I don't see how he could skulk around twenty-four-hour convenience stores late at night without being noticed."

Trask eyed the phone. "He could be using someone else to do the dirty work."

"In any event, the McClelland scandal isn't exactly a state secret. At least not in the art world."

"But someone outside that world would have to do a little digging to find it, right?"

"I should think so, given that the story is over a year old now. There hasn't been an article in the trade press on the McClelland forgeries in months." She shuddered. "Believe me, I'd know."

"Yeah, you probably would."

"You're a good example." Her brows rose. "You didn't even find out about the McClelland scandal until *after* you bought a fortune in early-twentieth-century art and antiques. And you're what most people would call pretty sharp about not getting conned."

"I don't claim to be sharper than the average guy when it comes to avoiding a con, but I'm probably a lot meaner than some folks if I find out I've been had."

She was dismayed to realize that his not-so-casual warning had the power to hurt her. What had she been thinking? That their adventures together during the past few days had formed a deep and lasting bond? Sheer fantasy, as Trask would be the first one to tell her.

"I'll keep that in mind," she whispered.

He did not move. He just continued to watch her from the shadows near the bed. But there was a disturbing stillness in him now that had not been there a moment ago.

"For the record," he said quietly, "I don't give a damn if it turns out that I'm the new owner of the best collection of fake Art Deco in the known universe."

For an instant, she felt nothing at all. And then fierce rage flowed into all the empty places inside her.

"Just what the hell do you mean by that?" she demanded.

"You heard me." He took a step closer to the bed. "I'm trying to tell you that what's going on between us isn't connected to that damn art collection."

"What is this? Am I supposed to be grateful?"

He stopped at the edge of the bed. "I'm trying to explain something here."

"I know that." She scrambled to her knees and gathered the sheet around her as if it were a chainmail cloak that could protect her from his words. "And I know where you think you're going with your stupid explanations, but it won't work."

"Where did I think I was going?"

"To bed. With me. For another one-night stand." She felt the heat rise in her face, but it did not slow her down. Her anger was stronger than her embarrassment. "Forget it."

"Alexa—"

"Talk about lousy seduction lines. Did you really believe an insulting remark like that would persuade me to hop back into bed for a little convenient sex?"

His eyes glittered in the shadows. "How did I insult you? I was trying to tell you that I don't give a damn about the art collection."

"That's supposed to make me feel all warm and fuzzy?" Her voice rose. "Telling me that you still think there's a good possibility that I defrauded you, but that you're willing to overlook it because you've got a hard-on is your idea of irresistible sweet talk?"

"That's not what I meant."

"That's sure what it sounded like."

"It came out all wrong." He took one more step and stopped at the edge of the bed. His hands closed around her shoulders. "I meant that I didn't care about that art collection."

"You don't care about it tonight, but how will you feel tomorrow when you're no longer trying to get laid?"

His hands tightened around her shoulders. "I'm going to feel just fine tomorrow because I know you didn't cheat me."

"Oh, yeah? How can you be sure of that?"

"Because I trust you," he roared.

"What makes you think you can trust me? Nothing's changed in this equation. I'm still the same woman I was when you first met me. I'm still the art consultant with the shady past. You haven't yet got any confirmation that the art and antiques in your new hotel aren't fakes, frauds, and forgeries."

"You're wrong. Things have changed. You and I are in this together."

"What does that change?"

"Everything." His voice softened. "Hell, I wouldn't be here tonight if I didn't trust you."

"And just when did you come to the conclusion that you could trust me?"

To her astonishment, he fell silent for a few seconds. She sensed his anger transmuting into something that was probably infinitely more dangerous.

"I don't know," he said simply. "I've probably known it for twelve years."

"What are you talking about?" She stared at him in disbelief. "Twelve years ago you only saw me for a few minutes. You were in a rage at the time. I'm surprised you even remembered me."

"I remembered you the instant I saw you again." He searched her face. "In fact, I never really forgot you or the way you looked that night when you told me to get out of the house. You were so thin. Nothing but skin and bone and big, haunted eyes. You were scared to death of me, weren't you?"

"I was scared of a lot of things in those days."

"But you didn't run and hide. You came down those stairs, grabbed the phone, ordered me out of the house, and threatened to call the cops."

"And you left."

"Of course I left." His mouth curved wryly. "I knew you'd do just what you said you'd do. I knew you'd call the cops. I could see it in your eyes."

"And I knew that you'd do just what you said you would do, too," she whispered. "I knew that someday you would come back."

"When you looked me in the eye and told me that I was going to discover that Avalon Resorts, Inc., was the proud owner of the best collection of Art Deco on the West Coast, I believed you, too," he said. "But I didn't admit it because I was pissed at the time."

"Where you angry because Edward had asked me to consult for him without telling you about my past?"

"No." He raised his hands from her shoulders and sank his fingers into her hair. "I was mad because the minute I saw you, I knew that you would be standing between me and Lloyd Kenyon again. And I didn't want you involved."

She let the sheet fall from her fingers and reached up to clasp his wrists. "Why not?"

His hands sank deeper into her hair. "Because I knew that I wouldn't be able to get at Kenyon if it meant hurting you."

"Oh, Trask." She smiled tremulously. "I didn't understand any of that when you said you didn't care about your art collection."

"Not your fault. I didn't do a great job of explaining myself. That kind of thing tends to happen to me when I get into—" He broke off. "Never mind. It doesn't matter. Everything's okay now."

She searched his face. "Is it?"

"Isn't it?"

She turned the possibilities over in her mind. "There's an ancient bit of metaphysical philosophy that probably applies to this situation."

"Okay, I'll bite. What is it?"

"Life is short. Eat dessert first."

His smile was slow and deliberate. "That kind of metaphysics I can grasp."

He bent his head and brushed his mouth lightly across hers. Alexa held her breath, but she did not resist. She was conscious of the heat in him. She could feel the pulse of her own desire.

He put one knee on the bed. "You were right when you said my seduction line was lousy tonight. You were also right about something else."

"What's that?"

"I do have a serious hard-on. How did you know? Was I that obvious?"

"Uh-huh." She settled her hands on his waist. "You forgot to zip your pants."

He glanced down, groaned, and rested his forehead on hers. "Just call me Mr. Cool."

She moved her fingertips lower, until she touched the heavy, rigid length of him. "I think hot would be a more accurate description."

"You can say that again." He eased her onto her back and sprawled heavily on top of her. "Does this mean that you're willing to overlook my crummy line about the art collection?"

"It's the thought that counts."

He kissed her, long and deep. A light, delicate shiver passed through her. A curious euphoria bubbled up inside.

"My thoughts were pure," he said against her throat.

"Were they?"

"Sort of."

She kissed his bare shoulder, and then she moved her lips through the crisp hair on his chest.

She made the kisses last. She experimented with making them wet. And then she used her teeth, very lightly. A shudder went through him. She felt the sleek muscles of his back flex and grow taut.

She savored the knowledge that she could have such an unmistakable effect on him.

Wild woman lives.

He slid one hand up along her leg to the inside of her thigh. She felt open and vulnerable. Probably because she was open and vulnerable, she thought. But it was okay. For now. Wild woman could handle it.

He sank two fingers into her.

Her whole body convulsed.

"On the other hand," she got out in a thick whisper, "my thoughts aren't pure at all."

"I can't tell you how happy I am to hear that."

He rolled onto his back and took her with him. A glorious excitement spiraled through her. She flattened her hands on his chest, rejoicing in the heat and strength in him.

After a while she kissed a path down his body, all the way to his sleek belly and beyond. He groaned and sucked in air.

He caught her up and pulled her down so that she sat astride him.

He eased himself into her, filling her and stretching her until the sensation became unbearable, until something inside her exploded in a shower of brilliant sparks.

The part of her that had felt open and vulnerable earlier, reveled in the sense of feminine power that swept through her now.

"You were wrong about one thing," he whispered. "I'm definitely going to be thinking about getting laid again tomorrow."

Trask stirred a long time later. He opened one eye and saw that it was still dark outside. He closed the eye and gently shifted the weight of Alexa's soft, warm body until she nestled more snugly against him. He could get addicted to the scent of her, he decided. Maybe he was already hooked.

"Alexa?"

"Hmmm?"

"Are you awake?"

"No."

"I just wanted to make a point."

"Keep it short."

"I will." He fell silent.

"So?" She stretched out one leg and wriggled her toes against his calf. "What's your point?"

"You can't call it a torrid one-night stand anymore."

It was her turn to go quiet for a while.

"You're right," she said eventually. "Is there a term for a torrid two-night stand?"

"Yeah." He leaned over her and kissed her until he knew that he had her full attention. "It's called a relationship."

25

Alexa felt Trask leave the bed shortly before dawn. She opened her eyes. He was headed toward her bathroom.

"Trask?"

He paused in the doorway. "Go back to sleep."

She saw that he had his pants in his hands. "Where are you going?"

"I have to take care of some business." He continued on into the shower.

"Business? At this hour? What are you talking about?" She tossed aside the covers and bounded out of bed. "Hold it right there, that's my bathroom. You're not going in there until you tell me what's happening here."

He switched on the light and scowled at her. "I was going to leave a note."

"Oh, sure. A note. That's just great. Saying you'll leave a note is right up there with promising to call me sometime."

"Okay, okay." He rubbed his stubbled chin. "I

was hoping you wouldn't notice that I was gone until later, but since you're awake . . ."

She eyed him. "This had better be good."

He shrugged. "I woke up a few minutes ago and it occurred to me that the job of finding Liz Guthrie might move a little quicker if I took a look around her place. There might be something there that would point to where she went. Something it will take Okuda much longer to find with his computer."

She felt her jaw unhinge. "Good grief. Are you telling me that you're trying to sneak out of here so that you can go break into Liz's house?"

"Put like that, it lacks a certain air of innocence, doesn't it? But in a nutshell, yeah, that's about it. I was afraid that if you realized what I was going to do, you'd insist on coming along."

"You got that right." She marched past him into the bathroom. "I'll be ready in ten minutes."

She stepped into the shower and reflected on the vast sense of relief that was welling up inside her. The fact that she was about to accompany Trask on a little jaunt that could land them both in jail was a mere bagatelle compared to her fear that he had been walking out after their torrid two-night stand.

Correction: Torrid two-night *relationship*.

"Trask?"

He got into the shower beside her and reached for the soap. "Yeah?"

"What if Liz is home?"

"In that case, I've got some questions for her."

An hour later Alexa stood with Trask in Liz Guthrie's kitchen. She was aware that, technically speaking, dawn had arrived, but no one would ever know it here in the depths of Shadow Canyon. Outside the window, the trees that surrounded the house were dark, hulking specters.

A chill of unease swept through her as she studied the darkened kitchen. She grimaced at the smell of rotting garbage. "So much for hoping Liz would be back by now."

"She definitely left in a hurry. Didn't empty the trash. Forgot to lock all the doors and windows." Trask swept the beam of a small flashlight across the kitchen counter. "The question is why."

"You think something scared her?"

"Something or someone."

Trask glanced back over his shoulder. "You okay?"

"Yes." She was lying through her teeth, but she was not about to admit that part of her was braced to see a faceless figure armed with a knife explode out of a closet.

"I told you it would be a bad idea for you to come with me," Trask said.

"Yes, you did. But I'm here, so there's absolutely no point saying I-told-you-so. Let's just get this done."

His brows rose. "We're a little tense this morning, aren't we?"

"We haven't had our morning tea," she reminded him. "What, exactly, are *we* looking for?"

"I'm not sure." Trask moved slowly into the gloom-filled hall. "But in keeping with the old adage about following the money, I'd very much like to find some business files."

Alexa opened a cupboard with gloved fingers.

"You're still convinced that whatever is going on is business-related?"

"Dimensions Institute is, first and foremost, a business. And like I keep saying, this thing is linked to Dimensions. Got to be."

She could not argue that point, she decided. She took out her own small penlight, switched it on, and trailed after Trask as he explored the dark, silent house.

"The officer who responded to my call was right," she said, taking in the sight of the expensive-looking stereo in the living room. "There's no sign that anything has been disturbed. No wonder he told Strood that I must have been hallucinating."

"He didn't tell Strood that you were seeing things."

"Yes, he did. I overheard them talking when I came back from the ladies' room at the police station. He implied I was an hysterical female who had spooked at a shadow. Don't bother to deny it. Strood probably said as much to you."

Trask opened a closet door.

"Didn't he?" Alexa repeated grimly.

Trask closed the door. "He did say something to that effect. I told him he was an idiot."

She was oddly touched. "Thanks. I appreciate your faith in my mental health."

"Hey, we paranoid conspiracy theorists have to stick together. After all, they're out to get us." He opened a door off the hall and aimed the flashlight inside. "We're in luck. There's a desk and some file cabinets in here. Looks like a home office."

"Help yourself. I'll go check out the bedroom."

"Remember, don't move anything," he said as he disappeared into the small office.

"Don't worry, I've read enough mystery and suspense novels to know how to do this. I'll be careful."

She walked down the hall and stopped in front of an open door. There was enough of Shadow Canyon's perpetual twilight coming through the windows to reveal a bed and a chest of drawers.

A squeak sounded behind her. She jumped and swung around so quickly she nearly lost her balance. Another dose of adrenaline poured through her, making her palms go cold.

"Trask?" she whispered.

"What?" His voice came softly through the open door of the office. It was accompanied by another squeak.

She realized that what she had heard was the sound of a metal file cabinet drawer being opened.

"Nothing." She exhaled deeply, tightened her grip on the flashlight, and stepped into the bedroom.

Her first impression was that there was nothing out of the ordinary. The bed had been made. The closet doors were neatly closed.

She used the flashlight to illuminate the titles of the volumes on the nightstand. *Dimensions in Our Lives. A Daily Journey Through Dimensions. Losing Weight the Dimensions Way.*

"You're really into this Dimensions thing, aren't you, Liz?" she whispered.

She crossed the room to the closet and cautiously opened the doors. The flashlight beam revealed a large gap between a pair of dark blue slacks and a little black cocktail dress. It was as if someone had grabbed all of the garments that had hung between the pants and the dress and yanked them out of the closet.

As if someone had packed in a huge hurry.

There was also a large, empty space on the shelf above the rod. It looked to be about the right size for a suitcase.

Turning, she walked quickly into the adjoining bathroom. She opened the medicine cabinet and aimed the light at the shelves. They were virtually empty. Only a box of ear swabs and a half-filled bottle of mouthwash remained.

She went back through the bedroom and out into the hall. She stuck her head around the doorway.

"I think you're right," she said. "It looks like Liz not only left in a hurry, she intends to stay gone for a while. A bunch of clothes and all of her toiletries and cosmetics are missing."

Trask did not look up from the contents of one of the file cabinets. "Something scared her off, all right."

"The guy with the knife, probably."

"Maybe. The only thing we can be sure of at the moment is that it's going to be impossible to get Strood to take this seriously. There's no hard evidence that anything's wrong here."

She realized he was fully occupied with Liz's files, so she turned and continued to the end of the hall.

One of the shoji screen panels stood open. Her stomach flip-flopped when she realized that the panel had been left in that position by the intruder. It was proof of her story but not the kind that Strood would buy.

The dim light of the Shadow Canyon dawn filtered through the pale drapes of the meditation room. Nothing had altered here. The rose-colored crystal sat in the same position on the low table. The pillow was exactly where it had been the last time she was in this room.

She played the flashlight beam around the small chamber. It splashed across the crowded bookcase. A chill of awareness went through her.

Trask came up quietly behind her. "What is it?"

"I'm not sure. This room feels different."

She ran the flashlight over the bookcase again. The various Dimensions titles still stood packed together on the shelves. She was about to give up when it hit her.

"The journal is gone," she said.

"What are you talking about?"

She turned slowly to look at him. "Liz's Dimensions personal journal. It's gone. If she hasn't been back, then *he* must have taken it."

"The guy with the knife?"

"Yes. But why on earth would he do that?"

"Beats me. What's a Dimensions personal journal?"

"It's used for recording your progress toward a heightened state of peace and serenity. You get one when you take a course at the Institute. Liz's was sitting right there on top of that bookcase yesterday. Now it's gone."

"What kind of stuff would she record in the journal?"

"I don't know. A journal is supposed to be a very personal thing. It's a sort of diary. Liz probably used it to jot down her feelings about her meditation exercises."

"How about the name of her personal meditation

guide?" Trask asked thoughtfully. "Would she have written that down?"

Alexa swallowed as she realized where he was headed with that question. Liz's personal meditation guide could well have been the last person to see her before she disappeared.

"Yes." She took a deep breath. "Now that you mention it, she might have made some reference to her guide. Oh, lord, Trask, it's just the kind of thing that she *would* have put into a personal journal. Do you think it was one of the Institute's meditation guides who chased me with that knife?"

"No way to know. But if all he took was Liz Guthrie's journal, there must be something in it he wanted."

"Do you realize what this means?" Alexa spun around to face him. "If we can find out who her personal meditation guide is, we'll have a handle on this thing."

"Maybe. But in the meantime, some interesting new questions have been raised."

"What do you mean?"

Trask held up a buff-colored folder. "According to the contents of this file and some of the others in her office, Liz and Dean Guthrie not only continued to sleep together after the divorce, they invested together."

"What?"

Trask smiled with the grim satisfaction of the hunter who has sighted prey. "It looks like they were partners in several ventures. Apparently they decided not to let a little thing like a divorce spoil a good financial relationship."

Alexa felt her mouth go dry. "Were they both

involved in the new Dimensions Santa Fe project? The one you said Guthrie wanted to pull the plug on?"

"Probably." Trask tucked the folder under his arm and led the way down the hall. "There are no records on that particular venture. The guy who took the journal probably took that file, too. Hell, he could have taken several files. There's no way to know."

"You're overlooking the possibility that Liz herself took some of her files with her when she left yesterday."

"True." The gem-hard gleam in Trask's eyes did not waver. "There's one more thing I haven't mentioned. If she and Guthrie were partners in the Dimensions project in Santa Fe and if that partnership was structured the same way their other ventures were, then a very interesting fact emerges."

"Which is?"

"Liz Guthrie now controls everything Dean Guthrie left behind, including his investment portfolio."

Alexa absorbed that. "Maybe someone got rid of Dean because he knew that Liz would inherit and he figured he could control Liz."

"You're getting very good at this conspiracy theory stuff. I may have to promote you."

"To what? Head Conspiracy Buff? No thanks."

"Suit yourself." Trask tightened his grip on the folder and started toward the door. "But as far as I'm concerned, everything in this file just adds weight to the evidence against Webster Bell. He's got motive and he's got opportunity. He's also got plenty of minions out there at the Institute."

"I know this doesn't look good for Bell." Alexa hurried after him. "But I have a hard time picturing him as a murderer."

"Maybe that's why he gets away with murder. But if I'm right, I can tell you one more thing."

"What?"

Trask glanced back over his shoulder. "Liz Guthrie may have bigger problems than having her personal finances controlled by Webster Bell."

"What's worse than having your money controlled by a weird metaphysical guru who wants you to pour all of your cash into his Institute?"

"Getting murdered by a weird metaphysical guru who decides he doesn't need you around anymore," Trask said.

Alexa chilled. She paused to close the door. "There would be no point in killing Liz. If you're right, she's the goose that lays the golden eggs. If something happens to her, there won't be any more eggs."

"There would be lots of golden eggs for Dimensions if Webster Bell has managed to persuade Liz to leave everything to the Institute in her will."

A sense of dread settled on Alexa as she went down the steps. "People do stuff like that, don't they? Put foundations and universities and trusts and things into their wills?"

"All the time."

"Maybe that's why she took off for parts unknown."

"Maybe," Trask agreed. "Disappearing would certainly be the logical thing to do under the circumstances. At least until she gets her will changed."

26

Trask walked into the hotel lobby shortly after ten and found it thronged. The milling guests were preparing to board a gleaming bus parked in the circular drive. A placard in the front window of the vehicle announced that it was bound for a tour of local "Hot Spots."

Only in Avalon would the words *hot spots* refer to points of metaphysical interest, Trask thought. In any other resort town the phrase would imply a scenic tour of trendy bars and nightclubs.

"'Morning, Trask." Pete Santana greeted him with the jaunty smile of an innkeeper with a full house. "I've been looking for you. Thought you'd like to see this." He raised his hand to reveal the newspapers he held. "We've got full-page feature spreads in both the Phoenix and the Tucson papers. They love us."

"Let me see those." Trask took the papers from him. Both were folded back to the articles on the resort.

A NEW JEWEL IN AVALON'S CROWN

Avalon Resorts, Inc., opened its newest and most luxurious hotel and spa in, appropriately enough, Avalon, AZ, last week. The gala reception that marked the occasion was hosted by the corporation's president and CEO, John Laird Trask.

"It was time that we came back to where it all started," Trask stated in an interview before the festivities. "Turning the old Avalon Mansion into a resort was a long-held dream of my father's. What you see here tonight is his vision made into reality."

Trask ran his eye quickly down the column until he spotted the words *Art Deco.* Then he paused to read more carefully.

The resort houses the corporation's new collection of Art Deco. The items were assembled by Edward Vale, a well-known consultant to businesses and wealthy collectors. The collection drew several prominent figures in the Southwest art world to the reception.

Members of the Avalon City Council were enthusiastic about the economic impact of the new resort . . .

Trask stopped reading and refolded the papers. A single paragraph in a daily newspaper noting the hotel's collection was not going to be enough for Alexa. She needed more than that to make her big comeback.

He handed the papers back to Pete. "Looks like we're off and running."

Pete grinned. "You can say that again. They called the resort a desert fantasy. We're getting a fresh surge in convention bookings."

Trask inclined his head to indicate the crowded lobby. "Looks good."

Pete studied the guests with undisguised satisfaction. "The Avalon Spring Festival is a huge draw, of course. We opened at the perfect time. Avalon is hot and getting hotter."

"Dad was right all along." Trask started toward the staircase. "It was just his timing that was off. It always was."

He went up the steps to the second floor and walked the length of the west wing to the door of his suite. He exchanged winks with *Dancing Satyr* as he opened the door.

"You're looking better every day."

He let himself into the room and went straight to the desk to check his messages. There were three from the Seattle office. He listened to them, concluded they were of minor nuisance value only, and erased them.

He took the time to grind some of the dark-roasted beans from his precious stockpile and made himself a decent cup of coffee.

Then he picked up the phone and dialed Phil Okuda's number.

Phil came on the line immediately.

"It's Trask."

"I was afraid of that," Phil said dryly. "I still haven't got a lead on Liz Guthrie, if that's what you're calling about. She's definitely trying to hide.

None of her friends have heard from her. There's no close family. Looks like she's using cash only, not credit cards or checks or anything else that can be traced easily."

"Can you find her if she's living on cash?"

"Sure. Just takes a little longer, that's all."

"Put some extra people on it, Phil. I think we need to get to her fast."

"What's the problem?"

"It's possible that someone else is also trying to find her. I think he wants her dead. If not now, then in the very near future."

"Talk to the cops?" Phil asked.

"They think she just took off for a little vacation. Anything new on Bell?"

"Nothing that we don't already know," Phil said. "He looks legit. Can't say the same for his pal, Foster Radstone, though."

"Is that so?" Trask settled in a chair. "What have you got on him?"

"For starters, until he went to work for Dimensions, he used to go by the name of Fletcher Richards."

"Any idea why he changed his name?"

"Probably because the Florida authorities are looking for him. In his previous career as a financial planner, he apparently bilked a bunch of senior citizens out of their life's savings."

Dylan tapped a spoon against a glass to get the attention of the small crowd gathered in Café Solstice.

"Hear ye, hear ye, this meeting of the Avalon

Plaza Business Association will now come to order," he intoned.

Alexa glanced around, swiftly counting heads. "Joanna isn't here yet."

Stewart looked up from a large tub filled with loose tea leaves that he was blending by hand. "She didn't come in today. Left her assistant in charge of the shop. I don't think she was feeling well."

"Joanna's been acting weird for quite a while now," Brad remarked.

There was a rumble of assent from the other shopkeepers.

"I'm starting to worry about her," Margie Ferris, the proprietor of the toy shop, said. "I wonder if one of us should say something to her brother."

"Talk to Webster?" Dylan frowned. "I don't know about that. Joanna wouldn't appreciate our interference in something this personal. Besides, she and Webster are really close. If she wanted to discuss something with him, she would."

Margie's expression darkened. "We can't just ignore the fact that she may be sliding into some sort of clinical depression."

Alexa studied the familiar faces around her. They were all concerned, she thought. But no one could think of the next move.

Dylan shifted slightly. "Tell you what, if you feel it's the right thing to do, I'll call Webster this evening after work and have a heart-to-heart talk with him. We've known each other for years. Maybe I can convince him that Joanna needs professional help."

Stewart and the others nodded quickly, relieved that someone had volunteered to take action.

"Okay, then, that's settled." Dylan picked up a stack of papers. "Back to business. Alexa just gave me some handouts from the Festival Committee. You'll find the final schedule for the downtown activities. There are no major changes for us. The shops here in the Plaza will stay open for the Gallery Walk until seven tomorrow night, as planned. Any questions?"

Alexa listened absently to the handful of comments that followed. Her thoughts churned with images of Liz's shadowy meditation room. The sense of gathering urgency that had been pressing down on her since she and Trask had searched Liz's house that morning was becoming a heavy weight on her shoulders.

When the meeting adjourned ten minutes later, she picked up her cup of tea, bid her friends a good morning and walked toward the door.

"Should be a good day," Brad Vasquez said as he followed her outside. "The town is jammed with tourists. This is far and away the biggest festival weekend Avalon has ever had. The opening of the new resort really gave it a boost."

Alexa glanced toward the door of Crystal Rainbow. "Joanna must have been feeling very unwell not to show up on what could be one of the busiest days of the year outside of the Christmas season."

"You can say that again. Speaking of opening up, I'd better get moving. See you when the rush is over, Alexa."

"Right." She went down the walk to the door of Elegant Relic.

In spite of the warm sunshine and the festive

crowd of shoppers that consumed her morning, the sense of disquiet grew stronger.

At eleven o'clock she picked up the phone and called Joanna's home number. Relief shot through her when Joanna answered on the sixth or seventh ring. Her voice sounded slurred and flat.

"Hello?"

"Joanna? It's Alexa. Are you okay?"

"No sleep last night," Joanna mumbled. "Took some more pills this morning."

"Do you need anything? I can stop by after work."

"Tea," Joanna whispered. "I'm out of my special blend. I'd give anything for a cup."

"I'll bring you some."

"Thanks." There was a pause. "Alexa?"

"Yes?"

"Never mind. Can't explain now. Too tired."

The phone clattered loudly as it was dropped back into the cradle. The line went dead.

Two hours later there was a short lull in the tides of shoppers. Alexa stepped outside to get some iced tea for herself and Kerry.

Café Solstice was doing a landslide business. Alexa ordered the teas and a package of Joanna's special blend from one of the counter assistants.

"You look like you're swamped, Ted."

"We are." Ted gave her change. "And wouldn't you know it? The boss had to go take care of some problem at the bank. Right at the height of the noon rush."

"Hang in there," Alexa said. "It will all be over on Sunday."

Ted grinned. "That's what I keep telling myself."

Alexa picked up the Styrofoam cups and the package of Joanna's tea and walked back to Elegant Relic. Kerry was in the process of boxing up two medium-sized gargoyles for a customer.

Alexa waited until the transaction had been completed. Then she picked up the phone and called Joanna again.

She counted ten rings. This time there was no answer.

Alexa's anxiety deepened. She wondered how many pills Joanna had taken.

She couldn't stand it any longer.

She replaced the phone and looked at Kerry. "I hate to leave you alone, today of all days, but do you think you can handle things by yourself for an hour? I'm really worried about Joanna. I can't get her on the phone. I'm going to run out to her house and see if she's okay."

"No problem," Kerry said. "I'm at my best when I'm swamped with customers. And when I know that my day off is coming."

Alexa glanced at the clock. "I should be back by four at the latest."

"I'll be fine. Hope Joanna's okay."

"I'm sure she is. See you in an hour or so."

Alexa collected her satchel, walked through her cluttered stock room, and went out the rear door into the alley.

In the parking lot she found her Camry, opened the door, and removed the reflective sun shield from the inside of the front window.

She had been invited to Joanna's house in the hills on several occasions. The trip took less than twenty minutes. She spent the entire time telling herself to calm down, that nothing was wrong, that Joanna was just feeling a little blue because Guthrie's accident had brought back sad memories.

But as she drove the winding road up into the hills above Avalon her unease sharpened with every mile. Maybe she should have come out here earlier.

Joanna's home had been designed by the same architect responsible for the Dimensions Institute. It was all sleek angles and planes of glass. From its isolated hillside perch it commanded a sweeping view of the town and the rust-red landscape beyond. There were no close neighbors. Joanna had always treasured her privacy.

The first thing Alexa saw when she pulled into the drive was a Lexus. That answered one question, at any rate. Joanna was home.

She got out of the Camry, walked across the wide deck to the front door, and rang the bell.

When she did not get an answer, she pounded loudly on the wooden panels.

"Joanna, it's me, Alexa. Please open the door. I'm worried about you."

She waited for a response. The desert silence closed in around the house. When it became clear that Joanna was not going to respond, she walked around to the kitchen windows and peered inside.

Joanna lay crumpled on the tile floor. The folds of a turquoise blue terry cloth robe swirled around her. A bottle of pills sat on the counter. An empty mug and a small package of tea bearing the Café Solstice label sat next to it. Joanna had evidently found some of her special blend in her cupboard, after all.

"Joanna."

Alexa rushed to the kitchen door. It was locked.

For a few seconds she thought wildly about smashing a window. Then she remembered that this was the same Joanna who hid her spare shop key beneath a flower pot outside the door of Crystal Rainbow.

She glanced around. Sure enough, there was a large flowering cactus cradled in a heavy terra cotta pot near the door.

She found the key beneath the pot, shoved it into the lock, and twisted the knob.

The sulfurous, rotten-egg smell of gas wafted through the opening. She recalled Joanna telling her that she'd installed a gas tank when she'd put in a new range. The gas company had not yet run any lines out to this sparsely populated neighborhood.

"Dear God. Joanna."

She threw the door open, took a deep breath of fresh air, and dashed inside. How much gas did it take to create a danger of explosion? she wondered. She knew very little about the hazards of a gas leak. Her own home was all electric.

She seized Joanna by the ankles and heaved with all of her strength. Joanna wasn't much heavier than *Dancing Satyr*. Alexa got her out into the fresh air on the deck.

"Joanna, please don't be dead."

Frantically she searched for a pulse and felt light-headed with relief when she found a weak one.

"Joanna, can you hear me? Talk to me. What happened? Did you fall?"

Joanna groaned. Her hand twitched, but her eyes did not open. "Don't let them get me. Please. *Help me.*"

The panic in Joanna's slurred voice sent another

jolt of fear through Alexa. "Don't move. I'm going to call for help." She looked around for the satchel she had dropped a moment earlier, found it, and retrieved her cell phone.

"Alexa?" Joanna's lashes fluttered. "What're you doing here?"

"It's okay." Alexa stabbed the emergency number. "Help is on the way."

"Too late." Joanna gave up the attempt to open her eyes. "Too late. The monsters."

The 911 operator was rattling off a string of questions in Alexa's ear. She tried to concentrate on answering them.

"No, I don't know what happened." Alexa glanced back into the kitchen. "There's gas inside the house. We're outside. I've got the door open now. I see a bottle of pills."

"Any idea what kind of drugs?"

"Prescription stuff. Tranquilizers, I think. She said something about taking some earlier."

"The medics are on the way. Try to keep her awake and alert until they get there. Better not go back inside the house."

"Right." Alexa disconnected. She leaned anxiously over Joanna. "Tell me what happened."

"Monsters." Joanna's lashes fluttered again in sudden agitation. "It's with the monsters."

"What's with the monsters?"

"Get them away from me. Do something. They're going to kill me. *Get them away.*"

"Joanna, listen to me, you're hallucinating. There's nothing here."

"I can see them." Joanna's voice was shrill with terror now. She moved one hand in an ineffectual gesture apparently designed to fend off some unseen horrors. "Stop them. Please, make them go away."

Alexa clasped Joanna's hand very tightly. "I won't let them get you, I promise."

Joanna blinked rapidly and then, suddenly, disconcertingly looked up at Alexa with dazed, frightened eyes. "I'm sorry. Couldn't think of anything else. I was so afraid."

"Afraid of what?"

"That it was happening all over again." Joanna closed her eyes. "And it is. It is, don't you see?"

"What's happening?"

Joanna writhed and clawed at the air. "They're eating me. Make them stop."

Alexa heard a siren in the distance. She tightened her grip on Joanna's hand. "I won't let them hurt you, Joanna."

"Promise?" Tears leaked out of the corners of Joanna's eyes.

"I promise." Alexa heard a car pull into the drive. "The ambulance is here, Joanna. You're going to be fine."

Joanna moaned. "I'm sorry. I was desperate. Couldn't think of anything else to do. I'm sorry."

Someone knocked loudly. Alexa jumped to her feet.

"We're back here," she shouted. "On the deck."

"Don't forget." Joanna stared bleary-eyed up at Alexa. "The monsters. Be careful. Be very careful."

"I'll be careful," Alexa said soothingly.

Two medics swept past her, efficient and businesslike. It was only then that she saw who else had arrived.

"Trask. What are you doing here?"

"We had an agreement, remember?" His face was set in stark lines. "You weren't supposed to go off on your own."

"I could have sworn that rule applied only to nights. Besides, I wasn't exactly alone. I was with Joanna."

"This is not a good time to discuss the fine points of this partnership. I'm not in what you might call an expansive mood. What the hell is going on?"

"An interesting question."

He paused and then glanced through the open door. "Is that gas?"

"I think so." Alexa watched the medics as they moved around Joanna. "She recently had a gas range installed. Something must have gone wrong."

Half an hour later Trask picked up the phone on the table next to the sofa in Joanna's living room. The smell of rotten eggs was gone now. He'd shut off the gas at the outside tank. All of the windows and doors stood wide open.

He glanced at the number in the phone book he had just consulted. His call was answered on the second ring.

"The Dimensions Institute." The voice was warm, welcoming, filled with peace and serenity. "May I help you?"

"This is Trask. Avalon Resorts, Inc." He did not infuse his voice with any peace and serenity. "Get Webster Bell on the line."

There was a short, startled pause. Trask glanced at Alexa. She was standing at the window watching the ambulance drive off toward town.

"I'm very sorry, Mr. Trask, but Mr. Bell is unavailable at the moment. He's giving a seminar. We never interrupt him when he's teaching."

"Get him," Trask said. "Now."

"Uh, one moment please."

The receptionist put her hand over the receiver. Trask heard her speak to someone else. She sounded stressed.

She came back on the line a few seconds later. "Please hold, Mr. Trask."

Another voice came on the line. "This is Foster Radstone. What seems to be the problem, Trask?"

"The problem," Trask said deliberately, "is that I just watched two medics load Joanna Bell into the back of an ambulance."

"Joanna?" Shock disturbed Foster's cushioned tones. "Are you certain? What's wrong? Is she——?"

"She's alive, if that's what you're asking. Barely. Get Bell."

"Yes, of course. Hold on a moment."

There was another short silence before Webster Bell picked up the phone. Trask realized that Foster had not hung up. He was still on the line, listening.

"What's this about Joanna?" Webster asked urgently. "Is she all right?"

"She's on her way to the hospital," Trask said. "Alexa Chambers found her here at her house. It looks like she took some tranquilizers and there was a problem with her new gas system. She's hallucinating, but she's alive and partially conscious. The medics said that was a good sign."

"My God," Webster whispered. "She didn't . . . That is, they don't think it was deliberate, do they?"

"I don't know," Trask said quietly.

"I knew she was under stress, but I had no idea that she . . . Never mind. Foster? Are you still on the line? I've got to get to the hospital."

Foster answered in soothing tones. "I'll drive you, Webster. We can be there in fifteen minutes."

"Yes. All right. I'll meet you at the car."

There was a click as Webster hung up his extension, but the phone did not go dead. Foster spoke once more.

"Trask? Did you say Alexa found Joanna?"

"Yes." Trask watched Alexa turn away from the open window. She looked at a stack of magazines on the end table. The sudden stiffening in her shoulders was visible from across the room.

"Where is she?" Foster asked.

"Alexa? She's here with me."

"You're both at Joanna's place?"

"That's right."

On the other side of the room, Alexa finally moved. She walked toward the pile of magazines as if drawn by magnets. When she reached the table she leaned down and picked up the glossy journal on top of the heap.

"I don't understand," Foster said. "How did Alexa happen to find her?"

"Long story. Hadn't you better get moving? Bell said he'd meet you at the car."

"Yes. Right. I've got to go. But if you're at Joanna's house . . ."

"Don't worry, the gas is shut off and the house has been aired out. Alexa and I will lock up before we leave."

"Uh, well, thanks."

Trask replaced the phone. Alexa did not look up

from the magazine in her hand. She stared at the cover with an expression of fixed intensity.

"Radstone is driving Bell to the hospital," Trask said. "I told him we'd lock up the house."

Alexa finally raised her eyes from the magazine. There was an odd expression on her face. As if she'd just seen a ghost, Trask thought.

"How did Bell react?" she asked quietly.

Trask shrugged. "Like you'd expect any brother to react to the news that his sister may have tried to take her own life."

"She was hallucinating," Alexa said slowly.

"I heard. Sounded like she was really out of it."

Alexa looked down at the cover of the magazine. "She kept talking about monsters. But once or twice she seemed to recognize me. She tried to apologize."

"For what?"

"I didn't understand. When I tried to find out why, she went back to raving about some monsters that were trying to kill her. She was terrified."

Trask thought about the anxiety he had seen in Joanna's face the day she had met with him at the hotel. "She warned me to let the past stay buried."

"I think Guthrie's death really unnerved her."

"Maybe it's more than that," Trask said bluntly. "Maybe she knows something about what's going on. Or maybe she only has some suspicions. Either way, I doubt if she'll talk to us because of her brother."

"Her first loyalty is to Webster," Alexa agreed. "If she thinks he's involved in something wrong she would be torn about what to do."

"That might explain the stress that led to the overdose of tranquilizers."

"It might also explain this." She held up the magazine in her hand.

Trask studied the glossy cover. It featured a photo of a bronze nude. "What's that?"

"*TCA*," she whispered.

Trask frowned. "What?"

"*Twentieth-Century Artifact.* A year-old edition. This is the issue that printed the first rumors of the McClelland Gallery forgeries. It was the article in this magazine that linked my name to the scandal."

The implications hit him. He crossed the room, took the magazine out of her hands, and read the lead beneath the picture of the bronze. *Fakes and Frauds at McClelland?*

"Are you sure?" he asked.

"Trust me, I will never forget that cover as long as I live. I see it in my dreams." Alexa took back the magazine and flipped it open to a page that had been turned down at the corner. "Joanna is not into twentieth-century art. And this magazine is more than twelve months out of date. I can think of only one reason why she might have it here in her living room."

Trask read the title centered above the article. *Rumors of Fraud Strike McClelland. Assistant Implicated.* He met Alexa's eyes. "You said Joanna tried to apologize for something?"

"Yes. Do you think it's possible that she was the one who made those late-night calls?"

"Sort of looks that way, doesn't it? But why?"

"She must have realized that she couldn't stop you from digging into whatever she thinks is buried here in Avalon," Alexa said. "So she tried to frighten me into staying away from you. I think she wanted to protect me."

27

Trask leaned back in the lounger and looked up at the stars that gleamed above Alexa's patio. "What with all the excitement today, I haven't had a chance to tell you a couple of things. The first stories on the resort appeared in the Tucson and Phoenix papers."

Alexa stretched out in the adjacent lounger. "Good press, I hope?"

"Yeah."

"Did they call your hotel a fantasy come true?"

"What else?" He paused deliberately. "The articles mention the art collection."

"That's nice."

"Not excited?"

"I'm not going to get excited until *TCA* does a story that calls the collection the finest display of Deco outside of New York."

"I was afraid of that." He paused. "You don't think you're expecting a little too much under the circumstances?"

"No. The Avalon collection *is* the best outside of New York. One of the best in the country. When

TCA acknowledges that, I can go public and take the credit."

Trask contemplated the stars while he considered various strategies for bringing leverage to bear on the publishers of *Twentieth-Century Artifact*. He did not know many people in the world of magazine publishing, but he knew people who had contacts in that world.

"Don't even think about it, Trask."

He assumed his most innocent expression. "About what?"

"About trying to intimidate *TCA* into printing a rave review of the hotel's collection."

"You never let me have any fun."

"It's a sweet thought," she assured him. "But I doubt if it will work, and it could easily backfire. I don't need any more nasty press, thank you very much."

"You underestimate me, my dear. I know how to apply pressure in very subtle ways."

"I'll just bet you do." She smiled. "Forget *TCA*. We've got bigger problems on our hands at the moment. What's your other news?"

"Radstone's a professional con man."

She sniffed. "He always speaks highly of you."

"I'm serious, Alexa. The guy used to go by the name of Fletcher Richards. Ripped off a bunch of seniors with some scam he ran as a so-called financial planner."

Her head came around swiftly. She stared at him. "Are you serious?"

"Yes."

"I can't believe it. He's Webster's righthand man." She waved a hand. "I *dated* the guy."

"Until I saved you from his clutches by keeping you too busy with my art collection," he said. "Makes you wonder if there might be something to this metaphysical stuff after all, doesn't it?"

She looked at him askance. "I beg your pardon?"

He moved one hand in a broad arc. "You know, it's as if there was some mysterious force at work all along."

"Mysterious force?"

"Trying to bring us together," he explained.

"I suppose that is a point of view."

"Right. It's my point of view and I'm sticking with it." Satisfied, he decided to move on. "Tell me again why you drove all the way out to Joanna's house in the middle of the afternoon?"

"Like I said, I was worried about her. She didn't open her shop this morning. Stewart said she wasn't feeling well. I tried calling her, but she didn't answer the phone."

"So you just hopped into your car and drove out to see her? I don't suppose it crossed your mind to let me know what you were up to? We're supposed to be working on this project together, if you will recall."

"That reminds me, how did you find out where I was?" she asked.

"Sure. Change the subject. Just when I'm really getting into my lecture." He eyed her. "I called your shop. Talked to your assistant, Kerry."

"Oh."

"About this partnership of ours—" He broke off at the sound of a car in the drive. "I think you've got company."

Alexa tilted her head, listening. "I wonder who would come by at this hour of the night?"

"Let's find out."

Trask got to his feet and started around the side of the house. Alexa swung her legs off the lounger and hurried after him.

A gleaming Range Rover was parked in the drive. The driver cut the lights and the engine just as Trask rounded the corner of the house.

Two of the vehicle's doors opened. Foster Radstone got out from behind the wheel. Trask watched him flash his cap-toothed smile at Alexa. It hit him that no price would have been too high for his new Deco collection as long as working on it had kept Alexa from getting seriously involved with Radstone.

Webster Bell climbed from the passenger seat. The porch lights gleamed on the silver in his necklace and belt. His looked ten years older than he had the night of the hotel reception.

Alexa stepped around Trask. "Is Joanna okay?"

"She'll be all right." Webster gave her a weary smile. "Thanks to you. I stopped by to say thanks. You probably saved her life today."

"We hadn't realized that she was so deep into a state of clinical depression," Foster said gravely. "She obviously needs intensive psychiatric care. Webster is going to make arrangements for her to go directly from the hospital into a private facility for a while."

"Are you sure she tried to commit suicide?" Alexa gazed thoughtfully at Webster. "Maybe she just took too many tranquilizers by mistake."

"I'd like to think that's the case," Webster said quietly. "But I'm afraid she's very ill. She's still hallucinating."

"The doctor allowed Webster to see her for a few minutes," Foster said. "She wasn't very coherent. Apparently she's anxious about her journal. We went to her house to get it for her, but we couldn't find it. You didn't happen to notice it when you were there earlier today, did you?"

"Are you talking about her Dimensions personal journal?" Alexa asked slowly.

"Yes," Webster said. "Did you see it, by any chance?"

"No, I'm sorry," Alexa said. "I didn't notice it."

"We weren't in the house very long," Trask added. "Things were hectic. After the medics left with Joanna, I called you, and then we locked the doors and left."

Webster ran a hand across his face as though trying to erase the weariness etched there. "She wouldn't talk to me very much, but she seems to want the journal very badly."

"I'm sure it's a source of comfort to her," Foster said. "Webster and I hoped we could find it."

"Maybe it's at her shop," Alexa volunteered helpfully.

Trask barely managed to subdue a strong impulse to plant his heel on her toes.

"No, it's not there, either," Webster said. "We checked the shop after we couldn't find it in her house." He gave a dispirited shrug. "I guess that's all we can do for now. Maybe when her mind clears she'll remember where she left it."

"If there's anything I can do, please let me

know," Alexa said. "Joanna is a friend. I want to help in any way I can."

"Thank you." Webster smiled gently as he slid back into the front seat of the Range Rover. "Think positive thoughts."

"I will," Alexa promised.

Foster raised a hand in farewell. "Peace and serenity."

The heavy vehicle's engine roared to life. Trask took Alexa's arm and turned her away from the blinding headlights. He guided her back to the patio.

He was furious with himself.

"Damn it to hell, after what happened at Liz's house, we should have thought to look for a journal at Joanna's place," he said.

"Hey, we aren't exactly trained detectives." Alexa gave him a wry smile. "Besides, as I recall, we were busy making another brilliant deduction at the time. Those late-night phone calls, remember?"

"I wonder what the hell she knows about all this."

"From the sound of things, we won't be able to get close enough to her to ask any questions for a while. You heard what Foster said. Bell is making arrangements for her to go into a sanitarium."

"Whether she needs one or not," Trask said dryly.

"I know you've concluded that Webster is behind all this, but I'll tell you one thing," Alexa said.

"What's that?"

"I got a good look at his face tonight. Whatever is going on, I can almost guarantee you that he never intended to put his sister at risk."

* * *

The monsters surrounded her. Some hung by serpentine tails from the ceiling and leered. Others stood three deep, slathering jaws agape. Perched atop the backs of their scaled companions, a few glared down at her with menacing eyes.

None of them moved. It was as if they were all frozen . . .

"Alexa, wake up. You're dreaming."

"Go away." Annoyed by the interruption, sensing she had to get back to the dream before it evaporated, she turned her back to Trask and snuggled into the bedding.

Trask shook her gently. "It's okay, it's just a dream."

"I know that," she grumbled into the pillow. "Important. Leave me alone."

"I guess that tells me where I rank in the general scheme of things around here." Trask sounded only slightly amused.

Alexa opened one eye. There was no recapturing the dream now, anyway, she decided. She turned back to face Trask.

He was propped on his elbow, looking down at her. The sheet had fallen to his waist. His bare shoulders blotted out a very wide swath of moonlight.

"I changed my mind." Alexa drew a finger slowly down his biceps. "You're more interesting than the dream."

"I can't tell you what that does for my ego."

She blinked and yawned. "How come you're awake, anyway?"

"I've been doing some thinking. When you reached out to grab me I got distracted. I assumed that you were feeling in the mood."

"Umm." She frowned, trying to call back the images of her dream.

"Someone interesting?" Trask asked in a suspiciously polite tone.

"*Something* interesting. Monsters, I think."

"I can guess where the inspiration for that came from."

Alexa thought about Joanna lying on the deck floor clutching at her and begging her to keep the monsters away. She winced. "Yes. Poor Joanna. I hope she's resting comfortably tonight. What kept you awake?"

He shoved his pillow up against the headboard and sprawled back against it. "The Dimensions Institute."

"What about it?"

"I want to get inside."

Alexa yawned again. "Take a guided meditation class. Or a tour of the grounds."

"I mean inside the offices. Specifically, Bell's and Radstone's offices."

Alexa stilled. "Trask, that sounds like a very risky, possibly even stupid, idea."

"Stupid, huh? Lucky for me I'm man enough to be able to rise above that kind of remark."

"What do you expect to find in Webster's and Foster's offices?"

"Answers. Okuda says that his computer people have gone as deep as they can. They haven't turned up much that's useful. I have a hunch that's because

Bell and Radstone are too smart to store the incrimnating stuff on a computer, at least, not one that's on-line."

She was quiet for a moment. "You still think this is all about money, don't you?"

"The Institute is all about money. And thus far everyone who has died has been standing in the way of the Institute's cash flow."

"We're talking about *two* people who have died." Alexa realized she was once again trying to be the voice of reason. "Your father and Dean Guthrie. The authorities have said that both were killed in accidents. Furthermore, twelve years separated the deaths. No one is going to buy your conspiracy theory involving Dimensions. We simply haven't got any solid evidence to show to the cops."

"Hell, don't you think I know that? It's the reason I want to take a look around inside Bell's and Radstone's offices."

"I don't like it," she said.

"Neither do I." He looked at her. "But I can't think of anything else, and something tells me we may not have a lot of time."

Her hands went cold. "Liz Guthrie?"

"Yeah. Liz Guthrie. I have a hunch that the clock has already started ticking for her. And maybe for some other people, as well."

She sat up. "Lord, you can't mean *Joanna?*"

"I don't want to scare you, but personally I find her collapse and impending incarceration in a sanitarium a little too convenient. If you hadn't gone out to her house today, she'd be dead by now. What do you want to bet that, either way, dead or committed to a psychiatric hospital, Bell takes control of her finances?"

Alexa flopped back onto the pillows. "What a mess."

"That's why I have to get inside those offices at the Institute."

She watched the shadows on the ceiling for a while.

"I'm probably going to hate myself in the morning for saying this, but . . ."

"I'm listening."

"The Institute grounds will be very crowded tomorrow night because of the festival activities. There's a psychic fair, a public talk by Bell, and fireworks. I have a good idea of the schedule because I've been working with Foster on one of the coordinating committees."

Trask said nothing.

"I know my way around the Institute and the seminar building, which is where the offices are, because of that meditation class I took."

Trask shifted onto his side. "You can draw me a map."

She turned her head on the pillow. "I'll do better than that. I'll go with you."

"Not a chance."

"Wanna bet, partner?"

28

Dylan Fenn stuck his head into the door of Elegant Relic shortly after three o'clock the following afternoon. He grinned when he saw Alexa emerging from the back room with a box full of small gargoyles in her arms.

"Good day?" he asked.

"Are you kidding? This is the third time I've restocked these little critters since this morning." She looked at Kerry. "I thought you were going to take a quick break. Better grab it while you can. This quiet spell won't last more than a few minutes."

"I'm on my way out the door even as we speak, boss." Kerry came around the corner of the counter. "Want me to bring back some tea for you?"

"Thanks, I'd appreciate that. Make it iced."

"You got it. Hey, Dylan." Kerry smiled at him as she went through the doorway. "How's it going?"

"I've been swamped." He made a face. "Four more hours including the Gallery Walk to go and then the worst will be over. We can all head for

Dimensions to take in the Psychic Fair and see the fireworks."

Kerry laughed. "Next week you and Alexa will both be whining about the slowdown in business."

Alexa looked up from arranging gargoyles. "We're small-business people, Kerry. Whining is what we do. Don't forget my tea."

"I won't." Kerry disappeared in the direction of Café Solstice.

"I'd better get back to Spheres." Dylan started to turn away. "See you up at the Institute tonight?"

Alexa kept her bright smile pasted firmly on her face, but her palms went cold. "Wouldn't miss Dimensions Night. But it'll be tough to find anyone in that crowd. Everyone's saying that the festival has drawn more people this year than any year in its history. Tonight the Institute is the center of attention because of the fair and the fireworks. It will be thronged."

"We could drive up there together in my car."

Alexa concentrated on positioning gargoyles. "Thanks, but I've already made arrangements."

Dylan paused. "Going with Trask?"

"Yes."

"I was afraid of that." His face clouded with concern. "I guess there's nothing I can say."

"No," Alexa said gently. "There isn't."

He smiled ruefully. "None of my business, anyway. All the same, take care, okay?"

"Don't worry, Dylan. I know what I'm doing." *Sort of*, she added silently.

"Don't mind me," Dylan advised gently. "I've been feeling kind of down all day, in spite of the sales volume."

"Because of the news about Joanna?"

He nodded. "I can't stop thinking about it."

"I know what you mean."

"We're her friends, Alexa. We should have realized how close to the edge she was."

"We're not exactly mental health experts," Alexa reminded him.

"Still . . ."

"Hey, if it makes you feel any better, we're all feeling a little guilty today."

"It's easy to look back and see the signs that we missed at the time," Dylan said. "She'd been getting more and more anxious and upset during the past few weeks. And she has a history of depression. There was that time right after Harry Trask died . . ."

"The important thing is that she's going to be okay."

"Thanks to you. What made you go to her house yesterday anyway?"

"It was just an impulse."

Dylan looked wise. "I think it was more than an impulse. When are you going to admit that there's something to Webster Bell's theories about psychic energy waves and positive vortices?"

"I'll buy into that theory the same day I start seeing aliens and Abominable Snowmen."

Dylan's eyes widened. "Don't tell me you missed them. They arrived on a tour bus from Tucson this morning. Checked in at the Avalon Resort."

"Go back to work, Dylan. You're missing customers."

"True. See you later." Dylan backed out of the

doorway and sauntered off down the shaded path that led to Spheres.

Alexa put the last gargoyle in place, straightened it, and picked up the box.

Her palms were still cold. Her anxiety level was climbing by the minute. At this rate, she would find herself sharing a room with Joanna at the no-doubt very expensive, very private, sanitarium Webster Bell had selected.

She had spent most of the day worrying about Trask and his plans to break into the Institute's files tonight. On those rare occasions when she had not been fretting about him, she worried about Liz and Joanna.

It was all too easy to succumb to Trask's dark conspiracy theories.

The doorbell chimed, announcing the arrival of a customer. Alexa was relieved. Selling gargoyles and fake swords took her mind off what lay ahead that evening.

29

Alexa peered through the Jeep's windshield. The headlights revealed a long line of vehicles parked. beside the road that curved down the hill from the entrance to the Dimensions Institute.

"Foster was right when he said there would be a problem with overflow parking. The Institute's lots must be full."

Trask slowed the Jeep. "I see why Pete Santana thought it would be a good idea to put on a special shuttle for the resort guests. It looks like we'd better park here and walk the rest of the way."

He eased the Jeep to the side of the road and stopped it at the end of the line. Alexa opened the door on her side. She hesitated when she realized how dark it was. The nearly full moon did not compensate for the lack of streetlights. She turned away from the glare of the twin beams of an approaching car.

"We'll need flashlights," she said, slinging the strap of her satchel over her shoulder.

"In the glove compartment." Trask was out of the car, leaning into the backseat. "There should be two of them. Same ones we used at Liz Guthrie's house."

Alexa fumbled with the latch of the glove compartment, and finally got it open. She retrieved the two small flashlights, closed the compartment, and then shut the door on the driver's side.

Trask walked around the back of the vehicle to join her.

"Mind putting this in your purse?" he asked very casually.

She aimed the flashlight at the bulky black leather case he held out. "It looks heavy. Why do I have to lug it?"

"Some of us red-blooded types haven't got with the New Man program yet. We still feel conspicuous carrying something that looks like a purse."

"That's not a purse."

"Of course it's not a purse. Why the hell would I have a purse?" He pushed the soft leather bag into her hands. "It's a laptop computer case."

It took a second for the implications to strike. By the time she realized what it all meant, Trask was several steps ahead of her, moving toward the entrance to Dimensions.

She dropped the case into her already overburdened satchel and jolted forward, pursuing Trask alongside the row of parked cars.

"What the heck do you think you're going to do with a laptop?" she demanded breathlessly when she caught up with him.

"I'm no hacker, but I am a businessman who uses

a personal computer on a regular basis. I have a reasonably good working knowledge of routine business software applications."

"So what?"

"So if it turns out that Bell and Radstone keep their files on personal computers instead of hard copy, I want to be prepared."

"Why not just take a couple of disks with you, stick them into Bell's and Radstone's computers, assuming you find them, and copy the files you want?"

"I won't have time to stand around their offices picking and choosing the files that look promising. But with the laptop I can copy everything from Bell's and Radstone's hard drives onto my own and I can get it done fast."

"What if the computers are password protected?"

"I'll be out of luck, just as I will be if they've encrypted the critical files."

Alexa hitched the satchel higher on her shoulder. "I can tell you've given this a little thought."

"Believe it or not, that's one of the things we CEOs get paid to do. Think."

"Wow. I always wanted a cushy job like that. But my high school guidance counselor said I would probably have to work for a living. When do you plan to perform your little act of B&E?"

"I looked at that schedule you gave me. I'll go into the seminar complex during Bell's talk and the fireworks display. I'm betting everyone will be outside to catch the big show at that time."

She glanced at him. His face was unreadable in the shadows, but she sensed the controlled anticipation in him. "The real reason you want me to haul this laptop around in my purse is so no one will notice you carrying it and wonder why you brought a computer to a psychic fair."

"A computer might raise a few eyebrows," he agreed. "Of course, I could always say that I use it to channel with, but I'm not sure anyone would buy that story."

Alexa looked at the impressive stone and wrought iron gates that marked the glowingly lit entrance to the Institute. The night was balmy and warm, but she suddenly felt chilled to the bone.

"Probably not," she said.

The grounds of the Institute were crammed with tourists and local Avalon residents. Several rows of booths had been set up in the vast gardens that surrounded the sleek, modern buildings. The crowd that filled the winding garden paths that separated the stalls moved at a sludgelike pace.

Balloons bobbed from strings attached to the wrists of children. The scents of aromatherapy candles mingled with the smell of tofu hot dogs and soy burgers. There was a general air of festivity that Alexa would have found contagious under other circumstances.

She glanced at some of the signs as she and Trask forged their way through thick clumps of fairgoers. One read *Pyramid Power*. She looked at the counter beneath it and saw an array of small crystal pyramids for sale.

Next to the pyramid booth was a gaily striped tent. The painted board in front invited fairgoers to step inside and get themselves tested to determine the level of their latent psychic abilities. *Find out if you have the potential for telepathy or psychokinesis.*

Farther along the path were booths featuring books purporting to reveal the secrets of Alchemy, Atlantis, Stonehenge, and Roswell. *Learn how to access alien energy sources to gain control over your financial affairs.*

There were a number of costumed street musicians wandering through the crowd. Alexa noticed one dressed as a medieval court jester complete with pointed cap and mask. He held a flute to his lips. She could not hear the music above the general din.

"I can't believe the size of this crowd," Trask muttered. "There must be several thousand people here tonight. I knew this metaphysical junk was a big draw, but I didn't realize it was this popular."

His scorn made Alexa feel oddly defensive. Avalon was her home, after all. "Metaphysics isn't junk philosophy to a lot of people. It's been around in one form or another for several thousand years. What you see here is a manifestation of the innate human desire to seek meaning in the universe and to explore the unknown dimensions of the mind."

"Uh-huh. You get that out of one of the Institute's brochures?"

"How did you guess?" She watched a woman dressed in flowing robes deal from a pack of tarot cards. "But it's true, you know. Humans have been into metaphysics one way or another for eons. Probably part of what makes us human."

"I'll stick to spreadsheets and laptops."

She glanced at him. "What makes you think your business software isn't just another form of metaphysics?"

He eyed her. "You're joking, right?"

"Maybe." She smiled. "Maybe not. Think about it. You use your business applications programs to give yourself the illusion of control, don't you?"

"It's not an illusion, it *is* a form of control."

"Hah. If that were true, no business today would go bankrupt. All CEOs and corporate honchos would make the right decisions all the time. There would be no surprises when the Asian markets fluctuate or when the dollar goes soft. This fancy computer I'm toting around for you is nothing more than our generation's version of the old alchemists' equipment."

"Come off it, Alexa. You're too smart to actually believe in any of this garbage."

She looked around at the milling fair crowds. "You don't have to believe in something in order to respect the power it generates."

He paused to sweep the crowd with a considering glance. "Okay, you've got me there. Anything or anyone who can attract this many people and their money has power."

"And you don't have to believe in something to respect the impulse that prompts belief in others," Alexa concluded softly. "The bottom line, Trask, is that we don't have all the answers."

He raked a psychic reading booth with a disapproving glance. "You're right. But no one is going to find them by going to a fortune-teller."

"That may be true." She smiled. "On the other hand, sometimes it's fun to get your fortune told. Ever tried it?"

"Hell, no. If I want to read my fortune, I pick up a copy of the *Wall Street Journal*."

"That certainly sounds entertaining."

"I suggest we move on to a different topic," Trask said evenly. "Give me a rundown on which Dimensions building houses what."

"All right." She looked up at the brightly lit glass walls of the Institute's structures. "The large one in the center is the main seminar complex. As I told you, it's divided into classrooms and offices."

"Anything else in there?"

"It's been several months since I was last inside." She tried to recall the exact layout. "There's a reception desk in the lobby area. And a bookstore that stocks a lot of metaphysical titles and the Dimensions publications."

"What's the long, low building to the left?"

Alexa glanced at the structure nestled into the hillside. "That's where the people who come here on retreat stay."

"Basically, it's a hotel."

She nodded. "Right. A pretty pricey one at that."

"You said Bell's home is here on the grounds?"

"It's that house on the hill just above the retreat. The building with all the glass."

"Got it."

Something whispered across the back of Alexa's neck. Instinctively she glanced over her shoulder. Out of the corner of her eye she saw the jester again. He disappeared behind a booth before she could get a close look.

Trask looked at her. "Something wrong?"

"I don't know." She shrugged her shoulders to loosen the tension coalescing there. "Ever have the feeling that you were being watched?"

"Yeah." He gave her an enigmatic look. "Are you telling me you've got that kind of feeling now?"

"Yes. Sort of ridiculous. After all, we're surrounded by a few thousand people. Of course someone is bound to be looking at us at any given moment."

"There's a difference between having someone look at you and having someone watch you," he said quietly.

"I'm sure it's just my imagination."

Trask said nothing.

"Trask?"

"Okay, I'm feeling a little weird, also."

"The guy with the flute?"

"You noticed him too?"

"He moved," she said. "Perfectly normal thing for a street musician to do."

"I'm not into this metaphysical stuff, but I do have a healthy respect for my own instincts." He took her hand and tugged her toward another aisle of booths. "Let's see if we can get lost in this crowd."

They threaded their way deep into a knot of people drifting slowly along a path. Alexa glanced at the man and woman next to her and noticed that they were both wearing badges that read *Tesla Lives*.

The small crowd swept them up and carried them off in a seemingly haphazard direction. A few minutes later, Alexa felt Trask's fingers tighten around her wrist. He pulled her toward the fringes of the group.

"Now what?" she asked.

"I think we lost him, assuming he was following us. But just to be on the safe side, let's get our auras read."

"Our *auras*?"

"Why not? You said this fortune-telling stuff was fun."

Trask used his grasp on her wrist to haul her through the opening of a yellow and white tent. Alexa glanced at the whimsical sign and managed to read part of it.

AURAS READ AND ANALYZED

The flap fell closed behind her before she was able to make out the fine print. The interior of the tent was enveloped in gloom. A single small lamp glowed at the rear.

A woman spoke. "Ah, customers at last. About time."

Small bells tinkled. A figure garbed in a gown shaded in a dozen hues of green rose from a green, tasseled cushion. The green silk scarves that covered her head cast her features into deep shadows.

"Came to get our auras examined," Trask said with a stunning nonchalance.

Alexa was impressed. He sounded as if he got his aura read twice a month on a regular schedule.

"Wonderful. I've been bored all evening." Bells chimed softly again as the woman in green motioned to two large, fringed cushions. "Please be seated."

Alexa looked around as she sank down onto a plump cushion. "Slow night?"

"Very." The aura reader took her seat in a graceful, practiced movement. "But that's generally the way it is in my business."

"I'm surprised," Alexa said. "I would have

thought that aura reading would have been a major attraction at a psychic fair."

The veiled head inclined in agreement. "Some of my colleagues will do quite well tonight."

"There's a huge crowd outside," Alexa said. "How come you're not swamped with customers?"

Trask frowned as if it had just occurred to him to question the fact that they hadn't had to stand in line.

"Not everyone wants a true reading," the aura reader said. "But that's fine by me. It takes energy to read auras, you know. I can't do a lot of them in an evening. Now, if you don't mind, I'll get rid of some of the light."

"Why do that?" Trask asked as she reached out to turn down the small lamp.

"It's easier to see auras in darkness," the woman said matter-of-factly. "At least for me. I can sense them in any light, but to do an accurate reading, I must have darkness."

"Sure," Trask said. "Everyone knows that." He glanced back at the closed tent flap.

Alexa followed his gaze. She flinched when she saw a great, looming shadow of a man outlined against the wall of the tent. Memories of her encounter with the intruder in Liz Guthrie's house came back in a rush.

The shadow moved on. It was soon replaced by another, much smaller outline. A child. Alexa breathed out slowly in relief. The outside lamps were casting the shadows of any fair-goers who passed close by onto the fabric of the tent.

She turned back. There was just enough of a glow

coming through the tent to make out the figure of the aura reader.

"Hmm," the reader said eventually.

"I take it we don't have interesting auras?" Trask said. He did not sound overly concerned at the prospect of having a dull aura.

Alexa sensed that his attention was on the shadow play taking place on the wall of the tent. She wondered if he was watching for the outline of the man in the jester's costume.

"On the contrary," the reader said. "Both of you have extremely intriguing auras." The dark outline of her veiled head turned toward Alexa. "Yours is strong and bright. The hues have great clarity and energy."

"I take it that's good?"

"Yes." The reader turned toward Trask. "Your aura, sir, radiates a degree of power that could be dangerous in some people. It requires a lot of control, but I see that you've got enough to handle it."

"I'm into control," Trask said easily.

"The hues are dark," the reader continued, "but they are clear and pure."

"The result of good, clean living," Trask said absently. He was still watching the shadows on the tent fabric.

The reader cleared her throat. "I should mention that I sense an element of tension in both auras."

"Can't imagine why," Trask said. "We're just sitting here getting our auras read."

Annoyed by his rudeness, Alexa poked his shoulder. "Ignore him," she said to the reader. "He's hungry. I promised him we'd get a bite to eat right after we finished this."

"I understand. Go feed him."

Trask turned back, scowling. "Is that all there is to the reading?"

The reader moved slightly. Bells tinkled. "I could elaborate on how well-matched your auras are. Great yin-yang stuff going on. Together you've got darn near a full spectrum."

"Is that anything like a full house in poker?" Trask asked.

"In the metaphysical sense," the reader said. "I can also give you the details on how the light, bright colors in the lady's aura complement the dark shades in yours, sir, and how the tesla psychic currents harmonize. But I'm sure you two already know all that."

Alexa stared at her. "Why would we know anything about it?"

There was a short, charged pause. The outline of the reader's head swiveled again as she looked from Alexa to Trask and back. "Sorry. I assumed that the two of you have a, ah, personal relationship."

"Relationship?" Trask repeated ominously. "What do you mean by that?"

"Calm down," Alexa muttered.

He ignored her. He kept his gaze on the hapless aura reader. "Have you been talking to someone about us?"

"Of course not." The reader sounded indignant. "I'm a professional. I've got standards."

"Are you connected to the Institute?" Trask demanded.

"No," the woman said quickly. "I'm an independent operator. I just rented booth space for the fair. That's all."

"Then what's all this talk about a connection between Alexa and me?"

"Hey, I just read 'em the way I see 'em."

Alexa groaned. "Trask, I really don't think you want to go down this road."

"The hell I don't," he said. "I want to know exactly what she knows about us and how she knows it."

"It's no big deal." The reader turned up the lamp. "I'll try and explain it without getting technical. The fact that your aura has begun to resonate strongly with the lady's in certain ways is usually an indication that two people have established a mutual bond."

"A bond," Trask repeated in a perfectly neutral voice.

"Yes," the reader said. "A bond."

Alexa thought about the uneasy partnership she and Trask had formed. "I think you could say we've been through a bonding experience of sorts."

Trask gave her a strange look. "Is that what you call it?"

"For want of a better phrase," Alexa said demurely.

The reader hesitated. "Uh, look, sorry if I put my foot in it. I figured you two were already engaged or, at the very least, involved in an affair or something."

Trask regarded her in Sphinx-like silence.

"Good grief." Alexa went hot all over.

"I knew this stuff was garbage," Trask said grimly.

"Look, are you implying that I didn't give an accurate reading?" A belligerent, defensive tone had entered the reader's voice. "It's not my fault that the two of you came in here with a couple of auras that have obviously begun to resonate."

"No," Alexa said cautiously, "it's not your fault."

"Judging by your reaction," the reader snapped, "I assume you're trying to keep your relationship a secret."

"The thing is—" Alexa began.

"In my opinion, people who are involved in illicit love affairs shouldn't wander into an innocent aura reader's booth, ask to have their auras read, and then get indignant when the reader tells them what she sees."

"It's okay, really, it is." Alexa scrambled to her feet. "No one's blaming you."

"I should hope not. Like I said, I'm a professional. I've got standards."

Alexa nudged Trask, who still had not moved. "Come on, we'd better get going. We've got a lot to do tonight."

"Hold it." The aura reader put out her hand. "That'll be fifty dollars."

"*Fifty bucks?*" Trask finally emerged from his frozen state. He surged to his feet. "For a carnival show fortune-telling session? Forget it."

"I didn't tell your fortunes, I read your auras." The reader rose from her cushion. "Furthermore, this is no carnival sideshow. It's a serious business and I resent the implication that I'm a huckster."

"This is a psychic fair." Trask swept out a hand. "Hell, all the booths are run by hucksters."

"You're entitled to your opinion." The reader's veils shivered with the force of her icy indignation.

"But I'm entitled to my fifty dollars. The sign out front clearly states the fee. If you didn't want to pay the price, you shouldn't have come in here."

"Pay her," Alexa said through her teeth.

Trask's jaw clenched in stubborn lines. "I'll be damned if I'll fork over fifty bucks for a two-bit performance."

"This was your idea," she reminded him.

"I'm not about to let this . . . this charlatan take advantage . . ."

"Okay, okay, stop making a scene." Alexa fumbled with the catch of her satchel. "We'll split it."

"It's not the money, it's the principle of the thing," Trask declared.

"Sure." Alexa got a twenty and a five out of her wallet. "That's what people always say when they're too cheap to pay the tab."

"I am not cheap, damn it." Trask dug out his wallet. "I'll pay for the reading."

"Just worry about your share." Alexa handed the reader the twenty and the five. "I wouldn't dream of forcing you to pay for my half. After all, this is a *partnership*, isn't it?"

"I said I'll pay her." Trask ripped the two bills out of the reader's fingers and slapped them back into Alexa's hand. Then he gave the woman fifty dollars. "There. Satisfied?"

"Yes," Alexa said.

"Yes," the aura reader said.

"Terrific. Let's get out of here." Trask shoved his wallet back into his pocket, seized Alexa's arm, and hauled her toward the entrance of the tent. "I think we now know why there was no line of people standing in front of this booth. Who in their right minds would pay fifty bucks for an aura reading?"

"We did," Alexa said.

The aura reader slipped the bills into her veils. "You get what you pay for."

Trask did not bother to respond to that. He yanked open the tent flap and ushered Alexa outside.

Once back on the garden path they blended quickly into the crowd. Alexa glanced around. She saw no sign of the man in the jester's costume. She relaxed slightly and looked at Trask's grim face.

"I realize that was a bit awkward," she said. "Nevertheless, I think you're overreacting."

"Fifty bucks to have some fortune-teller tell us that we're having an affair? Give me a break."

"She wasn't a fortune-teller," Alexa said patiently. "And she didn't exactly tell us that we were having an affair. She said she just assumed as much because our auras resonate in certain ways."

Trask gave her a speaking glance.

Alexa exhaled deeply. "I think we've exhausted that subject. Let's get back to business." She surveyed the group of fair-goers on the path. "I don't see our jester friend."

That got Trask's attention. He looked over his shoulder. "Neither do I."

"Probably a false alarm."

"A false alarm that cost me fifty bucks," Trask muttered. "Resonating auras. What bull."

Alexa glared at him.

"Okay, okay."

"The main activities of the evening are about to

begin." Alexa glanced at her watch. "Webster's talk will start soon, and then they'll set off the fireworks."

"Let's work our way toward the seminar building."

Alexa acquiesced with a sense of relief. She decided not to tell him that she had a strong hunch "resonating auras" was psychic-speak for falling in love. She was having enough trouble coming to grips with the ramifications of the aura reader's words as it was.

30

He had been right about the effect of Bell's speech and the timeless allure of fireworks. The combination of attractions had emptied out the seminar building. Even the receptionist had left his post to wander outside.

Trask stood in the shadows of the darkened hallway and took morose satisfaction in the knowledge that at least this part of the evening was going according to plan. After it was over, he would worry about the way the phony aura reader's mumbo jumbo had poleaxed him.

He glanced down the hall behind him. It was shrouded in shadows. Only the lobby of the building was lit.

It had been easy enough to get into the seminar facility without being noticed. He had simply joined the crowd milling around the Dimensions bookshop. When the others had left to see Bell, he had slipped into the nearest men's room and waited a few minutes. When he had emerged, he had the place to himself.

But not for long, he thought. He had to move quickly.

He adjusted the strap of the computer case on his shoulder and started along an unlit corridor. The passage was lined on each side by twin rows of glass-paneled office and seminar room doors. Assuming nothing had changed since the time Alexa had spent here, Radstone's office was up ahead and to the left.

He had made the decision to search Radstone's files first because everything he had indicated that it was Radstone who managed the Institute's money. And money was at the core of this. It was the only motive that explained both his father's death and Guthrie's as well.

He reached the junction of two hallways, turned, and started along the corridor that led to his destination.

A squeak sounded, unnaturally loud in the darkness. He recognized the noise immediately. It was the sort that was made by the soles of a pair of running shoes on hardwood floors. It emanated from the intersecting hallway.

So much for the theory that he was alone in the seminar facility.

Trask halted and looked at the door directly across from where he stood. There was a small sign printed on the translucent glass, but he could not read it in the dim light. He had to get out of sight. Whoever was coming down the hall might decide to turn right and walk along this passage.

He crossed the corridor in two strides and tried the doorknob. It refused to turn in his hand.

He swore silently and tried the next one. It, too,

was locked. He was thinking up reasonable excuses for hanging around dark corridors when he passed a third door. This one did not have a glass panel in it. It opened easily.

He caught a glimpse of a toilet and a gleaming washbasin before the door swung shut, leaving him in absolute darkness. It looked like he'd picked the women's room this time. At least it made a change of pace.

It occurred to him that he was spending a lot of time in rest rooms this evening. He hoped that was not a bad omen.

He heard the squeak outside in the hall and knew that whoever had come down the intersecting corridor had turned in to this one. It had been close. Five seconds later and he would have been seen, Trask thought.

He wondered who had just walked past the rest room door. A member of the Institute's faculty, possibly. Someone with an office in this hall. But if that was the case, why hadn't he turned on the lights?

Trask waited until the squeaks had receded into the distance. Then he counted to ten and cracked open the rest room door. He glanced down the shadowy length of the corridor.

There was a figure at the end of the hall, barely visible in the darkness. As Trask watched, the dark shape disappeared through the doorway into an office.

Trask reviewed the map in his head. Radstone's office was at the end of this hall. First big deduction of the evening: It was Foster Radstone himself who had walked down the hall in squeaky running shoes.

In the dark.

So much for searching that office. The only option left was Bell's. That meant backtracking to the intersection and turning left.

"I got your message. What the hell do you want?"

The angry, muffled voice came from the far end of the corridor. It belonged to Foster Radstone. Trask stopped.

"Are you crazy? Get the hell out of my office."

Trask gazed into the shadows at the end of the hall.

"You're outta your fucking mind." Radstone's voice echoed through the glass panel on the door, loud and getting louder. *"You can't threaten me. Get the hell out of my office, you bastard."*

Second big deduction of the evening: There was someone else besides Foster in the office.

This was simply too interesting to pass up.

Trask went silently back down the hall toward Radstone's office. He glanced at the bottom of the door as he approached. No light showed beneath it. The glass panel was luminous, however. Inside, the office was flooded with moonlight and the glow of the lamps that lined the path outside.

Why wasn't Radstone turning on any lights tonight?

He reached the door and saw the shadowy outlines of two figures etched against the glass. There was something wrong with the head of one of them. Strange, pointed shapes stuck out from the skull.

The jester.

As Trask watched, the jester raised one arm in an ominous movement. The shadowy fist clutched a small, blunt object.

"No. *No*," Radstone's voice rose. "Wait. How much do you want? Name your price."

The jester mumbled something, low and incomprehensible.

Trask decided not to waste time trying the knob. If the door was locked he would lose the element of surprise.

He yanked the strap of the computer case off his shoulder and hurled the laptop through the glass panel.

Someone screamed. Radstone.

Outside, the first of the fireworks erupted, small bombs in the night. The sharp explosions mingled with the sound of breaking glass.

Simultaneously there was another explosion, closer to hand. The figure in the pointed cap bolted for the window. Radstone crumpled to the floor without a sound.

Trask reached through the jagged glass, wrenched open the door, and went in, fast and low.

The jester had one leg over the sill.

Trask launched himself forward. The toe of his low boot collided with Radstone's outflung arm.

Trask staggered, managed to catch his balance, and vaulted after the disappearing jester. He reached the window just as the fleeing figure tumbled awkwardly over the sill.

Trask grabbed for whatever he could catch hold of and succeeded in getting a handful of sleeve. The jester made a fist and lashed out wildly. Eyes glittered with rage and panic behind the holes in the mask.

Trask turned his head at the last instant. The blow glanced off the side of his jaw. He tightened his grip on the jester's sleeve and hauled backward.

The jester twisted frantically. Trask heard thin fabric rip. He made another bid to get a better grasp on his opponent. His fingers snagged on a bracelet.

The delicate band snapped. The jester slipped free and fled into the night.

Trask put one leg over the sill, straining to keep the jester in sight. A groan from the man on the floor stopped him. Reluctantly he eased back into the room.

Something hard crunched under the heel of his boot. He ignored it to cross the room. He found the light switch, flicked it on, and looked down.

Foster Radstone lay sprawled on the carpet. There was an unhealthy grayish cast to his face. He was gasping for breath. Blood soaked the front of his turquoise polo shirt.

Trask went to the desk and grabbed the phone. Given the size of the crowd on the Institute's grounds tonight, there was bound to be some emergency personnel in the vicinity.

He listened to Radstone's increasingly labored breathing as he rattled off the details.

"There's an aid car standing by outside the front gate," the operator said. "I'm dispatching it now."

"Tell 'em to hurry." Trask hung up the phone and went to crouch beside Foster. He saw no sign of an exit wound.

"Help is on the way," he said. He shrugged out of his denim shirt, wadded it up, and shoved it over the hole in Radstone's chest. "Who did this to you?"

Foster gurgled. His eyes fluttered again. There was barely any color left in his face.

He was not going to get any answers tonight, Trask realized.

"Take it easy," he said quietly. "The medics will be here any minute."

He glanced toward the window and saw the turquoise beads scattered on the floor. A Dimensions bracelet. He recalled feeling it snap in his fingers when he had tried to retain his grip on the jester.

Great. That meant Strood would be able to limit his pools of suspects to the entire staff of the Dimensions Institute, most of its seminar students, and half the people in Avalon.

"Guard . . ." Foster whispered hoarsely. "Guard."

Trask heard footsteps in the hall. "It's a little too late to call security."

Foster shook his head fretfully. *"Guardian."*

Trask stilled. Then he leaned closer. "Tell me about him, Radstone. Who is this guardian?"

Foster opened his mouth, but this time no words emerged. He had stopped twitching, but now he was not moving at all. He still breathed, however. Trask held the shirt firmly in place and listened to the approaching footsteps.

"In here," he shouted.

Two uniformed medics came through the door. They were followed by a couple of anxious-looking men dressed in the blue and white colors of Institute personnel.

The first medic through the door looked at Radstone and then at Trask. "What happened here?"

"Gunshot," Trask said.

The medic glanced at the blood on Radstone's

polo shirt. "Yeah, I can see that. Okay, out of the way, we'll take over now."

Trask rose and moved aside.

One of the Dimensions men eyed him warily. "What's going on?"

"I was outside Radstone's door when I heard an argument and a gunshot." He gave them the rest of the story in short, simple sentences without a lot of details. These were not the people who would handle things, after all. Strood and his small force were the only real cops in Avalon.

When he was finished, the men exchanged baffled looks. They were obviously out of their depth.

"I'd better notify the town cops," one man said. "Tom, go find Bell and tell him what's happening."

"Right."

They disappeared into the hall.

Trask saw that both medics were still very busy with their patient. He took another step back and picked up the computer case that lay on the floor. He wondered if the laptop had survived the impact.

For the first time he noticed the top of Radstone's desk. It was littered with files. He looked across the room and saw that one of the drawers in the gray file cabinet stood open.

He read the labels on the files that were faceup on the desk. All of those that he could see contained the words *Dimensions Trust*.

He moved unobtrusively to the open file drawer and looked inside. There were a handful of folders left. One of them was clearly labeled, *Chambers, Alexa. Priority One.*

Footsteps sounded again in the hall. Voices called out. He only had seconds.

Both of the medics had their backs to him now. He reached into the drawer, removed the slender file marked *Chambers, Alexa,* and stuffed it quietly into the computer case.

It wasn't what he had come here to find tonight, but sometimes, in business, you took what you could get.

31

"Did you get the feeling that Chief Strood was a little ticked?" Alexa sank deeper into the overstuffed chair. She watched Trask. He had his back to her as he stood in front of his desk on the other side of the hotel suite. "It's almost as if he's upset because you saved Foster's life."

"*May* have saved his life. The hospital says he's in critical condition. They don't know if he'll make it or not."

"Well, he wouldn't have any chance at all if you hadn't arrived on the scene when you did." Alexa shuddered. "When I think of how close you came to getting shot, yourself . . ."

"The guy freaked out when I threw the laptop through the glass window. All he wanted to do was get away," Trask said absently.

"I still don't understand why Strood got so annoyed with you."

"Strood's pissed because he knows he's finally going to have to open a genuine, honest-to-God investigation." Trask glanced at her over his shoulder. "I'm going to order some sandwiches from room service. Want anything else?"

"Tea," Alexa said at once. "A nice big pot of it. Forget the food, though. I'm not very hungry. My stomach is still tied up in knots."

"Personally, I'm starved." He picked up the phone.

Alexa surveyed the suite as she listened to Trask's end of the short conversation with the hotel staff. The room was sleek, sophisticated, boldly defined, and unabashedly exotic. A perfect example of neo-Art Deco. Her chaise longue would fit right in here. She decided that if she were not so keyed up from the events at Dimensions, she would have been suitably impressed. Obviously it paid to own a hotel empire.

Trask looked at her as he hung up the phone. "What's the matter?"

"Nothing. I was just thinking that this is an incredible room."

He looked around with a curiously enigmatic expression. "Pure fantasy."

She smiled wearily. "Fine by me. But then, I don't share your bias against fantasy."

"I know you don't." He touched his jaw in a gingerly fashion.

She frowned. "Are you sure you're okay?"

"Uh-huh. The guy clipped me as he went through the window."

"Do you think you should put a cold compress on it?

"Nah. It's not that bad." Trask lowered his hand. "That reminds me, I brought you a little souvenir."

He walked to the laptop case, unzipped it, and

reached inside. Alexa watched him withdraw a folder.

"What's this?" she asked.

"I didn't have a chance to take a good look, but at first glance it appeared to be a dossier." Trask put the folder into her hand. "On you."

"Me? What on earth . . . ?" She opened the folder and glanced at the contents. A shock went through her when she saw her own name at the top of a neatly printed page.

Chambers, Alexa
Potential: Level One Candidate for Circle of Enlightenment

She read quickly through the pages of notes Foster had made on her. With every sentence her outrage increased.

Note: This candidate is to be handled by me personally.

Financial Analysis: Sole beneficiary of a large inheritance from grandmother. In addition, target appears to be the primary beneficiary of Lloyd and Vivien Kenyon. . . . She is unmarried, no offspring . . .

Alexa looked up and saw Trask watching her intently. "This is amazing. He knows all about my financial status."

"Why am I not surprised?"

She glared at him and went back to the dossier. "He notes that I'm an ideal target. The creep actually calls me a target. Of all the unmitigated nerve."

"Target for what?"

She scanned the next page quickly. "Apparently to become a major donor to the Dimensions Trust. He says that with proper handling—" She looked up again, furious now. "*Handling*. Can you believe it?"

"Go on."

Alexa read the next section aloud.

> We have her established as a tenant at Avalon Plaza, which will ensure her continued association with Institute activities and influences. . . .

She gritted her teeth. "So that's how I lucked out with the lease at Avalon Plaza. Wait until Lloyd hears about this."

"Anything else?"

Her fingers tightened on the page. "Here's another entry. It's dated shortly after I stopped going out with him."

> Target is obviously sexually repressed. She is strongly resistant to a physical relationship with a man. I don't believe she's interested in women, either. Will urge her to attend Sexual Enlightenment seminar. . . .

She broke off once more, cheeks burning. "Just because he didn't turn me on, he calls me repressed."

"Shows how much he knows," Trask murmured.

She did not look up. She could hear the satisfied amusement in his voice. The sight of the sexy gleam in his eyes would be too much. She concentrated on reading swiftly through the remainder of the document.

> . . . Refused Sexual Enlightenment seminar.
> Attempts to keep target involved in Dimensions activities continue. . . . Target accepted position on festival committee. *I* feel certain that she can eventually be persuaded to join the Circle of Enlightenment. . . .

Alexa turned the last page and read Foster's final notes silently. "Hmm."

"What does that mean?" Trask asked with grave interest.

"This last entry is dated the day after you and I had dinner at the country club," she said. "Guess the little twerp was starting to get worried."

"About what?"

She cleared her throat. "About you."

"Let me see that." Trask took the dossier from her and read the final paragraph aloud.

> Critical to get target away from Trask's sexual influence. Don't know why she has responded to him, but his agenda is obvious. He intends to use her somehow against Kenyon. Best guess is that Trask has come up with a scheme to hurt Kenyon financially. Gaining control of target's inheritance would be one way to do it as Kenyon frequently combines her trust income with his own resources in his deals. Losing access to her funds would probably cut his leverage options in half. . . .

Trask abruptly stopped reading. He closed the file and carried it back across the room to the desk. He tossed the dossier down onto the polished surface with a short, brutal motion of his hand.

"Son-of-a-bitch," he said very softly.

Alexa steepled her fingers. "Well, I guess that gives us a pretty clear idea of where Foster fits into this thing. He was focused solely on the bottom line."

There was a short, charged silence. Trask looked at her. Belatedly she recalled that he prided himself on his own ability to focus on the bottom line.

"I mean," she said quickly, "that all he cared about was getting his hands on my money."

"I told you so."

"You're biased. You think everyone involved in the metaphysics business is a con artist. However, even if we grant that Foster really is a bad guy, that doesn't explain why someone tried to murder him tonight. Strood will have his hands full trying to figure that one out."

Trask folded his arms and leaned back against the desk. He looked at her with a darkly thoughtful expression. "Not if Foster Radstone has been true to his professional calling as a con man."

"Explain."

"What do you want to bet that Radstone was siphoning money out of the Dimensions Trust?" he said.

She pondered that briefly. "You think he might have been fleecing Webster Bell and the Institute?"

"Someone, presumably the shooter, scattered a whole bunch of files involving the Trust on Radstone's desk tonight. I think he did it while he waited for Radstone."

"You believe that he wanted those files to be found together with the body?"

"That's what it looked like to me." Trask crossed the room to the yellow lacquered cocktail cabinet and opened the door. "If I'm right, if someone tried to kill Radstone tonight because he was skimming from the trust, then it fits with the pattern."

"I see what you mean," Alexa said slowly. "Radstone may qualify as someone else who was a financial threat to the Institute."

Trask took two miniature bottles out of the cabinet, broke the seals, and emptied the contents into two snifters. "Like I said, it fits."

"Did you tell Strood that Radstone tried to say something about a guardian?"

"I told him." He handed her one of the snifters. "He didn't pay too much attention. Thinks Radstone was trying to say *guard*, not guardian."

Alexa inhaled the brandy fumes in her glass. "Theoretically, all we have to do now is wait for Foster to recover and hope that he'll be able to tell us the identity of the person who tried to kill him."

Trask stopped and looked at her. "He may not know who he is. The guy was masked. Even if Radstone can identify him, he may have no interest in doing so."

"Why not?"

"Because in the process he'd probably have to admit that he was trying to bilk the Dimensions Trust. Radstone is guilty of something. I got the impression that his first assumption was that the jester would be open to a payoff. He acted like a man who had been threatened with blackmail."

Alexa winced. "It does sound like you're right about his being a con man."

"Something tells me that when Foster recovers, he'll fade away into the sunset. He'll figure that if he decamps, he'll be safe. Hell, he may be right. After all, if he takes himself out of the picture, he'll no longer be a financial threat to the Institute."

"And threats to the Institute seem to be the main focus of whoever is behind all this." Alexa paused. "That still leaves Joanna. Maybe she'll tell us something when she recovers."

Trask swallowed brandy and looked grim. "I'm not too sure that we can depend on her to help us get to the bottom of this. She's gone out of her way to try to keep the past buried."

"If her close call with the gas was not an accident, she may be at risk again when she gets out of the hospital." Alexa sighed. "How are we going to convince her that she may be in danger?"

"If she's trying to protect someone, there may not be anything we can do," Trask said quietly.

Alexa sat up very straight in the chair and wrapped her fingers around the glass. "The only person she would go that far out of her way to protect is her brother, and I still can't see Webster as a murderer."

"We all have our little biases," Trask said dryly. "But there's something else we need to consider. If Radstone survives, and if Joanna's accident wasn't an accident, it will mean that between us, we screwed up the shooter's plans at least twice in the past few days."

Alexa shuddered. "Yes."

Trask carried his glass to the open French doors and looked out over the darkened desert. "Whoever he is, he's probably not a real happy camper right now. In fact, I have a hunch he'll be getting desperate. Which means he's more dangerous than ever."

"We don't even know if the killer is a he. Could be a she."

Trask hesitated, thinking about the frantic grappling at the window of Radstone's office. Reluctantly he nodded. "Could be a she, but I don't think so."

"Why not?"

"This is going to sound a little primitive, but the fact is, he didn't smell like a woman."

"You mean no perfume? I don't think you can depend on something that vague . . ."

Trask shook his head. "It's a little more basic than that. Women smell different than men. At least, they do to a man. This guy was sweating and he smelled like a guy. For all the good it does. Still not much to go on."

Alexa shivered in the warm night air. "You said he wore a Dimensions bracelet. Could be some crazy out at the Institute."

"Half the town wears those bracelets."

A knock on the door interrupted Alexa's bleak thoughts.

"That'll be room service," Trask said. "I'll get it."

He turned and went back into the suite to open the door.

Alexa watched a young man in Avalon hotel livery roll a cart into the suite. China and silver clinked gently.

When the server finished setting up the tray, he looked expectantly at Trask. "Will there be anything else, sir?"

"No," Trask said. "That's it."

"Shall I pour the tea, sir?"

Alexa stared at the teapot. A vision of the empty mug and the nearly full package of loose tea in Joanna's kitchen flashed in her mind.

"Good grief," she whispered.

The server looked as if he had just glimpsed his own doom. "Something wrong, ma'am?"

"No." She gave him a reassuring smile. "No, nothing's wrong. Just hungry, that's all."

The server left hurriedly.

Trask waited until the door closed. Then he looked at Alexa. "What's the matter?"

Alexa could not take her eyes off the gleaming teapot on the cart. "There was an empty mug and a package of loose tea sitting on Joanna's kitchen counter yesterday when I pulled her out of the house."

Trask watched her intently. "What of it? Half of Avalon drinks tea. Just like half the town wears those Dimensions bracelets."

"Yes, I know." She wrapped her arms around herself while she allowed her intuition to leap recklessly to the wild conclusion. "But when I spoke to Joanna earlier on the phone that morning, she told me she wished she had some of her tea. She said she was out of it. I told her I'd bring her some after work."

"Maybe she found an extra supply in her cupboard after she talked to you."

"Maybe." Alexa dragged her eyes away from the teapot and looked at him. "That's what I assumed at the time. But what if that's not what happened?"

"I'm listening."

"Shortly before lunch that day I went to Café Solstice to get some sandwiches for myself and Kerry. Stewart Lutton, the owner, wasn't there. One of his employees said he'd had to leave for a while, even though it was one of the busiest days of the year."

"Go on."

"This is a terrible thing to suggest without any proof, but what if Stewart took some tea out to Joanna?" She trailed off.

"And hung around to make sure she took a couple of tranquilizers, waited until she went to sleep, and then sabotaged the gas coupling inside the house?"

"Stewart lives in an old RV. He uses propane. He'd probably know how to rig the line. Of course, a lot of people know how to do stuff like that, don't they?"

"*Some* people know how to do stuff like that," Trask corrected softly. "But if you're right about the tea and the fact that Stewart was gone from his café for a while earlier in the day, it doesn't look good."

"Stewart is very committed to Dimensions. He wears a bracelet."

"From what I've seen, a lot of people wear them."

"Yes, but they're not all the same. People who are deeply involved with the work of the Institute usually have very expensive, unique designs. Stewart's is like that. Unique. And expensive."

Trask looked intrigued. "Meaning he couldn't replace it in a hurry?"

"Not unless he had a duplicate, which seems unlikely."

"So, all we have to do is get a close look at your friendly local purveyor of fine teas tomorrow and see if he's wearing a Dimensions bracelet."

Alexa looked at him very steadily. "You're going on the assumption that he'll stick around after what happened tonight."

"Damn. You may be even better at this conspiracy theory stuff than me." Trask reached for the phone.

32

"What the hell do you mean Strood isn't available?" Trask could feel the renewed sense of urgency clawing at his insides. Alexa's theories were starting to sound much too plausible. "I was with him in his office not more than an hour ago. He told me he was going home as soon as he closed out the paperwork on the Radstone shooting."

"The chief never made it home." The woman on the other end of the line sounded weary and impatient. "He was called out again. Vehicular incident."

Even in a town the size of Avalon it had to be rare that a chief of police was summoned to the scene of a routine car accident. Trask hung on to his patience with an effort.

"Look, I know Strood isn't real fond of me. He probably told you to keep me out of his hair for a while. But this is serious. I've got to get through to him."

"I'll give Chief Strood your message, sir."

He was wasting his time. "You do that. Tell him

it's important and that it involves the Radstone case."

"I'll tell him."

Trask slammed down the phone and looked at Alexa. "Strood's unavailable. All we can do is wait until he returns my call."

Alexa flopped down into one of the red tapestry chairs. "I sure hope we're right about this. It could be extremely awkward if we're wrong. Not to mention stressful and embarrassing."

He looked briefly amused. "What's this 'we' stuff? Lutton is your candidate for suspect of the year, not mine. I've got my own."

She winced. "I admit the link is a weak one. It's just that your candidate for suspect poster boy feels even more wrong. I just can't see Webster Bell deliberately endangering Joanna's life."

"I agree that it's worth mentioning Lutton to Strood." He walked back to the open French doors and braced one hand on the edge of the frame. "Alexa?"

"Yes?"

"Do you happen to know when Lutton moved to Avalon?"

He felt her sudden stillness behind him. He glanced over his shoulder and saw from the expression in her eyes that she understood.

"You're wondering if Stewart was here twelve years ago when your father died, aren't you?" she asked gently.

He looked back out into the night and made himself sound casual. "It would tie up the loose ends. Assuming he's involved in this."

"I'm sorry, Trask. I don't know when Stewart

came to Avalon. All I can tell you is that he's been around for a few years, at least. He said something once about having been one of the original tenants in Avalon Plaza."

"When did the Plaza open?"

"Five or six years ago. I don't know the exact date."

That told him nothing. "It shouldn't be hard to find out when Lutton arrived in Avalon."

"No." Alexa hesitated. "Now what?"

Trask glanced at the room service cart. "Now we eat. Then we go to bed and try to get some sleep while we wait for Strood to call."

Her gaze went to the doorway of the darkened bedroom. Trask watched her eyes slide quickly away from the shadowy entrance.

"I'd better go home," she said. "I'll need a change of clothes and other things in the morning before I go to the shop."

"Let your assistant open Elegant Relic."

"I promised her a couple of days off after the big rush was over. She said something about going to Tucson to see her boyfriend."

Trask reached out and took Alexa's hand in his. He ran his thumb lightly over the soft skin on the inside of her wrist and savored the shiver of awareness that went through her.

"You can stay here," he said softly. "I'll drive you home in the morning in time to take a shower and change clothes."

In the muted light the depths of her eyes appeared limitless. "It's one thing for you to stay with me at my place. It's another to spend the night with you here in the hotel."

Anger sparked in his gut. Or was it fear? He wondered. "What difference does it make?"

"Like you keep saying, this is a small town."

"Right. And everyone in it already knows about our relationship. Hell, even that phony psychic who read our auras tonight guessed that we were involved in an affair."

"There is such a thing as discretion," she muttered. "Staying here in the owner's suite with you and walking out through the lobby tomorrow morning in front of your front desk staff and the concierge does not qualify as discrete."

He tightened his grip on her wrist. "You're making excuses. Why?"

"Please, Trask. It's been a long night and it's not over yet. I'm tired . . ."

"I said no more excuses. Tell me the real reason you want to leave."

She glared at him. "Stop arguing with me. This is my decision. If I want to go home, I get to go home."

He exhaled deeply. "It was that aura reader, wasn't it?"

"What on earth are you talking about?"

"She made you nervous."

"Don't be ridiculous," Alexa said.

He narrowed his eyes. "She made you nervous about me. About our relationship."

"Maybe it's time I did stop and think about it," Alexa said carefully.

"Don't tell me you actually believe in any of that psychic nonsense."

"No, I don't believe in it. But she did make me consider some aspects of the situation."

"Such as?"

Alexa looked out the doors toward the moonlit spires. "Such as how quickly everything has happened between us."

"Damn. I was afraid of that."

She slanted him a sidelong glance. "We've both been under a lot of stress."

"Uh-huh."

She wriggled her hand until he reluctantly let her go. "Stress tends to magnify emotions. Makes them seem much more intense."

"Yeah, sure. So what?"

Irritation glinted in her eyes. "Look, you started this conversation. You asked me to talk to you about my feelings. I'm trying to do that, but I'm getting the distinct impression that you're already bored with the topic."

"Okay, so I'm not good with this kind of discussion."

"That's obvious."

"Maybe I just don't want to hear you say that you don't think our so-called intense emotions are worth jack squat."

She stiffened. "I didn't say that."

"Sounded like it to me."

"I'm trying to inject a little reason and logic into this relationship."

"Like hell. You're running scared all of a sudden, and it's the fault of that little con artist who said she could read our auras."

Alexa rolled her eyes. "For heaven's sake, don't blame her. If anyone's innocent in this mess, she is."

"I ought to find her and demand my money back." He walked out onto the balcony and gripped the iron railing. "Fifty bucks to screw up a perfectly good relationship. Talk about getting ripped off."

There was a short, stark silence behind him.

Alexa made an odd sound at the back of her throat.

A sudden, dark suspicion swept through him. He turned quickly.

Alexa gasped and slapped a hand over her mouth. Her eyes glinted above the edge of her palm.

He stared at her, incredulous. "Are you laughing at me?"

"Sorry." She got control of herself and gave him a placating smile. "I don't know what came over me."

He set his jaw. "I'm glad you find something amusing in this fiasco."

"Trask, we're both exhausted, tense, and, generally speaking, not at our best. Let's get some rest. We can resume this conversation at another time."

A wave of dejection welled up inside him. "I don't think it will go much better the next time." *It never does.*

The last of the laughter died in her eyes. "I see. Well, in that case, there's no point pursuing this. Will you take me home or shall I call a cab?"

"You know damn well I'll take you home." He watched her collect her big purse. "And I'll stay the night, just like I did last night. I'll sleep on the couch if that's the way you want it. But I'm not leaving you alone. No until this thing is finished."

"All right." She started toward the front door. She did not look back at him.

Something inside Trask snapped. He took three long strides, caught her by the shoulders, and pulled her around to face him.

"I don't believe in auras and psychics, but I do believe in mutual attraction." He tightened his grip on her shoulders. "I think we've got plenty of that going here."

She searched his face. "It's not enough."

"You said it was intense."

"Intensity is nice." Her smile was wistful. "Better than I imagined it would be. But I don't think it's enough, either."

"Personally, I would like to go on the record as stating that this is the most intensity I've felt for a long, long time. Maybe it's not enough for you, but it beats whatever is in second place for me. And, frankly, my dear, I don't give a damn if it is the stress that's doing it for us."

"Trask . . ."

"It feels good." He shook his head to clear it of the frustration he felt at not being able to find the right words. "It feels very good."

"I thought you were the one who didn't want to get sucked into a good fantasy."

"I've never been involved in a fantasy that was this . . ." Once more he groped for the right word. "This real."

Damn. That had come out all wrong. He'd blown it.

For a few seconds she seemed frozen in place. He could not read the emotions that swirled in her eyes. It occurred to him that he had just staked a fortune on a desperate gamble and lost everything.

Then, very slowly her hands glided up his arms and twined around his neck.

"Maybe you're right," she whispered. She

brushed her mouth across his. "After all, how often does a really terrific fantasy come along?"

A euphoric sense of relief sluiced through him. He captured her face between his hands and crushed her lips beneath his own.

Fantasy or not, this was enough for now, he told himself.

He scooped her up into his arms and carried her across the lush, elegant chamber into the ebony and silver bedroom.

He put her down on the gleaming black lacquer bed and came down on top of her, starved for the tight, hot warmth of her, thirsting for the salty perfume of her body.

The phone warbled.

His first instinct was to ignore it. He put his fingers on the buttons of Alexa's silk shirt. She opened her eyes and looked up at him.

"Strood," she said.

He groaned. Reluctantly he rolled to the side of the bed and plucked the phone off the nightstand.

"You got Trask. This had better be good."

"Sorry if I'm interrupting anything important on your end." Strood's sarcasm was laced with weary exhaustion. "I realize you big-time CEOs have lots more critical things to do than talk to a hick cop. But I just got your message, so I figured maybe you actually had something important you wanted to tell me."

Trask groaned and sat up against the lipstick-red velvet-covered pillows. "I was in bed."

"Lucky you."

Trask heard the sound of voices and a heavy truck engine in the background. "Where are you?"

"Scene of an accident. To tell you the truth, I was a little surprised that you weren't hovering in the vicinity. Lately you seem to be nearby whenever anything dramatic happens around here."

"I've had all the drama I want tonight."

"Me, too. Unfortunately, I've got a mountain of paperwork ahead of me so if this can wait until morning . . ."

"No. It can't wait. Listen, Strood, Alexa and I have been talking. For a variety of reasons, we think you should look into the possibility that Stewart Lutton, the guy who runs Café Solstice at Avalon Plaza, may know something about what's going on."

"Lutton?"

"I'll be glad to give you our thinking on this. We may be totally off base, but it's a place to start."

Silence vibrated on the other end of the line.

"Huh," Strood said.

Trask heard the scrape of metal and what sounded like the grinding of a heavy-duty winch.

"Strood?"

"Yeah?"

"Where, exactly, is the scene of that accident?"

"Funny you should ask. Avalon Point."

Trask shut his eyes. He felt Alexa's hand close around his shoulder. "Not again."

"Apparent suicide," Strood said quietly. "Even left a helpful note."

A sense of grim certainty settled on Trask. "Who's the victim?"

"Stewart Lutton. Drove his motorcycle off the cliff. In the note we found in his RV, he says something about the Guardian's work being finished."

33

She dreamed of monsters again that night. Jaws gaped, eyes gleamed, teeth protruded, tongues lolled. But none of the beasts had the power to truly scare her. She walked among them casually, as if they were familiar pets or, at the very least, business associates.

She was searching for something but the monsters kept getting in her way . . .

Alexa was worried about Trask. She knew that he was waiting for an answer to the phone call he had placed earlier. He had asked his investigator to find out when Stewart Lutton had moved to Avalon.

They still did not know much more than they did after Strood's call last night. The chief had been too busy to give them all the details. In any event, the investigation was still ongoing. From what Alexa could gather, the note Stewart had left claimed responsibility for the attempted murders of Joanna Bell and Foster Radstone and for the death of Dean Guthrie. According to Strood, Stewart had made some bizarre claim about having had a vision in which the ghost of King Arthur had appointed him the Guardian Knight of the Dimensions Institute.

Stewart's note had not, however, mentioned Harry Trask or the events of the past.

She watched Trask covertly across the breakfast cart as he drank coffee and munched eggs with methodical efficiency. She could feel the prowling tension in him. He would not be able to relax until he had the answers to the questions that had haunted him for twelve years.

She had to admit, she was more than a little curious herself, now. How long *had* Stewart lived in Avalon? she wondered.

She took a sip of the tea that the hotel kitchen had prepared in a china pot. The label read English Breakfast and carried the resort's signature logo. Some generic blend, she decided. It was okay, for hotel tea. Nevertheless, the executive chef would have done well to consult with Stewart before selecting a supplier.

Stewart.

The phone rang. Alexa was closer to it than Trask so she picked up the receiver. "Hello?"

There was a short, startled pause before a deep masculine voice said, "I'm calling for JL Trask. Did I get the wrong number?"

"No, he's here. Just a second." Alexa handed the phone across the cart.

Trask took it from her. "Phil? What? No, that wasn't the maid." He flashed Alexa a sudden, amused glance and then looked away. "A friend."

Alexa considered that closely. Anyway you looked at it, "a friend" covered a lot of ground.

"What did you get on Lutton?" Trask asked.

Alexa realized that he was talking to the investigator he had mentioned, Phil Okuda. Very slowly she put down her cup. She watched Trask's face, conscious of the tension in her own stomach.

"Five years ago? You're sure?" Trask met Alexa's eyes. "No chance he was involved with the Institute before that?"

Her heart sank. He was not getting the answers he had wanted. So much for tying up the loose ends.

"I see. All right, that settles it," he said much too evenly. "That's what I wanted to know. Yes, keep looking for Liz Guthrie. When you find her, have her give me a call. Right. I'll talk to you later."

He hung up the phone and looked at Alexa with stony eyes. "You heard?"

"Stewart came to Avalon five years ago?"

"Yes." He rubbed the back of his neck. After a moment he picked up his empty coffee mug and got to his feet. He went to the counter and grabbed the pot. "Lutton was living in the San Francisco Bay area when Dad went off Avalon Point. He was doing eighteen months on a drug conviction. There is no record of any connection to Dimensions until he moved to Avalon."

"*Drugs?*" Alexa was flabbergasted. "When I think of all the tea I bought from that man. He was a drug dealer?"

Trask said nothing.

Guilt assailed her. Stewart's former career was of little interest to him at the moment. He had other things on his mind.

She was not certain what to say. She stood and

walked across the room to put her arms around his waist from behind. She leaned her head against his strong, warm back. His muscles were rigid.

"I'm sorry, Trask."

"I told myself that I could deal with the answer, even if it wasn't the one I wanted. But I was so damn sure that Dad's death hadn't been an accident."

She tightened her arms around him. "You had no control over what happened."

"Dad was so angry that night after we talked—"

"Stop it." She dropped her arms, took hold of his shoulder, and turned him around so that he was forced to look at her. "Whatever you said that night, you did not cause your father to go off that cliff. He was a mature adult. If he was too angry and upset to drive safely, he should have known better than to get behind the wheel of a car."

Trask just looked at her with an unblinking gaze.

"Look at it this way," she said. "If you quarreled with your brother and then got into the Jeep and drove it into a ditch, who would you blame? Yourself or your brother?"

He scowled. "It would be my own fault if I ended up in the ditch."

"Because you're an adult, and part of being an adult is taking responsibility for your own actions. Right?"

He hesitated. "Yeah. Look, I know where you're going here, but—"

"The least you can do is show enough respect for the memory of your father to give him credit for being an adult who made his own decisions. Right or wrong, he made choices and they were his to make, not yours."

Trask said nothing.

She cradled his hard face between her palms. "You came back to Avalon for answers. You've got them. Now the only healthy thing you can do is let go of the past."

He pulled her into his arms, wrapped her close, and buried his face in her hair. For a long time he did not speak, but Alexa felt the tension gradually ebb from him.

She relaxed, too. It was going to be all right, she thought. Trask would deal with the answers he had gotten here in Avalon. He might not like them, but he could handle them.

The shoppers who sauntered along the shady paths of Avalon Plaza that morning were oblivious to the dark cloud of gloom that hung over it. But Alexa could feel the weight of the shock and horrified dismay that had descended on all of the tenants, herself included.

At the far end of the square Café Solstice brooded, its windows darkened, its doors locked. A bright yellow crime scene tape had been strung across the front door.

Dylan Fenn put his head inside Elegant Relic shortly after opening time. "You want any tea, Alexa? I'm making a pot in my back room."

"Thanks, I've had enough this morning." Alexa carried a fresh stack of illuminated manuscripts out of the stock room and began to arrange them on a display table. "I'm surprised any of us are even interested in tea today, given the news about Stewart. You'd think we'd all convert to coffee."

"You can say that again." Dylan shook his head. "I still can't believe it. Incredible, isn't it? Lutton, of all people. A killer."

"Goes to show you can't tell a psychopath when you see one."

"Ain't that the truth." Dylan glanced down the path toward the darkened café. "I was one of the first in line this morning to say those immortal words, *He seemed like such a nice guy.*"

"Must have been crazy for years." Alexa adjusted one of the brightly decorated manuscripts. "Apparently he saw himself as some sort of defender of the Institute. Remember what he said the other day about how Dimensions had changed his life?"

"I recall when he first came to town," Dylan mused. "He was a loner who looked like he had reached the end of the line. Then he got involved in Dimensions, and it was like he'd found an anchor in a storm. He got his act together and opened Café Solstice. Never would have guessed he'd go off the deep end the way he did."

"He must have become obsessed with Dimensions."

Dylan shook his platinum blond head. "Webster was right when he said that the opposing vortices were out of synch here in Avalon. Maybe now that this is all over, they'll start resonating properly again."

"I certainly hope so." She glanced down at the vividly decorated reproduction of an ancient map in her hand. It featured a host of dragons and strange beasts at the edge of the known world. *Monsters.* "I just hope Joanna will be all right."

"Have you heard anything about her, yet?"

"No. The hospital says she still isn't seeing visitors. Not even Webster."

Dylan looked alarmed. "You don't think there's a chance she'll be permanently—" He broke off to lower his voice. "You know, brain-damaged or something? I mean, gas and pills sounds like a pretty wicked combination."

"Webster says she's expected to make a complete recovery, at least physically. I got the impression that her real problem now is a combination of depression and anxiety."

"Poor Joanna. She kept saying that the past should stay buried."

Alexa stared at the golden-eyed monster on the map. "But none of what happened here during the past few days had anything to do with the past."

"Maybe not directly, but you have to admit that it was Trask's return to Avalon that set things in motion. If he hadn't come back . . ."

"Trask had nothing to do with anything that happened." Alexa whirled around, sudden rage welling up from an inner spring of emotion that she had not suspected she possessed. "Nothing at all. I don't want to hear any more talk about how Trask set a bunch of negative vortices in motion, do you hear me, Dylan?"

Dylan blinked a couple of times and took a hasty step back. "Uh, sure."

"That's garbage. Absolute bull. Understand?"

"Right." Dylan's head bobbed up and down. "Complete bullshit."

Alexa knew from the wary look on his face that she was in the process of losing it. She took a deep, steadying breath. "Sorry," she said gruffly. "I didn't mean to yell at you. But I really do not want to hear any more of those stupid theories about negative vortices."

Dylan smiled weakly. "Got it. No more stupid theories."

"So, when are you coming back to Seattle?" Nathan asked.

Trask gripped the phone and looked out the balcony window at the surreal landscape. "I'm not sure."

"Damn it, JL, you just told me that it was finished. You said you were finally convinced that Dad's death was an accident. Why not come home?"

Trask studied the starkly sculpted red spires outside the window and wondered why the cool green-and-water world of Seattle did not beckon, why it no longer felt like home.

"I haven't finished my vacation," he said.

"Finish it at one of the Hawaiian Avalons."

"I like it here." Saying the words out loud sent an unexpected spark of awareness through him. It was the truth, he thought. In spite of everything that had happened and the things that had not happened, he liked it here in Avalon.

"I distinctly recall hearing you say that Avalon, Arizona, was one weird place," Nathan reminded him.

"Yeah, but weirdness has its charms."

"What about all the loopy metaphysical types and the psychic nonsense?"

"You get used to them."

"What about the fact that there's no water? No lakes, no Puget Sound, no Elliott Bay?"

Trask thought about the afternoon he had sat with Alexa beside Harmony Spring. "There's water around. It just comes in different forms here in the desert." *Nothing is so seductive . . .*

"Okay, what about the lousy coffee?"

"I'm working on that problem."

Nathan paused. "Are you feeling all right, JL?"

"Yeah."

"You sure you're okay with the truth about Dad's accident? You were so damned obsessed by your theory that he was murdered . . ."

"I'm okay with the facts. This is Bottom Line Trask talking, remember?"

Nathan fell silent for a moment. When he spoke again there was a note of disbelief in his voice. "It's the Chambers woman, isn't it? Alexa? Is that her name?"

"Yeah," Trask said. "That's her name."

Nathan went quiet again for a while.

"Are you sleeping with her?" he asked eventually in an unnaturally neutral tone.

Trask said nothing.

"You *are* sleeping with her," Nathan said.

Trask did not respond.

"I guess that's okay." Nathan sounded cautious now. "Maybe an affair is what you need right now. Might be therapeutic."

"I wasn't asking for your approval, and I'm not interested in therapy."

"You're probably a little vulnerable right now," Nathan said gently.

Trask considered hurling the phone off the balcony. "Vulnerable? Where did you pick up that kind of language? You sure as hell didn't learn it from me."

Nathan chuckled ruefully. "Got it from Sarah. If you don't want her advice, remember your own."

"What advice is that?"

"Don't get caught up in the fantasy."

"Since when have you ever known me to get sucked into a fantasy?"

"Hey, I'm just spouting off words of wisdom from my esteemed elder brother."

"Give my best to Sarah." Very deliberately Trask disconnected the phone.

After a while he got up and went out onto the balcony. He sank down into one of the loungers and brooded over the spectacular scenery.

What the hell was the matter with him?

It took a while for the truth to surface. But when it did he knew he had a serious problem.

This time he wanted the fantasy to be real.

At four-thirty that afternoon Alexa sold the last gargoyle from the display, an engagingly ugly little creature with pointy ears and a lolling tongue.

She went into the stock room to fetch another supply. For some inexplicable reason, the little monsters had been selling like hotcakes all day.

She selected a box of small gargoyles that were each about the size of a man's fist and carried it back to the display table.

Opening the box, she began arranging the surprisingly heavy little statues in a whimsical design.

Little monsters.

She paused, a gargoyle in hand, and glanced into the stock room.

After a moment she set down the gargoyle and walked slowly back into the cluttered room.

She came to a halt and stared at the boxes full of gargoyles stacked against the far wall. From out of nowhere fragments of a dream shimmered in her mind.

The monsters surrounded her . . . as if they were all frozen . . .

An eerie sensation crawled up the skin of her arms and stirred the hair on the nape of her neck.

Jaws gaped, eyes gleamed, teeth protruded, tongues lolled.

She glanced through the doorway that connected the stock room to the front portion of the shop. There were no customers in sight.

Reluctantly she turned back to study the boxes of gargoyles. Joanna had tried to tell her something about monsters.

. . . It's with the monsters . . .

Impossible.

Ridiculous.

But what if Joanna had not been entirely out of her head that day when she had nearly died from the pills and gas. What if there had been some truth mixed with the hallucinations?

Talk about a fantasy. It was a crazy notion, but there was no help for it. She would not be able to put the bizarre thought out of her mind until she had satisfied herself that Joanna's strange words had had nothing to do with the little "monsters" in the boxes.

She waded through the ranks of winged lions, gothic dragons, and ancient Egyptian mummy masks to where the gargoyle boxes were heaped against the wall.

She reached up, took down the nearest carton, and unsealed the lid. She glanced inside. Cheerfully menacing little gargoyles gazed up at her out of their nest of plastic packing material.

She shut the lid and opened another box. This time lascivious gargoyles laughed at her, mouths open in rakish grins. She tried a third carton. Gargoyles with sly expressions winked at her.

A small sound from the outer room startled her. She nearly dropped the box of gargoyles.

"I'll be with you in a minute," Alexa called loudly.

"There's no rush, dear."

The warm, grandmotherly voice chilled the blood in Alexa's veins. She put down the heavy carton and turned very slowly to look at the petite, silver-haired woman with the sparkling blue eyes who hovered in the doorway.

"Well, shoot." Alexa fitted her hands on her hips. "I should have known you'd turn up sooner or later."

"How lovely to see you again, dear." Harriet McClelland glowed with pleasure. "It's been a long time, hasn't it?"

"Not long enough, Mac. Not nearly long enough."

34

"I thought we should talk, Trask." Webster rubbed the bridge of his nose in a world-weary gesture as he paced back and forth in front of the balcony window. "Compare notes, as it were. You risked your neck and saved Radstone's life last night. Thought you'd like to know what my accountants have discovered so far."

Trask looked up from pouring his unexpected guest a cup of coffee. Webster was in his trademark black clothes this afternoon. His silver and turquoise jewelry gleamed as brightly as ever. But the lines at the corners of his mouth appeared more deeply etched, and his eyes did not glow with the usual expression of benevolence and deep-seeing perception. It was obvious he'd gotten little sleep in the past twenty-four hours.

"I'll admit I'm interested in the details." Trask handed Webster the coffee. "But, first, how is Joanna feeling?"

"She still won't talk to me. All she wants to do is sleep. The doctors say they think she may have ingested something besides the tranquilizers. An hallucinogen of some sort."

"Some drug Lutton gave her?"

"Yes. All her vital signs look good now, thank God, but they won't be able to assess her mental state for a while." Webster's hand closed into a fist. "Every time I think about that bastard, Lutton, and what he tried to do to her . . ."

"You were going to tell me what you'd found out about Radstone," Trask prompted.

Webster exhaled heavily. "The doctors say he'll make it. The sneaky son-of-a-bitch was bleeding the trust dry."

He took a sip from the cup and grimaced. Trask could not tell if it was the taste of the coffee or the thought of Foster Radstone that induced the expression.

"I understand that Lutton was convinced that he'd been charged with some mystical duty to protect the Institute," Trask said. "But as far as I've been able to learn, his only experience in business consisted of drug dealing and running a small café. Any idea how he uncovered the work of a sophisticated con man like Radstone?"

Webster's brows came together in a thoughtful frown. "I suppose we'll never know for certain. He volunteered a lot at the Institute. Worked in the trust offices for a while."

"You think he just stumbled into some data that indicated Radstone was skimming from the trust and knew how to interpret it?"

Webster shrugged. "That's the only way to explain it. Radstone wouldn't have had to go to great lengths to hide his scam from me. Fool that I was, I turned over the entire financial operation to him."

"Even so, you've got accountants, bookkeepers, and the tax folks involved in any business the size of Dimensions. None of them noticed anything wrong, yet some ex-drug dealer figures it all out?"

Webster eyed him. "You're saying it doesn't feel right?"

"Yeah, that's what I'm saying."

Webster studied the view through the open French doors. "Strood says Lutton's note indicates that, with Guthrie, Radstone, and Joanna out of the way, he considered his job finished."

"But he'd botched at least two out of three of those jobs. Joanna is still alive, and he couldn't be sure that Radstone was dead. The only one he actually got rid of was Guthrie. Why commit suicide now?"

"Who knows?" Webster's jaw tightened. "He was crazy. Crazy people do crazy things. Maybe he killed himself because he had failed too often."

Trask walked forward to join Webster in the open doorway. "There are still some loose threads in this thing."

"Such as?"

"I'd like to know what happened to Liz Guthrie, for one thing."

A troubled look passed across Webster's face. "Yes. I'm starting to worry about her myself. Strood still thinks she simply left town for personal reasons. He believes she's safe because there was no mention of her in Lutton's note."

"I've got someone looking for her. This morning he told me he thought he was getting close. With any luck he'll pick her up today."

Webster nodded, clearly relieved. "It sounds as if he expects to find her alive, thank God."

"I've got a question I want to ask her."

"What's that?"

Trask glanced at him. "I want to know the name of her personal meditation guide. The one who was with her the morning she suddenly left town."

Webster's expression tightened. "We don't assign personal guides who make house calls. Must have been part of Radstone's con. He probably pretended to be her guide and used his influence to get her to write checks to that account that he controlled."

Trask considered that. "Maybe."

Webster smiled slightly. "I can see you're a long way from satisfied."

"I'm a hard-to-satisfy kind of guy."

Webster nodded. "Probably what makes you so successful. Trask, I know this is none of my business, but, like everyone else in town, I'm aware that you came back here to Avalon to look for answers relating to your own past. I'm also aware that you didn't find them."

"I found them. They just weren't the ones that I expected, that's all."

"That is often the case in life, isn't it? The end result of the harmonic convergence is rarely what we anticipate. But that does not mean that the energy vortices do not resonate."

"Bell, if you don't mind, I'd prefer to skip the metaphysical lecture today. I'm not in the mood."

"I realize you don't hold with a lot of our theories, but I can't help thinking that you were drawn back to this place at this time for a reason."

"There was a reason, all right. I had a new hotel to open."

Nathan was right, he thought. He'd finished what he'd come here to Avalon to do. He had no more excuses for hanging around.

The only thing holding him here was a fantasy.

Harriet gave Alexa a cheerful smile. "It's almost time to close your shop, dear. Why don't we go somewhere and have a nice cup of tea together? We can talk over old times."

Alexa opened another box of gargoyles. "The last thing I want to do is have a cup of tea with you, Mac."

"Coffee, then," Harriet said irrepressibly. "I noticed a cute little café at the end of the walk."

"It's closed indefinitely." Alexa examined the monsters inside the box and closed the lid. "What do you want, Mac?"

"Oh, dear. I see you're still a trifle upset with me."

That was too much. Alexa shoved the carton of gargoyles back into place in the stack and swung around to confront Harriet.

"Upset? Why should I be upset, Mac? You pretended you were my friend and mentor, but you set me up to take the fall when your forgery scheme fell apart. You left me to face your irate clients. You disappeared without a trace, leaving me holding the bag."

"I know you won't believe me, dear, but I never intended for you to get into trouble because of my little side business."

"Side business? You're an art forger. You cheated some very powerful people. They were not happy when they found out they'd been taken to the cleaners. Experts hate it when someone makes a fool out of them."

"I suppose I should be ashamed at having duped the so-called experts and the critics." Harriet twinkled. "But you must admit, some of them had it coming. Such an arrogant, prissy lot."

"That arrogant, prissy lot tore my reputation to shreds. I was found guilty by association. I've had to go to ground for over a year to let the worst of the gossip dissipate. I may never fully recover."

"Nonsense. Ultimately, the publicity will serve you well. Trust me."

"Trust you? Mac, I did trust you once and you betrayed me."

"There's no need to go all melodramatic." Harriet smiled benignly. "You'll do just fine, believe me. When the reviews of your wonderful Art Deco collection at the Avalon Resort & Spa hit print, you'll be hailed as the brilliant expert who exposed the McClelland forgeries."

"If the word *McClelland* ever appears next to my name in print again, I'll be doomed."

Harriet shook her head sadly. "You've got fantastic instincts when it comes to early-twentieth-century art, my dear, but you still have a great deal to learn about how things work in the art world."

Alexa folded her arms. "In the past year, I've learned more than I really want to know, thank you very much."

"Nonsense. What you fail to grasp is the importance of mystique."

Alexa raised her brows. "Mystique? Is that another word for stupidity?"

"No, dear, it's another word for presence. For fascination. For excitement. For charisma. For glamour. In short, for all the qualities that captivate those who make a living in the world of art."

"Oh, yeah?" Alexa swept out a hand to indicate the cluttered back room full of imitation marble statuary, cheap tapestries, and fake swords. "Does this look like I've got a lot of mystique in my life?"

"Give it time, my dear." Harriet looked wistful. "Young people are always so impatient."

"Impatient?" Alexa yelped. "Is that what you—?"

There was a movement in the doorway. She broke off to glance between two towers built of Greek pedestals and saw Dylan. He had a Styrofoam cup in one hand. He gave her an awkward smile.

"Uh, sorry." He glanced uneasily at her and then at Harriet. "Am I interrupting anything?"

Harriet gave him her charm-the-client smile. "Not at all, dear boy. Alexa and I are old friends. We haven't seen each other in a while. We were just renewing our acquaintance."

"I see." Dylan looked dubious. He turned to Alexa for guidance.

She managed to unclench her teeth. "Was there something you wanted, Dylan?"

"Brought you some tea." He held up the plastic cup. "Iced. I'll, uh, just put it down on your front counter."

"Thank you, Dylan."

"Sure. Any time." He stepped back and came up hard against the full-sized suit of sixteenth-century armor. There was a loud clang. One of the metal gauntlets clattered to the floor.

"Oops." Dylan's pale face flushed a dark red.

"Careful, there," Harriet said brightly.

Dylan winced. He stretched out his arm to scoop up the fallen gauntlet. Then he stood holding it with an abashed expression. "I'm not sure how to put it back."

"Just set it down on the table," Alexa said. "I'll reattach it later."

"Sure. Okay." Dylan set the heavy glove on a table. "See you tomorrow, Alexa." He nodded politely at Harriet. "Ma'am."

He disappeared in an embarrassed rush.

Harriet turned to Alexa. "Your friend is the anxious sort, isn't he?"

"Your fault. You made him nervous."

"But, dear—"

"You make me nervous." Alexa waved that aside. "Just tell me why you're here, Mac."

"It's very simple really." Harriet's smile would have soothed a disgruntled devil. "I need a little help from one of my dearest friends."

Alexa stared at her aghast. "Me?"

"You."

"Forget it." Resolutely, Alexa turned back to the stack of gargoyle boxes. "I'm busy."

"I can see that. But this won't take long. It's a simple request, really."

"There is no such thing as a simple request where you're concerned." Alexa lifted another box down from the stack and yanked open the lid. More gargoyle eyes goggled up at her. "You're bad news,

Mac. I gave you the best years of my life, and look what you did to me."

"Because of me, my dear, you will one day be a legend in the business. You will surpass that twit, Paxton Forsyth, himself, in prominence. In the future your verdict on any objet d'art created in the first half of the twentieth century will be accepted as the final authority."

"Yeah, sure." Alexa was aware of a growing sense of anxiety. The deeper she dug into the heap of gargoyle cartons the more convinced she was that Joanna had been trying to tell her something important. "Let's have it, Mac. Why are you here?"

Harriet cleared her throat. "Well, dear, as it happens, I have recently acquired a rather important client."

"Client?" That stopped her for a moment. Alexa looked at Harriet over her shoulder. "I knew it. You're still in business, aren't you?"

"Yes, of course." Harriet chuckled. "Can you envision me just sitting back in my rocking chair, knitting?"

The thought of Mac not involved in the art world was mind-boggling, Alexa admitted silently. "What, exactly, are you doing these days, Mac?"

"The usual," Harriet said airily. "I assist my clients in acquiring the very finest early-twentieth-century art and antiques."

"Who are these clients?" Alexa asked suspiciously.

"Wealthy, discerning collectors who, for one reason or another, prefer not to do business with the customary galleries and auction houses."

"Why not? Afraid they'll get arrested?"

"In some cases, yes." Harriet smiled candidly. "In others, there is a fear of deportation. Some simply are obsessed with maintaining their anonymity. Collectors are an odd lot, you know that. I cater to those who like to keep a very low profile."

"So, you're working for criminals and lowlifes who don't dare come out in the light of day. Congratulations, Mac. Sounds exciting."

"It certainly has its moments. Now then, the reason I need your assistance, my dear, is that I have recently acquired a very fine Icarus Ives piece for my client. *Dancing Satyr.*"

Alexa groaned. "I should have known."

Harriet's eyes widened innocently. "I take it you're with me on this so far."

"I knew that Ives piece that Edward bought from Forsyth was one of your forgeries. I was sure of it."

"Lovely, isn't it? I understand it's in the new Avalon Resort & Spa collection."

"West wing. Right outside the owner's suite." Alexa glowered. "I wondered what had happened to the real one. You stole it, didn't you? And then arranged to leave your fake in its place."

Harriet glowed with pride of craftsmanship. "Paxton Forsyth never knew the difference. And Edward Vale, being the charming dunce that he is, purchased it for the new Avalon collection. I knew I was in trouble when I heard the rumor that you were vetting Vale's acquisitions."

Alexa was briefly distracted by that news. "The rumors about me are already on the street?"

"Of course, dear. I told you that you were well on your way to becoming a legend."

Alexa narrowed her eyes. "What's the problem? You've got the real *Satyr* for your client."

"The problem," Harriet said delicately, "is that my client unfortunately obtained Vale's catalog of the Avalon collection. He noticed that *Dancing Satyr* was listed among the items housed in the hotel, and he naturally wondered a bit about the authenticity of his own *Satyr*."

A short silence descended. Alexa bit her lip. And then, from out of nowhere, the humor of the situation swept over her.

"Oh, lord, this is wonderful." Laughter welled up. She succumbed to it. "This is great. Shot yourself in the foot, huh, Mac? Your new client is afraid you've foisted off a forgery on him. He thinks the real *Satyr* is in the Avalon Resort collection. He's afraid you sold him the fake."

"That's about the size of it, I'm afraid." Harriet coughed discreetly. "Unfortunately, my client is inclined to take a somewhat dim view of the situation."

"Serves you right. What do you expect me to do about it?"

"My client wants a second opinion on his *Satyr*." Harriet paused meaningfully. "And he wants it from the expert who exposed the McClelland forgeries."

Alexa straightened slowly. "He wants a second opinion from me?"

"Yes, you dear." Harriet smiled broadly. "A droll predicament, is it not?"

"Hilarious."

"I promise you that once you have convinced my client that his *Satyr* is the real one, nothing more will be said about the matter. The fake can stay in the Avalon Resort collection forever, and no one will be the wiser. My client has no interest in exposing the fraudulent *Satyr*. He merely wishes to be assured that he has the real one."

"Mac, if you really think I'm going to help you out of this mess, you've slipped a cog since the last time I saw you."

"Come now. Surely our friendship can sustain a small misunderstanding."

"Is that what you call it when you leave a friend to take the heat for a bunch of fake statues? A misunderstanding? I don't— Oh, wow."

"Alexa? What is it, dear?"

"I knew it was here somewhere." Alexa stared at the corner of the turquoise and white cover of a Dimensions meditation journal. "She didn't hide it inside one of these cartons, she hid it *behind* the stack."

She went back to work with a will, dragging the rest of the cartons aside so that she could get at the journal.

"Do be careful, dear." Harriet frowned in concern as she watched Alexa stagger under the weight of a large carton. "That looks rather heavy. Can I give you a hand?"

"Yes, you can, as a matter of fact." Alexa reached for the journal.

And froze.

Hand.

The image of Dylan reaching down with his right hand to pick up the fallen gauntlet blazed in her mind.

"Oh, damn," she whispered.

Harriet looked concerned. "What on earth is wrong now, dear?"

"I just remembered something."

"Something important?"

"Maybe."

"Well, dear?" Harriet prodded. "What is the matter?"

"Dylan wasn't wearing his Dimensions bracelet."

3 5

The phone rang just as Webster was preparing to leave the suite. Trask grabbed the receiver.

"Trask, here."

"I found Ms. Guthrie," Phil Okura said without preamble. "She's with me now. Safe and sound, but scared to death."

"Where are you?" Trask motioned to Webster to come back into the suite.

"In a hotel near the Tucson airport. She's been staying here since she left Avalon. She won't talk to me. Says she can't trust anyone except her guide, whoever that is."

Trask watched Webster close the door and come back into the suite. "Ask her if Stewart Lutton or Foster Radstone was her guide."

Webster's black and silver brows bunched with concern as he listened to Trask's side of the conversation.

Phil paused to repeat the question. Trask heard a muffled response.

"What did she say?" he asked.

"She won't answer the question. She won't talk to anyone except her guide."

"Ask her if she'll talk to Webster Bell."

There was another short pause while Phil relayed the question. He came back on the line a few seconds later.

"She says of course she'll talk to him, but she doesn't believe that he's there with you. The lady is really frightened, Trask."

"Hang on." Trask handed the phone to Webster. "Ask her for the name of her personal guide. The one who was with her the morning she left Avalon."

Webster took the phone. "Liz? Is that you? We've been worried about you."

The deep music of his voice resonated through the room. Trask knew that on the other end of the line, Liz would be reassured. There was no mistaking Webster's voice.

"Yes, Stewart's death was a shock to all of us," Webster said gently. "The poor man was clearly very disturbed. Yes, it's safe to come home now. The vortices are no longer in a state of flux. Do you mind if I ask why you left Avalon?"

Another short pause.

"I see." Webster glanced at Trask. "You say your personal guide knew that the vortices were going to become violent? Yes, he was obviously very much in tune with the harmonic energies. Very wise of him to advise you to stay out of the area for a while."

Exasperated by the slow pace of the conversation, Trask began to prowl the room. He knew that Webster was probably handling Liz Guthrie the right way, but that did not make it any easier to control his impatience.

"Liz, I'm not in my office and I don't have access to my records," Webster said casually. "As you know, I've been a little busy lately. Can you remind me which personal guide Dimensions assigned to you?"

Trask halted.

"Are you sure?" Surprise echoed in Webster's voice. It disappeared at once beneath a soothing balm of honey and warmth. "Of course. Thank you, Liz. Take care of yourself, my dear. I'll see you when you get back to Avalon."

Webster hung up the phone and looked at Trask.

"Well?" Trask prompted.

"I don't get it." Webster frowned. "It doesn't make any sense. She says her personal meditation guide was Dylan Fenn."

"Damn." Trask grabbed the phone.

"This is all very exciting, dear." Harriet's eyes gleamed with enthusiasm as she followed Alexa across the stock room. "But would you mind telling me why we are about to sneak out of your shop through the rear door?"

"Because if we leave by the front door, Dylan will see us. We'd have to walk straight past his shop window to get to the parking lot."

"He'll think we're going for a cup of tea."

"No, he won't. The only café in Avalon Plaza is closed."

The decision to leave was an impulse that was too strong to deny. An overpowering sense of urgency was riding Alexa. Given the events of the previous few days, she thought, it might be best to follow her instincts.

"If you think this is a matter for the police, why don't you call them?"

"That's the problem. I don't know yet if it's a police matter." Alexa forged a path through a row of pedestals toward the rear door. "Chief Strood has already concluded that I'm a little on the flaky side. If I call him with a lot of wild accusations and no proof, he'll think I've gone over the edge. As far as he's concerned, he's already closed this case."

"You think you'll find proof in that book that this Dylan Fenn person is involved in something nefarious?"

"Maybe. Right now I only know two things for certain. The first is that Joanna felt she had to hide her journal. The second is that Dylan wasn't wearing his Dimensions bracelet. He never takes it off."

"Which means?"

"Which means he may have been the person Trask discovered in Foster Radstone's office last night."

"This is all very complicated, dear."

"Yes, it is. Which is why I want to get this journal someplace where I can sit down and read it without worrying about Dylan walking in on me."

"Shouldn't you lock the front door of your shop?" Harriet asked.

"No. If Dylan comes for another visit and finds it locked with all the lights on, he might get suspicious. This way he'll just assume that I went down the alley to dump some garbage or something."

"If you say so." Harriet glanced around the stock room as Alexa reached for the doorknob. She wrinkled her elegant nose in gentle disdain. "Now that I consider the matter, I must admit there is probably no pressing need to lock up this particular collection. Who would want to steal any of this stuff?"

Alexa glared at her. "Don't start. I'm in this line of work because of you, Mac."

"Now, now, dear, it's only temporary, after all. And we have agreed to let bygones be bygones."

Alexa yanked open the door. "No, we have not agreed—" She took one step outside and came to an abrupt halt. "Damn, damn, damn."

Dylan stood there. He had a gun in one hand and a sad little smile on his face. He flicked a glance at the journal Alexa held.

"I see you found it. I wondered where Joanna had hidden it."

Anger blazed, clean and strong. It burned away some of the fear and shock that was coursing through her. "What is this all about, Dylan?"

"It's about sacrifice, Alexa. I worked so hard, but you ruined everything. I'm afraid only another sacrifice can realign the vortices now."

"I ruined things? You're crazy."

Dylan's eyes glittered with sudden fury. "Joanna and Radstone should both be dead by now, along with Guthrie. The vortices should have come back into balance. Peace and serenity should have been reestablished here in Avalon. But because of you and Trask, the harmony of the energy forces is still deeply disturbed."

Harriet pursed her lips. "What's this talk about sacrifice, young man?"

Alexa tightened her grip on the journal. "Don't you see, Mac? The little creep thinks he's sacrificed himself for the sake of the vortices. But he screwed up. Things didn't go the way he planned."

"No, no, Alexa." Dylan used the gun to motion the two women back into the store room. "You don't understand," he said as he followed them through the door. "You, Alexa, are the sacrifice. Your death will calm the vortices. Unfortunately, I'm afraid your friend, here, will also have to die. Sorry, ma'am. One of those wrong-place-at-the-wrong-time things, you know?"

"She's not answering the shop phone or her cell phone." Trask cut the connection.

"Take it easy," Webster said. "Maybe she's busy with a customer. Or maybe she just stepped out for a moment."

"I don't like it." Trask picked up his keys and went to the door. "I'm going to drive over to Avalon Plaza. Want to come along?"

"Yes." Webster went after him. "On the way, you can tell me what you think is going on here."

"I've got a question for you first." Trask reached the hall and went swiftly toward the stairs. "How long has Dylan been associated with Dimensions?"

"Since the beginning." Webster descended the staircase behind Trask. "He came to work for me when I opened the Institute."

"I knew it," Trask said. "I always knew it. Should have figured it all out a hell of a lot sooner."

"Are you implying that Dylan is the killer?"

"Yes. He'll be very desperate and very frustrated by now. He'll be looking for someone to blame." Trask hit the first floor and shifted into a run.

Webster huffed after him. "You think he's a danger to Alexa?"

"He has the shop two doors down from her, and

I can't get her on the phone. What do you think?"

"I think there may be a problem," Webster muttered.

"I should have answered the phone," Alexa said. "Someone might wonder why I didn't." *Someone like Trask, for instance.*

"Not likely," Dylan said. "Whoever it is will think you're in the rest room or something."

The call had been from Trask. She was sure of it. Or was desperation causing her to conjure fantasies of rescue?

Mentally she projected a vision of Trask getting into his Jeep and driving over to the Plaza to see what was going on. It was a weak vision, at best. Maybe she should have paid more attention to some of Webster Bell's theories of positive image projection.

"What's the plan, Dylan?" Alexa clutched Joanna's journal and tried hard not to look at the gun. Beside her, Harriet appeared uncharacteristically anxious, even dithery.

"The plan," Dylan said, "is to wait until after five o'clock. When the rest of the shops have closed and everyone has gone home for the day, the sacrifice will be made."

Alexa stared at him. "You think you can just kill me and go on with business as usual?"

"Unfortunately, I'll have to leave Avalon with my work only partially accomplished." Dylan's eyes slitted. "All because of you. I tried to keep you out of this. I knew that you would disturb the vortices. But you insisted on continuing to interfere. You got involved with him. You slept with him."

"Trask?"

"Yes, Trask." Dylan frowned. "It wasn't supposed to end like this. It was supposed to be neat and tidy. All of the forces were supposed to be back in proper alignment by now."

Harriet put a hand to her throat. "Oh, my, I'm feeling a little dizzy."

Alexa doubted that Harriet had ever been dizzy in her life, but she refrained from commenting. Instead she looked at Dylan. "Let my friend go. She doesn't know anything about any of this."

"I can't do that." Dylan glanced at his watch. "She'll cause trouble."

"She won't go to the cops, if that's what you mean. She has a few issues with the police herself."

"Really, dear," Harriet said in a weak, breathy voice. "There is no need to air dirty laundry in front of strangers."

Dylan scowled. "I don't care if she's wanted for murder. I can't trust her. I'm not letting her leave."

"Is it hot in here or is it just me?" Harriet asked.

Alexa summoned up what she hoped was an anxious expression. "Maybe you'd better sit down, Mac."

She used her eyes to indicate a rank of winged lions. Understanding flashed in Harriet's gaze.

If they could put a few of the cartons full of stone pedestals and imitation statuary between themselves and Dylan, they might be able to use them as a barricade. With luck, one of them, at least, might make it into the outer room when the shooting started.

"Yes, I suppose that would be best." Harriet tottered to the row of heavy lions and started to lower herself onto a carton. "My doctor told me to avoid undue excitement."

"Don't move," Dylan said sharply. "Stay right where you are."

"Whatever you say," Harriet murmured. She straightened with what appeared to be painful effort. "Would you mind if I got my pills out of my purse?"

Dylan glanced at her handbag. "You won't need them."

Alexa looked at him. "You know you won't get away with this. Trask will figure out what happened. He won't give up until he finds you. He's that way about some things. A little obsessive."

Dylan tightened his grip on the gun. "I'll take care of Trask later. After the sacrifice calms the vortices."

"You do realize that all this talk of a sacrifice makes you sound less than sane, don't you?" Alexa asked casually.

Dylan uttered a disgusted sound. "You don't understand any of it, do you?"

"Why don't you explain it to me? Start with how you found out that Foster Radstone was skimming funds from the Institute."

"I've always kept close tabs on the Institute's financial status. It was one of my duties as the Guardian. I suspected Radstone was skimming months ago. I added him to my list."

Harriet peered at him with wide-eyed interest. "Forgive me, young man, but you don't appear to be the type who takes an interest in financial matters."

Dylan gave her a brief, chilling smile. "I was a

corporate financial officer for over a decade before I found the path to Dimensions."

"And you seemed like such a nice man," Alexa muttered. "What was this list you mentioned?"

His expression implied that she was not very bright. "The list of people who had to be removed so that the message of Dimensions could expand farther into the world. There were three of them on it at the beginning. Dean Guthrie was at the top. Radstone was next. Liz Guthrie was to be the last."

"My God," Alexa whispered.

He ignored that. "I meditated for a long time on how to proceed."

"Not long enough, apparently," Alexa said. "Why did you wait until Trask arrived in Avalon?"

"If it had been necessary to get rid of Guthrie immediately, I would have done so. But I knew that I could afford to wait for a few months to begin the process of getting rid of those who stood in the way. The problem was that I had to arrange for several deaths rather close together in time."

"And you wanted to be sure that Chief Strood didn't conclude there was a link between them, is that it?" Alexa asked.

"Exactly. I knew that having Trask in town at the time of Guthrie's accident would provide a distraction in case Strood got suspicious."

"Which he didn't," Alexa said.

Dylan's mouth tightened with disdain. "Chief Strood was his usual incompetent self. He never seriously questioned Guthrie's crash."

"After Guthrie's death went off without a hitch, you figured you were on a roll, didn't you?"

"The vortices were in flux. There was an enormous amount of negative energy available for me to tap. It was a sign that I was to continue with my plan."

"But after Guthrie, things started going wrong, didn't they?"

Dylan's jaw locked in fury. "I had everything planned so that each killing would look different. Unrelated to any of the others. But the only one that went right was Guthrie. You and Trask screwed up the others."

Out of the corner of her eye, Alexa saw Harriet give her a speculative glance. She realized that the older woman was willing to take her cue from her.

The only thing Alexa could think of to do at that moment was keep Dylan talking while she and Harriet tried to maneuver behind a makeshift barricade.

"Tell me about Liz," Alexa said. "Is she okay?"

Irritation flickered in his eyes. "It's much too soon for her to die. It would look weird if her accident followed too closely on the heels of her ex-husband's death."

Alexa sank her nails into the journal. "I can see where that might raise a few questions. Sooner or later everyone's going to find out that Liz inherits Dean's entire estate, right? And I'll bet she, in turn, has left her entire estate to the Institute."

Dylan blinked owlishly. "You know about the wills?"

"Trask and I figured it out."

"Ultimately everything Liz possesses will go to the Dimensions Trust," Dylan said with evident satisfaction.

"You're her personal meditation guide, aren't

you? You're the one who sent her away the morning that I went to see her."

Dylan's fist tightened around the gun. "When she hung up the phone and said you were planning to drop by after her meditation session, I realized you were starting to ask too many questions. And you were involved with Trask. It was all getting very complicated."

"You couldn't risk having me talk to Liz, could you?"

"No. You might have put doubts into her head. I didn't know how much you and Trask already suspected, you see."

"How did you get her to leave so suddenly?"

He gave her his impish smile. "She trusted me implicitly. I warned her that the vortices had become extremely dangerous for her. Which was true enough, when you think about it. I told her she had to leave the area at once and stay away until I let her know that it was safe to return."

"And then you hung around her house to terrorize me, didn't you?"

The gun in Dylan's hand trembled slightly. "No, I left right after I saw Liz off. Then I realized that her personal journal was still in the house. In her rush to pack, she had forgotten it and so had I."

"You didn't want me to find it and browse through it, did you?"

"No. I was afraid that she might have mentioned me, you see. If you saw my name in her journal you would only ask more questions. I went back to get the damned thing. But I saw your car in the drive."

"And you knew that I was already there."

"Prowling around like a burglar." Dylan fixed

her with an accusing look. "I decided to give you a good scare. I parked farther down the road and put on the robes that I wear when I guide Liz's meditation. I entered through the front door while you were looking through the garage window. Got a knife from the kitchen. All I intended to do at first was frighten you off so that I could get the journal and leave."

"I don't believe that."

"It's true." He scowled. "But then it occurred to me that our encounter was a sign. I realized the vortices had provided me with an opportunity to get rid of you."

"But you failed again, didn't you?" Alexa said. "Tell me, did I do any damage when I sent that little landslide down on top of you?"

"Bitch." Dylan leveled the gun at her. "When I think about how I actually tried to keep you out of this . . ."

"I'm very sorry," Harriet quavered. "But I'm afraid that if I don't sit down, I shall collapse. I really don't feel at all well."

Dylan hesitated. Then he made an offhand motion with his free hand. "Go ahead. Sit down."

Moving with a fragile air, Harriet sank gracefully onto a small box behind the row of winged lions.

Once seated, only her head and shoulders were visible above the backs of the stone beasts. She gave Dylan a weak, pitifully grateful smile. "Thank you, dear boy. So kind."

Dylan paid no attention. He glanced at his watch again. "Only a few more minutes. Then it will all be over."

Alexa was keenly aware of the distant, muted

sounds of cars pulling out of the parking lot. Most of the shoppers would have left by now. Her fellow tenants would be finished counting the day's receipts soon. It would not be long before Avalon Plaza would be deserted.

Keep Dylan talking and pray that Trask was on his way.

Think positive.

"How did you kill Dean Guthrie?" she asked as casually as possible.

"Guthrie was easy. He was drunk, as usual, when he left the bar that night. I hid in the backseat of that big car of his. When he got behind the wheel, I hit him on the head. He went out like a light."

"Then you drove him to Avalon Point?"

Dylan nodded happily. "I got out, wedged his foot against the gas pedal, and put the car in gear. It went straight over the edge."

Alexa shuddered. "You chose Avalon Point because of the connection to Trask, didn't you?"

"Sure. Like I said, if any questions were asked afterward, I wanted Strood to look in Trask's direction. Besides, it was sort of symbolic, you know?"

"Symbolic?"

Dylan's smile was snake-thin. "That's the same place where I forced Harry Trask off the road twelve years ago."

Alexa took a deep breath. "So Trask was right all along. His father was murdered."

Dylan raised one shoulder in another dismissing motion. "I had to get rid of him. He stood in the way of the expansion of Dimensions."

"But why did you murder poor Stewart? He wasn't on your list."

Rage flickered in Dylan's eyes. "I did not murder Stewart. He was a sacrifice, just like you."

"There's a difference between murder and sacrifice?"

"A world of difference. Stewart was my loyal, gallant squire. He was as committed as I am to the cause. But after things went wrong again last night, I realized that it was necessary to feed the dark vortices. Besides, he had failed to get rid of Joanna. It was only fitting that he pay the price."

"You weren't trying to pacify the vortices," Alexa shot back. "You figured that if Stewart conveniently committed suicide, it might satisfy both Trask and Strood. Get them off your back. Why did you send Stewart to kill Joanna, anyway?"

Dylan's hand tightened on the gun. "In her efforts to keep the past buried, she was doing great harm. She was starting to ask her own questions. She and Liz are close, you see. They began to talk about the similarities between the deaths of Guthrie and Harry Trask. I couldn't allow that. I appointed Stewart to get rid of her."

"What's in her journal? Why do you want it?"

"I don't know," Dylan said harshly. "But that idiot, Liz, contacted her after she went into hiding. She was warned not to talk to anyone, but when I called her, she admitted that she was so scared the day she left Avalon that she called her closest friend."

"Joanna."

"Yes."

"And now you're afraid that Joanna might have written something in her journal that implicates you."

"Looking back," Dylan muttered, "I think she'd had her suspicions all along."

"But she kept quiet," Webster said in a great rolling voice that filled the little stock room to the brim, "because deep down she was afraid that I was the killer."

Everyone's head snapped around to stare at Webster, who stood in the alley doorway.

Dylan jerked as though one of the energy vortices had delivered a high-voltage shock. "*Webster.* No. You're not supposed to be here. You're not supposed to be involved in this."

"Put the gun down," Webster said in a commanding voice. "It's all over."

"Don't come any closer or I'll kill her." Dylan edged closer to Alexa as he spoke. "I swear I will."

"Give me the gun," Webster said quietly.

"But, Webster, I'm your Guardian Knight. Don't you see? I live to serve the Dimensions Way. You must trust me to handle this."

"Put down the gun, Dylan."

Harriet shot to her feet with a high, keening shriek. "My heart. My heart." She clawed wildly at her throat and toppled sideways into a tower of cartons. The boxes cascaded around her.

Dylan's face worked in fury. "You stupid old woman." He aimed the gun at Harriet.

"Don't hurt her." Alexa seized the first thing at hand, a box of medieval maps. She raised it high over her head and flung it at Dylan.

Dylan sidestepped the box. He swung the gun back toward Alexa, hand tightening on the grip. "You've ruined everything. It wasn't supposed to end like this—"

A sickening thud cut off his shrill words.

He collapsed to the floor with such suddenness that Alexa did not even realize what had happened until she saw that his gun had fallen to the floor.

Dylan lay unmoving. He was neatly pinned between a carton emblazoned with a picture of Stonehenge and the words *Some Assembly Required*, and a three-foot-tall sculpture of Sir Lancelot.

"Alexa." Trask vaulted over a recumbent dragon and seized her. "Are you all right?"

"Yes." She leaned into his big, strong body. She was definitely not the clinging type, she thought. But right now Trask felt awfully good. "Yes, I'm all right."

"You scared the hell out of me. When I realized that Dylan . . ."

"What did you do to him, anyway?" She raised her head from his chest and saw the small, fist-sized stone gargoyle lying on the floor beside Dylan's head. "Good grief. No wonder he went down. Nice shot."

"I told you that I used to play a little ball." He moved his right shoulder in an absent way, as if remembering an old ache.

Alexa gave him a tremulous smile. "I remember. Your father dreamed that you might turn pro someday."

Trask nodded. He said nothing.

"I think that your father's crazy dream just helped save my life," Alexa whispered.

Trask refocused on her face. "Dad always was a little ahead of his time." He pulled her hard against him, crushing her. "Christ, Alexa. You scared the living daylights out of me."

"I was a little nervous, myself," she mumbled into his shirt. "Maybe I've pushed the envelope on this wild woman stuff far enough."

"You can say that again," he muttered into her hair.

She turned her head against his chest to watch as Webster gallantly assisted Harriet to her feet.

"Are you sure you're all right, ma'am?" Webster studied her with grave concern. "Maybe I should call 911."

Harriet smiled beatifically. "No need for that. I'm as fit as a fiddle." She looked expectantly at Alexa. "Aren't you going to introduce me, dear?"

Alexa sighed. "Webster Bell, Trask, allow me to introduce Harriet McClelland, my former employer. The woman who taught me everything I know about early-twentieth-century art and then some."

"A pleasure," Webster said politely.

Trask contemplated Harriet in silence for a long moment. Then his mouth curved slightly at the corners. "Well, I'll be damned."

Harriet's blue eyes sparkled approvingly. She winked at Alexa. "I must say, dear, your taste in men has definitely improved since we last met."

36

"The little sociopath had us all fooled." Webster sank wearily into one of the suite's red tapestry chairs. "I still can't believe it. So Harry Trask really was murdered. You were right all along."

"I was right, but for the wrong reasons." Trask lounged against the back of the red tapestry sofa. "Fenn admitted to Strood that he got rid of my father because Joanna was set on marrying him. He didn't even know that the partnership between Dad, Guthrie, and Kenyon had gone bad. Fenn wanted to make certain that Joanna's inheritance remained linked to Dimensions."

"I'm so bloody sorry." Webster massaged his silver temples. "For everything."

"No one in this room is to blame," Trask said very steadily. "Fenn was the killer. He bears full responsibility."

Alexa, seated on the sofa below him, looked up. Her eyes were shadowed with concern. He put one hand on her shoulder and squeezed gently. He had been finding excuses to touch her all evening, he realized. He did not want to let her out of his sight. He had a feeling that some of his old nightmares were soon going to be replaced with a new batch.

He took a swallow from the glass of very expensive single malt scotch he had retrieved from a locked case behind the resort's bar. Alexa, Webster, and Harriet followed suit. A short silence descended on the small gathering.

The confrontation in Elegant Relic showed every indication of turning into a major bonding experience, Trask thought. He had brought them all back to the suite for a late dinner and an informal debriefing after Strood had finished taking down their statements.

It was nearly midnight now. The French doors were open to allow the desert night into the room. He took a deep breath of the clean air.

"I must say, that young man, Fenn, is clearly bonkers." Harriet gave a delicate shudder.

Trask watched in amused awe as she tossed back a healthy gulp of the potent scotch. Other than a slight brightening of her blue eyes, she appeared unfazed.

"He said he wanted to sacrifice Alexa to some things he called vortices," she continued. "Can you imagine?"

"I'll tell you what I find hard to believe," Alexa said. "It's that Fenn was a hot shot corporate financial officer before he quit to follow the Dimensions Way."

Harriet made a tut-tutting sound. "We all take odd turns in our lives from time to time. Who would have believed that a woman with an unerring instinct for early-twentieth-century art and antiques would have opened a shop that specialized in tacky museum reproductions, for example."

Alexa turned on her. "Of all the unmitigated gall. How dare you call my shop tacky? It's your fault that I had to open Elegant Relic in the first place . . ."

"Now, now, ladies," Trask said soothingly. "We're straying from the subject."

Webster walked to the open doors. "From what I can gather, Stewart was so zealous about the Dimensions Way that he was an easy target for Fenn to manipulate. In addition, because of his past, violence was not foreign to him."

Trask thought about what he had learned during the talk with Strood. "Dylan appointed himself Stewart's personal meditation guide and swore him to secrecy, just as he did with Liz. They both went along with it because they believed he really could teach them how to ascend to a higher plane of consciousness."

Alexa looked at Webster. "How is Joanna doing?"

"Much better." Webster gave her a wan smile. "I talked to her for a few minutes after Strood finished with me. She said that, deep down, she had always wondered about the circumstances surrounding the death of Harry Trask."

Alexa glanced at Trask and then turned back to Webster. "But she never said anything because of you."

Webster hesitated. "In some distant corner of her mind she was secretly afraid that I might have killed Harry to keep him from getting his hands on her money. I can see where she got the idea. She and I had some almighty quarrels over the subject of her marriage."

"This Joanna was obviously caught between a rock and a hard place," Harriet observed.

"Bad enough to lose the man she loved," Alexa said quietly. "She could not endure finding out that her only living relative, her beloved brother, might have been the killer. No wonder she wanted the past to stay buried."

Harriet looked at her with a fond expression. "I had no idea you'd been living such an exciting life since we dissolved our partnership, dear."

"We didn't exactly dissolve our partnership," Alexa said through her teeth. "You disappeared in the middle of the night and left me to face the music."

"It amounted to the same thing," Harriet said cheerfully. She looked at Trask. "I understand that you're the proud new owner of Icarus Ives's *Dancing Satyr.*"

"I own a statue called *Dancing Satyr.*" Trask glanced at Alexa. "I'm told it's a fake."

"It is," Harriet said. "One of my best pieces."

Trask nearly choked on his scotch. "It's a McClelland?"

"Yes, dear." Harriet smiled. "I wonder if I might ask a small favor of you . . ."

"Whatever you do," Alexa warned. "Don't listen to her."

Several hours later Alexa awoke to find herself alone in the black lacquered bed. She turned and saw the solid, dark shape of Trask outlined against the window.

"Are you okay?" she asked softly.

"Yeah."

She sat up and folded her arms on her knees.

"You've got the answers you came here to find."

"Most of them," he agreed.

She braced herself to ask a question of her own. "How long will you be staying in Avalon?"

"That depends," he said.

"On what?"

"On the answer to my last question."

A lightheaded sensation passed through her. "What is your last question?"

He watched her from the shadows. "Before you abandon your wild and reckless lifestyle entirely, will you take one more risk?"

"What kind of risk?"

"On me?"

A glorious rush of warmth rose within her. The sense of weightless happiness was so great she wondered that she did not levitate off the bed. She pushed aside the covers, got to her feet, and walked across the room to join him.

She put her arms around his neck and raised her mouth to his.

"I kept telling Dr. Ormiston that I wouldn't have a problem with commitment when I met the right man," she said.

A long time later Trask rolled onto his back and put one arm behind his head. He had never been more satisfied, more content, more at peace, he thought. And the sex was terrific, too.

"What are you thinking?" Alexa asked in a sleepy voice.

He smiled to himself and gathered her close. "Wild woman lives."

37

Three weeks later . . .

"You were certainly busy while your mom and I were out of town." Lloyd stretched out on Alexa's patio lounger and reached for his beer. "Scared the bejeezus out of us when we found out what had happened."

"What can I say?" Alexa smiled. "I went through a wild period. Probably just a phase."

"Let's hope so. Don't think I could take too much of that kind of excitement." Lloyd eyed her. "Trask, I assume, is not just a phase?"

"No. Trask is permanent." She watched the setting sun paint the desert with the uncanny light of other dimensions. "I'm going to marry him."

"Figured as much." Lloyd gazed out over the glowing red and purple landscape. "That why you asked me to come over before Trask and Vivien got here tonight?"

"Yes. I wanted to discuss something with you in private."

He nodded. "You probably want to talk prenups.

I know I've always made a big deal about them. You've got a fair amount of money to protect."

"Thanks to you."

Lloyd shrugged that off. "All I did was take what your grandmother left you and put it to work. Anyhow, like I said, I know I've drilled the idea of the importance of a prenuptial contract into your head since you started to date."

"Good advice, Lloyd. I've never forgotten it. Think I'll need one with Trask?"

Lloyd gave her a searching look. "Do you think you need one?"

"Nope."

Lloyd smiled slowly. "That's pretty much how I see it, too. Does he want one?"

"Nope."

"Figured he wouldn't. Forget the contract. Twelve years ago that stubborn son-of-a-gun wouldn't take a dime from me. He hasn't changed much from what I can tell. If the marriage doesn't work out, he won't touch your money. And you wouldn't touch any of his. You're just as proud and bullheaded as he is."

"The marriage is going to work just fine."

"I think you're right." Lloyd took a swallow of beer. "Trask turned out okay. Had a feeling he would."

Alexa smiled. "You were the only one around who wasn't worried when you heard that he was coming back to Avalon."

Lloyd snorted. "Probably should have worried some, after all."

"But not about Trask."

"No, not about him." Lloyd arched one thick

brow and gave her a long considering look. "Always knew you'd recognize the right man when he came along."

"That's what I tried to tell Dr. Ormiston."

"So how come you wanted me to come over early tonight?"

"So that I could ask you if you'd walk me down the aisle."

Lloyd paused, the beer halfway to his mouth. A slow smile curved on his face. Warmth gleamed in his eyes. "I would be proud to walk you down the aisle, Alexa. Nothing would make me happier."

"Thanks." She blinked away some moisture that was causing the twilight scene to shimmer a bit in front of her eyes. "Thank you very much, Lloyd."

They were both quiet for a while.

"Tell me something," Lloyd said eventually. "How'd you know Trask was the right man?"

"I think it was because, in some very important ways, he reminded me of you."

EPILOGUE

Two months later . . .

Harriet handed her engagement gift to Alexa with a flourish. "You'll want to open this one first, dear."

Alexa took the silver and white present from her. "I'll put it with the others."

"I think you should open it now," Trask said.

Alexa waved a hand at the huge crowd gathered on the grounds of the Avalon Resort & Spa. "What about our guests? Most of the town is here today, in case you haven't noticed."

"I've noticed," Trask said. "We'll get back to them. Open Harriet's gift."

"But everyone's waiting for us to do the first waltz bit."

"Go ahead," Vivien urged. "Open Harriet's present."

Lloyd smiled at Alexa. "Our guests can wait five minutes."

Edward Vale hoisted his champagne glass. "To Harriet's gift."

Alexa ignored him. Edward had been drinking champagne all afternoon. Luckily he was staying at the hotel, she thought. He would not be fit to drive by the time the reception ended.

She looked at the circle of faces gathered around her. This was one of the happiest days of her life, she thought. She was officially engaged to the man she loved and she was surrounded by good friends and family. It probably didn't get much better than this.

She could afford to be flexible.

"Okay, okay, I'll open Harriet's gift."

She ripped into the gorgeously wrapped package and uncovered a white box. She raised the lid, tossed aside the tissue, and saw a copy of *Twentieth-Century Artifact*. A very new copy.

Alexa stilled.

"Hot off the presses," Harriet said. "Won't be on the stands until next week. I prevailed on an acquaintance to get it for me. Page twenty-three."

Alexa fumbled with the cover. It was not easy to get to page twenty-three, she discovered. Her fingers were trembling.

"I'll do it for you." Trask took the glossy magazine from her and flipped through it quickly. "Here we are."

Alexa took back the magazine and looked at the Insider's Notes column.

CORPORATE COLLECTION STUNS
DECO COLLECTORS

Insiders were enthralled by the glittering collection of Art Deco housed in the sumptuous new Avalon Resort & Spa in Avalon, Arizona. "I wanted the best," Edward Vale, the corporate art consultant who supervised the project told *TCA*. "Naturally I went to the expert who exposed the McClelland forgeries, Alexa Chambers. She has an incredible eye for early-twentieth-century art and antiques. The client was delighted with the result."

Avalon's collection is the envy of several major museums and galleries. Its breadth and depth is remarkable. Indeed, it stands comparison with the finest collections in the country.

Never has the notion of the "modern" been so well defined as it was by the artists and craftsmen of the Art Deco period. Ms. Chambers has done a magnificent job of capturing that sensibility.

Of interest to insiders is the fact that the original catalog of the collection listed an Icarus Ives sculpture, *Dancing Satyr*. That piece, we are told, although purchased for the Avalon resort, was later sold to an anonymous collector before the hotel opened. "It was a personal decision," said JL Trask, president and CEO of Avalon Resort, Inc. "I was never a great fan of Ives's work."

Trask went on to say that, although the hotel's collection will be limited to the very finest examples of the Deco period, he himself has begun a unique private collection. It will be limited to the infamous, quite brilliant forgeries created by the anonymous sculptor whose work brought down the McClelland Gallery over a year ago.

Collecting rare and interesting forgeries has long been in vogue in the art world among a certain eccentric type of collector . . .

"Eccentric?" Trask snatched the magazine out of Alexa's fingers. "Let me see that. Damn it, Mac, it

was your idea to claim that I was starting a private collection of McClelland forgeries. You never told me that I'd get labeled eccentric in the press."

"It's all right to be called eccentric in the art world, dear," Harriet said airily. "There's a certain mystique involved."

"Well, it's not okay in the business world," Trask growled. "*Eccentric*. Of all the—"

"Relax." Alexa gently took the magazine from him, closed it, and handed it to a smiling Vivien. "Someday the McClelland forgeries are going to be worth five times what Icarus Ives's work is worth."

Harriet beamed.

Trask looked at Alexa, eyes gleaming. "Think so?"

"Yep." She smiled complacently. "I'm an expert, remember?"

"Well, as long as you're sure."

"Think positive," she said. "You live in Avalon, remember? Thinking positive is the local motto."

"Uh-huh."

"Cheer up, the bottom line is that you've made a brilliant investment," she said.

He smiled. A slow, sexy heat gleamed in his eyes. "Well, that's okay, then. You know me when it comes to the bottom line."

He caught her hand, drew her to him, and led her away toward the assembled guests.

Alexa smiled. "You know something? Back at the beginning I told myself that falling in love with you would be the most reckless act of my life."

"Was it?"

"No," she said. "It was a sure thing."

"Funny you should say that." His fingers tightened around hers. "Back at the beginning I told myself I wouldn't get caught in the fantasy."

"Did you?"

"Yeah," he said, "but it turned out okay. Bottom line was that it wasn't a fantasy. It was real."